DON'T LET ME BREAK

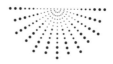

KELSIE RAE

DISCLAIMER

Please note: Don't Let Me Break involves a character with epilepsy. Her seizures are described in detail and may be triggering for some people.

Don't Let Me Break
Cover Art by Cover My Wagon Dragon Art
Editing by Wickedcoolflight Editing Services
Proofreading by Stephanie Taylor
Published by Twisty Pines Publishing, LLC
January 2023 Edition
Published in the United States of America

PROLOGUE

KATE

My head is pounding. No, it feels like it's being sliced in half. Scratch that. It feels as if someone is stabbing it over and over again with little razor blades, leaving ribbons of brain instead of a single mass. Feeling like this can mean only one thing: I had another seizure.

I blink slowly, taking in my surroundings. I don't know where I am. I know it isn't home, though. It's too bright. The ceiling has thick wood beams and gold fixtures. And there are people. So many people.

The restaurant. I'm at the restaurant. With Ash. And Mia. And Colt. And Theo. They invited me to celebrate. I remember now.

It's okay.

It's going to be okay.

Or maybe it isn't, but things haven't felt okay for a while now, so I'm not sure why I'm surprised.

The restaurant is quiet as I open my eyes again, blinking slowly. A stranger is next to me. Brown, wavy hair cropped short on the sides and longer on the top. Kind eyes.

1

Assessing eyes. A strong jaw. And pretty, full lips pulled into a frown. I don't recognize him. And it isn't the seizure displacing my already shitty memory, either. Not this time, anyway. I would've remembered him. I know I would have. Maybe he's come into Butter and Grace before? His light blue eyes are like the sky on a sunny day. And yummy full lips. And soft hair.

Whoa, girl. You're going in circles here.

Where am I again?

"Hey," the stranger murmurs, pushing my hair away from my forehead as his pretty blue eyes bounce around my face, evaluating me.

Such pretty eyes.

With dark lashes and little flecks of navy spread throughout the sky-blue color.

Blue. Blue. Blue.

"You okay?" he asks, his brows pinched in concern.

I laugh, nearly choking on the lump clogging my throat and the guilt squeezing my chest. "I'm sorry."

His pretty lips pull into a frown. "You have nothing to apologize for."

"Debatable," I argue. My head is throbbing, and my muscles are already sore from the strain of the seizure. I try to push myself up, but the room spins. Strong, warm hands grasp my arm and back as the stranger helps me sit up.

I'm on the ground. I guess I shouldn't be surprised. It's usually where I end up when a seizure hits. Especially a bad one.

Everyone's standing around me.

Looking down at me.

All of my roommates are here. Ashlyn, Mia, Blakely. Theo and Colt are here too. Theo's dating Blake, and Colt's dating Ashlyn.

Dating.

The word brings a memory to the surface. Wes. My ex. He'd brought a girl to Butter and Grace, the restaurant where I'm a waitress. I had to serve the bastard before coming here. It's why I was stressed. Why I downed Mia's wine without giving a shit it could trigger a seizure.

It's my own freaking fault.

I know better.

Ash's eyes are rimmed with redness, hinting she's holding back tears as she stares down at me. Colt's embracing her against his chest the same way Theo is with Blakely.

But none of them say anything. They're watching me. Waiting to see if I'll start shaking again. If I'll have another episode.

It must've been a bad one.

Seizure, that is.

The word alone is like nails on a chalkboard but combined with the evidence surrounding me and how uncomfortable I must've made everyone feel? It might as well as be… What's worse than nails on a chalkboard?

Man, I can't even think of a solid metaphor right now.

My head is throbbing.

I press my hand to my temple and close my eyes.

Kill me now.

"Are you strong enough to sit up on your own?" the stranger asks. His hands are still on me. Like everyone else, he's probably worried I'll collapse again, so he's reluctant to let me go.

I turn and look up at him again.

He really is good-looking. A little older. Maybe thirty? Thirty-five? Definitely not anyone from my classes at LAU. I would've remembered him. Maybe he's come into Butter and Grace before.

Gah. I'm still going in circles.

3

I squeeze my eyes shut and try to shrug out of his grasp, but he doesn't let me. "I'm fine."

"Give yourself a minute," he suggests.

"But I'm fine," I repeat.

"Kate, are you sure you're okay?" Ash asks. She squats down beside me and the stranger, her sweet expression filled with concern.

She's never seen me have a seizure. And clearly, now that she has, she'll never let me live it down. The girl's a mother hen on a good day. Now that she's seen me at my worst? She'll never let me out of her sight again. We've been room-mates for almost two years. It's a miracle I was able to keep her shielded from this for so long. Guess my luck's run out.

Shocker.

"I'm fine, Ash," I mumble. "Can we...not do this? I just want to go home--"

"The ambulance will be here any second," Mia chimes in.

My eyes widen in surprise as I register her words.

Ambulance?

Noooo.

"You called an ambulance?" I choke out, blinking back tears. "Why? I'm fine. This isn't a big deal. I'll go home, and..." My voice trails off as the pounding in my skull heightens, drowning out my thoughts or whatever I'd been rambling about.

Shit, why is the room still spinning?

"Breathe," the stranger reminds me.

I let out a shuddered breath and close my eyes, letting a single tear slide down my cheek while attempting to block out my friends' faces. The pity. The concern. The fear.

Don't they get it?

It's just another day in the messed-up life of Kate Winchester.

Lucky me.

1
MACKLIN

y buddy, Felix, is on duty and took Kate's vitals
as soon as he arrived on the scene with Remi,
his girlfriend and fellow paramedic. Felix didn't
care that I insisted on riding with Kate to the hospital, but
the bastard did shoot me a look when she told him it wasn't
necessary. One of the girls offered to take my place as her
plus-one in the back of the ambulance, but apparently, Kate
was even more anxious about a friend joining her than a
stranger. When her friends told her going by herself to the
hospital wasn't an option, she chose me instead.

After a quick conversation with my little brother, Theo, I
promise to text him with any updates, and we're off.

It's funny how quickly an evening can turn upside down.

Theo had invited me to join him and his friends who
were celebrating something. My guess is Colt, Theo's childhood best friend, suggested extending the offer to me. Or
our mom intervened. She's been worried about me since the
divorce, calling in favors and asking anyone and everyone if
they know any young women who'd agree to go on a blind
date with a recently divorced man. Or, if it wasn't too much

trouble, she'd ask if they could swing by and bring me some cookies she'd made earlier in the day in hopes of cheering me up.

I can't even begin to count how many strangers have shown up on my front porch in the middle of the fucking woods with cookies all because Mama Taylor asked them to. I gotta give the woman credit. She's a stubborn, convincing lady when she wants to be.

The blind dates, though? Well, I had to put my foot down somewhere.

Hanging out with Theo and his friends, however, I could swallow.

And even if it was a pity invitation extended by my little brother, I needed to get out of the house. It's my oldest daughter's birthday, but she doesn't want to see me. Didn't even bother to reply to the happy birthday text I sent. She's avoiding me, convinced the bullshit my ex is spewing about me is true when it's the furthest thing from it. Don't get me wrong. I'm not a saint. But Summer's the one who called off the marriage and tore our family apart. Then again, maybe it is my fault. As soon as my winnings from the lottery hit our joint bank account, she took half of it, packed her bags, and sent me a text, informing me her lawyer would be in touch.

I didn't even bother fighting her.

We were both done with the marriage.

Done fighting for something neither of us wanted .

But I wouldn't have called it quits if she hadn't pulled the plug. Because I'm not a quitter. Never have been. Not when she showed up on my front porch with a positive pregnancy test when we were sixteen. Not when she convinced me to use my college fund to pay for the new two-bedroom apartment in the city since I could only afford a studio in the suburbs.

If anything, it's the saying *no* part I suck at. Like when she took the house and convinced our two girls I'm bad news.

The ambulance hits a minor bump, and Kate winces, yanking me back to the present. Remi and Felix are in the front of the rig since I'm a trained paramedic, and I told them I'd keep an eye on the patient until we arrived at the hospital.

Doesn't mean she's said a word to me.

In fact, the girl looks pissed.

With her arms crossed and a nasty scowl marring her pretty face, she stares blankly at the back door of the ambulance. Like I don't exist.

"How you doin'?" I ask her.

Silence.

I clear my throat and shift on my seat. "I should probably introduce--"

"Don't bother."

A snort slips out of me as I tilt my head to the side. "I'm Theo's--"

"Were you the one who told them to call an ambulance?" she interrupts, finally gracing me with a look. Those gray eyes are stormy. Even stormier than in the restaurant when she first woke up. Like it's my fault she wound up on the floor. My fault she's in the back of an ambulance. My fault she can't ignore the entire situation and go about her day as if she didn't have a seizure in the middle of an Italian restaurant.

Leaning forward, I rest my elbows on my knees and hold her turbulent gaze. "Yeah. I was."

Her scowl deepens. "Why?"

"Because your friends didn't know what to do, and someone needed to take charge."

"And you thought it was your right?" she demands.

7

"Yeah, I guess so. Ya know, since you were a little preoccupied and all."

It's a dick thing to say, but if she's offended, she doesn't show it.

"You had no right to make that call," she spits.

She's seriously pissed at this moment, and I don't have the energy to fight her on something so small in the big picture. Not tonight.

With a sigh, I pinch the bridge of my nose and mutter, "Look, it's not a big deal. They'll check you over. Make sure everything's okay. Call your doctor. Your parents--"

"They can't call my parents," she rushes out. The blood drains from her face, making her already pale skin even whiter.

Hell, you'd think she's been caught with drugs on her and will be locked up for the rest of her life with how panicked she looks.

My hand drops to my lap. "Why?"

"Because."

This girl really is a piece of work.

With a scoff, I prod, "Gonna need more to go on than that."

"Because I don't want them to worry."

"They're *parents*," I tell her dryly. "It's what they do."

"Then why feed the fire? I'm fine."

I shake my head, fucking flabbergasted. "You're a prickly little thing, aren't you?"

"I'm not prickly. I'm annoyed."

"Annoyed you had a seizure?"

"No. I'm annoyed with how you're not minding your own business and that you want me to call my parents when it has nothing to do with you."

Well, fuck.

If I hadn't already been sure the girl was pissy, I am now.

Why is she fighting me on this? Why are we even having this conversation? Why do I even care what she does? Actually, I know exactly why I care. Because I have a kid who's avoiding me like I'm a criminal or some shit. And I know it isn't about me, and she can do whatever she wants on her birthday, but I'm still her dad. And if Kate can be so dismissive of her parents, so can Hazel. Which is exactly what she's doing with me. Not her mom. The woman's a damn saint in my daughters' eyes, but me? Their terrible father? Yeah, it's a bitch.

Shoving my own shitstorm of a life into the back of my mind, I tell Kate, "Look. Your parents care about you. They have a right to know––"

"I'm over eighteen. Well over eighteen," she spits. "They don't have a right to anything . Not if I don't want to tell them. And since I'm conscious and coherent, I can make the call for myself."

She's serious. I pull back, surprised by the acid on her tongue and how determined she looks despite the splitting headache I know is cracking her skull in two.

"Fine," I concede. "Since you won't call them, I'm staying with you."

"What?" she screeches.

"I'm staying with you."

"You don't know me."

"You're right. I don't. And we can keep it that way if you want, but I know proper protocol after someone with epilepsy has a seizure, Kate."

She flinches as the word epilepsy slips past my lips, but I don't call her out on it. Instead, I continue, softening my voice. "You're not supposed to be alone. If you don't want your parents around, I'll be by your side until the doctor discharges you. Once he or she does, I'll drive you home,

9

confirm one of your roommates is around, and leave you in their care."

"I'm not a baby."

"And I'm not treating you like a baby."

"That's exactly what you're doing."

"No, I'm treating you like you have epilepsy, Kate." She squeezes her eyes shut, the word hitting her like a lash from a whip, the same way it did a moment ago. I take a deep breath adding, "And there isn't anything wrong with it. But there are good days and bad days. And if I had to guess, today's a particularly bad one, considering how your roommates responded. So yeah. We're going to treat it like a bad day. And we're going to acknowledge it. And we're going to get through it."

She shakes her head, then presses the heel of her hand against it, wincing.

My frustration dissipates instantly. But I don't reach for her. I don't offer any comfort. She doesn't want it, anyway.

With another sigh, I murmur, "Headache?"

She drops her hand back to her lap and stares blankly in front of her again. "I'm fine."

Sure, she is.

"You know it isn't a weakness, right?" I mutter, scrubbing my hand over my face and spreading my legs wide in front of me as the ambulance pulls up to the emergency room. "Asking for help. Acknowledging you have a battle most people couldn't even dream of fighting."

Her nostrils flare, but she doesn't look at me.

"You're a badass, Kate," I add as Felix shifts the ambulance into park. "A prickly badass, but even prickly badasses are allowed to have bad days sometimes."

Without another word, we head inside the hospital, where the nurse asks Kate a bunch of questions after confirming I'm allowed to stay in the room with her. Kate tells them it's fine but doesn't bother acknowledging me the rest of the time we're here. The doctors run a bunch of tests, eventually concluding there's no reason to admit her to the hospital. And when I drive her home, thanks to Theo dropping my car off at the hospital after he and Blakely parted ways, Kate slams the car door behind her. With folded arms, she walks toward the townhome she shares with her roommates, not bothering to look back at me.

The front porch lights flicker on as Kate reaches the steps and walks to the door. It opens, revealing one of her roommates, who pulls her into a hug almost instantly. We haven't been introduced, but she has a sleeve of tattoos on one arm and piercings along the shell of her ear as she meets my gaze over Kate's shoulder. She dips her chin in gratitude as she guides Kate inside.

Kate's right about one thing.

She's definitely well over eighteen. My guess is closer to twenty-five or so. Doesn't make it okay for me to be attracted to her. She's still young. Too young for a guy like me. A guy with my shitty baggage.

I shake my head and shove my car into reverse.

Guess my job here is done.

2

KATE

A few weeks later

"Seriously, this is going to be *so* good for you," Blakely tells me as she turns off her car.

I peek up at the large brick building and frown. The new gym opened a few weeks ago. The owner decided to give LAU students a promo code when signing up, only charging us eight dollars a month for the first year.

Which is great.

If you like exercise.

And being around your fellow classmates who also like exercise and a good deal.

Maybe I'd also be a fan of the circumstances if I wasn't such a recluse.

Except I am.

A recluse.

Usually, anyway.

Blakely, however, is an exercise junkie. She's practically a bean pole and has the energy to prove it. Meanwhile, I'm curves upon curves despite my morning walks. Which I'm fine with. It's not like guys are on my radar right now, anyway. Not after Wes broke up with me after finding out about my condition. Besides, I have other things to figure out. Like, why the hell I had a seizure a few weeks ago, and if I need to mess with my medication. Or, ya know, how I'm supposed to get to work with my license suspended for three months, thanks to said seizure.

Epilepsy's a bitch.

Plain and simple.

But it's really a bitch when it hits out of nowhere after being dormant for almost a year. And to think I was mad at myself when I woke up on my parent's kitchen floor last fall. At least they didn't call an ambulance or recruit an exercise junkie to drag me to the gym like Ashlyn. I sigh and look up at the big building again.

If I'd driven myself, I could turn around and head back home. Unfortunately, Blake's driving, and she's insistent on kicking my ass today. As soon as Ash told her exercise is good for epilepsy, Blake's been determined to whip my butt into shape.

Lucky me.

I know she's trying to help. I do. But this is…a lot.

It's easier when people don't know. When they don't witness a seizure firsthand. When they hear the word epilepsy without tying it to a memory or an experience. But as soon as they can connect my diagnosis with a personal encounter, everything spirals. My parents are the same way. Then again, I'm their only child, so maybe they were always helicopter parents. I guess I'll never know for sure since I was diagnosed when I turned eight. And my memories before then? Well, they're hazy at best.

At least I had almost a solid decade of normalcy. It has to count for something, doesn't it?

"You comin'?" Blake asks me.

I blink away the memory and smile at her. "Yup. No time like the present." Glancing at my phone, I check the time, do the math, and add, "But I have to be home in an hour so I have time to shower before my shift."

Blake salutes me. "Yes, ma'am. Let's go."

We head inside, scan the little barcodes on our keyrings, and move to the locker room to drop off our things. Once our stuff is secure, it's weightlifting time.

Yuck.

Don't get me wrong. I'm all about physical health. But I like to walk. And hike if the occasion calls for it. Swimming? Sure. Sounds great as long as there's a hot tub soak in my future. But weights? And huffing and puffing? And sweating? Thanks, but no thanks. I'll pass.

Well, I would if Blake wasn't so freaking bossy.

She helps me warm up for a few minutes. Once I'm ready, she motions to the free weights lining the wall as if I'm a contestant on *The Price is Right*. "Pick your poison, Kate. We'll start with squats and lunges, then move to deadlifts."

What the hell are deadlifts?

With wide eyes, I give her a look like she's crazy but keep my feet planted as a massive bodybuilder saunters around me and grabs the heaviest weights on the rack. He checks me out, glances at Blake, and smiles. "Hey--"

"I'm taken, so back off. And"--Blake waves her hand around again, this time motioning toward the opposite side of the gym--"go work out over there, dude. My girl and I are about to get our sweat on."

"Your girl?" He looks at me a second time, his mouth lifting in appreciation. "All right. I can get in on that."

"Nope. We're good. Thanks, though." Blake rolls her eyes and turns to me, effectively ignoring the meathead like he's a pesky fly. "Let's start light since this is your first time. Why don't you grab the ten-pound weights? One for each hand."

I grimace but grab the weights imprinted with a one and a zero, letting them hang at my thighs. "Now what?"

"Now, my dear Kate"––she grabs a pair of twenty-five-pound weights and rests them on her shoulders––"we get to work."

~

Sweat drips down the side of my face as Blake stands beside me, ordering me to do one final squat because, apparently, she has a thing for torture.

Balancing the weights on my shoulders, my legs shaking, I glower. "Are you trying to kill me?"

"Come on. You got this. Look at yourself in the mirror and say it. Say, 'I got this.'"

I ignore the mirrors, staring at a spot on the padded gym floor instead, and grit out, "I got this," as I lower my ass into my final squat.

Holy freaking crap, this is hard!

I push myself back to a standing position, and my butt screams in protest, another droplet of sweat trickling along my spine.

"You," I pant, glaring at Blake. "Are the devil."

She grins. "Never said I wasn't. Come on. Let's put the weights away."

My legs feel like Jell-O as I stagger toward the row of weights. I'm setting them down when a familiar face grabs my attention in the mirror.

I pale, glancing over my shoulder and quickly staring at the ground, my cheeks heating with embarrassment.

It's the stranger. The stranger from the restaurant. The one who escorted me to the hospital and demanded to stay with me since I refused to call my parents. I still can't decide if he's an asshole or a gentleman for being so damn pushy about it.

Regardless, the entire ordeal was a real joy, and I'd prefer to never face him again after giving him front-row seats to the whole thing and all my epileptic glory. Yeah, talking to him again? Even a thousand years would be too soon.

I puff out my cheeks, avoiding the reflection in the mirror like it's a death sentence while praying I go unnoticed.

Oh, what I wouldn't give to blend into the walls and disappear at this moment.

"Blake?" the familiar deep voice calls. I recognize it instantly, though I refuse to acknowledge why or how well my dreams like to replay it every time I go to sleep.

Nope.

No, thank you.

Blake turns around and squeals when she sees my white knight from Hell striding toward us. "Mack!"

Ah, so the stranger has a name.

I refused to learn it, which was made easier by the pounding headache basically blocking out any and all conversation around me, creating a haze over the whole experience. Well, everything except *him*.

In the mirror's reflection, I watch Blake throw her arms around Mack's shoulders and pull him into a full-bodied hug, causing a sharp twinge in my chest. I refuse to acknowledge what it is.

Annoyance, I decide.

Yeah. That's it.

Instead, I stare at the ground, fighting between eavesdropping and booking it to the locker room like my yoga pants are on fire.

"Hey! How are you?" Blake asks.

I peek up at them again, unable to fight my curiosity, as the stranger returns Blake's hug, wrapping his arms around her slender waist before letting her go. "I'm good. How are you?"

"Great! Working out with my friend." She hesitates, and I stare back at the ground, pretending if I'm quiet enough, I'll be able to fly under the radar or maybe disappear entirely.

If only God loved me that much.

"You remember Kate," she adds.

So much for disappearing.

I clear my throat, lift my head, meet Blake's gaze, then turn my attention to Mack. The bossy bastard's as attractive as I remember. Same chiseled jaw. Same warm smile. Same knowing gaze.

Son of a bitch.

Pasting on a fake smile, I grit my teeth and offer, "Uh. Hi."

"Hey." He stretches his hand out for me to shake like I wasn't an absolute brat to him the last time we were together. "I didn't have a chance to introduce myself last time."

Liar. He had a chance. I simply refused to let him.

"I'm Macklin," he continues. "*Mack*."

I take his hand and shake it awkwardly. It's worn and tan and calloused and warm and––

I clear my throat again, forcing myself to hold his gaze.

Yup. Same blue eyes I remember.

And boy, do I remember them.

Blue. Blue. Blue.

They've become a regular appearance every night in my dreams, along with his warm, slightly gritty voice. Which is annoying. And inappropriate on so many levels.

"Kate," I reply, forcing myself to concentrate on our conversation and not on how attractive he looked in my dreams last night. "My name's Kate. Hi."

"Hey."

"Hi," I repeat for what, the third time?

Seriously. Kill me now.

To be fair, I've always been somewhat awkward around guys. I blame it on the lack of alcohol experience and desire to attend parties. You know, since alcohol has a way of making social interactions a little easier, and parties seem to have the same effect when you've been to enough of them.

What I wouldn't give for a strong shot of something right about now to get through this interaction.

I still can't believe I was so mean to him on the way to the hospital. I turned all my anger and frustration on the stranger who demanded to ride with me in the back of the ambulance. I didn't even make an effort to ask his name, and when he offered to give it, I full-blown told him not to bother. Once we reached the hospital, I silently stewed, ignoring everyone and everything. The doctors. The nurses. I closed up like a little clam, choosing silence and avoiding the situation altogether until I could get home and process it in my room. Alone. It's easier that way.

However, the consequences of my actions have a way of catching up with me, and this one is currently standing three feet away.

When I realize I'm still holding Mack's hand, I let it go and wipe my palm against my black leggings, catching a glimpse of myself in the mirror.

I look like a cherry. A sweaty cherry. Seriously. My hair is so wet from perspiration it's sticking to my temples, making me look like a drowned rat or something. Which is great.

First, a seizure. Now, this.

Could I be any more embarrassing?

"How you doin'?" he prods.

"Fine." I fold my arms and rock back on my heels, caught between my upbringing––and the need to be polite––and my desperation to get the hell out of here.

"I'm good too," he replies, a smile teasing his pretty lips, despite the fact I most definitely did not ask how he was doing. "You're still prickly, I see."

"Excuse me?" I balk.

He turns to Blake. "Is she always like this?"

"Prickly?" Head cocked, Blake studies me carefully and taps her chin. "Not usually. Apparently, you bring it out of her."

"Can we please stop talking about me like I'm not even here?" I interrupt.

"Okay," he answers. I don't miss the slight lift at the corner of his full lips.

My own purse. "Good."

"Good," he repeats.

"Good," Blake chirps. I'd say she's drowning in the awkwardness the same way I am, but the girl doesn't feel awkward. *Ever.* Pretty sure she doesn't even know the meaning of the word. If anything, she basks in it.

"So," she continues. "Since when do you come here?"

"I've been coming here before work since the gym opened. It's right by the hospital."

"You work at the hospital?" I blurt out, interjecting myself yet again into a conversation I have no desire to be in.

He turns to me, surprised by my curiosity. "Yeah. Well, sort of. I'm a paramedic."

That's why he was so friendly with the other paramedics, I realize. "Is that why you were at the restaurant?"

"Huh?" Blake asks. She's looking at me like I'm a crazy person until it dawns on her. "Oh. This is Theo's older brother. Sorry, I assumed you knew."

The day I seized is still fuzzy. Fragments rise to the surface, but piecing them together from A to Z is easier said than done. I tuck my dark hair behind my ear and offer another forced smile. "It's fine. We should probably get going, though. I have work and need to shower"––I motion to my still-red face––"so…"

"Good to see you again, Kate." He turns to Blake and adds, "Give my brother a dead leg for me, all right?"

She laughs. "Deal."

I tear my attention from his backside as he saunters away and suck my lips between my teeth, choosing to focus on my scuffed-up Nikes and the ground again in hopes of it swallowing me whole.

No such luck.

Shocker.

"Ooooh. So that's how it is," Blake notes.

"How *what* is?"

"You and Mack." Her eyebrows bounce up and down. "What happened between you two?"

"Uh… Nothing?"

"Uh-huh, sure." Folding her arms, she stares down at me, waiting for me to cave. But I won't. Because I have nothing to say. Not now, and not ever. Not when it comes to Mack.

When I don't answer her, she warns, "Fine. If you won't tell me, I'll ask Mack." She turns on her heel as if she's going to walk over to the guy and talk to him again but my arm darts out, holding her in place.

"Blakely, stop," I beg. "Seriously. Nothing happened."

Her attention drops to where I'm holding her, and she quirks her brow. "If nothing happened, why were you blushing?"

"I wasn't blushing."

"Dude."

I let her go and cross my arms over my chest, resisting the urge to book it into the locker room and get the hell out of here because if I do, Blake will hunt Mack down and demand non-existent answers. Then again, I'm afraid if I don't start talking, she'll grow impatient and hunt him down anyway.

"Fine," I concede, finally cracking. "Nothing happened--and it really didn't--but I have no interest in getting to know the guy."

"Why not?"

"Because I don't," I argue.

"Yeah, okay." She gives me a thumbs up. "Way to *not* be defensive, Kate."

"I'm not being defensive!"

"Seriously?" Her pointed look feels like ants crawling under my skin.

Annoyed, I blurt out, "What do you want me to say?"

"Nothing, I guess. But Mack's right. You do seem...prickly."

"I'm not prickly," I start, but she points at my face and laughs.

"See? *Prickly*. And you're never prickly. You're like the nicest girl I know. So, what's up?"

"Nothing's up," I argue because I'm sure as heck not going to bring up the fact I may or may not have had a dirty dream or two involving her boyfriend's older brother, and the idea of voicing it aloud makes me literally feel like I'm going to puke.

"Okay, sure. Nothing's up. Regardless, Mack's basically a golden retriever and is the sweetest person I've ever met, despite you being kind of rude to him. So, my question is... why don't you want to get to know the guy?"

"Uh, because he's old?" I offer, the first excuse rising to the surface like oil in water.

She picks up her set of weights from the ground and props them on her shoulders. "Uh, first of all, pretty sure that's age discrimination, and second of all, he's only like eight years or so older than you. What's your next excuse?"

"First of all," I mimic, "eight years is a decent amount of time, and second of all, he's Theo's older brother."

"So?"

"So even if I was delusional enough to go down that road, what if things got messy?" I ask. "We have mutual friends. It would be weird."

"Uh, what road?" she challenges.

"Uh, what do you mean? I didn't mention a road."

"Uh-huh, sure. You said you're not delusional enough to go down that road because things could get messy. Do you like him?"

"I just told you I didn't."

"Yeah, but I don't believe you," she decides. "And as for things getting messy, you do remember you're talking to the girl who's dating her brother's best friend, correct?" She wipes her set of weights with some Clorox wipes and puts them back onto the stand, then grabs mine, wiping them and setting them back onto the rack. "What's your next excuse?"

Resting my hip against the stand, I point out, "Okay. I just got out of a relationship with Wes."

"Who's an ass," she reminds me. "So?"

"So, maybe I'm not ready to date anyone."

"Also, debatable, but so far, it's your most believable excuse. Any other reasons why you don't want to get to know Macklin?"

"He saw me have a seizure," I blurt out. The truth hits harder than she probably realizes, but it doesn't make the reality of the situation go away. He saw me have a seizure. Actually, not only did he see it, he had a front-row seat to the whole thing. And seizures? They're messy. And uncontrollable. And heart-stopping. Not only for the one experiencing them but also for the people who witness them. It's not like I can let my guard down with someone who sees me like I'm a ticking time bomb. It isn't fair to me, and it sure as hell isn't fair to them, either.

This is why I didn't want to tell Wes about my disability.

Because I didn't want him to look at me differently. And starting a friendship––er, whatever––after having already witnessed said disability? Nope. No, thank you.

"So?" Blakely prods.

"So, he saw me have a seizure," I repeat.

"And that's a problem because…?" Her voice trails off as she pushes out her hip, resting her hand on it.

I glance over my shoulder, confirming we're relatively alone and our conversation is still somewhat private. Satisfied, I keep my voice low and mutter, "Because he'll treat me differently."

"No, he won't."

"Yes, he will."

"No," she repeats with a laugh. "He won't. The guy doesn't get squeamish over anything, Kate. And I'm not even kidding. Trust me. One time, he was playing roller hockey on the street with a bunch of kids from the neighborhood, and one of them fell. Hard. His bone was literally sticking out of his arm, Kate. *Literally.*" Her nose wrinkles as if she can still picture the damage. "No one wanted to come within five feet of the kid except Mack. The guy broke his hockey stick and used it as a splint, tying it with his T-shirt to the kid's arm as we waited for the ambulance to show up. He was fifteen."

"Seriously?"

Blake nods. "Yeah. Seriously. So, trust me when I say your little seizure was a cakewalk for the guy."

We both know she's lying and is trying to downplay the event to prove a point, but I'm grateful for it nonetheless. It isn't going to convince me to give the guy a chance, but still. I *am* grateful.

"Well, regardless," I mutter, "I'm not looking to make any new friends. *Period.* So…"

"Why not?"

"Because I'm just not," I tell her.

"So, you're being a butt," she concludes. "Got it. Come on," she hooks her arm through mine. "Let's take you home so you can shower before your shift."

"Thanks."

"You're welcome," she returns. "But if you ever change your mind and decide you might sorta kinda be okay with making new *friends*"—she lifts her hands and does air quotes around the word—"I think you and Mack would make a cute couple."

"Oh, so now we're a potential couple, Blake?" I say dryly. "You're delusional."

"Optimistic," she clarifies. "There's a difference."

I shove the locker room door open and exhale loudly.

Sure, there is.

KATE

"**H**ey, Mom." I pin my phone between my shoulder and ear as I put the mascara back into my makeup bag.

"Hey, baby! How are you?"

"I'm good. Getting ready for my shift."

"Great!" my dad chirps. They must have me on speaker. I'm not surprised. It's kind of par for the course with these two.

"Yeah. How are things with you guys?" I ask.

"We're doing great. Thought we might stop by Butter and Grace and say hi."

I shove my makeup bag into the bathroom drawer and flick the light off. "Oh, you don't have to––"

"I know," Mom interrupts. "But we miss you. Are you still coming home this weekend?"

With a grimace, I head back to my room and slip on some shoes, searching for an excuse not involving the truth or the fact I *can't* come home until my driver's license isn't suspended.

"Honey?" Mom prods.

"I have a big exam coming up in Palmer's class, so…"

"You can always study at home," Dad offers. "We'll give you privacy and will only interrupt to drop off caffeine and chocolate."

I laugh. "While that sounds like a treat, I'll have to pass this time. Thank you, though."

"We miss you, baby," my mom repeats.

"I know. And I miss you guys too," I tell them.

And I honestly do. I love my parents even when they're overbearing, leaving me feeling like they're smothering me at times. They're still super sweet and super caring and super hands-on and also super good at making me feel like a child. I sigh and add, "How 'bout we talk about this later? Ash is giving me a ride to work, so I gotta go."

"Why is she giving you a ride?" Mom asks. I swear the woman's a damn detective. "Are you sure everything's okay? Is your car giving you trouble?"

My shoulders hunch, and I rest my forehead against my bathroom doorjamb.

Crap.

"Uh…no," I answer. "Everything's great. I, uh, thought I'd save some gas."

"Do you need any money, baby?" she quizzes me. "We can Venmo--"

"Seriously, I'm fine," I reply.

"Honey, it's no trouble," Dad placates.

"I know." My sneakers slightly scuff against the hardwood floor as I head down the hall to the family room, where Ash is waiting for me on the couch. "But this isn't about money. Saving the environment is important, ya know? My friends and I are trying to do our part by carpooling a little more," I lie. I mean, technically, it's true. We are carpooling more, but it has less to do with the environment and more to do with me not being able to drive for the next little while, but still. Two birds with one stone and all.

"Well, as long as you're taking your turn, too, baby," Mom returns.

"Of course," I lie. *Again.* "Look, I gotta go, but I'll talk to you guys later, okay? And don't worry about stopping by Butter and Grace tonight. I'll see you after my exam."

"You sure?" they ask in unison.

"Yup. Positive. Love you guys."

"Love you, baby!" Mom calls out as Dad adds, "And don't forget to take your medicine!"

I hang up the phone and shove it into my back pocket as Ashlyn pushes herself up from the couch. "Hey. Sorry I took so long."

"No problem. Colt won't be done with practice for another thirty minutes anyway. And P.S., your parents are the sweetest."

"They're *something*," I mutter.

"Oh, come on. They love you. And trust me. Having loving parents isn't something to bat your eyes at."

Ash's relationship with her parents has always been a little rocky, but after Colt chewed them out the first time they met, things had been going pretty smoothly. At least, I thought so.

"How are your parents, by the way?"

She shrugs. "Fine. Baby steps, right?"

"I guess so. Thanks again for taking me to work," I add, grabbing my black jacket from the back of the couch and sliding my arms in it. The weather is getting colder and colder as the months pass, and the idea of leaving our house without an extra layer is full-blown ludicrous at this point.

"No problem." Ash shoves her hands into the pouch of her LAU hoodie and pulls out a set of keys on a baby blue lanyard. "How have you been feeling?"

As I open the front door, my gaze thins in silent warning. "Ash––"

She holds up her hands in defense. "I know, I know. I'm not treating you differently or anything. I'm just curious."

"Uh-huh, sure you are," I mutter.

"To be fair, I'm also worried about Mia, so you aren't the only roommate who's a..."

"Shitshow?" I finish for her.

"Not what I was going to say," she argues.

"I'm only half kidding." I close the door behind us and walk down the driveway toward her beat-up car. "But you definitely have a good point. I'm a little worried about Mia too."

"Blake's been running with her every morning since she saw Mia's pepper spray purchase, but she said nothing's been out of the ordinary or anything," Ash tells me as she puts the keys into the ignition and turns the heater on full blast.

"Blake said that, or Mia did?"

With a pointed look, Ash deadpans, "Who do you think? You know Mia. The girl's a freaking vault. Of course, she hasn't said anything."

"At least Blake's running with her. That's something, right?" I warm my fingers in the air blowing from the dash-board vents while Ash backs out of the driveway and turns onto the main road.

"I guess so," Ash says. "Still feels like something's up, though. A few months ago, I was at SeaBird with Colt, and I overheard her talking to her boss, asking if she could have an advance to make rent. But when I brought it up to her after-ward and offered to help cover her rent for a few weeks or something, she said she'd found a solution and wasn't having any issues with money . But then," Ash continues, "when I asked Mia what the solution was, she got super weird and wouldn't tell me. And now, she's scared to run by herself?

Well, I think we can all see the trajectory she's on, and it isn't exactly a good one."

My eyes widen in surprise. Don't get me wrong, Ash, Blake, and I are all poor college students. But we've always been able to make rent, and we all have enough support around us for help in case money is ever an issue. And Mia? Her aunt's married to a rockstar. *Literally.*

"Maybe she asked Fender or Hadley for a loan?" I offer.

"Come on, Kate. You know Mia as well as I do. The girl doesn't ask for anything. Ever. You really think she'd borrow money or ask for a handout from anyone, let alone her famous aunt and uncle?"

The girl has a point.

"And even if she did, it wouldn't explain the pepper spray situation. Don't get me wrong. Mia's smart to carry it. But what triggered the idea? I dunno. I feel like there's something I'm missing. I just wish she'd talk to me." Ash gives me the side-eye. "Like how I wish you'd talk to me."

"There's nothing to talk about."

"Uh-huh. Sure."

"Seriously, Ash," I mutter. "I'm fine. And I'm sorry you had to see me have a, uh, an *episode*, but––"

"I'm not," she interrupts.

I lift my hand and silence her. "I'm fine, okay? But I'm begging you to please stop treating me differently. Please. I need normalcy."

She nibbles her lower lip, her gaze drifting to me from the corner of her eye as she flips her blinker on. "I know. I just love you, Kate."

"I love you, too, Ash."

"Can you promise me something?" she asks.

"What?"

"I wouldn't pry if I didn't feel like I needed to for you to open up to me."

"Was there a request in there or…?"

She laughs. "My request is for you to promise me you'll let me know if you ever need anything. Okay?"

"I mean, I did ask you to take me to work today," I argue.

"Only after I found out you were planning to take the bus."

Again, the girl has a point. I hate asking for help. I hate being a burden. But it's hard. Being the broken one. The one who struggles to stand on her own. The one who's a ticking time bomb, despite every single effort I put into being stable and impenetrable. The truth is I'm not stable. I'm not impenetrable. And I'm not sure I ever will be. But knowing it and embracing it are two things I've yet to master.

When Ash sees me grimace, she adds, "Exactly. I'm all about independence. You know I am. But take it from a girl who never felt like she could rely on anyone without being a burden to them before finding a guy who convinced me to rely on him. It's pretty great. Being able to count on someone. And I want you to be able to count on me. That's all I'm saying."

"I know," I murmur.

"Good. All right, I'll drop it." She pulls up to the curb outside Butter and Grace and shifts her car into park. "Have fun at work. What time do you get off?"

"At ten."

"Perfect. I'll see you then."

"Ash," I start.

"Kate," she warns.

I grab the door handle but give in. "Fine. I'll see you after my shift."

Her expression lights up. "Perfect. Bye!"

4

KATE

Work was fine. Long but nothing bad happened. The monotonous chaos at Butter and Grace suits me. Which is weird when I think about it. But I'm a good waitress. I'm friendly. Personable. Good at taking orders. My memory's shit, thanks to my medication, but as long as I have my trusty notepad, it isn't a problem.

Ash picked me up after my shift, and I went home desperate for sleep.

The next morning, I wake up without Blake ordering me to slip on some exercise clothes, and a spark of excitement flows through me at the prospect of having a day off with only one thing on the to-do list: pick up my prescription.

At least, it *was* the only thing on my to-do list until Mia bombarded me at 11:52 in the morning. The girl works as a bartender at SeaBird and rarely wakes earlier than noon. But apparently, she's *also* been recruited to be my own personal gym buddy and insisted we grab some endorphins before her evening shift tonight.

"I thought you had tonight off?" I question while spreading some mayonnaise on a slice of wheat bread.

Mia's hair is still askew. Her bright pink sleep mask is shoved on top of her head as she covers her mouth with a yawn.

"Figured I'd take another shift," she answers.

"Oh?"

"Yeah. Sammie wanted a night off with Hawthorne, and since Ash and Blake already made plans with their boys, I didn't think I'd be missed too much."

"Uh, I'll miss you," I argue, grabbing some sliced turkey and provolone from the fridge. "You're really going to leave me all alone with the lovebirds?"

She grimaces. "I'll make it up to you. Promise. You can even swing by SeaBird and hang out with me if you want. First drink's on me."

Mia doesn't know alcohol can be a trigger. None of them do. After the episode a few weeks ago and all of her research, Ash suspects it's a trigger for me, but I lied and told her it wasn't. By some miracle, she hasn't questioned me on it. I don't want them to feel like they have to walk on eggshells around me. Nor do I want them to feel like they can't go out drinking or hang out at SeaBird or play Beer Pong at the Taylor house without making me feel left out. And honestly? I don't regret it. Keeping the truth from them. But it does make invitations like this one a little sticky. Because I'd love to hang out at SeaBird while Mia makes drinks for other customers. And no, I don't need alcohol to make it happen. I could always sip a Dr. Pepper or something, but I'm not in the mood. Not today.

"I actually have work, too, so you're off the hook," I tell her. The lie slips out of me with ease. Well, for now, it's a lie. My boss is always asking me to pick up extra shifts, so I'll text her to let her know I'm available. Making a mental note to do exactly that once I have a bit of privacy, I finish making my sandwich, cut it in half, take one side, and push the plate toward Mia.

The girl looks mildly hungover with last night's makeup still smudged under her eyes, and I have a feeling some food might do her good. Without protesting, Mia takes the second half of the sandwich and bites into it, almost groaning. "Mmm...food."

"Glad I can be of service."

She swallows and adds, "Now, go change into some gym clothes. I promised I'd take you before my shift."

"What am I? The co-owned dog in need of a walk?" I counter. "Do you guys have a schedule or something?"

"Aww, I want a puppy! If I'd known it was an option––"

"Aaaand, I'm gonna go get ready." I slip around the edge of the granite counter, heading toward the hallway leading to our bedrooms. "I'll meet you out here in ten?"

She takes another bite of turkey sandwich and mumbles through her mouthful, "Deal."

~

WHEN WE REACH THE GYM, MIA HEADS STRAIGHT TO THE treadmill. Her arms pump back and forth while she listens to whatever emo music makes up her playlist. She's always been this way. More independent. Less in your face. I think we're kindred spirits in that way. The way we can tell when the other person needs some alone time instead of smothering them with love and attention.

Don't get me wrong. I'm all for love and attention. But there's something about being overstimulated when a lot of people are in the room. It's nice not having to worry about offending Mia when I need space, the same way I know she isn't afraid to tell me when she needs some alone time.

As for now, however, it means I need to figure out what

to do in the weights area without Li'l Miss Blakely here to boss me around.

I stare at the row of free weights in front of me like a lost puppy. My teeth dig into my lower lip while I glance around, avoiding the muscular dudes scattered around me like confetti, then turn back to the free weights.

What to do. What to do.

"Fifteen minutes of lifting, and I can escape to the hot tub," I remind myself as I pick up a set of ten-pound weights.

Feeling their stares, I glance at a few gym rats to my left but take a deep breath and ignore them. I have just as much of a right to be here as they do.

Don't I?

"Squats," I mutter under my breath. "I'll start with squats."

Finding a relatively quiet corner, I spread my legs shoulder width apart and lower myself into a squat before pushing up and squeezing my ass the way Blake taught me. Over and over again, I repeat the movement, mentally counting to ten. Next, I switch to stationary lunges, my left leg first, then my right. Once I finish the lunges, I start another set of squats while I attempt to ignore how out of place I feel.

But the worst part? I'm actually starting to like exercising. Not one hundred percent in love with it. I'm not crazy like Blakely and Mia. But enough. Enough to appreciate what my body can do. Enough to recognize I'm growing stronger. Enough to understand this is good for me.

Mentally. Physically. Emotionally.

Sure, it'd be nice if I couldn't feel the stares from everyone around me. But, hey. It is what it is.

I'm continuing my reps, refusing to try anything fancy without Blakely here to guide me when a throat clears behind me.

"Uh, hey, Kate," the low voice mutters.

I glance over my shoulder, nearly dropping my weights. It's Macklin. In a white T-shirt stretched across his very toned torso and a pair of joggers hanging low on his hips. The guy looks as good as my dreams make him out to be. Which is weird and wildly inappropriate on so many levels.

Unfortunately, my buffer's missing.

Way to ditch me in my time of need, Blakely.

Rocking back on my heels, I force a smile, pray my face isn't on fire, and say, "Oh. Hey, Macklin."

"Hey. How's, uh"––he squeezes the back of his neck, looking awkward as hell––"weightlifting going?"

"It's…fine?" I answer, looking down at the dumbbells in my hands.

Seriously? That's why he walked up to me? To ask how my weightlifting is going?

The awkward silence grows thicker, and I click my tongue against the roof of my mouth, waiting for him to say something. Like maybe why he came over here in the first place. But he doesn't. He only stands there looking around the room, avoiding anything and everything to do with me.

"Ooookay," I mutter, resting the weights onto my shoulders, preparing for another round of squats because really? Why is he talking to me? And why does this entire interaction feel so much more awkward than every single, already terrible conversation we've had?

Choosing not to overanalyze this encounter until I'm alone in my own room and can overthink to my heart's content, I adjust my stance a bit more and lower myself into a squat.

"Wait," Mack urges.

I stand up again and drop the weights back to my sides. "What do you want, Mack?"

Clearing his throat once more, he steps closer and drops his voice low. "Your leggings…"

I look down at the black fabric stretched across my lower half. "What about them?"

"They're, uh, they're see-through."

Convinced I've heard him wrong, I blink slowly. "I'm sorry, what?"

"Your leggings," he repeats, motioning to them. "They're see-through. When you bend over, you can see everything."

My jaw drops. "*What?*" I shake my head, convinced I'm having yet another dream––though this one is much less appealing––involving the infamous Macklin Taylor.

"I said––"

"You can see *everything*?" My voice cracks as the words leave through gritted teeth.

The bastard has the decency to look ashamed and confirms, "Everything."

My palms grow sweaty as I fight off a panic attack.

I bend down to drop my weights, but he stops me. "Don't."

The severity of my clothing situation hits full force, and embarrassment rushes from the top of my head to the tips of my toes as I groan. "You've got to be kidding me."

"Here." He takes the weights from my grasp and sets them down by our feet.

Covering my face, I try to get a handle on my mortification, but it's freaking impossible. "Kill me now, kill me now, kill me now," I repeat, the words falling out on uneven breaths.

The heat from his chest warms the small space separating us. "For what it's worth," Mack consoles, "you don't have anything to worry about."

I drop my hand to see him looking down at me sheepishly. "What do you mean I don't have anything to worry about? Everyone saw...*everything*!" I almost screech, backing myself into the corner until I'm relatively covered by the wall behind me.

I knew I shouldn't have bought these online. I was too trusting. Too excited about a good deal. But it's how they get ya. Give a girl a good deal, and she's sure to pounce. Just don't let her see what they look like when she's squatting, or *bam!* Big mistake.

Macklin follows me, practically pinning me against the mirrored wall as he keeps his voice low. "Calm down, Kate. It's not a big deal."

"Not a big deal?" I glare up at him. "You're joking, right? Now everyone in this gym has seen me, and compared to the other girls--"

"Trust me," he glances over his shoulder, confirming we're still alone. "I don't think any of the guys are complaining."

I look around his toned body to find multiple meatheads staring at me. One of them lifts his chin. A shameless grin spreads across his face as his gaze slides down my body.

"The black lace is a nice touch," Mack adds wryly.

I tear my attention from the meathead and meet Mack's stare. "Tell me you're joking."

"You honestly think I made a lucky guess on what you're wearing, Kate?"

My hand covers my mouth as the reality of the situation hits full force. He's serious. He was able to see everything.

He saw my black thong.

But I don't know what to say.

Seriously.

Ground, please open up and swallow me whole. Please? Pretty please?

"Breathe," Macklin orders with a laugh. "If anyone's embarrassed, it sure as hell shouldn't be you."

"What's that supposed to mean?" I demand.

He bites the inside of his cheek to keep from grinning and shakes his head like he can't believe we're actually having this conversation. "Trust me. You don't wanna know."

"Tell me," I insist, practically stomping my foot as another wave of shame rolls through me. Might as well rip it off like a Band-Aid. Hell, maybe I started my period, too, and the blood seeped through. And it would definitely be the cherry on top of a craptastic day.

Macklin bends closer to me until his breath tickles the shell of my ear. "You're not the one who's walking around with a woody thanks to your little show."

Balking, I glance down at his... Oh. My. Gosh.

Sure enough, Macklin's dick is up, and holy cannoli, he's hung. I can't decide whether I should pat the guy and congratulate him for clearly having a massive penis or if I should book it to the locker room and burn my leggings on the spot. I snap my gaze up toward the ceiling and swallow thickly. I still don't know what to say. Do I apologize for making him hard? Do I beeline to the exit and swear off gyms for the rest of my life? My face feels hot, and I fan it with my hand. This is almost as bad as waking up after a seizure and––

"Breathe," Mack interrupts my mental freak out as if he can actually see the wheels turning in my head. I clench my hands into fists at my sides. "You have nothing to apologize for. I felt like you'd probably want to know why the guys are staring at you. Not that they wouldn't normally, but––"

"Trust me. It's not usually an issue," I snap, digging my teeth into the inside of my cheek while staring at the ceiling, avoiding Macklin's baby blues and reminding myself to breathe.

"Debatable," he mutters. "And just so you know, when you're not bent over, it's not bad. It's only when you're doing squats and shit can I see..." His voice trails off, and he clears his throat. "Aaaand, I'm gonna go sit in my car until things calm down." He glances at his crotch. "See ya around, Kate."

He backs up, giving me space, and my lungs expand shakily as if only now remembering how to breathe. But Mack's stare is what does me in. The way he's managed to make me feel attractive without making me feel embarrassed or slimy from our interaction. Pretty sure if any other guy approached me, it would've turned out differently. I probably would've left the gym and vowed to never come back. But with Mack?

He was so kind. Even when I was biting his head off. Blake's right. He's a big golden retriever and was looking out for me. I shouldn't have been a bitch. And honestly, I'm not one. Not usually. Not unless he's around.

As he pivots and walks away, leaving me in peace, I grudgingly call out, "Hey, Mack?"

He pauses and faces me again. "Yeah?"

"Thanks for..." I scratch my temple and tuck my hair behind my ear. "Thanks for the heads-up."

"No problem."

And I swear his smile could melt a freaking glacier as he nods and turns away.

5
MACKLIN

I shouldn't be considering this.

Fuck.

I know I shouldn't.

It's inappropriate on so many levels.

But I'm harder than a fucking rock, and if I don't take care of this, I'll have blue balls for days.

I glance behind me, but the parking lot is empty. My steps quicken as I rush toward my car in the far corner of the lot shaded by the large pine tree. Fitting since I'm contemplating doing something as shady as jerking off in my car to the memory of Kate's sweet ass.

But those damn leggings.

I climb behind the wheel and look down at my joggers, the ridge of my cock taunting me.

"Don't do it," I mutter under my breath.

Fisting my hands in my lap, I close my eyes and drop my head back, imagining my mom in a bikini and hockey stats from the last LAU game.

But it's been too long.

Too long since I've been with someone.

Too long since I've even *wanted* to be with someone.

An image of Kate bent over, her black thong separating her round ass and leading to her core spurs me on. Teasing me. Tempting me. Convincing me to do the unthinkable. And in a fucking parking lot, no less.

I grit my teeth, tugging at my pants and shoving them down until my dick pops free.

Bad idea, I remind myself.

Obviously, there's some merit behind the saying about guys only thinking with their dicks, because mine's clearly in control at the moment.

Forcing my eyes open, I look out the windshield, taking in the empty parking lot one more time as I grip the base of my cock and rub my palm up and down it.

Bad idea. Bad idea. Bad idea.

The words play on a constant loop as I go over my conversation with Kate. Only this time, I give my imagination free reign.

"If anyone's embarrassed, it sure as hell shouldn't be you," I grit out.

"What's that supposed to mean?"

"Trust me. You don't wanna know."

"Tell me." She stomps her foot and glares up at me, looking sexy as hell.

I bend closer to her, my lips dragging against the shell of her ear. "You're not the one who's walking around with a woody thanks to your little show."

Her breath hitches as she finds my dick standing at attention, and I growl low in my throat. Her fingers reach forward, toying with the drawstring of my joggers.

I pump my hand faster.

"What are you doing?" I rasp.

Her fingers trail south, brushing against the head of my cock. It twitches. Straining. Begging. Fucking weeping.

"I'm thinking I should return the favor. You know...since you were the only guy here nice enough to tell me my leggings were see-through."

I groan and shift in my seat, my chest heaving.

I bet she'd feel so good. All soft and pliable.

My hand moves faster, and I squeeze tighter, my balls already tightening.

Fuck.

I grit my teeth harder and turn my head.

Oh, shit.

Kate.

Kate's in the fucking parking lot.

She sees me.

She's *watching* me.

With her little purse hiked on one shoulder and her jacket zipped up almost to her breasts, showcasing her sports bra and cleavage. Her eyes are what do me in. The stormy gray pinning me in place.

I fall apart, my dick jerking. Ribbons of cum hit my palm as I hold her gaze.

Her brows pinch, and she turns away.

Prickly as ever.

Only this time, she might have a good reason.

What the hell was I thinking?

6

KATE

"**H**azel!" I snap.

The new girl jumps, slips her phone back into her dark jeans, and leans on the hostess stand, looking like a damn Girl Scout. "Oh. Hey."

Closing a bit more distance between us, I glance over my shoulder to where our manager is currently yelling at the kitchen staff and drop my voice low. "Dude, that's like the sixth time. If Anna catches you, she'll be pissed."

"Sorry. I just met this cute guy, and…" She waves her hand around. "You know how it is."

I don't, but that's beside the point.

I shouldn't be so on edge, yet here I am, anxious and annoyed.

I have been since I saw Macklin in the parking lot. His jaw was so tight, and his head pressed against the headrest. And his eyes? They were hooded and dark, like in my dreams.

What was he doing?

Okay. Probably a dumb question.

I've replayed the moment a thousand times since I left the gym, but the unknown is killing me.

He wouldn't have...touched himself.

Would he?

He seemed so unfazed by the whole legging debacle. Other than the physical evidence between his legs, he was as cool as a cucumber. But he only pointed out the...physical evidence to make me feel better about my own mortification. And when he said he was going to let things calm down in his car, I didn't think he meant like *that*.

I should find it gross and repulsive. Yet I don't.

Which is messed up on so many levels.

Anna's lucky I texted and offered to come in tonight because two waitresses didn't show up for their shifts, and I've yet to receive a tip for more than ten percent of my tables' bills. Added to the fact I'm a little sexually frustrat-ed––and majorly embarrassed––thanks to my encounter with Macklin at the gym, along with having to ride the bus to work, I'm ready to go home and call it a day.

Reeling in my annoyance, I keep my voice low and argue, "I'm just reminding you to keep your phone out of sight if you want to keep this job. The girl before you was literally fired because she was obsessed with TikTok, and––"

"Okay, I got it," Hazel interrupts, curling in on herself.

She started working here a few weeks ago and is still figuring out the do's and don'ts in the industry. She's nice. A little snooty sometimes, but I have a feeling it stems from the fact this is her first job, and she wants to be taken seriously, even if it's a bit off-putting sometimes.

The irony isn't lost on me.

She's definitely friendly, though. She gets along with the customers, is always willing to help, and even offered her arm to an old couple earlier tonight when she led them to their table. Needless to say, all of these are great qualities to have in the restaurant business. Now, if I could only convince her to let down her walls a bit and be more teachable, we'd be golden.

It's not like I plan to work at Butter and Grace for the rest of my life or anything, but being on good terms with my coworkers is a solid goal of mine, and I like my job here. Usually, anyway. It's predictable. And when a girl like me could convulse at any second, I crave predictability. I like the comfort it brings. The monotony.

And I like Hazel. I really do.

She's nice, and she hasn't heard the rumors about the incident a few weeks ago, which means she doesn't look at me differently. If anything, she's almost becoming a friend.

With a reassuring smile, I add, "You're killing it. Keep your phone out of sight, and keep up the good work." I slip past her, grabbing the drinks for table nine. Once I've taken their orders, I head back to the front of the restaurant and find Anna next to the hostess stand.

Crap.

With her hands on her hips, she's talking to Hazel. I don't hear what's said, but I don't need to.

I warned you, Hazel.

"Yes, I understand," Hazel returns, her cheeks flushed with embarrassment.

Satisfied, Anna walks away, and Hazel's confidence crumbles like a stale cookie. Shoving my notepad into the front pocket of my black apron, I approach her and ask, "Everything okay?"

"Fine. It's just annoying, ya know?"

I glance over my shoulder at Anna, but she's already preoccupied with a customer. Anna's mom put her blood, sweat, and tears into Butter and Grace. Because of how hard her mom worked to build the restaurant's reputation, she's always been a stickler for rules, presentation, and a strict mindset. And when one of her employees doesn't feel the same way? Well, she makes your life a living hell.

"What's annoying?" I ask, pretending to be oblivious.

"Like, no one's here." Hazel waves her arm at the empty waiting area in front of the hostess table. She's right. There's not a soul in sight. Which makes sense considering the time. We should be closing any minute.

"I told you she's a stickler when it comes to phones."

"Yeah, yeah. I know," she mutters. "Oh, and P.S., you're welcome."

My brow quirks. "For what?"

"I put your ex in Shelby's section even though your table was up next, but I highly recommend you steer clear of the bar area." She angles her head toward the opposite side of the restaurant to drive her point home. Sure enough, Wes is sitting there with three of his friends. His brown hair looks a little tousled, and his smile is as boyish and carefree as always. Thankfully, his back is mostly positioned toward me, but it doesn't stop the slight dip in my stomach when I see him.

It's still weird to think about. That I could've loved him. That he could've loved me. We hadn't been dating for more than a couple months, but we were on the right track. And we could've made it there––to our happily ever after––if it weren't for my condition.

I didn't want to tell him I had epilepsy, but my roommates insisted he had a right to know. And in a way, I guess he did. Still, it doesn't make the sting from our breakup hurt any less.

But the weird part? It's figuring out how much I miss him versus how much I miss the idea of him. The idea of someone accepting me in all my messy glory. The idea of having someone by my side. The idea of having someone to call at the end of a particularly amazing or crappy day. That's what I miss. And it's what I was reminded I'll likely never have when he broke up with me after Googling epilepsy and the side effects.

Yup. I've chalked it up to one more thing epilepsy has taken from me.

A relationship worth having.

Tearing my gaze from the shitshow across the restaurant, I look at Hazel again. "Thanks."

She bumps her shoulder against mine. "I got you, girl. Speaking of guys, I literally just felt my phone buzz." She juts out her bottom lip. "Do you know how much it's killing me not to see if Johnny texted me back?"

I laugh. "I think you'll survive."

"Ugh. My dad used to always say the same thing. He had this rule where we were all supposed to put our phones in a basket during family dinner, and whenever I'd ask for it back or tell him why I couldn't put my phone in the basket, he'd say,"--she drops her voice an octave and paints a stern expression on her face--"I think you'll survive, Hazel."

My lips lift in the corner. "And did you? Survive?"

She scrunches her nose. "Barely."

With another laugh, I pat her shoulder. "And if you survived back then, I'm sure you'll survive for another fifteen minutes until we close for the night."

As I start to walk away, she quips, "Fingers crossed we don't get any late walk-ins, Kate. 'Cause if we do, I'm putting them in your section."

"No, thank you!" I call over my shoulder and go back to work, grabbing the next order from the kitchen. It's for a bunch of rowdy teenagers sitting in one of the back booths.

Balancing a plate of cheesy fries on one arm and a tray of drinks with the other, I head around the side of the restaurant when I run smack-dab into a hard body. The drinks stain my white shirt, soaking into the fabric almost instantly as the fries land on the ground in a scattered mess of cheese, chili, and chives.

"Oh, shit," a familiar voice says.

I look up to find Wes Templeton standing in front of me.

Fan-freaking-tastic.

"Good to see you again too," I mutter, my pulse thrumming with adrenaline as I bend down and start cleaning up the mess.

It had to be Wes, didn't it? Yup. It's official. Karma hates me. First, the legging debacle, then crappy tips all night, and the reminder of my lack of a love life. Now, this?

Stick a fork in me. I'm so done.

Scrubbing his hand over the top of his head, Wes asks, "Can I help?"

"Nope." I pop the 'p' at the end, gathering the ruined food into a pile. The melted cheese cakes under my fingernails, making me want to squirm as I ignore Wes's presence. I can feel him staring down at me, unsure of what to do or what to say. Hell, I can still see his shoes from the corner of my eye.

Go away, dude. I seriously don't want to see you.

"How've you been doing?" he asks. I can't decide if it's out of obligation or if he's genuinely curious. Regardless, it doesn't matter. That particular door is closed. Forever.

"I'm fantastic," I grunt, scraping up a few more fries from the floor while attempting to ignore him. Once the sludgy mess is back on the tray, I stack the empty cups and stand up, pasting on a fake smile as I face Wes again. Because why would he leave me alone when I'm clearly having a crappy day? Nope. It would be way too convenient. I bite my tongue to keep from lashing out at the poor bastard and wait for him to either say something or go back to his table. Instead, he looks at me like the ball's in my court.

Jackass.

Heaven forbid I speak my mind and tell him to go to Hell.

I know it's not fair.

At least he was honest with me. Honest about what he wanted. How he pictured his future. At least he told me before it went too far. Before I could fall for him any more than I already had. Before I gave myself a chance to hope I could be accepted, could be loved. At least he told me the truth.

A bit of my iciness melts, and I bite the inside of my cheek, shifting the tray of goo from one hand to the other. A few strands of hair stick to my forehead, and I wipe them away with the back of my hand, desperate to escape this conversation as quickly as possible. "I should probably get back to work, so…"

He tucks his hands into his front pockets as his attention drifts down my body. "You look good, Kate."

I snort, holding back tears while dropping my gaze to my soiled shirt. And I don't know if it's the compliment, the shitty day, or my frayed emotions, but I laugh. "Liar."

"I'm serious."

"Yeah, okay. I think we've had enough chitchat for tonight. I gotta get back to work. Goodnight, Wes." I start to walk past him, but he steps in front of me.

"You okay, Kate?"

"Like I said, *fantastic*," I repeat. My tone oozes sarcasm as whatever semblance of understanding from our past dissipates into thin air. "Now, if you'll excuse me." I turn on my heel and head back to the kitchen.

So much for tonight ending on a good note.

7

KATE

"Thanks again for picking me up," I tell Mia as I close the passenger door with a loud *thunk,* the last of my energy seeping out of me. I'm beyond thankful I didn't have to take the bus. That's something, right?

"Sure thing. You're lucky my shift ended early." She glances at me and gasps, noticing the caramel-colored stain plastered across my entire torso. "Whoa. What happened to your shirt?"

"Decided to swim in Diet Coke."

With a laugh, understanding dawns on her. "Been there."

As she pulls out of the parking lot, I unlock my phone and check my messages. I wasn't kidding when I scolded Hazel for using her cell at work. Anna is a stickler for those things, which means I need to catch up on everything I've missed, including three texts from Mom and one from Dad.

MOM

Hey! It's ten o'clock. Did you take your medicine yet?

My stomach falls as I read her message.

Oh, no.

I forgot to pick it up, and now, it's too late. The pharmacy's closed. My body tenses as I fight the urge to hit something, throw my phone, or just...scream. I close my eyes, count to ten, and attempt to rein in my temper before I read her next message. I already know what it'll say.

> **MOM**
>
> Hey. I know you're busy, but it's getting late. Will you please let me know you remembered your meds so I can get some sleep tonight?
>
> Hey, baby! Sorry to be a pain. Just worried. Message me back, okay?
>
> **DADDY**
>
> You're freaking your mom out. Will you please answer her text?

Groaning, I click my phone off, settle back into my seat, and lean my head against the headrest. I can't believe I didn't remember to pick up my meds from the pharmacy. I shouldn't forget. I know I shouldn't. But I did. And admitting as much to my mother, even though she insisted I pick up my meds from the pharmacy as soon as I woke up this morning, will only stress her out. I'm already burnt out enough, thank you very much. No need to fan the flames.

A couple extra pills should be in a Ziploc bag in my backpack, so it'll be fine. And if not? Screw it. What's one more seizure to add to the books? It's not like I'm guaranteed to have a seizure if I miss a single dose. Still, Dr. Reed has pointed out how I'm surprisingly sensitive to my prescription, and consistency is key. I shiver, almost hearing his voice in my head as I replay my last scolding at my follow-up appointment after I visited the ER a few weeks ago.

"Everything okay?" Mia asks, giving me the side-eye.

I shiver and drop my phone into my lap. "My mom's being…my mom."

"What do you mean?"

"I mean, she's stressing about something outside of her control and is anxious for me to check in with her." I roll my head toward Mia. "Enough about me. How was work for you?"

"Fine. Had to throw a few assholes out, but hey. Just another day in the life of a bartender."

"Guess so."

"Do any of your customers get rowdy?" she questions.

"Not usually. Butter and Grace has a two-drink cap on their customers."

"Gotcha. Sometimes, I wish SeaBird had the same cap. You should've seen these two assholes. I swear…" She shakes her head, her exhaustion almost matching my own.

"Hey, look on the bright side. As soon as you have your nursing degree, you'll be golden," I point out.

Her expression changes almost instantly. "We'll see."

"What do you mean, we'll see?"

"We'll see if I can get hired anywhere."

"I'm sure you will," I argue, but the memory of my conversation with Ash rises to the surface. Is Mia having money trouble again? I open my mouth to dig a little deeper, but my phone buzzes in my hand. I look down, caught between annoyance and gratitude for the distraction when I recognize my mom's name flashing across the screen.

Annoyance, it is.

I groan and squeeze my eyes shut while Mia turns onto our dark street.

"Who is it?" she inquires. "Your mom?"

"Yeah."

"Are you going to answer?"

"Maybe?" I offer. "Haven't decided yet."

"Why not?'

"Because I don't feel like hearing a lecture," I answer honestly.

Mia clicks her fingernails against the steering wheel, lost in thought for a few seconds. "You should answer," she urges as she pulls into our driveway, turns the car off, pushes the driver's side door open, and tosses me her keys. "I'll give you some privacy."

The door closes, blanketing the cab in silence, and I look at the bright screen in my hand.

I know Mia's right. And I know why the topic of parental figures can be a tricky subject for her. After all, her dad was murdered a few years ago, and her mom is Miss Independent, traveling for work and giving her daughter a wide berth. Not because she doesn't love her, but because she expects Mia to handle her own shit the same way her mom was forced to handle hers from a young age.

Regardless, Mia's always pushing family relationships, and I shouldn't be surprised she's encouraging me to answer my mom's call.

Grumbling under my breath, I slide my thumb across the cell phone screen and press the phone to my ear. "Hello?"

"Did you take your medicine?" my mom blurts.

"Seriously?" I sigh and pick at my still-damp shirt sticking to my stomach. "This is how you greet a person?"

"Well, I've been texting––"

"And I haven't had a chance to answer. I've been at work."

"I thought you weren't scheduled for today."

Pinching the bridge of my nose, I hang my head and pray for patience. "I decided to pick up an extra shift."

"Oh." She pauses. "Well, that's nice. How was work, baby?"

"It was fine. The usual."

"Well, it's good to see you working so hard."

"Thanks."

"But are you having fun?" she quizzes.

"Fun?" I wipe some dust from Mia's dashboard as the cold seeps in from outside. "What's *fun*?"

"You know what I mean. Putting your books aside every once in a while. Hanging out with friends. Letting loose..."

"You've got to be joking." I shake my head and breathe onto the cold window, drawing a sad face in the fog with my index finger.

"You know what I mean," my mom repeats. "Relaxing. Spending your Fridays without your nose stuck in a book or your hands juggling other people's orders. Actually having fun instead of distancing yourself."

"I'll keep that in mind."

"Hmm," she hums, unconvinced. "Now. Did you take your medicine?"

I snort. "Subtle subject change, Mom."

"I try," she teases. "And I've noticed you haven't answered me yet. Did you forget to pick up your prescription? I told you to put a reminder in your phone."

"I did put a reminder in my phone. And I would've picked it up before work, but I lost track of time."

"So you don't have it?" she demands. "Baby, you know how important it is to take your medication every day. And I mean every. Single. Day."

"Yeah, I know, okay?"

"Honey," she groans. "I swear you didn't used to be this forgetful. What's going on?"

Used to be.

It's one of my mom's favorite terms. She doesn't say it on purpose, and she has no idea how much it hurts. The way I used to be. The reminder of who I was and how I used to act. I'm not that girl anymore. Haven't been for a long time. But being a bit forgetful is better than having seizures, isn't it? And it is. Even she can't deny it. However, the reminder of how I'm not entirely who I used to be because of said medication? Because of said diagnosis? It freaking sucks.

With my elbow on the center console, I press my phone to my ear and relax my weight onto my arm, exhaustion creeping over me. "Nothing's going on."

"Don't lie to me. I'm your mother. You used to––"

"Yeah, I know. I used to be responsible. And on top of things. And I had straight A's. And I could concentrate. And I could be the perfect little girl you always wanted me to be. I hate to break it to you, Mom; I'm not perfect."

"I'm not saying you should be, baby. I'm saying you need to remember the importance of taking your medication every day at the same time, or else it could throw things off, and you could wind up––"

"I know what can happen," I snap, shoving my fingers through my hair and tugging at the roots. It's so frustrating. How she treats me like a child. And what's even more frustrating is the fact that I get it. I get that she doesn't mean to. I get that she wants––no, *needs*––to make sure I'm safe. To make sure I'm okay.

Sometimes, I envy Mia. How her mom trusts her. How her mom gives her space while still loving her. Even when she's caught in a bind. Even when she could use her mom's help. Her mother waits for Mia to reach out instead of sticking her nose into her daughter's personal life.

Because this? The relationship I have with my parents? Sometimes, it makes me feel like I'm suffocating.

Scratch that.

I've been suffocating ever since my diagnosis, and it isn't even their fault. Why would tonight be any different?

Sensing my frustration, she murmurs, "I'm sorry." She knows she's overstepped. She knows she's pushing when she shouldn't be. She knows I don't need a lecture, no matter how much she wants to give me one. "I love you, Kate. We both do."

"I know," I whisper.

"We want to make sure you're taking care of yourself. Are you sure you're okay?"

It's an excellent question. And it's one I'd love to answer without hesitation. But even I can't deny I screw up sometimes. I don't always take care of myself. I'm not perfect. And sometimes...it's hard to see the *why*. Sometimes, it's hard not to ask myself, what's the point? Why do I care? What does it matter?

So what if I don't take my medication? Maybe I'll have another seizure. Maybe I'll wake up on the floor with a dozen eyes staring at me again. It's not like the medicine is one hundred percent effective anyway. For some, it is. And I'm lucky enough to have found a pretty decent one. But still. I was taking my medication the last time I seized. Dr. Reed insisted on running some tests at the hospital, and his reasoning for how I ended up on the floor? Well, he told me sometimes, it just...*happens*.

Having your blood tested every few months and your memory turning to shit, not to mention all the money required to fill the prescription even if it isn't one hundred percent effective? It's a lot. And add in all the sacrifices, as well as trying to stay on top of things all of the time while knowing even if I am, it still won't be enough, *I* still won't be enough? It's exhausting.

"Kate, honey?" Mom murmurs. Her tone is softer. More gentle. Like I'm being handled with kid gloves. Like she knows how close I am to breaking.

"I have a few more pills in my backpack," I offer. "I'll take my dose as soon as I go inside, okay?"

"And you'll remember to pick up your prescription tomorrow?" she prods.

"Yes, Mom. I'll remember to pick up my prescription tomorrow."

"Thank you, baby."

And I hate it. How I can hear the gratitude in her voice. The relief.

"You're welcome," I mumble. "Tell Dad I said hi."

"Hi, honey!" he calls through the speaker.

"Hi," I choke out, not surprised he's been listening this entire time. Because he cares too. They both do. "I'll talk to you guys later."

"Okay, baby," Mom acknowledges.

I start to hang up the phone when she speaks again. "And, honey?"

"Yeah?"

"Don't forget to text me once you've taken it."

I close my eyes and fight the urge to cry. "Okay. Bye."

8

MACKLIN

"Dude, you should come out with us," Theo encourages me through the phone's speaker.

It's been a few days since we last talked. A few weeks since I've spoken to anyone outside of my job. Guess it's getting easier and easier to become the mountain my mom's worried I'll turn into. But I like the quiet. Usually, anyway. Just wish I had someone to spend it with.

"Did you hear me?" Theo asks.

"Yeah, I heard you. But now, I'm curious. Did Mom recruit you to get me out of the house again?" I grab a grocery cart from the front of the shop and head toward the produce section. It was a long day at work, and I'm exhausted. But I'm out of food and need to keep the house stocked in case a storm hits, and I can't drive back down the mountain.

"Nah," Theo starts.

"But I did!" Blake yells in the background of the call.

"Ah, I see. Apparently, you're a meddling Taylor woman in the making." I chuckle dryly and grab a couple of oranges from the bin.

"I *better* be," she replies.

I smirk, hearing the determination in her voice.

"Speaking of meddling, how's the dating life?" she prods.

"Fine," I lie as I pick up a lime and examine it, putting it back where it came from.

"Oh, yeah?" she challenges. "So you're bringing a date tonight?"

"Can't come, Blake." I snag a paper bag of Honeycrisp apples and a bunch of bananas, stacking them into the cart. "Sorry."

"Oh, come on," she whines. "It'll be fun! Mia even convinced her manager at SeaBird to let me in as long as I wear an orange wristband so no one serves me."

"That's supposed to be on the down-low, remember?" Theo mutters.

"Aren't you supposed to have a fake ID or something so you can get into the bar like a normal college student?" I ask.

Blake cuts off Theo's groan, her voice thick with snark. "I *had* a fake ID, but *someone* threw me under the bus before we were officially dating, and now, I've been flagged."

"I've already apologized," Theo reminds her.

"Not enough," she informs him. "Anywho, I still say you should come."

Reaching for a couple heads of broccoli, I slip them into my cart and mutter, "I dunno. SeaBird's usually packed with college kids, and––"

"Is there something wrong with college kids?" Blake interrupts.

I smile and shake my head, despite knowing she can't see me. The girl's so damn spicy I can't help it. No wonder Theo pokes at her like he does. "Nothing wrong with them, Blake. They make me feel old, is all."

"Come on. You're not old," she argues.

"When I'm surrounded by kids closer to my daughter's age than my own? Yeah, it makes me feel old."

"There's nothing wrong with dating a younger woman. Right, Teddy?"

"Nothing at all," he returns, and lip-smacking sounds through the speaker. My nose wrinkles, and I fight the urge to hang up until Theo adds, "You just gotta find the right one."

"Yeah." I pick up some cheese from the back of the store and make my way toward the frozen section. "I'll be sure to do that."

"We only want to see you happy," Blake chirps.

"You sure you haven't talked to Mama Taylor?" I question, but Blake barrels on.

"Even if it's just a friend for you to hang out with. You need someone who shares your same interests. Someone you can open up to and talk with about your day. It doesn't even have to be about sex or anything. Mack, all we're saying is… find a friend."

"Yeah, I hear you loud and clear." My attention catches on a familiar face in the frozen section, and I pause.

Speaking of sex...

I haven't talked to Kate since our run-in at the gym, and I'm still reeling from it. I probably shouldn't have told her I had a hard-on, but she was so ashamed of her leggings I couldn't help it. I had to take the attention away from her and her lacy black underwear.

Fuck, her underwear.

I almost groan as the memory rises to the surface before shoving it away.

Because Blake's right.

I could use a friend.

And it doesn't have to be about sex.

Honestly, it'd probably be smart if it *wasn't* about sex.

I don't need to get attached to anyone anytime soon, and I have a hunch Kate doesn't need to, either. Besides, she's young. I should remember that. She also kind of hates me, but I have a feeling it's a defense mechanism, and I don't scare easily.

"Mack?" Blake calls out through my cell. "You still there?"

"I'll, uh, I'll talk to you guys later," I tell her, dragging my attention from Kate and grabbing a gallon of milk from the opposite aisle. "Thanks again for the invite."

"You still coming to Mom and Dad's on Sunday?" Theo asks.

"Yeah, I'll be there."

"Good. We'll see you later!"

The call ends, and I shove my phone into my pocket as I sneak another look at Kate. Her long, dark hair swishes from side to side while she peruses the premade cookie dough options next to the eggs.

I push my cart toward her, but she's too distracted to notice me. "Hey, Porcupine," I greet her.

Her head snaps in my direction as if I've scared her. She crosses her arms and frowns. "Porcupine?"

"'Cause you're prickly," I remind her, pulling back a little bit when I notice the slight bags under her eyes. "You okay?"

"Yeah." She untucks her hair from behind her ear, using it as a curtain to shield herself from me. "You always shop here?"

"Sometimes." I push the cart a little closer to her and grab a carton of eggs next to the section she's been studying, opening it and making sure none of the eggs are cracked. I close it and set the carton into my basket. "Changed your leggings, I see."

She rolls her eyes but refuses to look at me and mutters, "Burned them is more like it."

"What a shame," I tease. "So...cookie dough, huh?"

She glances at me, then looks down at the Pillsbury section like it's the most fascinating thing in the world. "Uh, yeah. Not as interesting as your gray joggers from the other day, but hey. We win some and lose some."

I laugh, surprised by her bravado. I have a feeling she's almost as shocked she mentioned my joggers as I am. A light blush spreads across her cheeks. But instead of poking the bear the way I desperately want, I point out, "Mama Taylor has a killer cookie recipe, but she refuses to share it with anyone."

Her lips lift slightly as she turns back to me. "Sounds cutthroat."

"When it comes to her baking, she is."

"My mom always used the Nestle recipe on the back of the chocolate chip bag."

"Also a solid choice," I tell her. "I've never had the prepackaged stuff, though."

She glances at the tubes of dough again and grabs the classic chocolate chip flavor. "It's not homemade, but it'll do in a pinch."

"A pinch?" I cock my head. "Are you in a rush to catch up with everyone or something?"

"Huh?" A cute little wrinkle appears between her dark eyebrows. "Oh, you mean Ash and Blakely and the boys. No, I actually told them I had to study, so..." Her voice trails off, and she rocks back on her heels. "How did you know about it? SeaBird," she clarifies, her eyes thinning with suspicion.

"Don't worry, Kate, I'm not following you or anything. Theo invited me. Pretty sure Mama Taylor's twisting his arm to make me feel included."

Her mouth twitches, her stormy gaze sparking with amusement, but she hides it quickly. "So you're telling me meddling parents never grow out of...meddling?"

"Not in the slightest. At least my mom hasn't," I clarify.

"I guess I won't hold my breath for my parents, either."

"Your parents are meddlers and worriers, huh?" I ask.

Her lips thin, but she doesn't answer me, and damn if it doesn't turn me on.

Her silence, her walls, her aloofness...all of it intrigues me. The way she refuses to even talk to me unless I pry the words out of her. The way she gets nervous and fidgety anytime I'm around. It makes me want to poke the bear even more. Makes me want to peel back the layers she surrounds herself with. Makes me want to continue our conversations no matter how one-sided they feel.

Just like in the ambulance. Just like at the gym.

So damn quiet.

So damn intriguing.

"So you're not going to hang out with your friends tonight?" I prod.

"SeaBird isn't exactly my scene."

"Why not?"

"I dunno. Booze and I aren't exactly friends, and sometimes the lights are super flashy and..." Her voice trails off as she shrugs, her anxiety tainting the air around us like gasoline, needing only the tiniest of sparks to burn our almost pleasant conversation to the ground.

It doesn't take a genius to piece together what she's refusing to say out loud. Alcohol and flashing lights can be triggers for seizures. She's staying away to protect herself, even when it's isolating for her.

My stomach dips at the realization. It must be lonely. Dealing with something so inordinately heavy by yourself. However, I doubt she wants my pity. And honestly? She doesn't have it. We all have our baggage, and we all learn to carry it in different ways. Hers just happens to involve staying away from clubs and alcohol. It wouldn't be such a big deal if she wasn't in college. But for now, it's a bitch and leaves her more isolated than her friends probably realize.

"I'm getting too old to be hungover, so I get it," I admit. "It's not really my scene, either. Especially after I just got off work."

"And figured you'd do a little grocery shopping before heading home?" She tilts her head toward my cart, perusing my groceries. Her eyes widen with surprise.

"There a problem with my food?" I ask.

Realizing she's been caught snooping, her gaze snaps to mine, and she settles back on her heels. "Nope."

"You look surprised."

"No, I..." Her attention drops to my cart again, and she shakes her head.

"Tell me," I urge.

She lets out a light, embarrassed laugh and glances at the cart another time as if she can't help it. "No processed food."

"That's a problem?"

"No," she rushes out.

"Then, what is it?"

"I've never met a guy who doesn't survive off ramen noodles, protein shakes, and frozen pizzas."

"Not all of us have young metabolisms able to bounce back after eating like shit all the time."

Clutching the tube of dough to her chest, she challenges, "Are you coming after my cookie dough?" Her tone is a little lighter. Less guarded. More carefree than I've ever witnessed, at least during our conversations anyway. Probably because she's relieved at the subject change and how we aren't tiptoeing around her epilepsy. But what do I know?

Her smile, though. Damn. It's the first time I've seen it. The first time she hasn't tried to bite my head off or dismiss me at the drop of a hat. But I'm not sure whether or not I like her full attention. Actually, I have a feeling I do like it. Maybe a little too much.

I blink, forcing myself to stop staring at how gorgeous she is. "You think I'd come after your cookie dough?" I shake my head. "Of course not. But if I'm going to eat something sweet, I prefer to put the time and effort into making it worth it."

"Unfortunately, not all of us have Mama Taylor's recipe."

"Maybe I'll have to steal it from her so you can compare."

"Hmm," she hums, holding my gaze as she tucks her long black hair behind her ear. Apparently, the shields are down again.

Interesting.

As if realizing we're having an actual conversation where she isn't as cold as ice, she leans back a few inches and murmurs, "I should probably get going."

"If you want, I can pick up the ingredients, and we can make some real cookie dough tonight." The invitation slips out of me before I can help myself. But I don't rescind it. Because I kind of like her prickly side. Part of me wonders if others get to see it as often as I do. Not that I'm special or anything.

Besides, I think she needs the company as much as I do.

"I shouldn't," she decides.

"Why not?"

"I dunno? You've had a long day at work. I've had a long day at school. I need to study. You need to…"--she waves her hand at the grocery cart again--"put your groceries away. It seems like more hassle than it's worth. It's only cookie dough."

"*Only* cookie dough?" I step closer. "You see, when you say things like that, it makes me think you need to try some other recipes. Just sayin'."

"I'll see you around, Mack."

I nod and step away from her. "Next time, then. See you around, Kate."

She smiles stiffly but walks away, clutching the tube of cookie dough in her dainty little hands like it's a lifeline.

My girls used to love cookie dough. Every Sunday, we'd visit Grandma and Grandpa Taylor's house. They'd sit on the granite countertop, arguing over whose turn it was to scoop the flour, crack the eggs, and add the chocolate chips. The familiar dull ache in my chest heightens, and I pull my phone out, typing Miley a message. We've been chatting a little more over the last few months. Nothing crazy. But the girl responds every so often and always makes sure to at least like my messages, even if she doesn't know what else to say. And damn me if I didn't admit I live for those little thumbs-up notifications.

ME

Hey, Miley. I was talking with a friend about cookie dough, and it made me think of you. Do you remember when you and Hazel would help Grandma make cookies? Pretty sure I still have a picture of you eating from one of her spoons with the baking tray in front of you.

I hit send and pull up Miley's big sister's text thread. Countless blue messages line the right side of my iPhone, while the left side is pathetically blank. She's never responded to me. Not once. She's always been the stubborn one. The one who refused to cry when she was hurt, choosing to run into her room and slam the door instead of letting her parents comfort her. Part of me thinks it's what she's still doing. Keeping me at arm's length while she licks the wounds left from my divorce.

I'm so sorry, Hazel.

Refusing to let it bring me down, I'm trying to think of

66

something clever to say to Hazel when Miley responds, distracting me.

MILEY

Photo or it didn't happen, old man. Let's see it.

Old man.

I bite back my laugh and shake my head. The girl's a smartass, but I love her for it. Pulling up the photos app, I search through the pictures on my phone and find the image I'd been thinking about. Miley's in nothing but her diaper. She's barely two and is sitting on the counter, her face covered with cookie dough as my mom squishes her face against hers. They're both grinning from ear to ear while Hazel's posing in a princess dress with her hands held up high in the air, holding a dough-covered spatula like it's a magic wand as she stands on the counter with bare feet. They both look so little. So precious.

I send the photo to Miley and pull up the unanswered text thread between Hazel and me again, unsure what to say.

ME

Miss you, Haze!

I delete the message and try again.

ME

Took a short walk down memory lane tonight. Hope you're doing well.

Delete.

ME

Crazy to think you used to be this little.

I groan and try again.

67

ME

> You and Miley still argue over who gets to lick the bowl?

I hit send and share the picture, waiting for the *delivered* notification to pop up beneath the blue bubble on the phone, curious to see if it changes to *read* anytime soon.

They always do.

Sometimes it's minutes. Sometimes it's days. But Hazel always reads them. My texts. And it doesn't matter if she never responds because I'll always keep sending them no matter what.

Always.

9

KATE

S *hit, it's cold.*

I tug my coat tighter around me. The frigid wind cuts through it like an ice pick. It's darker too. I look up at the gray, angry clouds hanging heavy in the sky and pick up my pace toward the house. It was stupid of me to walk here, but I was craving something warm and sweet and gooey to take away my loneliness, and cookie dough sounded like the perfect choice.

Running into Macklin was unexpected. He wasn't the warm and sweet I was looking for, but his invitation still melted my insides in exactly the right way. At least it did before I remembered I'm not looking for...whatever the hell keeps happening whenever he pops up.

I fold my arms and quicken my pace, walking along the side of the road as an angry clap of thunder reverberates from the sky and into my bones. My body jerks at the deafening sound, but I keep my head down when a dark SUV pulls up beside me.

Fear claws its way up my throat as the *Dateline* headlines flash through my mind of Kate Winchester's disappearance.

The window rolls down, revealing a shadowed figure behind the steering wheel.

"Hey, do you need a––*Porcupine?*" the low voice rumbles.

The dashboard lights up Mack's familiar features, and I let out a sigh of relief.

Not a murderer. Noted.

"Hi," I answer, putting my head down and continuing my hurried walk along the street.

With the window still rolled down, Mack's SUV follows me. "What the hell are you doing walking home?"

Another clap of thunder makes me jump.

"Get in the car," he orders.

"It's fine," I yell back. "I think the rain will hold until I make it––"

"Get in the car, Kate."

Resisting the urge to defy him, I march closer to Mack's car. With the cookie dough clutched in one hand, I yank the door open, climb inside, and tug off my hood as Mack pulls back onto the road. But it's weird. Because for the first time since we've met, he isn't chatty. Nope. He's silent.

I peek at his hands on the steering wheel. They're tight, showcasing the veins along the back of his hands and on his wrists before disappearing beneath his black coat.

"I really was fine walking," I start.

"Why were you walking in the first place?" he demands. There's a sharpness in his tone. One I've never heard.

I lean away from him, unsure how to handle the new, not-so-golden-retriever-y guy beside me.

"It's nine o'clock at night, Kate. It's dark. Cold. The clouds look ready to burst at any second––"

"I told you I was craving cookie dough," I interrupt.

He grabs my hands and shoves them toward the vents. I almost moan at the warmth.

Holy shit, it feels good.

Goosebumps spread along my arms as the heat finds its way under my coat sleeves.

Giving me the side-eye, Mack's jaw clenches like he can't help it.

"Why didn't you drive?" he demands.

"None of your business."

"Answer the question, Kate."

"Oh, so I'm not a porcupine anymore?" I quip.

"Not when it comes to your safety."

"Well, if it counts for anything, you're not acting like much of a golden retriever right now, either."

"Golden retriever?"

"All nice and friendly and comforting and…"--*seriously, stop talking, Kate!*--"stuff," I finish awkwardly.

His jaw clenches, and he gives me the side-eye again. "Why the hell didn't you drive?"

"I felt like walking," I lie.

He grinds his molars. "I hope you're joking."

"Why is it funny?"

"Do you not have a car or something?" he asks.

"I have a car."

"Then why didn't you drive it?"

"I only live like a mile away. Turn right at the next light, by the way," I add, directing him to my house.

The blinker turns on with a flick of his fingers, and he merges into the right lane. "It's not safe to walk outside by yourself at night."

"Yeah, okay, *Dad*." I fold my arms, annoyed. I probably shouldn't be because the jerk has a point. But I don't like being told what to do, and I sure as hell don't like it when it's coming from someone like Mack. Someone who has their life together. Someone who feels like they know everything. Because it's bullshit. He doesn't know a thing about me. Sure, he had a front-row seat to literally my biggest insecurity, but it doesn't mean he knows me. Not even close.

"At least now it makes sense why your parents are so overprotective," he mutters. I'm not sure the words are meant for me. It doesn't stop me from hearing them. And it sure as hell doesn't stop them from hitting their mark.

"Excuse me?" I shift in the passenger seat until my back is plastered to the door, and I glower at him fully.

"I'm just saying." He waves his hand toward the angry sky as lightning cracks through the clouds. "You should know better, and if you have a car, you should use it. Especially at night when the forecast says it's going to--"

"I can't drive," I snap. "That's why I didn't take my car."

He frowns, glancing at me again, a bit of the judgment leaving his eyes. "What?"

"I said I can't drive," I repeat. "Not for another couple of months, thanks to my seizure, so don't assume anything, asshole."

We approach the next light, and he gently taps the brakes, slowing down but staying silent as he processes my word vomit. And oh boy, do I regret said word vomit. I should have never said anything at all. I should've let him assume I'm an irresponsible brat instead of allowing him to see the truth. Because the truth hurts worse. The truth is corrupted by things out of my control. And I hate being out of control. I hate having my license taken away. I hate how, even now, I could wind up unconscious, shaking in the passenger seat of Macklin's SUV since, apparently, my medication's going bonkers. Sure, the odds aren't particularly high, but still. They're there. And they're higher than for most people. I hate how no matter what I do, it still affects me. It still affects my decisions and how others look at me. Or *don't* look at me, considering Mack's gaze is currently glued to the road, his knuckles white with tension as he throttles the steering wheel.

I've pissed him off.

Or embarrassed him.

Or…something.

He's made me feel all of the above, too, so an eye for an eye, I guess. If only it made me feel better about lashing out at him.

He didn't know. Of course, he didn't. How could he?

I shouldn't have snapped.

He shouldn't have assumed.

So, where does this leave us?

In a silent car as he continues straight down the road without a word.

Say something, Mack!

You're the chatty one. Not me.

That isn't my job in this relationship.

You're nice, I'm mean, and you're cool with it. Remember? I silently remind him.

But nope. Mack stays quiet, his hands relaxing against the steering wheel as the clouds finally break and water splashes against the windshield.

My street comes into view a minute later, and I clear my throat, the sound practically deafening in the otherwise silent cab. "Turn right."

He follows my order without a word.

"It's the house on the left," I add.

The car stops in front of the driveway, and I reach for the door handle.

"Kate, I'm sorry," he murmurs. The softness makes me pause.

Hesitating, I glance at him, my fingers still clutching the door handle. I don't know what there is to say. He assumed. I snapped. And here we are.

But the guilt emanating from him? Well, it isn't exactly fair, either.

"It's fine," I mutter, unable to take the silent staredown any longer.

"No, it isn't. I shouldn't have assumed."

"Not everyone gets their license taken away because of a seizure."

"I shouldn't have assumed you were being irresponsible when you were actually being the opposite. I'm an ass."

"You're not an ass," I whisper.

And it's true. He's probably one of the sweetest guys I've ever met, and I've been treating him like crap because of it. Because I like him. I like how he's kind. I like how he's patient. I like how he notices people and isn't afraid to say hello when I'm accustomed to sneaking out in the opposite direction. Hell, I'm envious of him. Jealous of how comfortable he is in his skin, wishing I could feel the same.

"I made an assumption," he continues. "It was an asshole thing to do." His hand scrubs over his face, and he pins me with his stare. "I'm sorry."

"Apology accepted." I open the door, but he stops me again.

"Hey, Kate?"

I turn back to him. "Yeah?"

"Next time you need a ride––and I'm not just saying this––call me."

"Mack, I'm fine."

"You don't get it. I literally won't sleep at night if you don't make me this promise."

The sincerity in his eyes makes me pause, the light blue turning darker in the lack of light.

Blue. Blue. Blue.

"Promise me," he pushes.

"You hardly know me," I remind him.

"Guess it's just in my nature."

"To care about weak, pathetic people?" I question dryly.

"To care about my friends and their well-being."

Friends.

The word hits differently than when Ash, Blake, or Mia says it.

I hesitate, digging my teeth into the inside of my cheek and dipping my chin in a single nod. "Fine. If I ever need a ride, and there isn't anyone at home, and it looks like it's going to rain, *and* I'm craving cookie dough, I'll give you a call." I start to slide out of the passenger seat, but he reaches for me, grabbing my wrist.

The heat from his grasp warms my forearm through my jacket as I look down at his fingers encompassing it.

"Or if you feel stir-crazy and want to get out of the house," he clarifies. "Or if you start walking somewhere and decide you don't want to walk anymore. Or if you just want a fucking ride somewhere. Anywhere. *Period.* Give me a call."

He's serious. I can see it. Feel it. Taste it. Honestly, I've never met a more sincere man in my life other than my father, but even he doesn't count *because* he's my father. The man beside me? He's practically a stranger. A nice stranger. With kind eyes and a kind smile. But a stranger, nonetheless.

A stranger who probably has other things to worry about. Other *friends* to worry about.

"I'll be sure to give you a call," I lie.

His mouth quirks up on one side, and he lets me go. "Oh, you will?"

"Yup."

"Then, I should probably give you my number."

Dammit, the thoughtful asshole caught me.

"Are you always this bossy?" I ask.

He smiles, and my stomach somersaults.

"You know what? I have a better idea." He pulls out his

phone. "What's your number? This way, you can't fake saving my contact info or give me the wrong number."

He waits patiently, his thumbs hovering over the screen as the rain pitter-patters against the roof of his car.

"Mack," I warn.

"Kate," he returns, refusing to budge.

"You really won't let this go, will you?"

His smirk turns into a full-on grin. "Not a chance."

Annoyance simmers in my veins, but I rattle off my number, and he inputs it into his phone. My right ass cheek vibrates. I take out my phone and find an unknown number flashing across my screen.

"Now you have mine too," he tells me.

"I can see that." I tuck my phone back into my pocket. "Are we done here?"

"Unless you want to make cookies," he offers.

A dry laugh slips out of me before I can stop it. Gotta give the golden retriever credit. He's a persistent little bugger.

"Maybe some other time," I tell him.

"Can I ask you one more question?"

I sigh and close the passenger door, stopping the rain from ruining the leather seat as I face him fully again. "What is it, Mack?"

"Why'd you say no when your friends asked you to hang out tonight?"

"I already told you. I need to study, and SeaBird isn't my scene."

The light from the dashboard highlights the sincerity in his gaze––and the stubbornness. "So it really is because you don't like SeaBird?"

"I never said I didn't like it. It's like I already told you...the lights bug me sometimes, and I don't like drinking."

"Okay, but if the lights weren't flashing, and you didn't

drink alcohol while you were there. Would you still have said no?"

"It's complicated."

"Try me."

He's not going to let this go. My lips purse, but I give in. "Fine. But only because you were nice enough to give me a ride," I tell him. "I like going to bars. I like the atmosphere. It's fun. It's a great chance to hang out with my classmates and meet people, but…"

"But what?"

I swear he can see the indecision in my eyes. He knows I don't want to tell him and understands I'd rather keep this particular can of worms to myself. I can also tell he won't drop it until I give in, and I need to get away from the guy if I want a chance to reset and raise my walls again.

"Tell me," he pushes. "But *what?*"

"But if the shitty stars align, and I have a seizure, I'm kind of screwed," I answer. "A seizure––period––isn't safe, but a seizure in the middle of a dance floor, surrounded by people who are drunk off their asses? It's a recipe for disaster, and I promised my parents I'd be as safe as I could, even if it means I have to stay home sometimes."

"So your solution is to stay in, even when you want to go out?"

"It's not like I can ask one of my friends to be my babysitter on the off chance I have an issue. Especially when the odds vary from day to day as much as they do. It isn't fair to them."

"But is it fair to you?" He challenges, his brows pulled low. "Having to say no to things you want to do?"

"I guess it's one of the joys of having epilepsy." I reach for the door handle again, anxious to go inside and put this conversation to rest.

"What would you do if you didn't have to worry about it?

If you could go out knowing you were safe? What would you do?"

"I dunno? Dancing sounds fun." I push the door open, and this time, he lets me step outside. "Thanks again for the ride." The door shuts as the rain splats against the crown of my head, and I rush inside, my tube of cookie dough clasped tightly in my hand.

But it doesn't stop the sensation of his gaze on me as I hurry up the porch steps and unlock the front door.

If only I knew what it meant.

Or why I care.

10

MACKLIN

"**H**ey, Mama," I greet, kissing her on the cheek. The house smells like bacon and vanilla, thanks to the different foods scattered on the white granite countertops.

"Aww, my baby!" Mama gushes. Wiping her hands on her sunflower apron, she turns around and pulls me into a hug. "How are you?"

"I'm fine. Where's Dad?"

"He's at the office. Some kid got hit with a puck in the mouth this morning, and he's trying to save the boy's front teeth." She grabs my chin and shakes my head back and forth. "Reminded me of you and your brother."

I laugh and pull away from her. "So, Dad's allowed to miss Sunday Brunch, but I'm not?"

"Oh, because eating your Mama's delicious food is so hard to do." She smacks the back of my hand with her spatula as I reach for a piece of bacon.

With a laugh, I shake off the sting. "Can I help with anything?"

"Why don't you grab the trays and set them on the

kitchen table," she offers. "Blakely and Theo will be here any minute."

"Blakely's coming?"

"Yes. She also invited a friend, but I'm not sure if she's joining us. It was still up in the air, apparently. I invited Hazel and Miley, too, but they said they couldn't make it."

I pause as I start to pick up a tray of food.

I'm not sure if it'll ever get easier. Hearing my daughters' names while knowing they don't want to see me. I messaged them earlier today. Told them I was thinking about them. Miley said thanks, and Hazel didn't respond.

Part of me wonders if she's ever responded to her grandma's texts, but the other part of me doesn't want to know, terrified Hazel's only grudge is with me. That I'm the problem. The one who caused irreparable damage with no tools or opportunities to fix it. I should be glad she isn't icing out everyone on my side of the family. At least it's something. Some kind of connection she can build. Some sort of knowledge that she's loved. That she's missed.

It takes a few trips, but I grab the bacon, French toast, omelet dish, and blueberry muffins and move them to the sitting area as requested. I'm setting the last of the trays onto the table when the front door opens.

"Mama Taylor!" Blakely yells, and my mom's head pops through the kitchen entrance.

"Blakely Thorne!" Mama raises her hands in the air. "Get your cute butt over here, girl!"

Blakely races toward her and wraps her arms around my mom.

"Look how big you've gotten!" Mama gushes.

Blakely laughs and pulls away. "It's so good to see you!"

"You too. How's your mama?"

"She's good," Blake answers. "Told me to say hi."

"Good. You sure she doesn't want to come and eat some

breakfast with us?"

"She's actually hosting Colt and Ash this morning," Blake explains. Colt is Blake's older brother and Theo's best friend. Their family lived down the street from us growing up. They were all really close until Blakely and Colt's father died in a car accident a few years ago. My mom did everything she could to help, but the family needed time to process everything.

Life is weird.

How it can change at the drop of a hat.

Leaving everyone feeling like they're spinning out of control.

It takes time to adjust.

To find a new routine.

A new normal.

I can relate.

"Well, shoot," Mama pouts. "Next time, we'll have to all get together."

"Deal," Blakely agrees.

"Is your friend coming?" Mama looks around Blakely's tiny frame in search of her friend as if she might be hiding in the foyer, but Blake shakes her head.

"No, Kate said she couldn't make it. Thanks for letting me invite her, though. It was sweet of you."

"Of course. You know everyone's always welcome at the Taylor House. Now, come and sit down before the food gets cold." Mama ushers Blake to the table and welcomes her youngest with as much gusto as she greeted the rest of us.

Chair legs scrape against the wood floor as Blake pulls out the seat across from me while Mama grills Theo about school, hockey, and his intentions with Blake.

"You invited Kate?" I ask.

"Yeah," Blake answers, pouring herself a glass of orange juice. "She usually goes home on the weekends, but she was in the kitchen when I woke up, so I asked if she wanted to come. She claimed she had to study. I swear, the girl's even more of a recluse than you are."

Yeah. I have a feeling Blake has a point. And a girl like Kate shouldn't be a recluse. Especially when she feels obligated to be one. Like she's a burden or some shit. She basically told me that herself when I dropped her off at her place after the grocery store the other day.

"What would you do if you didn't have to worry about it?" I asked. "If you could go out knowing you were safe? What would you do?"

"I dunno? Dancing sounds fun."

Dancing.

"Does she ever date?" I ask Blake.

Her brow arches, and she drops the bacon, giving me her full attention. "Why? Are you thinking about asking her out?"

"Only curious if she has a secret boyfriend or something, and it's why she keeps turning you guys down when you invite her places," I clarify.

"Hmm," Blake hums, unconvinced, her eyes tiny slits as she studies me while reaching for the piece of bacon again. "But no. No boyfriend. The last one was an ass who broke her heart, and the only other guy who's caught her interest since is a bit of a recluse himself."

"Are you saying I've caught her interest?" I prod.

"I'm saying she could use another friend. One who isn't afraid to push her out of her comfort zone and treat her like gold." The crispy bacon crunches between her teeth as she stares me down. "But if you hurt her, I'll beat your ass, Macklin. Don't think I won't."

I chuckle dryly and clear my throat as Mama and Theo head toward the table, cutting my conversation with Blakely short. "I'll keep that in mind."

Then, we eat.

11

KATE

As the barista hands me my cup of coffee, I smile and thank her. Turning around, I almost bump into the person behind me.

My spine is rigid as I dig my heels into the ground, barely saving my pumpkin spice latte from drenching the poor soul in front of me.

"I'm––" My apology sits on the tip of my tongue as I recognize the culprit. "Oh." I scowl. "Hi."

Macklin smiles down at me. "Hey."

"What are you doing here?"

He lifts his chin at the barista behind me. "Grabbing coffee. Speaking of which," he turns to her and adds, "I'd like a black coffee, two Stevia. Thanks."

As he digs into his pocket for his wallet, I try to walk around him, but he steps in front of me.

"How'd your test go?" he asks, handing the barista his money.

"What test?"

"The one you needed cookie dough for."

"Oh. Technically it was a quiz." I shake my head. *Not the point, Kate.* "It was fine," I tell him.

I hike my bookbag a little higher onto my shoulder, unsure if I should stick around and finish this conversation like an adult or book it out of here, thanks to the dream I had––again––starring the man in front of me.

Seriously, I've gotta stop running into this guy. It's messing with my head. I don't even like him. And after our little car ride from the grocery store? I'm afraid we're crossing into dangerous territory. *Friendly* territory. And I'm not sure I can be friends with him. Not when my subconscious is already attached. Which is wrong and inappropriate on so many levels.

You're sexually frustrated and nothing more, I remind myself. It's normal. Completely. Totally. Normal.

"You gonna visit your family this next weekend?" he prods.

"Huh?" I shake my head and look up at him, attempting to focus on his question instead of an escape plan.

"Blake mentioned you usually visit family on the weekends but stayed home to study yesterday."

"Oh. Uh, yeah. I did. I have another test I need to prepare for, so…"

It's partially true. I *do* have a test coming up in Litwak's class, and I studied for a solid hour before turning on the television and watching a documentary on orcas. It was crazy. Sometimes, they hunt great white sharks and like to coordinate their hunting tactics with other members of their pod. They're also hella smart and mourn the loss of their loved ones. How insane is that? But it was nice having the place to myself. Kind of lonely, but it is what it is, and I'm not naive enough to think it's anyone else's fault but my own.

As the barista hands Mack his boring black coffee, I take a sip of my latte, practically burning the shit out of my tongue.

I hiss, my nose scrunching as he looks at me again and prods, "So, are you going next weekend?"

"To visit my family?"

"Yeah."

"I, uh, I haven't decided yet," I lie, blotting the dribble of hot coffee from my bottom lip and wiping it on my jeans. "Probably not."

"If you want me to drive you--"

"I'm fine." I head outside without a backward glance, the cool wind ruffling my hair as I cradle my cup of molten hot deliciousness to my chest.

I need to get out of here.

Because there's something about him. The way he saw through my lie so easily, getting straight to the point and recognizing the truth. I can't go see my parents until I have my license back, especially when they aren't even aware of the seizure leading to having my license revoked in the first place.

And even though my friends bought the lie about my test and my reason for deciding to stay home yesterday, Macklin didn't. Because he's as observant as shit.

And it's unnerving.

Not only does the way he watches me get under my skin, but he also makes me curious. I shouldn't be. I'll only wind up disappointed when he grows bored of our conversations and finds someone else to annoy--and intrigue. And I'm tired of being disappointed. But I can't help it. He isn't like anyone I've ever met. And the way he picks up on the tiniest of details? It's...dangerous. Especially for a girl like me who likes to keep herself closed off from the world. It's safer.

It's what I should be doing. Keeping my distance. Both physically and emotionally. And after our little chat at the grocery store? I'm afraid I've been failing on both accounts when it comes to Macklin Taylor.

I keep my head down and hurry along the asphalt path toward my next class, determined to put some much-needed distance between me and the guy with his boring cup of coffee who started popping up left and right as soon as he saw me at my most vulnerable.

Heavy footsteps echo behind me as Mack races to catch up, refusing to leave me alone. "Are you off to your next class?"

I stop short and face him fully. "Are you following me?"

"No?"

"Why are you on campus?"

"Theo left his laptop at my mom's house yesterday, so I dropped it off at his class and wanted to grab a cup of coffee before work. That a problem?" he challenges.

Oh.

"No. No problem." My lips pull into a thin line to keep from frowning. I turn on my heel and head toward the gray brick building for my next class.

"Hey, can I ask you something?" he calls.

Annoyed, I face him again and sigh. "What?"

He catches up to me, his stride long and confident as a laughing couple walks around me, their fingers entwined. They look so happy. So at ease. So...natural.

"You lonely, Kate?" Mack asks, his deep voice snapping me back to the present.

"What?"

"I asked if you're lonely." His gaze is soft, as if he knows how weighted his question is, but his stance is relaxed. Like we're discussing the weather instead of something pretty damn personal and intimate.

I shake my head, refusing to analyze his question or how close it hits to home. "What kind of a question is that?"

"A pretty simple one." He takes a sip of his coffee and

steps closer, pinning me with his curious stare. "Are. You. Lonely?"

"Of course not."

"You sure?"

"Why would you ask me that?"

"I dunno." With a shrug, he rocks back on his heels and takes another sip of coffee, the cool wind leaving the top of his dark brown hair tousled. But his eyes? They never stray from mine. I swear he can see into my soul with those bad boys. And I'm too weak to break the connection. Too weak to turn away and get the hell out of here. Too curious about what could happen if I don't.

"Maybe I'm thinking we're kindred spirits," he murmurs.

"Kindred spirits who are lonely despite having amazing friends who would kill for us?"

The guy has to see how ridiculous he sounds. Hell, I know his brother. I've heard of how sweet his mom is. How much she cares about him. Not to mention my family. My friends. Honestly, even Colt and Theo would take a bullet for me, and we aren't very close.

How dare he ask me if I'm lonely? I mean, sure, I miss intimacy. Even the platonic kind. But it doesn't mean I'm lonely. I have plenty of great friends. Plenty of people who love me and would do anything for me. I mean, yeah, I've been busy, and they've been preoccupied with their own lives. But that's normal, isn't it? We all have our own stuff to deal with, and life gets busy. It's no one's fault.

If anything, it's mine. I'm the one who's been distracted. Preoccupied. Distant.

It's on me. Not my friends.

Yup. It's official. The guy's delusional. But if that's the case, why do I kind of feel like crying all of a sudden?

Wowza.

I blink away the moisture in my eyes as Mack steps

closer, analyzing my expression like a seasoned detective. The heat from his chest practically melts me on the spot, but I don't step away.

I should.

I know I should.

No one's ever called me out like this. No one's ever been so blunt with me. Whenever people ask how I'm doing or if I'm okay, I tell them I'm good. And I am. On paper, I'm fine. Mentally, though? Emotionally? It's complicated. And having someone like Macklin Taylor see through my façade so quickly while offering a sense of camaraderie is…overwhelming. Really overwhelming.

As is his presence. I lift my head, peeking at him and those blue eyes.

Blue. Blue. Blue.

I never knew blue could be warm.

Inviting.

Honest.

Soothing.

I can almost feel the heat in them. Like a cloudless summer sky.

I shake off the comfort from his presence alone, refusing to acknowledge how close he hit the nail on the head when we both know how little sense it actually makes.

"I'm not lonely," I argue.

"Okay." He brushes my hair away from my cheek, his blue irises making my stomach flip-flop as they dance around my face. "You wanna not be lonely together?"

"What?" I breathe out.

"I said, do you wanna not be lonely together?"

"I just told you I'm not lonely."

"And I heard you loud and clear, Kate. But do you wanna know a secret?"

"What?"

"I was married for sixteen years, and I might've messed up on a lot of things, but there were a few things I did learn."

"Like what?"

"Like sometimes, a woman's eyes can say what her mouth refuses to."

My attention drops to his mouth. He's so close. When did he get this close? I swear I can almost taste the black coffee on his tongue.

"And what are my eyes saying?" I whisper.

His mouth quirks up in the softest of smiles. "They're saying you could use a friend."

My gaze flicks back to his. "A friend?"

"Yeah."

"I have friends," I remind him.

"Okay." His chuckle is warm as he grabs another stubborn strand of my hair blowing across my forehead in the wind and tucks it behind my ear. "I'm saying you could use a different kind of friend."

"What kind of different kind of friend?"

"The boring kind."

A breath of laughter escapes me. "Are you saying you're a boring friend?"

"I'm very boring," he admits, smirking. "Somehow, I think you might like boring. You already have friends who invite you to do crazy things. I'm the friend who invites you to do boring things."

"Like what?"

"Like hanging out. Making cookies. Watching movies. Reading books. Friends who stay at home and watch the rain. Friends who don't need to go out or drink or party or get laid. Just…friends. Friends you can feel safe with."

Damn him.

The idea sounds pretty freaking perfect if only it was

delivered by anyone else. But Macklin? He's different. Yet, I can't put my finger on why.

Against my better judgment, I whisper, "You wanna be my friend?"

His attention drops to my lips, and he steps away. "Yeah, Kate. I wanna be your friend."

For the first time in forever, the tightness in my chest eases, and I surprise both of us with a smile, all too aware of how dangerous this is for me.

I should leave.

I should say something mean and go to my class.

I should reinforce the boundaries I've created to keep myself safe.

But I don't want to.

I don't want to do any of those.

I want to be friends.

Boring friends.

I want to be with someone I don't have to make excuses with. Someone who understands my disease and doesn't make me feel bad about it. Someone who's okay with boring nights at home. With cookies and television and rainstorms.

"What do you say, Kate?" Mack asks. "You wanna be my friend?"

I bite my bottom lip but force myself to shake my head when all I want to do is the opposite. "You don't want a friend like me. Trust me."

"Why not?"

"Because being friends with me is messy."

"Kate——"

"I should probably get to class. I'll see you around, Mack."

I turn on my heel and get the hell out of there.

12

KATE

"I still can't believe you convinced me to come back here," I mutter, eyeing the rack of weights as if they could jump out and grab me any second. The last time I was here, a bunch of guys saw my underwear through my leggings––including Macklin Taylor––and I vowed to never come back.

Unfortunately, Blakely is even more stubborn than I am.

She laughs beside me. "Not gonna lie. Every single time you say yes, I consider it a modern-day miracle." She stops short and grimaces. "Shit, I forgot my water bottle in the locker room. Start warming up, and I'll be right back." She heads to the locker room while I wait near the weight racks when a familiar face appears in the mirror.

My breath hitches as Wes weaves between the treadmills on the opposite side of the gym with his best friend, Levi, at his side. They're heading straight for me, but I don't think I've been spotted. Not yet. I dart around a metal contraption for building butt muscles, my flight response kicking in at full force, and run into a wall.

At least, I wish it was a wall.

With wide eyes, I tear my attention from the damp, white T-shirt stretched across very muscular pectorals and travel up toward a pair of familiar blue eyes.

Kill. Me. Now.

"Whoa, you okay?" Mack asks, grabbing my arms to steady me.

Squeezing my eyes shut while ignoring how much I want a hole to appear on the Earth's surface and swallow me whole, I mutter, "Not particularly."

"What's wrong?"

I glance over my shoulder to where Wes and Levi are standing. Thankfully, they still aren't looking at me. They must not have seen me yet.

Maybe I do have a bit of luck left.

Mack follows my gaze and grits out, "Did one of those guys make you feel uncomfortable?" He starts to step around me. I grab onto his T-shirt to keep him in place.

"Nope. I'm good."

His eyes heat as he looks down at my tiny fists wrapped in his shirt, resting against his sternum. I don't let him go. I'm too terrified he'll approach Wes and Levi if I do. It's the last thing I need.

Head cocked, he stares down at me, silently demanding an explanation.

"Okay, maybe not," I concede. "But not for the reason you think."

"Start talking, Kate," he growls.

"I used to date one of them, and I don't feel like facing him again anytime soon."

A flash of frustration sparks, and he demands, "Which one?"

"What? Why does it matter?"

"Answer me."

I glance at Wes and Levi again, my heart squeezing. "The taller one. With olive skin. Wes."

Assessing my ex, Mack nods, his muscles relaxing. "I assume he broke it off?"

"Kind of a rude assumption, but yes."

His mouth quirks up as he looks down at me again. "Only made the assumption 'cause you look like you've seen a ghost. He cheat on you or something?"

I shake my head. "No. He broke it off when I told him about my…"--*man, I hate this part*--"condition."

His expression darkens, and his muscles turn to granite beneath my fist. "Then he's an asshole."

"Or honest," I offer.

Grinding his molars, Mack stares down at me as if at war with himself. Finally, he grits out, "Do you trust me, Kate?"

"Not really. Why?"

"I think it's time he sees what he's missing."

"No, Mack," I press my palm against his chest. "I don't want to cause a scene or--"

"Trust me." With his hands on my waist, Mack spins me around and pins me to the mirrored wall behind us. The air whooshes from my lungs as my back hits the cool surface, and he digs his fingers into me.

Yeah, he and I need to have a chat about what it means to be a friend because this position? His hands on me? The way he's looking at me? It's not exactly something I experience with Blake, Mia, or Ash.

The heat from his palms makes my knees weak as they brush against the bare skin beneath my tank top. My stomach coils with anticipation. Mack leans down, his wavy brown hair tickling my cheek as his lips brush against my throat.

"Laugh for me, Kate."

My eyes roll back in my head, his scruff tickling my sensitive skin while I try to focus. "W-what?"

He blows a raspberry on my neck, and my legs nearly give out. A squeal escapes me as his fingers dig into my waist, and he tickles the shit out of me.

"Macklin!" I slap at his shoulders, but he doesn't stop. Doesn't let up. He only makes me laugh harder and harder as I try to squirm away from him and his tortuous touch.

"Stop, stop!" I beg between bouts of laughter. "We're in public, for Pete's sake!"

He kisses my neck again, and my amusement catches in my throat. The feel of his lips against my skin is almost more than I can bear. His hot, minty breath. The low hum vibrating through his chest and into mine. The sound shoots straight to my core, and it clenches on reflex. He pulls away and drops a kiss on my forehead, leaving me reeling and way more turned on than I have any right to be.

"You're right, babe," he concedes. "I'll wait 'til we get home."

Home? My brain short circuits, overwhelmed by my pulsing core. What the hell is happening?

"Kate?" Wes interjects.

Mack's thumb brushes against my waist as he lifts his head, putting a few inches of much-needed distance between us. And boy, do I need it. Mack turns toward the culprit's voice like he's surprised and just remembered we're very much in public. But he doesn't let me go. He keeps his hand beneath the hem of my shirt, pinning me in place against the mirror while meeting my ex's gaze. I feel like I'm on fire. I can't decide if it's embarrassment or lust heating every inch of my skin. I'm not sure which is worse.

After all, jumping Macklin's bones, especially when we only recently established we're friends, is probably frowned upon.

I tuck my hair behind my ears, smoothing down the messy strands, pasting on the fakest smile known to man.

"Wes?" I say breathlessly. "Uh, hey."

"Hey."

Mack stands to his full height but tangles our fingers together, holding my hand as his attention shifts from Wes to me and back again. "Kate?"

"This is Wes," I offer. "My ex. Wes, this is…" my voice trails off, and I peek up at Mack, unsure what the hell I'm supposed to say.

"Macklin," Mack answers for me. He offers his hand for Wes to shake. "Nice to meet you, man."

"You too," Wes replies tightly. He looks at me again. "It's been a while. I stopped by Butter and Grace again but didn't see you."

"I've been busy."

Wes glances at Mack again and frowns. "Yeah. I can see that. Uh, it was good running into you. We should catch up when your friend isn't around."

I almost snort as the word *friend* rolls off his lips but choke it back. "Sure thing."

"Yo! Wes!" Levi calls from near the free weights.

Wes hooks his thumb toward his friend. "I gotta go."

"Good seeing you," I add.

His gaze slides down my body, hesitating on the slip of skin between my shirt and leggings, and lands on my hand intertwined with Mack's. He clears his throat and shakes his head. "You too."

He walks back to the free weights, leaving me alone with Macklin, my savior slash mindfuck.

Giving Wes my back, I face Mack fully, my veins swimming with frustration and confusion and attraction and every other freaking emotion in the book. "What the hell was that, *friend*?"

"It was me helping you. You're welcome, by the way."

I scoff. "Uh-huh. Thanks a lot. Maybe I want the guy back. Did you ever think of that, buddy?"

"Trust me. Your ex wants you back as well." He inches closer. "And while I *am* your friend, if I were you, I would be careful before going back to him."

"Why?"

"Because you deserve a guy who understands there's so much more to you than your diagnosis. And if he was willing to let you go once because of it, who's to say he won't do it again when things get rough?" He kisses my cheek, and my breath hitches. "You deserve more, Kate. A hell of a lot more."

I shouldn't like his kiss. I shouldn't like the feel of his hands on my waist or when they're intertwined with my own. It blurs the lines I've created even more, leaving me feeling whiplashed.

With a question on the tip of my tongue, I meet his gaze, but he shakes his head.

Leaning back in, he explains, "He's still watching us."

"Oh," I breathe out. His dark scruff tickles my jawline as I pull away. Desperate for space. For a chance to think and clear my head, no matter how impossible it feels.

His mouth lifts on one side, and he squeezes my fingers. Letting me go, he comments, "I'm gonna finish exercising. I'll talk to you later."

He walks away, his dark basketball shorts hanging low on his hips while the heat from his lips against my cheek mocks me.

Who are you, Macklin Taylor? And why do you care about li'l ol' me?

"Uh, what was that about?" Blakely interjects.

I blink slowly, realizing I've most definitely been caught checking Mack out. Turning to Blake, I paste on a smile. "I think it was Mack attempting to make Wes jealous."

Blake looks behind me and lifts her chin. "I'd say it worked."

I turn around. The bench press where Wes and Levi were is now empty.

"Did he leave?" I ask.

"Yeah. I saw him walk out the door."

Guilt floods my stomach, but it only lasts a few seconds as the memory of Wes and his date at Butter and Grace ahead of my seizure rises to the surface. Yeah, no. He's fine. And even if he isn't, he can cry on someone else's shoulder for all I care. Because Mack's right about one thing. If he doesn't accept my condition, he doesn't accept me. It's that simple.

The rest of the workout goes by in a blur. However, there's one thing I can't help but notice the entire time. One person. Macklin Taylor.

When he heads toward the exit, I tell Blake I'll be back.

And I chase after him.

13

MACKLIN

I shouldn't have intervened. I shouldn't have touched her. And I sure as shit shouldn't have kept watching her while I finished my workout. But I couldn't help it. I still can't help it. Fuck, half the time, I have a hard-on from being in the same room with her. But actually touching her? Her curves. Her neck. Her skin. She's so soft. So pliable.

And apparently, still hung up on her ex.

I cut my routine short, grab my keys and coat from the locker room, and head outside, anxious to clear my head. The morning rain iced up the asphalt, so I watch where I step as I stride toward my car in the gym's parking lot.

"Hey, Mack!" a soft, feminine voice calls.

I turn around to find Kate. She's still in her gym clothes, but her jacket's missing. The wind cuts through her tank top almost instantly, making her nipples pebble. I struggle not to stare.

"Where's your coat?" I demand. "It's freezing out here."

"I'm fine." She folds her arms, continuing to walk toward me. I bite my tongue to keep from arguing with her as I close some of the distance between us.

"Everything okay?" I ask.

With a nod, she rubs her hands up and down her bare arms while avoiding my gaze. "I just wanted to thank you for everything back there."

"Not a big deal."

"It kind of was." Her gaze flutters around the parking lot, choosing to stare at anything and everything except the guy in front of her. "I was feeling alone and insecure, and you helped me." She peeks up at me again, those stormy gray eyes practically hypnotic yet unsure.

I clench my hands at my sides to refrain from reaching out and holding her chin to prove she has my full attention. Because she does. She has my full attention. She's had it since the moment we met. Since the moment I saw her on the ground. Since the moment she woke up and looked at me with fear, determination, and strength. So damn lost. So damn strong.

"Thank you," she murmurs.

My Adam's apple bobs in my throat as the memory of what it felt like to have her in my arms assaults me. "You're welcome."

"You busy tomorrow?"

I smile. "What do you have in mind?"

"Nothing crazy. As you already know, I have a test to prepare for, but Mia's working at SeaBird, and the rest of the girls are taking their boys there to hang out while she's on her shift. So, I was thinking I could hang out with one of my new, boring friends while I study or something."

"You have multiple boring friends?" I challenge, stepping closer.

Amused, she lifts her chin, defiant as ever, as she murmurs, "Only one."

"Does that make me your *special* boring friend?"

"It makes you a guy who's willing to turn on a mind-numbing hockey game while I study for an upcoming test so we can be not lonely together. You know,"--she shrugs one of her shoulders--"if you're still interested."

"Yeah, Kate." My fingers itch to brush away the dark, silky strands sticking to her forehead, but I stop myself, fisting them around my set of keys and letting the cold metal bite into my skin instead. "I'm definitely still interested."

"Okay." She smiles again, but it fades slightly. "Any chance you'd be willing to come to my place? I have a little while until--"

"Why don't I pick you up and bring you to my place?" I offer.

She shakes her head and takes a step away from me as if the idea of accepting my help is almost more than she can bear. "Oh no, you don't have to--"

"It's no trouble, *friend*. I'll swing by on my way home from work around six, okay?"

Indecision mars her pretty features, and her straight white teeth dig into her tempting bottom lip before she gives in and lets out a sigh. "Okay."

"Okay?" I repeat, my brow quirking.

"Yeah. Okay," she returns with a little more assurance.

"Good. Now, go back inside. It's cold as shit out here."

"To be fair, I'm pretty sure shit is actually kind of warm, but--"

I shove her gently. "Go on, my little porcupine."

With a light laugh, she turns around and rushes toward the entrance, calling over her shoulder, "Okay, my little golden retriever."

Golden retriever.

If Theo ever found out Kate looks at me like I'm a golden retriever, I'd never hear the end of it.

Shaking my head, I wait until she's tucked safely inside

the building, refusing to acknowledge how impossible it is to keep my gaze from finding her curvy ass.

The girl's a damn siren, and she doesn't even know it.

Which can only mean one thing. This whole friendship scenario might be harder than I anticipated.

14

KATE

"You sure you don't want to come?" Ash asks as she lines her eyelids with soft brown makeup. The girl's beautiful on a bad day, but when she's decked out in makeup and dressed to the nines, she's drop-dead gorgeous. I can see why Colt's so obsessed with her. He better not screw this up.

Resting my shoulder against the bathroom doorjamb, I answer, "I'm okay. Thanks, though. I need to study."

"You study too hard, and that's coming from a girl who's a tutor and is trying to become a *teacher*." She quirks her brow and holds my gaze through the mirror as if confirming her point is made loud and clear.

I suck my lips between my teeth, then let them go. "Maybe some other time."

"You always say that."

"And sometimes, it's true," I argue.

She slips the eyeliner cap back into place, tussles her long blonde hair, and gives me her full attention again. "Sometimes. But not lately. Is it because of the seizure?"

"Ash..."

"Is it because we all have boyfriends, and you need another girl's night? Because trust me, I get it."

"It's not that."

"Then, what is it?" she asks.

"It's...nothing," I reply. And I hate not having a solid answer for her, but I'm not lying this time. Not necessarily. I can't put my finger on why there's more distance between us than usual. I can't understand why I'm craving space while hating my overwhelming loneliness simultaneously. It's confusing and complicated, but I don't know what else to do about it. The truth is, sometimes, our feelings don't come from logic or even conscious thought. They just are.

"We miss you, that's all," Ash murmurs.

"I miss you too," I answer honestly. "But seriously, I'm happy for you. I'm happy you found Colt. I'm happy Blake found Theo. I guess I'm trying to find my own happy too."

"That's literally all I could ever want for you." She pulls me into a hug, and I return it, wrapping my arms around her slender waist. When she lets me go, she studies me carefully and adds, "But are you sure you'll find your happy while hiding away in our house?"

"Actually, I'm hanging out with a friend tonight--while studying," I rush out.

Her expression lights up almost instantly. "Oo, a friend, eh? Is this a boy friend or a girl friend?"

"Boy," I tell her. "But it isn't like that."

"Oh?"

"What isn't like that?" Blakely interrupts from the hallway.

"Kate's hanging out with a boy tonight," Ash answers for me, turning back to the mirror and lacquering her lashes with mascara.

"I thought she had to study?" Blake questions. She takes my place near the doorjamb, so I sit down on the edge of the bathtub and make myself comfortable. I should've known they'd interrogate me tonight. Part of me misses it. The girl talks. The opportunities to open up about something other than epilepsy or school. It's nice. Refreshing. And a little scary.

I glance at Blake and announce, "I *am* going to be studying, but I'm going to do it at Mack's house instead. As *friends*," I reiterate.

Blake gasps. "No freaking way."

"What?" I shy away from her and all the scrutiny seeping from her stare. "Seriously. We're just friends."

"Who's just friends?" Mia calls from her doorway.

Seriously? Is there not an ounce of privacy in this place?

The girl's dressed in a black crop top and black jean shorts, showing off her plethora of tattoos and toned stomach I'd kill for.

"Shouldn't you be at work?" I ask.

"Catching a ride with the girls," she returns. "And who's your new friend?" she presses.

"Were you eavesdropping?" I demand.

"Do you really think any of us are able to keep secrets in this house?" she counters.

"*You've* been keeping secrets," I argue.

Her lips purse as Blake interrupts, "We aren't talking about Mia. We're talking about you and Macklin kissing in a tree. K-I-S-S-I-N-G."

"We're *just* friends," I repeat.

"Uh-huh. I tried just being friends once," Blake returns. "And now, I'm sleeping with him."

"You guys, stop teasing her," Ash interjects. "I think it's great she's making plans and getting out of the house, even if it's to hang out with a sexy, established paramedic under the guise of friendship."

"You forgot to add divorced and a hell of a lot older than me to the list," I quip.

"Okay, pause," Mia interrupts. "Let's cut to the chase, shall we? Blake, how old is Mack?"

Blake pauses, her nose scrunching. "I dunno. Thirty… four? I think?"

Mia turns to me and pops out her hip. "And you're…?"

"Twenty-five," I answer.

"Dude, you're old," Blake teases.

The girl's only nineteen and the youngest of the bunch. Mia and Ash are both in their early twenties, too, which means, in comparison, I *am* kind of old. To be fair, I'm in my master's program and took a year off between high school and college in hopes of making my college experience feel more carefree and less bogged down by my parents. It didn't quite work as I'd hoped. After a seizure hit during my freshman year, I moved back home and waited out the rest of the semester until I could sign up for more classes. Since my parents were afraid I'd push myself too hard, I started slow, only taking a few credits to appease them, gradually adding more to my plate as the years went on. Not gonna lie. Part of me wonders if it's because I'm too afraid to actually put my degree to use and move on from college life, but I'm too stubborn to acknowledge it. Nope, for now, I'm fine drowning in my biochemistry degree, no matter how difficult the courses are becoming, thank you very much.

"Okay, she's not *that* old," Ash defends, stepping in and passing around pointed looks, daring Blake or Mia to argue with her. When both stay quiet, she turns to me and adds, "And neither is Mack. A nine or ten-year difference doesn't matter in the big scheme of things. You're both two consenting adults, and you're allowed to like each other––"

"We don't like each other," I interrupt, but Blake cuts me off.

"That's not what I saw the other day. Seriously, you should've seen these two at the gym. Mack was all sweaty from his workout and had her pressed up against the wall with his hand on her hip and his head in the crook of her neck. If that's not some solid foreplay, I don't know what is." She lifts her hands as if to say, *I rest my case.*

"No shit?" Mia interjects, her expression filling with pride. She looks me up and down with a new sense of appreciation. "Damn, girl."

"It wasn't like that," I argue.

"Then, what was it like?" Ash questions. Her makeup is officially on point as she finishes tucking her mascara into her makeup bag. With her arms folded, she rests her hip against the edge of the bathroom counter, giving me her full attention like the rest of the girls. Apparently, someone's invested in my love life...er, lack thereof.

With a huff, I explain, "I saw Wes at the gym, got a little spooked, and ran into Mack, who thought making Wes jealous was the route to take instead of my plan, which was to run in the opposite direction. He was only pretending."

"And were you?" Mia challenges. "Were you pretending?"

"Of course, I was pretending."

"Uh-huh. Sure," Blake snarks when the doorbell rings, cutting off my rebuttal.

"I'll get it." I slip between the gaggle of gossipers, grab my backpack from the kitchen table, and head toward the front door without bothering to see if they're watching me from the hallway.

The hinges squeak softly as I open the door, revealing a very attractive Macklin in a pair of black pants and a white collared shirt with patches sewn into the material. It's his uniform. And damn, it looks good on him. I glance over my shoulder to find Mia pretending to smack an imaginary guy's ass in front of her while biting her bottom lip as if she's at a dance club or something. I send her a warning look and turn back to Mack.

"Hey," I greet him.

"Hey." He tugs at the collar of his black jacket, bringing it closer around his face as the winds howl outside. I should invite him in, but if I do, the girls will pounce, and I'm not ready for that.

"How was work?" I tug the door closed a few more inches, praying it'll give us some privacy.

"Good. Sorry I'm late. I had to stop by the grocery store and grab a few things for dinner."

"Dinner?"

His mouth quirks up in a smile. "We gotta eat, right?"

"Oo, he's making dinner for you?" Blake calls from the hallway.

Macklin presses his hand to the door and pushes it open a few more inches, revealing the girls in all their snooping glory.

"Hey, Blake," Mack greets her.

"Whatcha makin' Kate for dinner?" Blake quizzes.

"He's not making me anything," I argue.

"Uh-huh. Sure," Mia quips as Blake ignores me and calls out, "Have fun on your non-date, you two!"

I give Blake the evil eye over my shoulder for daring to say the D-word, but she only wiggles her fingers back at me in a half-wave. "Love you, too, Katie Kat!"

"Aaaand, we're leaving," I announce. Hooking my backpack over my shoulder, I head outside, close the door behind us, and walk to the passenger side of Mack's SUV. When he opens the door for me, I climb inside while ignoring the tiny voice inside my head questioning whether or not nine years is all that much after all.

15

MACKLIN

The wind rages, the clouds angry and gray as we drive toward my place. Kate deferred to me when it came to the music, but her pouty little lips mouthed along to most of the lyrics, so I think she was okay with my choices.

She's been quiet since I picked her up.

I shouldn't be surprised.

If I've learned anything about Kate Winchester, it's that the girl likes to keep her lips sealed tighter than a clam most days.

But it's nice. The silence. The ease. Summer hated silence. She felt like she had to fill it, no matter what. Even if she had to start a fight, gossip about her friends, or complain about my mom. She had to say something. Anything. Until it began to sound more like noise instead of an actual, genuine conversation. It's probably why she became so frustrated with me, convinced I didn't care about her thoughts or feelings. And maybe, in the end, I didn't. That's on me. I won't say it isn't. But still. This? This silence? It's comfortable. I miss feeling comfortable in silence when I'm around someone. I glance at Kate and find her staring at me.

"What?" I ask.

"What are you thinking about?" Her voice is soft. Like a caress. Less hostile than all the other times I've run into her.

This Kate is more dangerous. More tempting.

She's a friend, I remind myself.

"You don't have to tell me," she adds when I don't answer immediately.

"I was thinking about how quiet you are."

Her brows furrow. "Compared to what?"

"To my ex."

"Ex?" she questions.

"Yeah. I think I mentioned this, but I was married for sixteen years."

"But you're only thirty-four," she reminds me as if the math doesn't check out or some shit.

With a smirk, I look at her again. "How do you know how old I am?"

As if caught saying something she shouldn't, she clears her throat and shrugs one shoulder. "Uh, Blakely told me."

I nod, turning back to the dark road as we climb up the mountain. It's raining now. The droplets stream on the windshield faster and faster, blurring my vision as my wipers pick up their pace.

"It's not like we were *talking*, talking about you or anything," she rushes out. "And technically, Mia's the one who asked."

"Mia's the other roommate?"

"Yes?"

Interesting.

So, Kate was talking about me with her roommates. I don't know why it intrigues me, but it does. I glance at Kate again as she tucks her hair back behind her ear and rubs her lips between her teeth.

"Anything else Mia asked?" I prod.

"Not really." She turns toward the passenger window, entirely avoiding my side of the car. I bite the inside of my cheek to keep from grinning. Kate's a terrible liar, but I won't call her out on it. Not tonight. They were talking about me. Kate and her friends. Maybe I'm not the only one who's feeling out this *friendship*.

"When did you get divorced?" she asks, determined to keep the conversation on me and not how she confessed she was talking to her friends about me.

"We were separated for a long time, but it was finalized last year."

"I'm sorry."

"Don't be. My relationship with Summer was never"--I pause, searching for the best word--"*conventional*."

Her silence rings loud in the car as the rain pitter-patters against the roof and windshield. She wants to ask me to clarify but doesn't want to pry. I can feel it. Her curiosity. Her need for answers. Her need to find the boundaries in our friendship and which ones should or shouldn't be crossed.

It's adorable.

How much she wants to ask.

How much she wants to know.

When I catch her knee bouncing up and down, I laugh. "Ask me, Kate."

"I'm just curious what you meant by never conventional." She turns to me again. "Like...what does it even mean?"

I search for a way to accurately describe my relationship with Summer, but I come up empty.

How do you explain a seventeen-year relationship with someone you never even fully connected with in the first place? Sure, we were young when we first met, but what about the other years? Yeah. I stayed for the kids, and I wouldn't change it. But the fact that Summer left me? That I was the one who was left behind, even though I'd been miserable for more than a decade? It makes me sound like a pushover. Like a fool. Like a coward.

"You don't have to explain it to me," Kate murmurs.

"It's fine," I tell her. "It's, uh… My relationship with Summer was never easy."

Her head tilts. "What do you mean?"

"It's hard to explain unless you've met Summer."

"Humor me," she pushes.

"I was never able to let my guard down around her. She's a very…" I stop, searching for the right words again. "Loud, charismatic, bold, empowered woman. And don't get me wrong. None of those things are bad, but sometimes, it made our relationship a little more strained than if she'd been more willing to listen to me instead of talking *at* me. Which is why I was thinking about how quiet you are. It's different. Good different. I'm not comparing you to her or anything," I add.

Her mouth lifts with a ghost of a smile before it disappears in the blink of an eye. "I get it. I think it's normal to compare things and people and try to find the right fit, even if it's in a platonic way."

"Exactly."

"Why'd you get married so early?"

"Summer got pregnant when we were barely sixteen, so I asked her to marry me."

Kate's jaw drops. "I–– You have kids?"

"Two of them. Daughters."

"That's sweet. Wait. Do they live with you?" She looks out the windshield again, the dashboard light illuminating her worried features.

I chuckle and shake my head. "You won't be meeting them tonight, in case you're worried about it."

With a sigh of relief, she drops her head back and looks up at the cab's ceiling. "Hallelujah. I'm not gonna lie. I almost had a heart attack." She laughs. "I mean, I don't have a thing against kids or anything. I actually really like them. But it would be weird explaining how we're only friends, our age difference, and how I'm coming over to hang out and do nothing? Can you imagine?" She laughs a little harder and covers her mouth as I pull up to the front of my place. But I don't join her. I can't.

Sensing the change in my demeanor, she turns to me again, her tone softening. "Mack? What did I say?"

"Nothing. It's, um… My daughters don't really talk to me anymore, so the idea of introducing you to them is a little strange."

She frowns, reaching out and touching my thigh as if she wants to comfort me. The realization is foreign. I haven't had anyone try to comfort me in a long time.

"Why don't they talk to you anymore?" she asks.

I look down at her hand on my thigh. "It's like I said. Summer is…loud. She wasn't afraid to tell our daughters her opinion of me. And don't get me wrong. I know I'm not perfect, and I know they witnessed a lot of fighting between their parents. Still, I wish they could disconnect their opinion of *husband* Mack with *father* Mack."

"Makes sense," she replies. "Do you still reach out to them?"

"Every day," I answer, my tone a little lighter. "I send texts, memes, TikTok's. Something to let them know I'm thinking about them."

"Do they ever reply?"

"Every once in a while. I got a Happy Father's Day

message for the first time this year from Miley, so it's something."

She smiles. "That's amazing, Mack. Seriously.'

"It's something," I repeat wryly.

She squeezes my thigh again and places her hand back in her lap. "It's something amazing. Keep texting. Keep reaching out. They might not show it, but I can guarantee it matters. Everyone needs their dad, even when they're crappy at admitting it."

"Speaking of parents," I muse. "Have you told them about the incident yet?"

Her pretty lips clamp shut.

"I'll take that as a no."

"It'll only stress them out," she argues. "And trust me when I say I've already caused enough stress during my childhood to last them a lifetime."

"Yeah, but they love you."

"I know they do. And I love them," she adds. "Once I get my license back, I'm going to visit them again. They might be obnoxious and overbearing, but I do miss them. And overall, they're pretty awesome parents."

"I think it's great, Kate. That you have such a good relationship with them."

"It's something," she returns, throwing my own words back in my face. "Now, enough sad talk. Come on. I wanna see your house." She bounces her eyebrows up and down and pushes the passenger side door open, ready to get to work.

16

KATE

To say his house is gorgeous would be an enormous understatement. The place feels masculine yet homey, with dark green cabinets, maple-colored floors, white walls, and a huge stone fireplace in the family room on the opposite side of the open floor plan. Seriously. It looks like it belongs in a magazine or something.

"You designed this?" I ask, turning on my heel and peeking out the massive windows at the beautiful view of the entire town below.

"Yeah. Built it myself."

"Wait." I lift my index finger before waving it around. "You *built* this?"

"Most of it. Had to hire a few things out, but…"

"Holy crap, Mack. Are you serious?"

He laughs. "It's not a big deal."

"Uh, it's a huge deal. This"––I spread my arms wide and do a small twirl, showcasing the entire family room and kitchen––"is gorgeous."

"Thanks. Make yourself at home. I'm gonna take a quick shower. I had to clean up some vomit today, and––"

"Ew, gross." I shiver. "Definitely go shower."

Relieved, he rounds the edge of the counter, leaving the groceries he'd purchased scattered along its surface. "Do you want me to show you how to turn on a show?"

My backpack lands with a soft thump as I slip it off my shoulder and set it on the counter next to a bag of carrots. "I'm okay. I'll start on my homework and wait until you get back."

"Perfect. The guest bathroom's this way, in case you need it." He points to a closed door near the front entrance. "Let me start a fire real quick so you don't get cold. I'll be in the master bathroom if you need anything."

"Okay." I can't help but watch his backside as he bends down next to the hearth and starts a fire, then strides down the hall toward his bedroom. At least, I assume it leads to his room. When he rounds the corner and disappears, I clear my throat. After all, checking out your friend's butt is probably frowned upon. And it's most definitely *not* why I'm here. I'm here to be "not lonely" while I study and nothing more. Mack knows it. And so do I.

School.

Focus on school.

Clicking my tongue against the roof of my mouth, I pull up an assignment from Professor Litwak and scan the material, the words blurring together as the minutes tick by. Not sure why I assumed I'd be able to concentrate in Mack's home. Then again, I didn't exactly expect him to live in the middle of the woods in a gorgeous house like this, either.

He's different than I'd assumed.

And the fact he has kids? Kids who don't talk to him, thanks to his ex-wife? Who does that? She turned their kids on their father all because she's bitter about how things ended?

Ridiculous.

I bet he's a good dad. Patient. Kind. I mean, yeah, I guess I'm making assumptions about him, but am I really? He's never been anything but sweet and kind and patient with me. Even when I was acting out. Even when I was being a brat. He always took it in stride. And the only time he even came close to being frustrated with me was when I put myself in danger by walking home in the dark. Admittedly, he kind of had a good reason to be frustrated. He was *scared*.

Poor Mack.

Who are his daughters? And can I smack them upside the head for him?

Not your problem, Kate, I remind myself.

I scratch at my temple and scan the assignment again but barely make it through a paragraph when the image of Mack with his shirt off while under the showerhead rises to the surface.

Nope.

Not gonna think about a naked Macklin.

Bad idea.

Super bad idea.

I push myself away from the leather stool, head to the kitchen cabinets, find a glass, and fill it with water from the dispenser on the fridge as my curiosity gets the best of me. My steps are slow as I peruse the kitchen, then note the fresh veggies and fruits filling the refrigerator along with the six-pack of Redd's Hard Cider. There isn't a crumb on the counter or a single chair out of place. They're simply tucked beneath the dark round table near the windows. He's a tidy guy. I'll give him that much. And the fireplace is something else. Setting my glass on the counter, I head toward the hearth and rub my hands together in front of the flames. The wood crackles, and the glow warms my chest as well as my fingers. I'm staring at the red, orange, and yellow dancing together when a picture frame catches my eye on the mantle.

I reach up to examine it more closely.

Wait. Is that––

"Everything okay?" Macklin asks from the hall.

I drop my hand and turn to face him, feeling like I've been caught doing something I shouldn't, but it only lasts a second because I'm too distracted by the man in front of me to care.

Hot damn.

His hair is still damp from the shower as he runs his hand over it, watching me and leaving me speechless. My attention slides down his toned body, taking in his gray sweatpants hanging low on his hips and his navy blue hoodie. The color makes his cool blue eyes pop.

I kind of love how he changed into something so comfortable. So normal.

I force myself to stop checking him out, remembering the simple wooden picture frame on the mantle.

When he realizes what I'd been looking at, his gaze softens, and he steps closer, staring at the image. "These are my daughters."

My brain short circuits for a split second, and I blink slowly. "Y-your daughters?"

"Yeah. Hazel and Miley."

I knew I recognized her!

The image has to be at least five years old, and the familiar face is most definitely sporting a pair of braces and shorter hair, but it's her.

I pick the frame up and point to the girl on the right. "Hazel's your daughter?"

He pulls back, surprised. "You know Haze?"

I nod, shake my head, and nod again, still reeling. "Uh, yeah. I work with her. We're kind of...*friends.*"

Jaw slack, he looks at the picture again, his expression twisting with...pain? Regret? I'm not sure. But clearly, I'm not the only one knocked off-kilter by this turn of events.

He swallows thickly and takes the frame from my hands. His fingers brush against mine, his rough, calloused fingertips acting like a taser on my already fragile system, though he's too immersed in the photograph to notice. My breath hitches, but I don't say anything as he sets it back on the mantle, lost in his thoughts.

"Small world, huh?" I murmur.

"Yeah, I guess so."

"I didn't know," I add.

He forces a smile and looks down at me, snapping himself out of whatever funk he'd been lost in. "It's all good. Neither did I."

"You okay?"

"Yeah." He smiles again, and this time, it's more genuine. More...real. "How's she doing, anyway?"

My heart pinches at the reminder of how little he knows his daughter. How much time he's missed. But I know what it's like to be pitied, and I know the man in front of me would hate it as much as I do.

"She's good. Addicted to her phone like the rest of us but friendly. Thoughtful," I add. "The other day, my ex came into Butter and Grace, and she knew about my history with him, so she sat him as far away from my section as possible. See? Thoughtful."

"Sounds like it," he muses.

"Yeah." I pause, chewing on my thumbnail before I ask, "Do you think it's weird? That I know her? Like...do you want us to go our separate ways and call it a night? I know we're just friends and everything, but I totally get it if it's weird for you."

He shakes his head. "No. I don't think it's weird. But I'm sorry."

"Sorry?"

"If I'm making you feel uncomfortable or anything. I was

surprised. I haven't seen Haze since the divorce. Miley lets me follow her on Instagram and stuff. But Haze?" His gaze shifts to the photograph again. "She's been more adamant about me keeping my distance. Guess I was taken aback that someone's seen her out in the wild, ya know?"

I grab his hand and squeeze, desperate to take away the notch of discomfort between his brows. "I can imagine."

He glances at the photograph one more time, then turns toward the kitchen. "I'm gonna make some dinner. Are you hungry?"

"I'm okay. Thanks, though."

"You sure?"

"Yup. I'll...get back to studying."

"Okay."

17
KATE

My stomach grumbles as the scents of chicken, roasted vegetables, and warmth waft through the air. I didn't know warmth could be a smell, but it is. It's cozy and homey, and my mouth waters even more. With my back against the armrest and the couch cushions pressed to my side, I keep my knees to my chest and balance the textbook on them. Focusing, however, is difficult. Because watching a grown man in his element in the kitchen is a thing of beauty. And watching *Mack* cook? Well, it's dangerous, for sure.

Glancing over the edge of the couch for the thousandth time tonight, I bite the inside of my cheek to keep from grinning. A black apron is wrapped around Macklin's waist, and two LAU oven mitts cover his hands. He bends down and checks his dish in the oven. How can he look so freaking dorky *and* attractive like this? It seriously isn't fair.

When he stands up, he catches me staring and smiles. "It's ready. Want some?"

"What'd you make?" I ask, my curiosity getting the best of me.

"Chicken pot pie."

"You made *homemade* chicken pot pie?"

"Technically, the chicken was leftover from last night, but yeah. You want some?" he repeats, lifting the green ceramic dish for me to inspect.

Even from here, it looks amazing.

All golden and flakey and delicious.

"I'm good, thanks." I turn back to my textbook. Because it feels weird. Intimate, somehow. Mack cooking for me while I study. The fire crackling in the corner. And if Blake ever found out, I'd never hear the end of it.

Forcing myself to focus, I reread the same damn paragraph for the tenth time as Macklin putters around in the kitchen for another minute before rounding the couch with two plates in his hands.

"What are you doing?" I inquire.

He sets a plate loaded with chicken pot pie on the dark coffee table in front of me, then sits on the couch. "Just in case."

"I said I was okay," I remind him.

"Yeah. I know. So, what are you studying?"

"How aspartame metabolizes in the body."

"No shit?"

I glance at him. "You're surprised?"

"Had a hunch you were smart, but aspartame metabolizing in the body? Damn, Kate."

"Don't be too impressed. It's pretty much all memorization, which is why my brain feels like mush now."

"You wanna take a break?" He shovels chunks of carrot and potato into his mouth.

I shake my head. "Can't."

"Why not? You've been studying for almost an hour."

"Yeah, and yet, I've retained almost nothing," I mutter, staring at the textbook as the words jumble together.

"What's your major?"

"Biochemistry."

His eyes widen. "Damn."

"Like I said, not a big deal."

"Sounds like a big deal. Do you like it?"

"Used to," I mutter, scanning the pages of letters, unable to string a single syllable together.

"Not anymore?" he probes.

"It's complicated."

"Well, yeah. It's aspartame metabolizing in the body. It's supposed to be complicated."

I bite back my snort and glance at him again, refusing to give him my full attention no matter how impossible it is. "I meant why I don't enjoy it as much as I used to. Now, do you mind?" I motion to my textbook again.

"Of course not."

I suck my lips between my teeth, attempting to concentrate. It feels useless when I can sense him staring at me.

"I'm trying to study," I remind him.

"And?"

"And it's difficult when you're staring at me."

With a smart-ass grin, he shovels another bite into his mouth and reaches for the remote. The television hanging above the mantle flares to life as Mack balances his food on his lap, searching for something to watch.

"You said we needed a mind-numbing hockey game, didn't you?" he confirms.

"Huh?" I look at him again.

"When you mentioned us hanging out. You said you wanted a fireplace, your laptop––or textbook since it's currently what you're using to study––and a hockey game on the TV. Right?"

"Seriously?"

"I only want to make sure I don't miss anything."

"Well, I mean, I could've used some of your mom's famous cookies."

He laughs. "I'll keep it in mind for next time."

Finding a Ranger's game, Mack tosses the remote onto the cushion and eats his pot pie, the scent driving me crazy until I can't take it anymore.

I slap my textbook closed and pick up the extra plate of food Mack dished up for me.

With a smirk, he watches me but doesn't comment.

"How'd you know I'd give in?" I finally ask, digging my fork into the flakey crust. The steam swirls in the air as I bring it to my lips, blowing softly while Mack stares at my mouth but stays quiet.

"Hmm?" I press, taking the bite. It's good. Really good. Probably the best damn bite of chicken pot pie I've ever experienced. Not that I have a lot to compare it with. Other than the Marie Calendar's single servings my mom used to buy when I was little, this is my first chicken pot pie experience, but it definitely won't be my last.

"How is it?" he prods.

My mouth quirks up. "Not too shabby. But you never answered me. How'd you know I'd give in and want some?"

He laughs again and takes another bite of chicken and pie crust. "Give the girl the food despite her protests. It's basically rule number one when becoming friends with a girl."

"Ah, so there's a class for this kind of thing?" I quip.

"Maybe."

"What else does this class teach?"

"Let's see. Be a good cook, obviously."

I lift another fork full of carrots, pie crust, and creamy gravy. "Check."

"Let her choose the shows."

I look at the Ranger's game on the screen, which is interesting enough to watch but not so immersive I can't focus on my homework or the man beside me.

"Check," I repeat.

"Always listen," he informs me.

I roll my eyes but nod. "Double check. You're good at that one."

He laughs and squeezes my foot on the couch, gasping as my icy toes steal the heat from his fingers. "And never let a girl's feet get cold. Shit, Kate. You're freezing. Come here."

With a quick tug, he grabs my toes and shoves them under his thigh, pinning my feet between him and the couch. I nearly moan at the contact.

"How are you so warm?" I ask.

"It's covered in the advanced course." He winks. "But all the boys you're used to hanging out with haven't reached the elite level yet."

"Ain't that the truth," I mutter. He's right. None of the guys I've ever dated gave a rat's ass about my wants or needs. They were looking for a good time, and I gave it to them until things got serious. When they found out about my condition, they bailed on me.

But not Mack.

He's still here.

And I can't figure out why.

If the man wanted to sneak his way past my defenses, he's definitely doing a bang-up job. The ambiance. The food. The banter. This man is a freaking catch, and I still can't figure out why he hasn't been scooped up again.

We finish eating, chatting back and forth until my belly is full, my toes are warm, and my heart is lighter than it's been in weeks. Months, even.

A little while later, I'm catching up on aspartic acid and phenylalanine with my textbook in my lap when Mack groans and throws his head back. The Rangers missed a goal and are already down two to one, the seconds ticking by as the game winds to an end.

"Did you play?" I ask.

He looks at me, confused. "What, hockey?"

"Yes."

"Yeah. When I was a kid."

"Not in college or anything?"

"Nah. I didn't go to college. Having a baby at sixteen will do that to you."

"Good point," I concede. "Do you miss it? Playing?"

He pauses, considering my question. "Yes and no. I miss the camaraderie. The team. Cheering on friends. Feeling the adrenaline rush during a close game. But playing? Actually being on the ice? It was fun, but I didn't have the talent to go pro. Not like Theo." His smile softens, and he lifts my feet, placing them in his lap as he slowly starts massaging my arches. "It's funny. I haven't watched a game on TV in forever."

"Why not?" I'm distracted by his magic fingers and how good they feel.

"Summer hated sports. She didn't like having games on in the house, so I guess I kind of fell out of the habit of watching them on TV. The only time I ever watch is when it's for work."

"Work?"

"There's always someone on the premises during the college games in case someone is hurt."

"Like...paramedics?" I clarify, surprised I didn't know this beforehand.

"Yeah. And since my boss found out I'm related to Theo, I'm usually at the LAU games whenever they play at home."

"Really? How did I not know this?"

He shrugs, digging his thumbs into my instep and pulling a moan of appreciation from my lips.

"Man, that feels good." My eyelids flutter as I melt into the cushions a bit more.

"How to be an Awesome Guy 101. I highly recommend the course for your future significant other."

I laugh, shaking my head. "I'll keep it in mind."

18

KATE

Mack drives me home a couple of hours later. And it's nice. His company. The way he's thoughtful and seems to anticipate what I want or need even when I don't recognize it myself.

After saying goodbye, I head up the front steps and open the door. Mia, Blake, Ash, Colt, and Theo are all in the family room, making the relatively average space look like a can of sardines as the guys take up every inch of the couches while Mia and Ash go head-to-head in the center of the room.

"Look, it's not a big deal," Mia defends.

"Bullshit, Mia!" Ash snaps. "It's a huge deal. I can't believe you didn't tell me."

"I didn't want to stress you out––"

Ash laughs, though there isn't any humor in it. Theo and Colt push themselves up from the couch, exchanging worried glances.

"Aaaand, we're gonna go," Theo mutters.

Apparently, I missed something.

A big something.

"Hey, Kate," Colt greets me quietly when he sees me standing next to the front door.

"Hey. What's going on?" I keep my voice low as Ash and Mia continue bickering back and forth.

"I'll let them catch you up," he mutters. "You doing okay?"

"As good as ever, I guess."

Colt nods and squeezes my bicep. He slips out the front door, and Theo follows behind. It closes with a quiet click.

I flip the lock and turn back to the shitshow in front of me. I've never seen Ashlyn mad. She's the mother hen of the group. The caregiver. The cheerleader. The fact she's looking at Mia like she wants to strangle her is off-putting and so out of character, it takes everything inside of me not to run to my bedroom, close the door, and lock it to block out the noise. The anger. The frustration.

"Ash, calm down," Blake interjects from the couch. "Let Mia explain."

"What's there to explain?" Ash laughs, her tone bordering on hysteria as she throws her hands in the air. "Mia's been selling naked pictures of herself on the internet instead of asking for help for once in her damn life! And now look what's happened, huh? An absolute shitshow!"

"Okay, pause," I snap, marching into the family room and shoving myself between two of my best friends. "Someone catch me up. *Now.*"

Mia's arms are folded, and her lips are nothing but a slash of red across her face as she keeps her head held high, refusing to speak. Refusing to cower. Refusing to show an ounce of emotion other than pride. And Ash isn't any better. The girl looks like she's two seconds from blowing a gasket. I can practically see the steam coming from her ears.

Finally, Blake looks at me and lets out a slow, controlled breath. "Some drunk guy started groping Mia at SeaBird and was spouting off a bunch of gibberish we couldn't understand until Theo and Colt stepped in and put him in his place. The guy claimed it was okay because he'd already paid Mia for the photos and knew what she looked like. And then…" Blake's attention darts to Mia, like she can't decide whether or not she should continue.

"He'd bought my pictures on OnlyFans," Mia snaps. "It's not a big deal. At least it wouldn't have been if Shorty hadn't found my account and decided to announce my real identity to the entire fucking world on the internet. Now, I have stalkers to worry about. *There*. You're all caught up." She gives Ash a dirty look. "Happy?"

"You think I'm happy about this, Mia?" Ash growls. "Your safety––"

"I can take care of myself, Ash."

"Bullshit," Ash grits out. "What if Theo and Colt weren't there tonight? What if they hadn't stepped in? What if the guy cornered you after your shift when you were walking to your car? What then, Mia? Do you have any idea how scared I am for you? How much I love you and care about you, and how much I'm freaking out over the idea of any of those creepers being able to find you and possibly hurt you? And the fact you couldn't even trust me enough to tell me about your financial issues before all of this––"

"This has nothing to do with trust," Mia snaps.

"This has everything to do with trust!" Ash yells. "You're one of my best friends, Mia. Why won't you let me in?" Tears well in Ashlyn's eyes, but she doesn't wipe them away. She lets them fall. One after the other, they slip down her cheeks and drip off her chin as she shakes her head back and forth, staring at Mia. Waiting for an explanation. A reason. An apology.

"I'm sorry," Mia whispers, the crack in her exterior finally breaking free. She collapses onto the couch, resting her elbows on her knees as she threads her fingers through her long blonde hair and tugs. "I needed money, and things got out of control. I started out on TikTok and stuff. Nothing crazy. But I was good at it. Good at getting views. Holding people's interest."

"How did you never come up on our For You page on TikTok?" Blake asks.

"I blocked your accounts. I blocked everyone I knew," Mia explains. "When someone suggested I start an OnlyFans account, I thought, why not? I won't show my face. No one will know it's me, and I'll be able to make some quick cash. I didn't want anyone to know. I didn't want anyone to look at me differently." She drops her hands and peeks over at Ash, her eyes glazed with remorse. "Shorty found out what I'd been doing to make the extra money to cover rent and school, and he was pissed at me. So he told them. Told everyone. One fucking tweet and everything fell apart. I shut down the site, obviously, but once the photos and videos are out there, they're out there. There's no taking them back. No erasing them."

She looks so helpless. So hopeless. So exhausted.

I collapse onto the cushion beside Mia. "How often have people tracked you down?"

Mia shrugs. "Only a few times. Three, maybe four."

"And the pepper spray?" Blake prods.

"I bought it after a guy cornered me on my way to class a few months ago."

Blake nods, the pieces finally falling into place.

"What are you going to do?" Ash whispers.

"I dunno. I keep waiting for it to die down, but as soon as it does, something like tonight happens."

"Does your uncle know?" Ash presses, mentioning Mia's rockstar uncle with more connections than the president of the United States.

"If Fender or my aunt knew, I wouldn't even be able to pee without a bodyguard following my ass," Mia mutters.

"Maybe that's a good thing," I point out. "Maybe you could use a bodyguard. Only for a little while."

Mia shakes her head. "No. I can't. I don't want to. It'll be fine."

"Will it?" Ash demands. Her voice is stronger. Sharper.

"Yeah. It will," Mia returns, refusing to back down. "Because it has to be. If I've learned anything from my life, it's that we can't bitch about the hand we're dealt. We can't go back and ask for new cards. We have to play with what we have. And yeah, I fucked up. I have no choice but to deal with it and move forward. And I will. I'm going to move forward. And I'm going to wait for this bullshit to die down because it *will* die down at some point. And I will *never* sell pictures or videos of my body again. It's that simple. But I am sorry," she adds, her eyes gathering with tears as she looks at Ash, then Blake, then me. She sniffles and wipes beneath her nose with the back of her hand. "I really am sorry. I wanted to tell you, but I didn't know how."

"It's okay," Ash murmurs. She sits on Mia's opposite side and wraps her arm around her. "We'll move forward together. We'll wait for the bullshit to die down together. But you need to promise me something."

"What?" Mia whispers.

"Promise me you'll talk to us," Ash urges. "Promise me you won't run by yourself again. Promise me you'll keep the pepper spray in your hand when you walk to class or when you walk to your car at night. Promise me you'll let us help you if you ever need it, and you'll share your location with all of us just in case."

Mia nods. "I promise."

"Good," Ash decides.

"Can I say something?" Blake interjects. When all eyes are

on her, she announces, "If I ever see Shorty, I'm going to neuter him."

I let out a breath of laughter, grateful for the comic relief no matter how laced with sincerity it is.

"Here, here!" I chant.

Mia joins in as Ash wipes the tears from her cheeks. "Here, here!"

We enjoy a quick group hug. When I pull away and yawn, covering my mouth with the back of my hand, Blakely asks, "P.S., how was your date?"

I give her the side-eye. "It wasn't a date."

"Okay, how was your non-date," Mia chimes in.

Scrubbing my hand over my face, I mutter, "It was fine."

Blake grins. "What did you guys do?"

"He made chicken pot pie, and we watched a hockey game, and I studied, and he warmed my toes."

"Warmed your toes?" Ash pipes in.

I bite the inside of my cheek to keep from full-on gushing about how adorable the bastard is.

But Blakely sees right through it. "He's like an adorable golden retriever, isn't he?"

"He's really sweet," I admit grudgingly.

Blake's grin widens. "Told ya."

"So...do you like him?" Ash prods.

"I like sleep, which is why I'm going to bed." I pull Mia into another quick side hug and add, "I'm glad you're okay."

"Thanks," she murmurs.

"'Night, ladies," I announce and walk down the hall to my bedroom, closing the door behind me.

KATE

The restaurant is dead. Which would normally be fine, but ever since I found out Hazel is Macklin's daughter, I feel weird talking to her. Which is what I would be doing if I hadn't found out who her father is.

Instead, I'm hanging out on the opposite side of Butter and Grace, glancing at her every few minutes to see if she's some crazy psychic who knows about my connection to her dad or if I really am losing my mind.

I feel like I'm keeping a secret from her. Which is dumb. If she wanted to know what her father was up to, she wouldn't be ignoring him. And so what? I'm friends with her dad. Not a big deal. It's not like we've had sex or anything. He doesn't even look at me that way. And even if he did, he probably would've made a move already.

Right?

Not that I would want him to make a move, especially when I know Hazel, but he did keep my toes warm. And he knew I wanted some chicken pot pie when I was too stubborn to admit it. And he is so damn sweet and thoughtful it's not even funny.

Like…how? How is he so perfect?

Get a grip on yourself, girl!

My phone buzzes in my back pocket, and I pull it out, finding a text from the devil himself.

> MACKLIN
>
> Hey, what are you doing tonight?

I look around, confirming Anna isn't anywhere in sight, and I respond.

> ME
>
> I'm working until 9, but after that, I'll probably go to bed.

> MACKLIN
>
> Any chance you'd want to stay up late tonight?

> ME
>
> Depends on what you have in mind.

I hit send before I can talk myself out of it, well aware of how much I'm playing with fire.

You're gonna get burned, I remind myself as I watch the little blue bubbles blip on the screen. Macklin's replying.

> MACKLIN
>
> I may have convinced Mama Taylor to share her cookie recipe. Want to give it a try?

"Kate," a sharp, feminine voice snaps behind me. My phone slips from my fingers, clattering to the ground as I jump in surprise. Turning around, I find Hazel clutching her stomach and laughing over my reaction.

"Dammit, Hazel," I scold. "You scared the crap out of me."

"Yeah, but you should've seen your face." She bends down and picks up my phone, handing it to me.

Anxiety knots my throat as I take it from her grasp and shove it into my back pocket, praying she didn't notice her father's name plastered across my screen.

"Thought we weren't supposed to have our phones out," she teases.

"Yeah, well. Do as I say, not as I do," I quip, walking with her toward the hostess stand.

"Speaking of advice," Hazel replies. "Any chance I can pick your brain for a few minutes?"

"Uh, sure. Go ahead."

"It's about a guy."

I grimace as her father's face pops into my head. "Pretty sure I'm the last person you should ask for relationship advice."

"Whatever." She waves me off. "Wes is hot, and since he's clearly still drooling over you despite the breakup, I'm going to say you're the perfect person for relationship advice."

"He hasn't been drooling over me," I argue, picking at a piece of lint on my apron.

"He's been in here three times this week. If that isn't drooling, I don't know what is."

"Okay, fine," I mutter, giving in and folding my arms. Anything to end this conversation as quickly as possible. "What's your question?"

"How long do you usually wait before going all the way?"

My eyes pop. "I'm sorry, what?"

"You know. Sex. How long do you wait before getting down and dirty? I had a bad experience last year and would like to *not* repeat it, ya know?"

"Uh, I don't..." *Please don't blush. Please don't blush. Please don't blush.* "I don't know?" I offer.

"The last guy you were interested in...," Hazel prods, "how long did you wait?"

"Technically, I'm still waiting." The words slip out of me before I can stop them, and the blood drains from my face.

"Hold up. There's a *new* guy?" Hazel demands, grabbing my arm. "Is that why you were texting at work?" Her expression lights up. "I'm impressed. Who is he?"

Dammit!

"Uh, no one."

"Liar." She lets me go and taps her finger against her chin. "Is he cute? I bet he's cute. What's his name?"

"We're just friends," I rush out. "And I mean it literally. I'm not ready for anything more."

"Aww." Her head bobs up and down in understanding. "Good for you. Is he a nice guy?"

"Yeah, he's pretty great. But like I said, we're just friends."

"Friends who want to see each other naked?" She bounces her eyebrows like she couldn't be happier for me, but I shake my head.

If only you knew.

My mouth opens, but I close it again like a fish out of water, unsure what the heck I'm supposed to say.

Hey, girl. I kinda wanna screw your dad. Hope it's not a problem or anything.

Thankfully, the girl has the attention span of a gnat and waves me off. "Anyway, I've been talking to this guy for a few weeks now, and we've basically done everything but the actual deed. My dad was kind of old school and taught me I shouldn't be doing any of that unless I'm in a committed relationship, and even though he was kind of an asshat, I can't get the idea out of my head, ya know? Especially after my last experience, when the guy finally got what he wanted and ghosted me. So, long story short, what would you do?"

If Hazel was anyone else, I'd have my answer locked and loaded. But at the mention of her dad, I'm speechless. Is this crossing a line? Should we even be talking? It feels wrong.

Keeping this from her. Even if it isn't a big deal,––and it really *isn't* a big deal––it still feels like she deserves to know. But if she wanted to know anything about her dad, she'd keep the door open and actually talk to him. So, where does it leave me?

And what if I didn't know who her dad was? What if we were having this conversation before I met Mack? What would I tell her?

"Seriously, what would you do if you were me?" Hazel prods.

"Honestly?" I start. "I think your dad makes a good point. Being in a committed relationship is probably the smarter route to take. But even more importantly, I think you need to make sure you're both on the same page, whatever the page is."

"Good idea."

"Have you talked to the guy about it at all? Not like a define-the-relationship talk or anything, but has he hinted he wants a relationship, or is he only looking for a good time?"

She hesitates, clicking her long, pointy nails against the hostess stand, lost in thought.

"I think he'd potentially be interested in a relationship," she decides. "I'm not sure if I even want to be in a committed relationship anytime soon. But I like spending time with him, and I asked if he was talking with anyone else, and he said no, so that's good, right?"

"Yeah, I think it's really good."

"Okay, good. So…kind of feel it out?"

"Yeah. But make sure you're safe. And make sure you both agree on what you want. Because there's nothing wrong with a solid no-strings-attached hookup, but if you guys are both looking for different things during said hookup, the outcome will be messy. And trust me. Even the best sex of your life isn't worth the mess. Make sense?"

"Yeah." She hesitates, her fingernails clicking against the stand a little faster. "Yeah, I get it. Thanks, Kate."

Anna walks toward us, her gaze flitting over the empty restaurant as I prepare myself for a lecture about how we should be working instead of standing around. Instead, she finds Hazel and announces, "It's dead. Go home. We'll see you tomorrow, Hazel."

"Oh. Okay. Thanks." As Anna walks away, Hazel rummages through the stand and grabs her purse and keys. "Well. Looks like I'm off for the night. Thanks again for your advice."

"No problem, Hazel."

"And one more thing." She pauses. "I think you should take your own advice. Don't be afraid to feel out what you and your new mystery man want. You deserve to be happy."

"Thanks, Hazel."

"Sure thing." She wiggles her fingers back and forth, her finger looped in her key ring. "See you later."

"Bye."

As she walks away, I pull out my phone and respond to Mack, taking Hazel's advice no matter how intimidating it is.

ME

Sure. I'd love to make cookies.

MACKLIN

Perfect. Can I pick you up at the restaurant at 9?

ME

That'd be great. Thanks.

MACKLIN

See you then.

20

KATE

"So, I lied to you," Mack informs me as he sets a small sack of groceries onto the granite countertop.

"I'm sorry, you *lied* to me?"

He grimaces and rocks back on his heels. "Yeah. I told you my mom gave me the cookie recipe, but when she found out I wanted to make them with a *friend*, she made the cookies herself."

I nearly choke on my laugh and mosey the rest of the way into the kitchen, collapsing on one of the leather barstools tucked beneath the island. "Are you saying she refuses to give you the recipe all because she knows I could steal it?"

The guy almost looks shameful as he grabs the back of his neck and squeezes, causing his biceps to bulge in his short-sleeved uniform top. "Yeah."

"She's *that* serious about keeping it in the family?"

"Don't feel too bad. She refused to give the recipe to Summer, even after we were married."

I gasp. "You're joking."

"I wish I was."

"So, what's with the groceries?" I wave my hand toward the mishmash of ingredients littering his granite countertop.

"Well, thanks to Google, I looked up the highest-rated recipe and figured we could try it, then compare all three."

"Three?" I ask.

Lifting his fingers, he ticks them off, one by one. "The processed stuff, my mom's already baked cookies, and the ones we make together."

"You bought a tube of premade cookie dough?"

"Uh, yeah. Gotta keep the experiment accurate. What do you think?"

It takes everything inside of me to keep from gushing at his proposal, but I fold my arms instead and smile. If I didn't know any better, I'd say he's trying to impress me. However, I have a hunch he's this thoughtful all the time. So even though it might not be personal, I still think it's kind of adorable how well he planned tonight's activity.

"I think it's a great idea," I admit.

"Perfect. The Pillsbury dough is in the fridge," he adds, pulling things out of the paper grocery sacks and setting them in a nice, even row on the counter, along with a single plate of already-made cookies covered in Saran wrap. "Wanna start baking those while I grab everything for the other recipe?"

"Sure."

I reach for the plate of cookies, but he smacks my hand. "Not yet."

"Now, who's prickly?" I argue.

He grins. "Chop-chop, Kate."

A few minutes later, I place little dollops of premade dough onto the parchment paper as he grabs the brown sugar, flour, butter, eggs, and everything else the Googled recipe calls for, setting each ingredient onto the counter and next to the things he'd purchased earlier tonight. Stepping back, he scans the list one more time. I smile when I realize how focused he is. His brows are pinched, and his lips are moving slightly as if he's talking to himself, mentally checking everything off the list.

Does he have any idea?

How freaking cute he is? How he somehow has a direct line to my ovaries––and probably every other girl's ovaries on the planet? If he does, it isn't fair. Then again, if he doesn't, it's almost worse.

With great power comes great responsibility.

And man, this guy could easily have power over me.

When he catches me staring, he asks, "Everything okay?"

"Mm-hmm," I hum, biting my cheek to keep from grinning like a lunatic or blushing like Bashful from *Snow White and the Seven Dwarfs* since I most definitely was caught staring at the guy.

"Something funny?" he prods.

"Nothing."

"What were you staring at?"

"You."

"What about me?"

"Didn't know I'd be hanging out with Betty Crocker," I tell him.

"Oh, yeah." He snaps his fingers and pulls a pair of aprons from the bottom drawer next to the fridge. "Thanks for reminding me."

With a flick of his wrist, he tosses one to me, and I catch it. "Are you serious?"

"Gotta keep your clothes clean, Kate." He ties his own black apron around his waist. It's the same one from the last time I was here when he decided to make homemade chicken pot pie. The memory makes me smile.

As he defrosts the butter in the microwave, I watch him

move around the kitchen, dumbfounded. "You thought of everything, didn't you?"

He looks at me and smirks. "Tried to. Now, hurry up. Let's put those in the oven."

A few minutes later, the familiar scent of baking cookies fills the air and makes my mouth water as I stand in front of the hand mixer and glass bowl filled with butter, sugar, and eggs.

It's weird. How natural I feel. How comfortable I feel. In his space. Baking. Smiling. Laughing.

He's definitely charming, my golden retriever.

"So, Mr. Recently Divorced," I muse.

"Love the nickname," he mutters, his words dripping with sarcasm.

I laugh. "Thought you might. But tell me, have you started dating yet?"

He glances at me, an expression passing in his eyes. It's gone too quickly for me to analyze what it is, and he pulls a spatula from the drawer, handing it to me.

As I turn off the mixer and scrape the sides of the bowl, he answers, "Not really. Why do you ask?"

"Because this is a pretty perfect date activity despite us both agreeing we're only each other's boring friend. Which is fine, by the way," I lie. "But seriously. The fireplace. The smell of cookies in the air. The gorgeous house making you look like you have your life together. It's pretty much the perfect trifecta."

"Says the girl who's pretty easygoing and has been up for anything so far. Tell me what you like to do."

"Other than study, avoid bars, be dragged to the gym, and make cookies with friends?" I shrug. "Not much."

"So, no dancing?"

"Dancing?" I ask.

"You mentioned you'd like to go dancing, remember?"

The memory of our conversation after the grocery store fills my mind, and I nod, surprised by his attention to detail. "Oh, yeah. Well, I hate to disappoint you, but when I mentioned dancing, I didn't mean I actually knew how to do it. Only that I'd like to try it one day."

"Got it," he murmurs. "Anything else? No hobbies or anything?"

With another shrug, I dip my finger into the cookie dough and steal a small taste, sucking it off. "I guess I'm too busy focusing on school."

"Well, take it from someone a little older than you. Take advantage of this time in your life. Have fun. Go out. Do things."

"Things," I mimic. "Sounds very specific."

He chuckles as he reaches around me, grabbing the spatula from my grasp and setting it on the counter. "As long as you're having fun, I don't think it matters what you do. All I'm saying is, don't let life pass you by."

"Is that why you invited me over? So you wouldn't be bored on a Friday night?"

"I invited you over because we both agreed being lonely is a bitch, and being lonely together might not be so bad."

"So, no dating?" I push. I shouldn't. It's not like I care what he does or who he dates, but I can't help it. He seems so put together. So perfect. How is he still single?

"Yeah, no dating for me," he returns.

"Why not?"

"For starters, I still can't figure out the appeal of online dating. Everyone either wants to start sexting right away, or they want to know what my favorite color is and refuse to meet face-to-face. It's exhausting."

"Sounds exhausting." I add a teaspoon of baking powder into the mixture, pushing the bowl toward him so he can take a turn stirring. "But to be fair, I feel like dating, in general, is exhausting."

"It shouldn't be," he argues. "Not if you're dating the right person."

"Guess I'm bad luck, then."

"Debatable." His attention slips down my body before he looks at the bowl and continues stirring. "When did you stop dating your ex from the gym?"

"Who? Wes?" I confirm, surprised by the subject change.

Mack nods, his forearms flexing as he mixes the cookie dough like a sexy chef.

"Um…a couple of months ago."

"Were you two serious?"

"We could've been. He told me he loved me, and I told him I had epilepsy, which in my book is the closest testament to love I could get, but you already know how the story ended."

"You think he broke up with you because you told him you have epilepsy?"

"Uh, yeah." I nod my head. "Obviously."

His lips pull into a fine line, but he doesn't answer me, adding another cup of flour to the bowl. The familiar whir of the hand mixer breaks the silence. Once the flour is well combined, he turns the mixer off again and glances at me. "You like to keep your diagnosis close to the chest, don't you?"

Ignoring him, I take the premade batch of cookies from the oven, set them on the stovetop, and lean my hip against the counter. "It's complicated."

"Doesn't have to be. You have epilepsy. There. Simple."

"Having epilepsy isn't simple."

"But telling someone is."

"For someone who doesn't have it, maybe."

He shakes his head as if I don't understand. But I do. I get it more than anyone. If anything, I'm offended he thinks I don't.

"It isn't a crutch, Kate. If anything, it only made me like you more."

The topic hits way too close to home as I busy myself with the cookies, using a spatula to set them on the cooling rack while avoiding his gaze entirely.

"And how has epilepsy only made you like me more?" I ask, unable to help myself.

"Because it proves you aren't breakable."

"No, it proves I'm already broken."

A dark laugh laced with exhaustion slips out of him as he shakes his head. The cookie dough forgotten, he mirrors my stance, folding his arms and resting his hip against the counter, leaving barely a few inches between us. "A broken girl wouldn't get back up again after being kicked down, Kate. And yet, here you are."

Yeah, here I am. Barely holding it together in his house at the mere mention of my condition. Hell, barely holding it together, period. I don't like talking about this. I don't like the reminder of the massive weight on my shoulders all. The. Time.

And here he is, making it sound so simple. So matter-of-fact. He thinks I'm not broken? That I don't know why Wes broke up with me? That I don't know how hard it will be to let my guard down and fall in love with someone or have someone fall in love with me despite my baggage? It's bull-shit. Total. Complete. And utter. Bullshit.

Yet here I am under his roof, thinking maybe, just maybe, I could try having a relationship with him.

Bullshit.

I kind of want to cry at the reminder of how messed up my life can feel sometimes, but I swallow back the lump in my throat and stare at the cooling cookies instead.

"Do you have an extra cooling rack?" I whisper, praying he doesn't notice the slight hitch in my voice or how close I am to crying.

Seriously. What the hell is wrong with me?

He opens the cabinet behind me, and I step to the side, giving him more room as he rummages through the cupboard. The distance doesn't stop his scent from washing over me, from teasing me, no matter how annoyed I am. Our fingers brush against each other as he hands me the wire rack, but I ignore the jolt of adrenaline as I set it down next to the stove, my gaze never leaving his. "Thanks."

We work in silence for a few minutes, and I'm grateful for it. Grateful for the handful of minutes where I can rein in my emotions. Where I can shove down the helplessness and focus on something else. Ingredients. Measurements. Order. Anything to keep my feelings at bay. To keep my exhaustion from ruining this moment.

Because I hate epilepsy. I hate how it knows how to ruin everything. Like a constant, thick haze of bullshit contaminating everything it touches. Even the carefree moments like this one. The moments where I almost feel normal. Even if only for a minute. And I know it isn't Mack's fault. I know he cares. But what he doesn't understand is his genuine curiosity will only hurt me in the long run because by the time he has his answers, he'll be bored, and I'll be tossed aside.

And I'm tired of being tossed aside.

Once a fresh batch of homemade cookies is in the oven, and the Pillsbury ones are set nicely on a plate, I start to step around Mack, but he grabs my bicep, keeping me in place. It's as if the silence is suffocating him as much as it's starting to suffocate me, and he can't take it anymore.

"Look, I'm sorry," he murmurs, his voice low and throaty in the otherwise silent kitchen.

I shake my head. "It's fine."

"It isn't fine. I hurt your feelings."

"You didn't."

"I did. And it's not okay. I'm sorry. I shouldn't have over-stepped my bounds." He rubs his thumb gently against my bare skin, adding, "You're a catch, Kate. You're beautiful. Smart. Kind."

"I'm hardly a catch."

"You have no fucking idea," he mutters, his attention bouncing around my face. "I hate the idea of you thinking epilepsy could overshadow any of those things. Yes, you have epilepsy, but it isn't your identity."

"You don't know what it's like." My quiet voice slices through his declaration like a hot knife through butter. He stays silent, waiting for me to elaborate while refusing to let me go. But I'm grateful for it. His touch. His warmth. His strength. Pretty sure it's the only reason I'm still standing in this moment, though I refuse to acknowledge why.

"Wes isn't the first guy to break up with me once he found out about my condition." I bite my bottom lip, praying the slight sting of pain will be enough to keep my tears from falling. "So far, I'm three for three, Mack. You can't tell me it isn't something worth worrying about."

"Everyone has their shit, Kate. Everyone has their baggage."

Another light scoff slips out of me as I scrounge up the courage to peek up at him. "Says the guy who clearly has his life together."

"I'm thirty-four, divorced, with two kids who won't talk to me, Kate. Yeah, I have a home, a steady job, and money in my bank account, but I still have my shit like everyone else."

"Yeah, well, the guys I pick seem to have a habit of thinking mine is too much."

"Maybe you need to stop dating stupid boys who are too

weak to handle a little baggage. Because trust me, one day, they'll look back and realize yours was worth carrying."

The timer on the oven beeps, cutting off my rebuttal. I lick my lips, and he lets me go.

Which is for the best. Because if he hadn't, I would've asked if he was up for the job.

"Now, enough heavy shit." He sets the cookie tray on the stove and tosses his oven mitts onto the granite island. When he catches me staring, a frown marring my lips, he repeats, "I said enough heavy shit. Stop thinking about it."

With my ass against the edge of the counter, I fold my arms. "Oh, so I'm supposed to just turn it off?"

"Maybe." He turns to me, his eyes thinning. "Get out of your head, Kate."

"I'm not in my head."

"Yeah, you are. I can see it." He steps closer and taps his finger against my temple softly. "The wheels are turning inside this pretty little head. Overthinking. Overanalyzing." His hands grip the edge of the counter, caging me in on both sides. "Stop it."

"And how do I stop it?" I tilt my head back and hold his gaze.

"I dunno. But if you don't think of something quick, I might have to find something else for you to focus on."

My thighs press together as I refuse to back down, no matter how stupid it is. But there's something in his voice. Something in the way he's looking at me. Something in the air. The way it crackles around us like the lightning outside. Charged, maybe.

"Is that a challenge?" I ask.

"Maybe?"

"And what else would you like me to focus on?"

His attention drops to my mouth. He leans closer, the heat from his breath warming my cheeks. He's close. So damn close I can almost taste him. His mouth quirks up slightly as he reaches up and rubs his thumb against the side of my mouth. But it isn't warm and calloused. It's soft and cold and wet and--

Confused, I touch my cheek and pull my hand away, examining it. "Did you just put cookie dough on my face?"

The little granules of sugar scratch at my skin as I rub at the blotch of dough with my fingers again, trying to clean myself up.

With a smirk, Mack sucks his thumb still smattered with deliciousness into his mouth, his eyes promising very dirty things if I was only brave enough to take it. And, oh, how I wish I was brave enough to take it. To love someone like Mack. Someone who already took the How to be an Awesome Guy 101 course and could blow my expectations of a healthy relationship out of the water. But it's scary. Putting yourself out there. Especially when he's already drawn a line in the sand as to what we are.

Friends.

When I don't move, he turns toward the fireplace. "What show do you want to watch?"

21

KATE

The wind and rain rattle the windows as the fire crackles in the hearth. It was only sprinkling when Mack picked me up after work, but it's taken on a new force as the night progressed. I keep waiting for it to calm down, but the storm's growing more and more tempestuous with every minute.

I should be scared or tense, but I'm not. If anything, it's almost peaceful. After my mini-meltdown in the kitchen and his excellent distraction with the sexy eyes and the smear of cookie dough, we turned on Netflix and watched a show. No snuggling since we're just friends. Although I can't decide if it's Mack who's holding onto the title or me at this point. Regardless, I did get a free foot massage. And that, combined with munching on delicious cookies and getting lost in *House of Dragon*, is a pretty excellent combination.

Macklin's hanging out on the couch with his white sock-clad feet resting on the coffee table while mine are still in his lap. I don't know why the view makes me smile, but it does. He looks so natural here. In his element. Relaxed. Attractive. I blink and focus on the TV again, blindly grabbing another cookie from the plate on my stomach while resting my head against the armrest as the credits start to play.

The cookie's chocolatey and soft yet crunchy, with precisely the right amount of sweetness. Which means it's a Mama Taylor cookie. We've already done a blind taste test, and the results were unanimous. The recipe Mack found online was a solid second, and the premade tube took last place and is still sitting mostly untouched on the counter. But Mama Taylor's? Those are things of beauty.

I gotta steal the woman's recipe.

Mack looks out the large windows as the rain patters against the glass and lightning slashes the sky. "It's really coming down."

I twist my head to glance out the window at the dark storm. "Yeah. It is. What time is it?"

He looks at his Apple watch. "A little after midnight. You tired?"

"Actually, yeah. I'm beat."

"You want me to drive you––"

Lightning cuts across the dark sky again, causing the inside of Mack's home to glow for an instant, followed by a loud clap of thunder practically shaking the house.

"Is it *safe* to drive right now?" I ask.

He glances out the window again. "I think we could make it."

"You *think?*"

With a dry laugh, he turns off the television, setting the remote on the coffee table. "Okay, I know we could make it, but it might be a little rough."

"How rough?" I question.

"Nothing too crazy. Worst case scenario, I'll sleep at Theo's."

"You can't sleep at Theo's. I would feel terrible."

"Hmm," he hums, weighing our other options. "We could

151

always turn on another movie and see if the rain lets up before I take you home? Or if you're tired, you're welcome to sleep in my room, and I'll take the couch. I have two other bedrooms, but I haven't bothered buying any furniture for them since I don't usually have guests."

The idea of Macklin having other guests sleeping here does weird things to my stomach, but I shove the feeling aside, refusing to acknowledge it, let alone analyze why.

Nope. No, thank you.

I've already been through the emotional wringer once today. No use doing it again.

I *am* tired, though.

"What do you think?" he prods.

"Not gonna lie. I'm usually in bed by eleven," I admit. A yawn hits, and I stifle it behind my hand, proving how tired I really am. It's official. The day has finally caught up to me.

"Not a night owl, huh?" he notes, watching me with a smirk.

"Noooope," I drag out the word as another yawn takes over.

He laughs and taps my knee. "Come on, Kate. I'll take you to the bedroom."

I settle further into the cushions. "It's okay. I can take the couch."

"Not gonna happen." Mack stands up, stretches his arms over his head, and offers me his hand. "Come on. I'll show you the master bedroom."

It's kind of weird being in here. Intimate, somehow. A large mahogany bed sits in the center of the room with a navy blue comforter and thick, fluffy pillows. The idea of

Macklin picking them out at Bed Bath & Beyond makes me smile. Biting the inside of my cheek, I swallow it back.

Nope. I've already witnessed enough adorable quirks from the man. No need to add fuel to the fire.

As my toes dig into the plush carpet, I stare at the king-sized bed, unsure if this is a good idea or not. Sharing a bed with anyone can be tricky, but sharing it with a guy like Mack? It's gotta be a no-no. At least for my own sanity, anyway.

Without a word, Mack steps around me and pulls the comforter down, then heads to his closet and retrieves a white T-shirt and a pair of basketball shorts.

"Here." He offers them to me. "In case you don't want to sleep in your clothes."

The cotton is soft in my hands as I fight the urge to lift them to my nose and take a giant whiff, positive it'll smell exactly like the man in front of me.

Speaking of adding fuel to the fire...

I shake off the thought and murmur, "Thanks."

"Sure thing. The bathroom's over here." He points to the doorway on the opposite side of the room. "Come on. I'll find you a toothbrush."

The bathroom's as gorgeous as the rest of the house. With white granite countertops, thick, fluffy gray towels, and the scent of Macklin clinging to the air. It's breathtaking. And clean. So damn clean.

His back muscles flex beneath his cotton T-shirt as he rummages through the bottom drawer and offers me an unopened blue toothbrush.

"Thanks."

In silence, I open it while Macklin grabs a matching blue one from the cup next to his sink and offers me some tooth-paste. The white paste oozes onto my toothbrush. As he adds some to his, a charged silence washes over us. Our gazes connect in the mirror's reflection as we brush our teeth. This shouldn't be intimate, but it is. It's so normal. So ordinary. So domestic. Like two lovers getting ready for bed after a long day.

Lovers.

The word is so foreign.

Companions, maybe.

Partners.

Yeah. That one fits better.

Like we're partners.

Even though we aren't.

It doesn't matter how in sync I feel with the guy, whether in the bathroom, in his kitchen, or while we're watching TV. I shouldn't feel in sync with him. Not when I don't know where we stand.

I tear my attention from Mack's reflection and spit the frothy white foam into the sink, rinsing my mouth with water while he follows suit. Once he's finished, I stand there, my hands at my sides, unsure of what to do or where to go. This is awkward. I probably shouldn't be here. Not when I kind of want to kiss him. Turning around, Mack faces me again, a soft smile tilting his lips up.

"Something funny?" I ask.

He shakes his head and lifts his hand, touching the side of my face. My breath hitches as he runs his thumb along the edge of my mouth. It takes everything inside of me to keep from leaning closer. From soaking up his touch. From asking him to kiss me.

"What are you...?" My voice trails off as I look into his eyes.

Blue. Blue. Blue.

Freaking electric.

His minty breath fills my nostrils.

He pulls his hand away, showing me the small smudge of white on his thumb. "Toothpaste."

"Oh."

He tucks his hands into his pockets. "All right. I'll see you in the morning."

That's it?

Is he joking right now?

Seriously. The guy's playing with me. He has to be.

I nod anyway, watching as he walks past his bed toward the hallway.

"Wait." I step to him like I can't help it. And maybe I can't. I like Mack. I like being around him. I like being in his space. And I'm not ready for him to leave. I'm not ready to be alone again. I'm not ready to be lonely. Not yet.

He turns around and waits.

"Where are you going?" I ask.

"I'm gonna sleep on the couch so you can have the bed."

My shoulders hunch, and I shake my head. "I feel bad taking your room."

"It's not a big deal, Kate."

"Seriously," I argue. "It's a big bed. You're welcome to stay in here."

"I can stay on the couch."

"I know you can, but I'm not kidding when I say I literally won't be able to sleep if I know I kicked you out of your room. So, *please*. Stay. We'll each keep to our own side of the bed. It'll be fine."

He glances at the mattress, then back at me, his brows stitched together. "You sure?"

I nod. "Yeah. We're both adults. And I know you wouldn't do anything if I wasn't comfortable, so…"

He stares at me for another long moment. "You swear you won't sleep well if I take the couch?"

"Positive."

"One hundred percent?"

"Yup. One hundred percent," I confirm. And it's true. I'll never be able to sleep alone in his room, knowing I kicked him out of his own bed. And no, it most definitely does not have anything to do with the idea of sleeping next to him. Nope. Not one bit.

He's cute when he's concerned. Like I've ruffled his feathers and left him off-kilter. Honestly, it's kind of refreshing since I'm usually the one with the ruffled feathers, and he's usually the one who's relaxed and at ease.

Mack squeezes the back of his neck, glancing at the bed again like it might reach out and grab us both, and mutters, "Okay."

"Okay." Rocking back on my heels, I add, "I'm gonna change."

"Okay."

"Okay," I repeat with a laugh. "I'll, uh…" I hook my thumb over my shoulder, pointing to the bathroom and bee-lining it toward the restroom.

I take off my clothes but hesitate before slipping Mack's cotton T-shirt over my head.

Hello, fuel to the fire.

There's something about wearing a guy's clothes. About the way it feels against your skin. The way it hits your upper thighs. The way it makes you feel enveloped and…safe when said clothes belong to the right person.

I lift the collar of the shirt and bring it to my nose, proving how weak I am when it comes to Macklin Taylor. It smells clean. Like laundry detergent. But there's an underlying scent beneath it. It smells like him. Lifting the hem of the shirt, I press it to my nose and breathe a little deeper.

Yup. It smells like him. Like his entire house. Clean. Woodsy. Mouth-watering. I let the material go and slip my legs into Mack's basketball shorts. I fold my clothes, sit them on the corner of the counter, making sure they're out of the way, and head back into the bedroom.

Mack's back is pressed to the dark headboard, and his phone is in his hands as I flick the bathroom light off. Darkness blankets the room except for the light coming from his phone. It bounces off Mack's blue eyes as he watches me, his gaze sliding down my body and landing on my toes. He clears his throat and looks at his phone again.

"Texting someone?" I ask.

"Deleting notifications," he mutters as I slide under the covers.

Unable to rein in my curiosity, I peek at his screen and freeze. It's a dating app. The Birds and Bees app, to be specific. My mom suggested I give it a try after I told her about my breakup with Wes. Needless to say, I politely declined.

Is Macklin messaging other girls? The realization brings a tightness to my stomach and doesn't exactly leave me with any warm fuzzies. Not after tonight.

When he catches me peeking, he turns the phone off and sets it on the nightstand. "Do you have everything you need?"

"So, is she wanting to sext, or did she ask what your favorite color is?" I quiz him, ignoring his question.

He grunts a laugh. "Neither."

"Oh, come on. Don't stop on my account. What'd she say? Or is it a *they*? Are you flirting with more than one girl, Macklin?"

"Just clearing out my notifications," he repeats, "Guess I'm a little OCD."

"Any messages from anyone interesting?" I prod, my pulse thrumming faster than a hummingbird's. But I want to know. I want to know if he treats every girl like this. Like they matter. Like they're worth the effort. Does he invite lots of girls over? Does he let them in his bed when it's stormy outside? Does he watch movies with them and give them foot massages without asking for anything in return?

Mack's fingers thread through the longer strands on the top of his head, then he rests it against the headboard and looks down at me. "Are you asking if I'm interested in anyone, Porcupine?"

With my head propped in my hand, I turn onto my side and face him fully, mustering as much nonchalance as I can. "Maybe. Like I said, you're quite the catch, Mack. I'm sure you have plenty of girls interested in you. The question is... have any caught your eye so far?"

He scoots a little closer to me, his jaw ticking as his focus drops to my lips. It's so dark I can barely see his sharp features, but the shadows and lack of light only tempt me further.

"Cat got your tongue?" I push, feeling the shift in the air with every passing second.

But he stays quiet and watches me squirm. And boy, am I squirming. Curse his eyes. And curse the way they know how to burrow past my defenses, leaving me entirely too vulnerable for my own good.

"Is that a yes?" I whisper.

"You could say so."

Ouch.

I ignore the stab of jealousy. "Have they asked what your favorite color is yet?"

He shakes his head. "Not yet."

"Oh, so straight to sexting, then?"

His mouth quirks up. "Not yet, though I am looking forward to it."

My eyes narrow, well aware of how much fun he's having toying with me. "All right. Goodnight, Mack."

I roll onto my opposite side and set my phone on the nightstand.

"Hey, Kate?"

"What?"

"What's your favorite color?"

I snort. "Go to sleep, Mack."

"Hey, Kate?" he prods.

"What, Mack?"

"Have you ever sexted a guy?"

"None of your business."

"Hey, Kate?" he repeats, somehow finding the perfect balance between annoying and charming in a way I'll never fully understand.

Exasperated, I huff, "What do you want, Mack?"

"Do you know how to delete dating apps?"

I pause. "Why?"

"Thought you might be able to save me some time. That's what I was doing. In case you were wondering."

"And why would you delete your dating apps?"

"'Cause a girl caught my attention." The mattress dips, jostling me as he gives me his back and faces the window. "Goodnight, Kate."

I stare at the bedroom door, the hairs along the back of my neck prickling as his words hang in the air. "Goodnight, Mack."

22

KATE

A soft buzzing sound pulls me from sleep, and I rub my face against the warm, hard heat of my pillow before opening my eyes. Not a pillow. Nope. It's definitely a torso. I was rubbing my face against an armpit.

Lovely.

I squeeze my hand resting on top of a pectoral, convinced I'm still dreaming.

Nope. Definitely flesh. Hard. Hot. I lift my head and peek up at the very unconscious, very handsome man I'm snuggled against.

Great. So I was feeling up a guy while he was asleep. That's not creepy or inappropriate at all.

The soft buzz happens again, and I frown, turning over and grabbing my phone from the nightstand. It's a text.

MOM

So help me, Kate. Will you PLEASE let me know if you had a chance to take your medication?

I squeeze my eyes shut as the familiar waves of disappointment and shame hit me, one after the other.

I forgot.

Again.

Shocker.

Sucking my teeth into my lips, I sit up and look down at Mack, unsure of what the hell I'm supposed to do.

He's still asleep. Blissfully so. His long lashes are slightly curled at the end, and his lips are parted as he snores softly. The light from the moon filters in through the window, making him even more attractive in the dead of night than when he's in his paramedic uniform, and that's saying something.

My phone buzzes again in my hand. Mom's calling.

I silence it as a jolt of anxiety pulses through me.

How could I be so stupid? I forgot my medication.

And now it's the middle of the night on top of a mountain in a warm cabin tucked away from reality and drama and conveniences like a five-minute walk to my apartment instead of a twenty-minute drive when I don't have a car. And I definitely don't have the heart to wake the sleeping man to tell him I need a ride.

Which means…what, exactly? What are my choices here? I could always steal his car, but––

My phone buzzes again, and I ignore the call, sending Mom to voicemail.

Dammit.

Dammit, dammit, dammit.

"Kate?" Mack croaks, his voice rusty and raspy and oh, so attractive that if we were in any other set of circumstances, I'd probably jump his bones under the guise of being in duress and not thinking clearly.

Shoving aside the thought, I keep my head resting against his broad chest and mutter, "Hey."

"Why are you awake?" He stifles a yawn against his hand. "Is everything okay?"

"Um…no?" I offer dryly, fighting the urge to cry.

Sensing my hesitation, he sits up a little more and looks down at me. "What's wrong?"

Chewing my lower lip, I keep my gaze glued to the window and answer, "I, uh, I wasn't planning on having a sleepover."

His chuckle warms my insides. "Neither was I."

My phone buzzes again.

"You sure everything's okay?" he prods.

"Uh, yeah. It's my mom."

"You gonna answer it?"

I send the call to voicemail again. "Nope."

"Kate, what's wrong?" he demands. Whatever sleepiness had been in his tired features is officially gone, replaced with concern as he fully sits up in the bed.

My phone buzzes another time, and I close my eyes, regret pooling in my stomach.

"Answer it," he orders. "It's late. It could be an emergency."

"It isn't. She's calling because I usually text her to tell her when I've taken my medicine."

He hesitates, his forehead wrinkling. "*Did* you take your medicine?"

"Um…"

"Kate," he warns.

Grimacing, I mutter, "I forgot?"

"Well, is it here? Is it on you?"

"I usually keep my emergency pills in my backpack, but I forgot to replace them the last time I used them, so…"

He closes his eyes, the weight of his realization hitting like a sucker punch. "So, you don't have your medication."

Guilt sits like a stone in my stomach. "Nope. I'll be fine

without it for one night. It's already almost two in the morning--"

The incessant buzzing from my phone starts up again, and I groan.

"Answer it," he orders. "Tell your mom we're going to pick up your medicine right now."

"What?" I sit up, and my hair falls over one shoulder. "It's the middle of the night."

"I don't care. It's for your safety," he argues, standing up and searching for his clothes.

"Seriously, Mack. I'll be fine."

Slipping a dark T-shirt over his head, he demands, "What happens if you miss a pill?"

"I--" I pause and clear my throat as his head pops out through the hole in his shirt, and he gives me a pointed stare, daring me to lie to him.

"For one pill?" I clarify. "Probably nothing."

"And possibly something?" he surmises.

"I don't--"

"Kate."

"Fine. Yes. Possibly something. But like I said, it's almost two in the morning, and I don't want to be a burden or let my condition ruin someone else's rest for once. Why don't we go back to sleep and grab it in the morning?"

"I'm not gonna put your health at risk, Kate."

"My health is fine."

"Your health will be fine once we grab your medicine at home. Come on. The weather's calmed down, anyway." My phone buzzes again, and he adds, "And don't ignore your mom. She only wants to know you're okay."

Annoyed, I answer the call, bringing the phone to my ear. "Hey, Mom."

"Honey, are you okay?" she rushes out, her voice cracking.

My head hangs as I realize she's been crying. "You haven't been answering my texts or my calls, I thought––"

"I'm fine," I interrupt.

Releasing a shaky breath, she whispers, "Are you sure? Your dad and I have been worried sick. Did something happen?"

"Nothing happened," I mutter, hating how cold I sound. How detached. "I just forgot to text you back. I'm sorry."

"Well, where are you? Your GPS says you're out in the mountains somewhere? What are you doing away from home in the middle of the night?"

"You're tracking me?" I shove my hair away from my face, fuming. "Seriously?"

"You weren't answering my texts, baby. We thought something might've happened––"

"Do you have any idea how crazy you sound?" I snap. But it isn't fair. I'm not mad at her. I'm mad at myself. I can't believe this is happening. I'm so embarrassed it's not even funny. Why does this have to happen to me?

"You're right," my mom replies, her tone soft and laced with regret. "I am crazy and overprotective and overbearing, and I'm sorry, but––"

"No buts, okay?" I pause and let out a deep, long breath as I search for patience. "I'm fine. I promise. I fell asleep at a friend's house, but he's driving me home now so I can get my meds. Okay?"

She sighs. And I hate the defeat in it. The heaviness. The disappointment.

"Look, I'm sorry," I start. The familiar weight of guilt settles on my shoulders.

"Don't apologize, baby. You have nothing to be sorry about. Thank you for picking up the phone, for filling me in, and for going to get your medicine. I'm sorry for tracking you. I know how much you hate it. I…"

She insisted I share my location when I first moved away and promised to only use it in case of emergencies. And I agreed, knowing it was probably a good option no matter how childish it made me feel. But I get it. The need to know I'm okay. The need to know where I am when I'm not answering my phone in the middle of the night. I shouldn't have snapped at her. I was being unfair.

"It's okay," I murmur. "I understand."

"We love you, baby," Dad chimes in.

"I love you too," I reply, not surprised I'm on speaker. "I'll talk to you guys later, okay?"

"You coming home this weekend?" Mom asks.

I glance at Mack. He's by the doorway dressed in his T-shirt and jeans with a thick coat and heavy boots, his keys dangling from his hand.

I still don't have my license. I won't for a few more weeks. But the idea of disappointing my parents further is more than I can bear.

"It's late. Really late. And I'm exhausted. We'll talk about it later, all right?"

"Sure thing, baby," Mom replies. "And thank you. Again. For answering."

"No problem."

"Love you, baby."

"Love you too."

I drop my phone onto my lap, and Mack tosses me my clothes. "Chop-chop, Kate. Let's get your medicine."

As Mack opens the garage door and backs out of the driveway, a gust of wind shakes the cab of his SUV, and my eyes widen as I take in the white wonderland in front of me. Apparently, the temperature dropped enough for the rain to turn to snow, and it's quite the spectacle. Winter is officially here.

The headlights on Mack's car slice through the darkness as the wheels roll over the untouched snow. It's beautiful. Trees line both sides of the winding road, their branches hanging low from the weight of the snow.

There isn't another car in sight. There's not usually much traffic since Mack lives in the middle of nowhere, but in the dead of night? It's even more of a ghost town. The realization wracks me with guilt as I stare at the dark expanse around us.

"I'm sorry," I mutter, my voice carrying more than I expected in the silent cab.

Mack glances at me. "Sorry for what?"

"For a lot of things," I admit. "For forgetting my medicine, for losing my license and making you drive me everywhere, especially in the middle of the night. For waking you up in the first place and using all your gas since I was so spacey. I'm...I'm seriously sorry."

Reaching over the center console, he grabs my knee and squeezes. "Don't apologize for shit like that."

"I'm embarrassed. I made you get up--"

"You gave me the opportunity to make sure you're taken care of," he counters. "And if you haven't figured it out by now, let me make myself clear. I like taking care of you. I like knowing you're okay. Knowing you're happy, healthy, and able to be the best Kate you can be."

"Yeah, but taking care of me when it's broad daylight versus two in the morning are two very different things," I argue, no matter how freaking sweet he's being.

"Who needs sleep, Kate? I'd rather hang out with you in the middle of the night any day of the week than waste it in bed, snoring away."

My treacherous heart skips a beat as I look down at my lap.

"You don't snore," I mutter.

"Oh, I don't?"

"No. You do this––" I almost say *cute*, but stop myself at the last second and try again. "You do this little...this little breathing thing. It's kind of raspy and rumbly, but it isn't snoring."

He chuckles. "Okay. Well, I'd rather hang out with you than do the raspy, rumbly thing in my sleep. Better?"

"Maybe." I peek up at him again.

He's too damn sweet. Too damn thoughtful.

I wish I knew what he was thinking.

I liked sleeping with him tonight. I liked making cookies and hanging out. I liked being close to him and feeling his warmth.

And I even like how he insisted we get my medicine, even when I told him it was okay not to.

Yeah.

I'm starting to like a lot of things about Mack.

Maybe a little too much.

But I'm too weak to stop.

And honestly? I'm not even sure if I want to anymore.

23

KATE

MACKLIN

Good luck on your test today.

ME

Thanks. Were you able to get any sleep after dropping me off last night?

MACKLIN

Yeah, slept great. You?

ME

Liar. And I slept okay.

MACKLIN

Liar. Did you even bother going back to sleep after I dropped you off?

ME

Maybe.

MACKLIN

Any good dreams?

ME

Maybe.

MACKLIN

Was I in them?

ME

That's a secret I'll never tell.

MACKLIN

Were we in my bed again?

ME

I'm not sure why the environment in my dream matters to you, Macklin.

MACKLIN

Just curious. What were you wearing?

> **ME**
>
> Did you really just ask me that?

MACKLIN

Maybe. Is it an inappropriate question?

> **ME**
>
> Maybe.

Without waiting for his response, I text him again.

> **ME**
>
> Ya know, if I didn't know any better, I'd say you're trying to sext me.

MACKLIN

Or maybe I'm trying to get you out of your head again.

> **ME**
>
> Who says I'm in my head again?

MACKLIN

You were awfully quiet when I dropped you off last night.

> **ME**
>
> I was tired, so sue me.

MACKLIN

All right. As long as you weren't stressing about the E word, we're good.

> **ME**
>
> Why would I be stressing about the E word? Oh. Right. Because it ruined your beauty sleep. How could I forget?

MACKLIN

Are you saying I'm beautiful, Kate?

ME

I'm saying I'm sorry my "baggage" ruined your night.

MACKLIN

Never apologize, my little porcupine.
Besides. I go to the gym for a reason.

Porcupine.

I bite back my amusement and type my response.

ME

And what reason is that?

MACKLIN

So my manly muscles can carry any baggage you throw my way.

I let out a laugh and shake my head. Seriously. This man is insane. He's also awfully good at piquing my curiosity and finding ways to distract me from my embarrassment or my need to apologize, which is quite the talent.

ME

Manly muscles?? What manly muscles?

MACKLIN

Ya know, I would send a half-naked picture of me flexing so you could drool over them, but since we're not sexting and all…

ME

You're ridiculous. You know that, right?

MACKLIN

Maybe.

ME

Do you work today?

MACKLIN

Yeah. How about you?

ME

Yup. I work this evening. And I have a test starting in two minutes, so I have to go.

MACKLIN

Good luck, my prickly porcupine.

ME

Thanks. I'm gonna need it.

MACKLIN

I've seen how hard you've studied. You got this.

ME

We'll see.

I tuck my phone into my backpack as Mr. Litwak begins passing out our tests.

A few hours later.

MACKLIN

How'd your test go?

ME

No idea.

MACKLIN

You don't know?

ME

I never know for sure. I think I did okay, but I'll have to wait and see. Litwak said he'd post the results in a couple days. Fingers crossed.

MACKLIN

We should celebrate this weekend.

ME

Celebrate what?

MACKLIN

Your excellent test score.

ME

Someone's confident.

MACKLIN

And someone's getting lost in their own head again. Do I need to give you something else to focus on, Kate?

ME

What? Like a picture of your manly muscles?

MACKLIN

Who wants to sext now? ;)

A MILLION RESPONSES FLOOD MY MIND, BUT I DON'T TYPE A single word. Instead, I'm staring at the winking smiley face and chewing on my bottom lip when another message pops up.

MACKLIN

About our celebration…I was thinking of going country dancing. Have you ever been?

ME

Nope. I'm not much of a dancer, remember?

MACKLIN

Maybe you haven't found the right partner.

I stare at his message, unsure how to reply. I should respond. Leaving him on *read* is rude. But not knowing what to say or how I should take his text in the first place is messing with my head.

Because I like him. And liking a guy who's older than you is daunting.

And messy, considering I know his daughter.

But I can't stop thinking about him, and it's becoming a problem. Especially when I don't know if he's asking me out as a friend or if he's actually interested in dating me. I mean, the guy's a flirt when he gets going. Is he like this with everyone? And considering how we ended our night compared to what he said before I fell asleep in his bed? I have no idea where we stand or what he wants. Especially after the not-so-well-timed reminder of my condition and how inconvenient it can be.

I shove my things into the gym locker and close the metal door. I probably should've stayed home and tried to sleep since last night was rocky. After Mack dropped me off, I spent the rest of the early morning hours tossing and turning in bed.

Once everyone has put their things in their lockers, Blake, Mia, and I walk toward the main area, weaving between all the macho men lifting weights. Blake was right. It's getting easier to ignore their curious stares whenever we touch the weight machines or free weights. *Usually.* Unless Wes is here with Levi. He hasn't bothered approaching me since our last encounter, so that's something.

I scan the room for Mack, like every other time Blake's twisted my arm into coming, but he isn't here.

I shouldn't be disappointed, but I am. I probably shouldn't be relieved, either, yet the feeling floods my system nonetheless. I'm still not sure how I feel about drowning in such contradictory emotions. Still, Macklin seems to bring them out of me, leaving me almost dizzy with indecision.

Did last night scare him off? I wouldn't blame him if it

did. Driving a girl home in the middle of the night all because she forgot her medicine is quite the wake-up call. But he was so sweet on the car ride home, and his morning texts have been amusing, to say the least. Still, I don't know what to think.

"Kate." Blake snaps her fingers an inch from my nose. "Are you paying attention?"

I clear my throat and nod. "Yeah. Sure thing." I pause, shaking my head. "Wait, what did you say?"

"I said, we're going to focus on our upper bodies today. Let's warm up."

Following her lead, Mia and I go through the motions, swinging our arms and elevating our heart rates while jogging in place for a few minutes. When we're properly warmed up, Blake hands each of us a set of weights and shows me how to perform a shoulder press. My shoulders scream at me within minutes. Blake continues guiding our workout when Mia's attention catches on something behind me.

"Kate, you seriously need to tap that," she tells me, her breathing staggered as she pushes the hand weights above her head one more time, finishing the set.

I glance over my shoulder and nearly swallow my tongue.

Macklin, in all his sweaty glory, is drinking from his water bottle next to the leg press. His gray T-shirt is stretched tight across his pecs, showcasing how ripped the bastard is. His bottoms hang low on his hips, leaving little to the imagination.

Wow.

Hello, manly muscles.

The guy wasn't kidding.

And to think I was snuggled up against his chest last night when my phone had to go and ruin it.

Tearing my attention from the man behind me, I turn to

Blake and Mia again. "I don't know what you're talking about."

"If you don't tap that, someone else will," Mia tells me. "The guy's a catch, and we aren't the only ones who've noticed."

Ignoring the twinge of jealousy, I mutter, "You guys are forgetting something."

"What are we forgetting?" Mia asks.

"We don't know if he's interested in me like that."

Not after last night.

"Only one way to find out," Blake returns. Before I can stop her, she waves her hand and calls, "Hey, Mack!"

He looks over at us and smiles at her. When his attention lands on me, his gaze drifts up and down my body for the barest of seconds.

Mia laughs under her breath and whispers, "Not interested, my ass."

I give her a pointed look and tuck the wisps of hair falling from my ponytail behind my ears, hoping I don't look like a drowned raccoon like the first time we ran into each other here. I stare at the ground, attempting to look interested in the hard foam pads beneath my sneakers instead of the man across the room. Still, I swear I can feel him moving closer to us. It's like my body recognizes his anytime he's around. Like gravity. An invisible force tugging me toward him or him toward me. It's exhausting fighting it. But giving in is an entirely new level of danger I'm not sure I'm ready for.

"How you guys doin'?" Mack asks once he's reached us.

"We're good," Mia replies. "By the way, I don't think we've officially been introduced yet. I'm Mia."

Another twinge of jealousy settles at my sternum, but I ignore it, watching Macklin shake Mia's hand. He smiles kindly back at her. "I'm Mack, Theo's older brother. Nice to meet you." He lets her hand go and turns to me. "Hey, Kate."

"Hey," I murmur, smiling shyly.

What are you thinking? Did you figure out how to delete your dating apps? Did my smell cling to your pillow the same way yours is still clinging to my skin? Do you regret telling me you're interested in me? Do you wish we'd never met?

"So, Mack," Blake interrupts. "I was wondering if you could help us with something."

Breaking our little staring contest, he looks at Blake and nods. "Sure thing. What do you need?"

"Kate's been dying to learn how to do a pull-up, but she's not quite there strength-wise. I was wondering if you could help her."

Dying to learn how to do a pull-up? What's this girl smoking?

"Yeah, sure. How can I help?" Macklin asks.

"Basically, I need you to lift her up so she can reach the bar, then I want you to grab the bar yourself and face her so you guys are chest to chest. Once you're situated, Kate's supposed to wrap her legs around your hips, and I want you to assist her with the pull-ups by taking some of her weight and, ya know, doing the pull-ups *with* her. Make sense?"

My eyes bug out of my head as I attempt to register what she's talking about, but I'm still stuck on the whole *she's supposed to wrap her legs around your hips* part.

My voice squeaks as I interrupt, "I'm sorry, what?"

"I think I understand what you're saying," Mack tells Blake. He walks over to the pull-up bar a few feet away and stands under it. "You comin', Kate?"

Mia snorts and covers her mouth. "She will be when she replays this tonight."

I glare at her as Blake nudges me between my shoulder blades. "As your own personal trainer, I expect you to follow orders. Now, go on."

Kill. Me. Now.

I face Mack and paste on a fake smile, unsure what to do

or what to say since my friends have thrown down the proverbial gauntlet, and I have to deal with the repercussions.

It's not like he'll actually go through with this...

Will he?

"You ready?" he questions.

Letting out a soft breath between pursed lips, I look up at the bar and nod. "Yup."

His grip is soft as he grabs my waist. "Jump on three. One. Two. Three."

Mack lifts me as I jump. Reaching for the bar, my fingers circle the cold metal.

"Got it?" Mack asks.

"Yeah, I'm good."

My legs hang limply as Mack jumps up. His hands frame mine on both sides, clutching the bar, and his chest is pressed against me. I can feel the steady *thump thump* of his heartbeat, his heat warming me as I stare at his sharp jaw, refusing to look him in the eye. Not when we're this close. Not when my nipples are pebbling, and I know he can feel them brushing against his chest.

Yeah, no. This is a bad idea. A very bad idea.

"Kate, wrap your legs around his waist," Blake orders from below.

She can't be serious.

I don't move, forcing myself to hold strong even though my palms are sweating.

"Kate, ya good?" Mack prods, his voice quiet. So quiet it's only meant for me.

I peek up at him, those blue eyes melting my reservations one millisecond at a time.

"Yeah," I breathe out. "I'm good."

"Do you trust me?"

"Pretty sure you've asked me that question before."

"Yeah, well, I didn't like your answer the first time. Do you trust me, Kate?" he repeats.

I smile softly. "Yes."

He lets go of the bar with his left hand and reaches for my upper thigh, hiking it up and wrapping it around his waist. He grabs the bar again, and I wrap my other leg around him.

If I thought this might be a minorly precarious situation before, the warning bells are officially on full-blown siren mode. Because I can feel him. All of him. Against my lady bits. And he's...

I gulp. Yup. He's hard.

"On the count of three, we do a pull-up," he orders, his breath brushing against my red cheeks. "Okay?"

I nod and force my hips to keep from grinding against him, no matter how impossible it feels. But it's been so long. So long since I've felt connected to someone. So long since I've even wanted to feel connected to someone. And this? Feeling Macklin at my literal core? It's the best form of torture a girl could ask for. If only I could put myself out of my misery, preferably on his erection.

"One," Mack murmurs. His cock twitches against me. "Two." I shift slightly, my clit pulsing as I stifle my moan. "Three."

He pulls up on the bar, taking my dead weight with him as I remember to actually use my muscles to help him.

It's official. The guy's ripped. It's the only conclusion I can make considering the circumstances because I'm most definitely not lifting my body weight, and I'm most definitely not a twig, either. Not compared to every other girl at this gym. But Mack's taking it in stride, lifting us both as I attempt to do my part despite knowing it's barely a drop in the bucket.

It's nice. Feeling small. I'm not sure if it's some weird, evolutionary kink he's tapping into or what, but I've never been more turned on in my life. And call it a hunch, but I'm pretty sure he's enjoying this exercise too. My nipples rub against his chest as we go up and down, his dick nestled between my thighs, his breath kissing my cheeks. A soft sheen of sweat clings to his forehead, the tiny, rhythmic grunts clawing up his throat as he lifts us again and again.

Yup. It's official. This is the most erotic moment of my life. It's all downhill from here. But what a way to go.

Mia's right. I'm totally using this for my spank bank later. I don't care how inappropriate it is. Hell, part of me wants to drag him off to the locker room to ease the ache in my core. I wonder if--

"And that's ten," Blake announces. "Good job, guys!"

Her sharp feminine voice cuts through the lustful haze in my brain, and I unhook my ankles from around Mack. He lets go of the bar and lands on his feet, grabbing my hips and softening my fall like a damn knight in shining armor as I let go of the pull-up bar.

Once I'm on my feet, I look up at him and suck my cheeks between my molars, unsure what to say or do now that I know what it's like to feel him--all of him--moving against me.

"You busy Friday night, Kate?" he rasps. And damn the sound. His voice. Smooth, yet rough. Low and throaty.

Wait. What were we talking about? Oh. Yeah. He asked if I'm busy.

"Friday? Uh, I don't think so?"

"Wanna go out with me?"

"As what? Friends? Or...?" My voice trails off. But I need to know. I need him to spell it out for me. I need clarity, especially when my brain is still lost in a haze of desire. In the feel of his hands on my waist. His breath against my cheeks.

He frowns, his attention slipping to my lips as he towers

over me. "I'm too old to play games with you, Kate. I want to take you on a date. Where you get dressed up, I pick you up at your house, and we eat food and get to know each other."

"And after?" I whisper.

His mouth twitches. "With your permission, I'm gonna kiss you goodnight and watch as you walk inside your place."

"And after that?" I push, more turned on than I've ever been in my entire life. I can't help it. The foreplay we just experienced will be tattooed onto my memory for the rest of my measly existence. And since he's asked me out, I want to know where we go from here and if it involves his dick between my thighs again.

He bends closer, his mouth tickling against the shell of my ear. "I'm gonna jerk off to the memory of how good you felt against me, praying one day you'll like me enough to want the same thing. I want you, Kate. Physically, emotionally, intellectually. Sound okay to you, my prickly little porcupine?"

He wants me.

Physically. Emotionally. Intellectually.

I gulp and nod, realizing I haven't answered him.

His chuckle is low and husky as he pulls away. "Good. See you Friday. Seven sound good?"

"Sure," I squeak.

He grins. "Perfect. Wear something that looks good with cowgirl boots."

Without another word, he walks away.

24

MACKLIN

W hen I told Kate to wear something that looks good with cowgirl boots, I'd been kidding. But the girl outdid herself. I take in her white lacy top and brown leggings tucked into ankle boots, blown away she actually agreed to go out with me.

We drive to Rowdy's, chatting about random shit. When we arrive, I put the car in park and lead her to the front of the rough brick building. I'd debated on whether or not to bring Kate here for our first date, but honestly? I think she's gonna love it.

Being on a first date again is strange. I've dabbled with dating since my divorce but never found someone I was really interested in. Kate, though? Kate's been different from the beginning. Even now, standing beside me, I'm not sure what I should do about it. And considering our age difference? Fuck. I don't know. She doesn't want the same things I want. At least, I don't think she does. Then again, she isn't like other girls. She's kind and sweet and mature. She doesn't want to party. Doesn't want to waste her college years. She's hardworking. Gorgeous. Driven.

Stop overthinking shit, I remind myself, glancing at her again. But I don't know what to say.

When she catches me staring, she runs her hands along the white lace of her top, her nerves buzzing off her pale skin, seeping into the air around us.

"Do I stick out like a sore thumb?" she asks.

"Not at all."

"You sure?"

"You look gorgeous, Kate."

She peeks at me again. "Maybe if you convince me I don't suck at being a country girl, I might even invest in a pair of cowgirl boots."

I smile and grab her hand, guiding her into the building. It's surreal being here. The low lights. The country music. The massive dance floor and peanut shells beneath our feet.

My buddy stops short when he sees me at the entrance and squints his eyes. "Mack?"

"Hey, Rowdy––"

"Macklin!" he returns, his grin widening. He pulls me into a hug and slaps his hand against my back.

I return the gesture, and when I pull away from him, he asks, "How you been, man? It's been a while."

"Uh, I've been good," I answer. Remembering my manners, I grab Kate's hand again and tug her closer to me. "This is Kate."

His eyes widen as he takes her in and offers his hand for her to shake. "Hey, Kate. I'm Rowdy. I went to high school with our boy, Macklin."

She takes his hand and smiles back at him. "Nice to meet you."

"You too. Ever been country dancing?"

She shakes her head. "Nope."

"Ah, you'll love it. Right, Mack?"

"Maybe another night. Tonight, I wanna show her Bruce," I announce.

With a laugh, he slaps his weathered hand against my shoulder and argues, "Nah, you wanna check in on your investment, don't you?"

"Who's Bruce?" Kate interjects.

Rowdy chuckles. "He's a mean sonofabitch."

He's right. Bruce has put plenty of men on their asses, but first, I need food.

"Can we get a table?" I request.

"Sure thing, man." He grabs a couple of menus from the hostess table. "Follow me."

Once we're seated and Rowdy's finally given us some space, Kate quizzes me, "Investment?"

I squeeze the back of my neck and open my menu, pretending to read the options, though I don't see a word. I hate talking about my money. I hate talking about how I won it. I hate talking about how, in a way, it took my daughters from me. And I hate how people treat me differently as soon as they find out about it. I don't think Kate will. At least, I hope not. But if I've learned anything since winning it, it's you never know how people will react. What people will ask for.

"You don't have to tell me," she starts, drowning in my silence.

"It's not a big deal," I reply. "I came into some money a while back and ran into Rowdy. He started telling me about his idea, and I thought, why not? Can't take it with me."

"So, you invested in his restaurant?"

I shrug. "Yeah. The food's great, and I thought the idea of teaching country dancing along with some live music, well-priced alcohol, and a fun environment would be a good fit for the college kids who aren't interested in SeaBird."

She looks around the packed restaurant, taking in the

dance floor littered with people in cowboy hats, the bar along the back wall, and the stage dusted with peanut shells. Turning to me again, she notes, "Seems like you're onto something. Does this mean you bringing me here had nothing to do with the flashing lights at SeaBird?"

I should've known she'd catch onto one of the reasons I thought Rowdy's might be a better fit for her than SeaBird. I wanted to give her a night off from her disease instead of shining a light on it. I motion to the dance floor on our left. "You also mentioned you're interested in dancing."

"Technically, there's dancing at SeaBird."

"Yeah, but dancing at SeaBird makes me feel like an old man."

"And country dancing doesn't?" she quips.

"Guess it depends on the day."

"Does this mean you actually know how to country dance?"

"I may have picked up a thing or two."

Her lips thin as if she's holding back her amusement. "You'll have to show me whatcha got one of these days."

"Maybe after I brush up on my skills," I tell her. "It's been a while."

"Can't wait." Her mouth quirks as her gaze catches on something behind me. "Wait. Is that a mechanical bull?"

"His name's Bruce."

"*That's* Bruce?"

"Yeah. The one and only," I tell her.

She turns back to me and settles in the booth. "Okay, now that's hilarious. You're right. Drunk college kids would *love* riding him."

"You don't have to be drunk for it to be fun," I counter.

"Pretty sure the only way you could convince me to ride Bruce is if I had alcohol in my system."

I close my menu, taking the bait. I doubt she even knows

she's dangled it in front of me. "Come on, Porcupine. You should try it. You might surprise yourself."

"By riding a mechanical bull?"

With a smirk, I nod.

"Have *you* tried it?" she asks.

"Who do you think was Rowdy's guinea pig when he was learning all the programming for it?"

Impressed, she leans away from me and blatantly checks me out from head to toe as if she doesn't believe me. "No way."

"Come on. You said you don't know what to do socially without alcohol." I motion to the dance floor and mechanical bull. "Now, you've found an alternative."

"Mechanical bull riding *and* dancing? Someone's optimistic," Kate notes. "You forget I don't know any of the moves or the songs or…" She shakes her head. "Yeah, I'd be lost."

"Pretty sure you're a quick learner, and when you have the right partner, you might be surprised."

"But not tonight?" she challenges.

"Not until I'm confident I can lead you around the dance floor without either of us looking like an idiot, but I'll work on it," I promise.

"Mm-hmm."

"As for tonight,"––I lean to my left, bringing Bruce into view as someone falls on their ass after being bucked off––"we conquer the beast."

"How 'bout I just watch you conquer the beast?" she offers.

"No deal. As your designated babysitter for the evening, I insist you have fun and let your guard down. And, if you run into any issues, I'll be here to help."

Her brows knit, but she stays quiet.

I know she knows what I'm referring to. I know she

remembers our conversation about why she doesn't go out. I know she probably regrets opening up to me about such a vulnerable topic, but I also know she deserves to feel normal. To feel beautiful and appreciated. To feel wanted and safe while being given the opportunity to have fun and let loose without worrying about the potential repercussions.

And I want to give it to her. The opportunity to let her guard down. To have fun and let loose.

I want it more than anything.

Closing the menu in front of her, she shifts in the booth and adjusts her top but doesn't look at me. "Is that why you brought me here? So I could let loose without repercussions?"

I brought her here for a shit-ton more reasons. Like the fact that I like her. That I like it when she smiles. That I like being around her. That she makes me feel not lonely, and I haven't felt *not* lonely in a long time.

"I got you, Kate," I assure her. "You can let go tonight."

Those stormy gray eyes meet mine as she peeks up at me. Watching me. Waiting to see if I'm serious. If I pity her. If I mean it. And she knows I don't mean alcohol. She knows I don't mean she should do something stupid because I'm giving her permission or some shit. She doesn't need my permission for it, anyway.

No. What I'm saying is for the first time in her life, she doesn't have to worry about being all alone. Because I'm here. And I get it. And I'm not going anywhere.

"Okay, Macklin," she decides. "After we eat, I'll let you introduce me to Bruce."

I bite back my grin. "Oh, really?"

"Mm-hmm," she hums, though she looks as unsure as before. "Let's see whatcha got."

～

KATE SCRATCHES HER TEMPLE, EYEING THE FAKE BULL LIKE IT'S straight out of a horror movie. After our food, we talked for a while about family and vacations and our favorite foods—— and color. Finally, she couldn't put it off any longer, suggesting we get the bull riding over with.

She was brave when we first walked over. But after seeing the line and watching person after person being thrown on their asses, I have a feeling she's second-guessing her decision to let me introduce her to Bruce.

I catch her chewing on her thumbnail. "Are you nervous?"

Her glower deepens. "Are you sure this is a good idea?"

The person in front of her walks toward Bruce and climbs on, bumping us up to being the next in line. Kate doesn't budge.

I press my hand against her lower back to urge her forward. "Pretty sure it's a brilliant idea.".

"Pretty sure you only want to see me fall on my butt," she mutters.

"I mean, you do have a pretty cute butt."

She looks over her shoulder at me. "Yet here you are, wanting to see me bruise it."

"I can always kiss it better if you'd like."

She smirks but doesn't deem my suggestion worthy of a reply as she moves to the front of the line. Rowdy turns the bull on, adjusting the setting to easy as the girl raises one hand in the air and rides the thing like a pro. Thirty seconds later, she falls onto the soft, cushioned ground and laughs as her friends stumble in and drag her off to the dance floor.

Which means it's Kate's turn.

She grumbles, "I'm seriously regretting ever telling you I like to go out. You know that, right?"

"Just wait 'til I get you on the dance floor."

The ground in the sectioned-off area dedicated to Bruce is covered with foam, making it a soft landing when you're thrown off the contraption. Still, it doesn't erase the concerned lines between Kate's brows as she stares at the bull in front of us, not bothering to climb on.

"Try it by yourself," I suggest. "If you need help, let me know, and I'll jump on so I can show you how to do it."

"They let you do two riders at one time?"

"Probably not, but since I know the owner and all, I'm willing to bet he'll make an exception."

Unconvinced, she meets my eyes again. "And you're sure you know how to ride this thing?"

"Yeah, I got pretty good at it. You can do this. Piece of cake."

She takes a deep breath but nods and slowly makes her way toward Bruce as if he's her own personal Everest. Once she's fully seated, Rowdy turns it on, and the bull slowly jerks beneath her. The girl looks like she has a stick up her ass, her body held so tight she might literally shit a brick if she doesn't loosen up a little.

"Move with it," I yell, cupping my hands over my mouth.

Her eyes are wide with fear as she finds me on the sideline. "Get your ass out here or make it stop, Mack!"

Rowdy laughs behind the utility board and prods, "Go on, Mack. Let's see what you two got."

Well aware we're both breaking the rules, I wait for the bull to spin around again as Kate jerks on top of the thing. Timing my footsteps, I run toward the moving bull, jump, and, thankfully, land behind her.

"Roll your hips," I order, grabbing her waist and plastering my front against her back as the bull jerks awkwardly beneath us.

"How?" she screeches while Rowdy bumps the difficulty up a notch just to be an ass.

I exaggerate my movements, moving with the rhythm of the bull while simultaneously grinding against Kate's round ass. And fuck. If I thought the gym was torture, this is a whole new level.

"Let go. Feel it." I roll my hips again, and this time, she follows my lead.

"Keep your hand on here," I add, placing her fingers around the leather strap connected to the front of Bruce. Her muscles are still tense, but she grips it tightly, following my orders.

"Relax into me."

She leans back, the rigidity in her muscles melting further as the bull jerks forward and back beneath us.

"Good girl," I rasp.

Fuck, she feels incredible. All supple and warm. Smells good too. Like flowers. I lean closer and take a deep breath, committing her scent to memory.

My pillow and sheets smell like her. Not sure when I'll have the discipline to wash them again, knowing it'll erase her fragrance from the night we slept in my bed together. But even my sheets pale in comparison to this moment with Kate pressed against me.

Rowdy kicks the difficulty up another notch, and Kate's breath hitches, bringing me back to the present. Faster and faster, the bull bucks as Kate holds on for dear life, her ass rubbing against my hard dick while I try to calm the hell down.

Pretty sure coming in my jeans in public is frowned upon, and if I don't get off this damn bull soon, I might be in trouble.

"Go with it," I urge. "Lift your left hand up in the air."

"I'll fall--"

"Everyone falls, Kate. The trick is to enjoy the ride while it lasts."

Her eyes meet mine over her shoulder for the briefest of

seconds before she lets go of the handle with her left hand and raises it into the air.

"Woo-hoo," she hollers, riding Bruce like a damn champ. The bull starts moving faster. She grabs onto my neck, and I burrow my nose against her throat, my arm wrapped around her waist.

If I could stay here forever, I would. I wasn't lying to her moments ago. Everyone falls. And I'm falling hard.

Faster and faster, Bruce moves beneath us. Kate squeals as we fall off into a heap on the soft ground.

Her laughter is contagious as she throws her head back and lets go, clutching her stomach and staring up at the ceiling, her dark hair sprawled across the ground. "Okay, you win. That was amazing!"

I sit up and look down at her. "You liked it?"

"Uh-huh." She wipes the tears from her crinkled eyes as she lets out another laugh. "I liked it a lot, actually. Was it difficult for you at all, or were you humoring me by winding up on the ground when I did?"

"Definitely not humoring you," I counter as I stand up and offer Kate my hand. "You did good."

"Debatable. But seriously. We should ride Bruce again." She takes my hand. "It was a blast."

I pull her up, then we head to the back of the line so we can ride Bruce again like she suggested.

My butt aches from riding the bull so many times, and my cheeks still feel pinched from all my smiling. I haven't laughed this hard in as long as I can remember.

And it's nice.

Laughing. Feeling carefree. *Not* stressing.

It's really nice, actually.

So nice, I can't even let my insecurities bring me down as I peek at Macklin and smile.

With one hand resting on the steering wheel and another on my thigh, his lips mouthing the lyrics to some old Billy Joel song, I can't help but check him out.

So. Damn. Attractive.

As if he can feel my gaze, he looks at me, his blue eyes practically glowing from the light of the dashboard. "Did you have fun tonight?"

"I had a blast." My grin spreads. "Seriously. Thank you."

"Thank you for saying yes."

"Thank you for asking me," I quip, rubbing at the tightness in my cheeks, my smile softening. "Honestly, I don't remember the last time I had this much fun."

"Me either. Next time, I'll have to get you on the dance floor." He parks in front of my house and opens the driver's side door, climbing out. I watch in awe, blown away that I'm the girl in his passenger seat, I'm the girl he asked on a date, and I'm the girl he's interested in as he walks to my side and opens the passenger door.

"Only if you brush up on your country dancing skills so I don't look like an idiot," I remind him.

With a wink, he replies, "I'll see what I can do."

Hand in hand, we walk toward the porch. I don't know what to say. I don't know what to do. It feels different this time. This first date. I'm not sure if it's because we've already hung out as friends or if he's already proven he's more mature than every other guy I've dated. But I can feel it.

The differences.

The positives stacking up, one after the other.

The comfort.

The trust.

I was even able to let go tonight. To not focus on my surroundings or what to do if I had a seizure. I was able to just…be.

It's weird. How it's always in the back of my mind. The possibilities. The potential issues or repercussions. But tonight? All the warnings were silenced. And it was incredible.

As we reach my front door, I try to calm my breathing, my nerves getting the best of me as our date winds to an end, and I smile at him. Because I don't want to go inside. I don't want this night to be over. Not yet.

"Hey, Kate?" Mack murmurs.

My eyes meet his. "Yes?"

"If I kiss you, will you pull away?"

My pulse quickens. "No."

"And if I ask if you're busy tomorrow night, will you say you have plans?"

I smile. "No."

"And if I tell you I like you, will you tell me you only want to be friends?"

"No," I repeat, rising onto my tiptoes and grabbing the edge of his leather jacket to keep my balance.

He runs his hand along my cheek, lifts my chin an inch higher, and leans closer. But not close enough. Because he isn't kissing me. He's waiting.

One. Two. Three.

I count our breaths, mesmerized by his eyes and how they seem connected to a piece of me I didn't even know existed.

Blue. Blue. Blue.

Still, he waits.

The frigid temperature seeps into my coat and kisses my cheeks, battling against his warm breath as he looks down at me. It's cold. The night air. But I could stay out here all night as long as Mack stayed with me.

The porch light gives him a halo and shadows his face, making his strong jaw even more prominent. My fingers itch to reach up and touch the slight scruff, but I stop myself.

"You gonna kiss me yet, Mack?" I whisper.

"Give me a second."

"For what?"

"So I can memorize this." His gaze bounces around my face and lands on my mouth.

"Why?" I ask with a laugh.

"Because a moment like this doesn't come along every day, Kate. And neither does a girl like you."

Not waiting any longer, he bends closer and presses his lips to mine. Hell, it's barely a kiss. A simple brush of his slightly parted lips. Soft. Warm. Innocent. Yet so damn tempting my knees quake. He swipes his tongue against my bottom lip. Tasting me. Testing me. My boundaries. My desire. My patience.

My breath hitches as I snake my hand along his chest, over his shoulder, and around his neck. His chestnut waves are soft as I weave my fingers through them, tugging gently in hopes of pulling him closer. Of convincing him to give in, to stop teasing me. To put us both out of our misery. Because after the gym, the bull rides, and his hands on me the entire night? I'm pretty sure I'm ready to combust. He smiles against my mouth and nips my bottom lip with his teeth, causing my core to pulse as he pulls away. And damn, I'm not ready for him to pull away.

"Do you want to come inside?" I murmur.

He nearly chokes on his groan but doesn't budge. "You're killing me, Smalls."

"No, I'm inviting you inside," I clarify.

Tortured, he drops his head back and looks up at the night sky. "I can't."

"Why not?"

"'Cause I'm not like the other guys you've dated, Kate."

My brows knit together. "So, you're saying no?"

"Gotta earn you first."

"You haven't earned me yet?" I question. "Pretty sure you just took me on the sweetest date I've ever been on."

"Compared to the boys you're used to, sure. Compared to the standard you deserve?" He leans down and places a quick kiss against my lips. "Not even close."

"Is this another rule in your advanced how-to-woo-a-woman class?"

His laugh warms my insides as he tells me, "I'll see you tomorrow."

"Oh, you will?"

"Yeah. At the gym, remember? Gotta help you with your

pull-ups." He slips the keys from my hand, unlocks my front door, and pushes it open for me. "Goodnight, Kate."

"Goodnight, Mack."

The keys are cold as he hands them back to me. He takes the steps two at a time, stopping at the base of the stairs to look at me one more time. His expression is laced with boyish awe. It turns me into a freaking puddle in one second flat.

"Don't forget your medicine," he adds.

"Seriously?"

"Just taking care of you, Kate."

"Uh-huh." I fold my arms and pop out my hip. "Okay, *Dad.*"

With a smirk, he tucks his hands into his front pockets and rocks back on his heels. "You can call me daddy anytime."

Then, he turns and walks away.

26

KATE

Butter and Grace is bustling. I'm not surprised. It's six o'clock on a Saturday evening. Thankfully, I haven't spilled any trays, and Wes hasn't made an appearance, so I'm counting my blessings as I drop off table six's order.

Hazel's busy chatting with one of the customers. She looks on edge and almost frustrated, which isn't like her. The customer's a woman with long blonde hair, massive boobs, a tiny waist, and looks like a CrossFit junkie with a side of girl next door. She's gorgeous. Beside her is a cute teenager who seems weirdly familiar. I squint my eyes, assessing her closer.

Soft brown waves. Baby blue eyes.

It's the other girl from the photograph on Mack's mantle. His second daughter.

Miley, I believe?

I stop short and look over my shoulder, my heart galloping in my chest. I need to get out of here like yesterday.

A frustrated Hazel grabs two menus from the hostess area and walks them toward my section, pausing when she catches me staring.

"Hey, Kate," she mutters, her expression surly.

Snapping myself out of my daze, I rush out, "Uh, hey! What's up? Everything okay?"

"Yeah. My dad's being a dumbass." She rolls her eyes while I flinch at the harshness in her voice. "By the way, this is my mom, Summer, and my sister, Miley. You okay if I put them in your section?"

"Uh, sure." A sheen of sweat breaks out along the back of my neck, but I wave at them awkwardly. "And, hi. Nice to meet you both."

"Hi," Summer greets me. She slides into the booth before turning her attention back to her oldest daughter. "I'm serious. Rachel said she saw him with some girl at Rowdy's last night. Some girl who's apparently half his age, by the way. I still can't believe he invested so much cash into that money pit."

"Mom," Miley warns, but Summer waves her off.

"Rachel said they were…" Her lips purse, and she glances at Miley. "Well, they were rubbing against each other like a couple of teenagers on the mechanical bull." She shivers. "Like seriously. How inappropriate." With a shake of her head, she grabs her napkin, setting it in her lap while looking less than amicable.

Nope. The woman looks like she's sucking on a lemon.

"Are you sure?" Miley asks with a frown. "It doesn't really sound like Dad."

"Don't defend him, Miley," Hazel warns. "It's a waste of breath." She heads back to the hostess stand.

Yikes.

Poor girl.

If only I knew whether or not her anger is warranted or if it's because her mother warped her view of Mack. If I had to guess, I'd say it's the latter.

"Honey, your father and I sheltered you from a lot of

things," Summer continues, "but now you're getting older, and I'm not going to keep you in the dark. Clearly, the man needs therapy if he's dating a girl half his age." Her nose wrinkles, and she looks around the restaurant like she wants to keep the conversation private despite me standing two feet away from her. "Can you imagine? Like, what is your father thinking? He has two daughters who are probably close to her age. It's sickening." Summer scowls and flips her long blonde hair over her shoulder. "I'll tell you this much. It shouldn't surprise me."

As if barely realizing I'm still standing here, Summer hesitates and glances up at me again, her eyes glazed with unshed tears. "Hi. Sorry." Clearing her throat, she wipes at the corner of her eyes, giving me a sad smile. "Ex drama. I'm sure you know how it is. I'll have a Diet Coke, please." She turns to her younger daughter. "What do you want, Miley?"

"Um…" Miley opens her menu, closes it quickly, and looks up at me with a smile matching her father's. "I'll have one too. Thank you."

"You're welcome. I'll be right back."

Throttling my notepad, I leave the table, trying to slow my breathing and racing heart as my mind catches up with what the hell just happened.

They were talking about me. Me and Macklin. But who in the world is Rachel? How did she see us at Rowdy's? And how dare she say we were making out in public. All we did was ride the bull––which, okay, was a little sensual––but it's not like we were making out or anything. We didn't even dance, for Pete's sake. Either the woman's delusional, or she's fabricating lies to make Mack––and me––look bad. Maybe Summer is just jealous of the fact Mack is finally moving on. She seems genuinely flustered at the prospect of Mack dating again, but I guess it's normal when you've been with someone for as long as they were together.

Regardless, her accusations are a bunch of bullshit. We didn't even kiss until he brought me home. And even then, he was a complete gentleman. He could've gotten into my pants if he wanted to, but he didn't want to rush anything or make me feel pressured.

What a bitch.

The word feels harsh, considering Summer's glassy eyes. The tears sure as heck felt genuine, but still. Talking about Macklin like that to his daughters? His daughters who already have a rocky relationship with him? It's a low blow, and there's no excuse for it.

Flustered, I grab a freshly cleaned glass, fill it with ice, and watch the fizz permeate around it as I fill the cup with Diet Coke. Doing the same to a second glass, I fume as I glance at the table again, my curiosity getting the best of me. Summer's talking, though I have no idea what she's saying. Miley is frowning and shaking her head as if she doesn't like what she's hearing as she stares at the menu in front of her.

Poor girl.

I wouldn't want to be around the woman, either, not when she's clearly frustrated her ex is moving on. One thing's for sure. I wouldn't want to be on the woman's shit list.

Nope. No, thank you.

This means waiting on her table while knowing what it's like to have her ex's tongue down my throat is going to be a real joy.

Once I have their drinks, I ignore my shaking hands and force my legs to move. I walk back to their table, setting the glasses in front of Mack's ex and his youngest daughter.

Does he know they're here? Probably not. Does he know this mysterious Rachel saw us last night? I doubt it. Does he know his ex talks about him when he isn't around and makes some pretty crappy assumptions? Maybe. *Probably.* But it doesn't exactly make me feel any better.

After taking their orders, I slip my notepad into the black apron around my waist, ready to place their orders with the cook, when Summer stops me.

"I don't suppose you go to LAU, do you?" she asks, toying with the small gold locket around her neck.

I gulp. "Uh, yes. I do go to LAU. Why?"

"Do you happen to know Theodore Taylor?"

My heart stops. "Theo?"

"Yes."

"Uh, yeah. Everyone knows Theo Taylor," I reply, anxiety gnawing at me.

"I don't suppose you've seen him with his older brother, have you?"

I shake my head. "I'm not sure. Does he attend LAU too?"

"Oh, no. I'm afraid he might be messing with one of the students who goes there. And you know how it is. Some girls, especially young ones, can be quite naive. I'm simply trying to look out for whoever my ex is currently...hooking up with."

Eyes wide, I turn to Miley. I'm not sure why. Maybe I need someone to reassure me that I'm not crazy, and I most definitely heard what I thought I did. Unfortunately, Miley's head is down, and most of her hair covers her face as if she wants to block out the world, especially her mother. But I can feel her anxiety.

Then again, maybe it's my own.

Is this woman serious?

"I, uh... Are you sure it's any of your business?" I question her. "You said he went out on a date with a younger woman. Every girl at LAU is legally an adult and can date whoever they want, so I'm not sure how it involves you or if it's your job to make sure they know who they're hooking up with."

"Excuse me?" Summer demands, her tone squeaking. "I was only asking——"

"Mom," Miley snaps. She lifts her head and looks at the woman sitting across from her. "You're being weird. Stop it." She glances at me, reads my nametag, and adds, "Kate's right. Dad can do whatever he wants as long as he's dating a consenting adult. And we both know Rachel never liked him and probably blew things out of proportion in the first place. Now, can we *please* stop talking about Dad and let the waitress put in our order?"

As if she's been slapped, Summer's long lashes flutter as she reaches out and pats Miley's clenched fist resting on the table. "You're right, Miles." She turns to me again. "And you're right too. After the divorce papers were signed, it became none of my business, and I prefer it that way. Now. Is there any way you could put a rush on our meals? We're kind of on a time crunch."

"Sure thing."

Turning on my heel, I head back to the kitchen, give the cook their orders, and slump against the wall, trying to maintain an ounce of composure. Was I being a bitch? Did I overstep my bounds the same way she clearly overstepped hers?

Was I obvious?

Does she know?

No. There's no way she could know I'm dating Mack.

Right?

The room starts to spin, and I close my eyes, praying I don't have a seizure thanks to the stress from our conversation. I know I can't control my seizures. Most of the time, I can't even feel them coming. Regardless, it's the last thing I need. Especially today.

But if I learned anything from my conversation with Mack's ex, it's that he was right when he told me he has baggage. Baggage I never quite understood until she was literally sitting in front of me.

If I was smart, I'd keep my distance from the woman. But does it mean I need to keep my distance from Mack too?

I don't want to.

At all.

With a scowl, I drop my head back, tapping it against the wall as I stare at the ceiling.

Hello, rock and hard place. Nice to see you again.

MACKLIN

Hey! How's your morning?

ME

Fine. Weird, but fine.

MACKLIN

Weird? Sounds promising. Wanna tell me about it?

ME

I'm debating.

MACKLIN

Now, THAT sounds promising. Are you in your own head again, my prickly porcupine? You can talk to me, you know.

ME

Any chance you'd be willing to meet me at The Bean Scene today? 2:00?

MACKLIN

Sure thing. See you then.

I scan our text thread for the hundredth time since this morning, my indecision practically suffocating me as I shove my phone back into my pocket and order two pumpkin spice lattes. Seriously. I have an addiction. Multiple, actually. I push the thought aside and hand the barista my credit card.

"Kate?" a familiar voice calls.

My spine turns into a steel rod, but I don't turn around.

Despite being the one to ask him to meet me here, I'm still scared. Still uncomfortable with the position I've been put in. Still afraid I'm making a mountain out of a molehill or whatever the weird saying is.

"Kate?" Mack repeats.

He's right behind me. I can feel him. His heat. His presence.

I glance over my shoulder and force a smile. "Oh. Hey, Mack."

"Hey." His brows are tugged low as he looks me up and down.

"Two pumpkin spice lattes for Kate," the barista calls out.

"You already ordered?" he asks.

"Uh, yeah. I was early…"

"I would've bought it--"

"I know," I tell him. "I ordered one for you too. I didn't know what you preferred, but…"

"Kate?" the barista repeats.

"I'll, uh…" I clear my throat and head to the pick-up line, grabbing our lattes. Mack follows me, his gaze unsure.

This is so freaking awkward, and it isn't even Mack's fault. It's mine.

"Thanks for meeting me," I add, handing him his drink and blowing gently into the small slit at the top of my cup.

"Yeah, no problem. It actually worked out. I'm on call for the hockey game in a little while."

"Oh." I take a sip, but it scalds my tongue, and I hiss. "That's convenient."

He lifts his cup. "Thanks for the coffee."

"Mm-hmm."

The Bean Scene is relatively empty, thanks to it being later in the day, but it still feels stifling. Like I'm locked in a crowded room. Like I can't breathe. Maybe it's the uncertainty in Mack's gaze or how his scent wraps around me, making the entire situation with his ex seem like a distant memory.

"So, are you gonna tell me what's going on?" he prods, stepping closer to me. "Why you asked me to meet you here?"

Just say it, Kate.

Tell him you ran into his ex. Tell him what she said. Tell him how she's most definitely talking shit behind his back.

Tell. Him.

The words catch in my throat, and I take another sip of my coffee.

Still scalding.

His lips pull into a frown, and he drops his voice low. "What'd I do wrong, Kate?"

Wrong?

He thinks he did something wrong?

He has to be joking.

The guy's practically a saint and has been since the moment we met. No. Saint isn't the right word. But reliable? Sweet? Charismatic?

Yup.

He really is a golden retriever.

"Kate," he pushes, drowning in my hesitancy.

I hug my cup to my chest and square my shoulders.

"You didn't do anything wrong. It's…" My voice trails off. But I don't know what to say.

How do I make the run-in with his wife *not* sound like a big deal when I'm the one bringing it up in the first place? Doesn't the fact I want to talk about it mean it kind of feels like a big deal to me?

Mack steps even closer, the toe of his boot tapping my Uggs and the heat from his chest warming mine as I lift my chin, looking up at him.

"What'd I do wrong, Kate?" he repeats. "I don't want to play games. I'm too old for that shit. But I like you. And I had fun––"

"I had fun too," I rush out. "And it's nothing like that. Seriously."

"So, what is it?" he questions.

He looks so young at this moment. So innocent. Like a little boy who has found out Santa isn't real. And I hate how I put it there. The unease. The confusion.

Unable to take the tension another second, I murmur, "Your wife came into Butter and Grace, and––"

"*Ex*-wife," he growls, recognizing the catalyst as he squeezes his hands into fists. "What'd she do this time?"

"She came into the restaurant and mentioned someone named Rachel? Does her name sound familiar?"

He grabs my bicep and drags me to the corner of the coffee shop in search of more privacy. "What happened?"

He looks pissed, his fury practically wafting off him. It mixes with his natural scent until I'm pretty sure I've never experienced anything so sexy or mouthwatering, no matter how messed up this scenario is.

Not the time, libido.

But I like seeing him all possessive. And passionate. No one's ever been possessive of me. I've always felt replaceable. Forgettable. Seeing Mack like this? It makes my reservations after my run-in with Summer feel even more inconsequential.

"So the name Rachel does sound familiar?" I confirm.

"She's my ex's best friend and hasn't liked me for years." He scrubs his hand over his face. "Tell me what happened."

"Apparently, your wife's––"

"*Ex*-wife," he grits out. Again.

"Your ex-wife's friend saw us at Rowdy's last weekend and was telling your girls a bunch of bullshit about how you were rubbing up on a girl who's half your age. And then, she started asking me a bunch of questions––despite not knowing I was the girl in the scenario. She also asked if I'd seen any middle-aged men trying to hook up with LAU students, and…yeah." I take a deep breath, all amped up from opening this can of worms. "It was weird. I didn't know if I should bring it up to you or not. And when she said she's shielded your daughters from a lot of things in the past, it made me wonder if it's a normal thing for you to date girls who are a lot younger and more naive, and––"

"And she got in your head," he finishes, closing his eyes as his jaw almost cracks from the pressure of gritting his teeth. But I don't blame him. He has every right to be frustrated. I only witnessed Summer meddling with one specific scenario. I can't even imagine how he's feeling if this is something happening on a regular basis.

Shrugging one shoulder, I stare down at the black lid on my latte and sigh. "Yeah, Mack. I guess she did get into my head."

"Let me be clear about something." His calloused fingers tickle my chin as he grabs it and lifts my head up again, forcing me to look at him. "My ex isn't a bad person, but she has her shit like everyone else, and she doesn't want anyone to be happy unless she's the source of said happiness. It's always been this way, and while I didn't recognize it when we were first married, it became very apparent later on. It was drilled into me once we signed the divorce papers. As soon as she discarded me, she decided I wasn't worth her time, and therefore, I'm not worth *anyone's* time. Not even my own daughters' time." He lets go of my chin and grabs my hand not holding my latte, squeezing it softly and bringing it to his lips. "I am begging you not to let her make the decision for us too."

The blue in his eyes is darker now. More stormy. Less light. But there's an intensity making me pause. Making me curious.

"*Is* there an us?" I whisper.

Goosebumps break out along my skin as he brings his hand from my wrist to my arm, dragging his fingers along my collarbone and slipping them through my hair to cup the back of my head.

"I told you playing games and dating around isn't my thing," he reminds me. "It's never been my thing. I like you. I like spending time with you. I want to keep spending time with you. And I don't want to ruin it by playing a game and pretending I don't think about you when you're not around. I'm not asking if you want to be my girlfriend. I know it's too early." His mouth quirks up slightly. "But I am telling you I like you. I need you to trust me when I say I've only dated two girls in my entire life. Summer. And you. I'm not gonna fuck this up by talking to some random woman on the internet, and I sure as shit don't prey on girls, Kate. I need you to believe me."

"I do believe you," I whisper.

As if my words are a balm to his soul, he closes his eyes and lets them sink in. Looking down at me again, he presses his forehead to mine. "Like I said, Kate, I like you. I like baking cookies with you and watching you study. I liked kissing you, and I liked…" His jaw tics, and he pulls away slightly, looking down at his feet. Ashamed? Embarrassed? I squeeze his wrist, then cup his cheek, forcing him to look at me the same way he did to me barely a minute ago.

The blue in his eyes hits like a shot of espresso. My attention drops to his lips. The same lips I kissed not so long ago. The same lips I've been dreaming about ever since. Scratch that. Even before our kiss, I dreamed about them. About what they'd taste like. What they'd feel like.

"What else did you like, Mack?" I whisper.

"I liked how I didn't feel lonely anymore. Even when I was with Summer, I still felt alone. But with you?" A soft smile tugs at the corner of his lips. "It's different. It's more."

"It's more for me too," I breathe out.

"Then give me a chance, Kate. Don't push me away. Don't let my ex get in the way of this."

"I don't want to. But this isn't only about you and me. You should've seen her, Mack. Summer was almost..." The word catches in my throat, so I take a sip of my coffee, unable to look at him. I'm too embarrassed. Too scared.

"She was almost what?" he prods.

"Jealous," I choke out, dragging my thumb along the tiny opening in my cup while refusing to look at him. "What if she wants you back?"

Mack snorts. "She doesn't, and she won't. She knows we were as toxic for each other as I do."

"You weren't there..."

"I don't need to have been there to know how she feels, Kate. We were together for a long time. And like I said, I know her. She doesn't like letting things go or giving things away, even when she doesn't want them anymore. The idea of me moving on stung, but it doesn't mean she regrets giving me up. It was just a hard pill to swallow."

"Do you wish she hadn't given you up?" I ask. "If you could go back--"

"Look at me," he orders.

I swallow past the bitter taste in my mouth and meet his gaze.

"We were both miserable. I was too much of a coward to admit it, let alone do anything about it."

"What about Miley and Hazel?" I ask. "I could see her influencing them. I could literally hear it in the way she spoke, and they're your daughters. What if our relationship pisses her off, and she keeps talking crap behind your back? I can't...I can't be the cause of another rift between you and your kids."

Defeat seeps from his bones as his chin drops to his chest. "The rift is already there, Kate. Even if you weren't in the picture, Summer would still have hard feelings toward me, and she'd still be airing it out in front of our girls. It took me a long time to accept it, but Hazel's an adult, and Miley's sixteen. She's old enough to make her own decisions, and the more I pushed after the divorce, the more they retreated. So now, I tell them I love them, try to reach out every day, and hope it'll be enough until they decide to bridge the gap that was made as soon as Summer and I signed the divorce papers."

"But it's...crazy, isn't it? The way she can do that to you? To her daughters?"

"She isn't a bad mom," he argues. "In fact, she's a pretty great one. It's only when I'm involved do the claws come out. It's another reason why I don't push. The girls don't deserve it, either. Dealing with her when she gets like this."

"Doesn't make it okay, though," I push. "I'm not sure I want to rock the boat, especially if it could potentially mess with your relationship with your daughters."

"She's my ex, Kate. And yes, she's the mother of my children and isn't going anywhere, but she's not allowed to say who I can or cannot date. Or what's right or wrong when it comes to my decisions. And when I'm with you, it doesn't feel wrong. Honestly, it feels more right than any relationship I've ever been in."

"It feels right to me too," I murmur, surprised by how true it is. It does feel right. When I'm with Mack, life doesn't feel so complicated. It doesn't feel so lonely. If anything, it feels comfortable. Like coming home and warming up by the fire. Like movie marathons in your favorite pajamas. Like fresh-from-the-oven chocolate chip cookies.

But his ex? She's the opposite. She's like a lobotomy or a colonoscopy. Like an ice-cold shower at five in the morning or a queasy stomach after some questionable take-out.

"Tell me what you're thinking," he murmurs.

"I'm scared, Mack. Scared to open this can of worms with your ex. I mean, can you blame me for not wanting to walk into that particular field of chaos? She was asking me––a complete stranger, mind you––if I knew you or if I knew who you might be dating. How long until she finds out *I'm* the tramp from Rowdy's? What then?"

"I never said I didn't have baggage, Kate. Remember? I told you everyone has their shit. And I know mine might seem like too much for you, but everyone has it. Everyone. I'm asking you to set it aside. To trust me. I'll try to shield you from her. Make sure she keeps her distance, which, honestly, shouldn't be too difficult in the long run since she wants nothing to do with me. I've been off her radar for years now, and if Rachel hadn't said anything, we'd still be off her radar. It'll take a little time, that's all."

"But we aren't even together," I remind him. "Not officially or anything."

"Do you want to be?" he asks.

Is he serious?

"What about your dating apps?"

He smiles, enjoying the shift in our conversation a shit-ton more than I am.

"I already told you I deleted them," he reminds me.

"What about all of your other options? What if you get bored, or if I wind up having another seizure, or––"

"You think I'll break up with you if you have a seizure?" he demands, his amusement dissipating.

"I don't know?" I shrug. A prickling sensation hits behind my eyes, but I blink it away. "It wouldn't be the first time, Mack."

His touch is gentle as he cups my cheek, his light eyes practically swallowing me whole.

Blue. Blue. Blue.

"I'm not like the boys you've dated in the past, Kate. I'm not gonna run at the drop of a hat or when things get messy." He runs his thumb along my skin. "I promise you, Porcupine. I'm not going anywhere."

"Can you promise me you won't let your ex get in the way too?" I practically beg, leaning into his touch.

"I promise."

The words ease the ache in my chest as I shove aside the tiny voice inside my head. The one telling me I can't handle any more drama. The one telling me Macklin will be bored by the end of the week, and this conversation will be a moot point anyway. The one telling me I'm opening myself up to heartbreak, and it's only a matter of time before Mack realizes I'm not worth the effort. Not worth the fallout.

But I hate that voice. I hate how long I've lived with it. I hate how many times it's made me feel like I'm worthless. Because when I'm with Mack? I don't feel so worthless anymore. In fact, I'm starting to feel pretty damn valuable.

Closing my eyes, I nod. "Okay, Mack."

His lips are on mine in an instant. Kissing me. Making my toes curl.

It isn't soft and sweet like our first kiss. It's needier. More desperate. Like he's trying to prove a point. Trying to erase his ex from my memory. Trying to tattoo himself on me.

When he pulls away, he presses his forehead to mine and rasps, "Come to the game with me."

I shake my head. "What?"

"I'm on standby in case anyone gets hurt. Come with me. Hang out with me. Watch the game from the tunnel with me."

"And if someone *does* get hurt?" I counter dryly.

"You can catch a ride with Ash or Blake. Theo said they'll be at the game, too, when I asked if he'd seen you lately."

I can't help the smile as it spreads across my face. "You asked him about me?"

"Of course, I asked him about you." He lifts my hand and kisses the back of it again. "Let's go."

28

KATE

"Thanks again, Russ," Macklin says to an old guy with a red and black LAU lanyard wrapped around his neck. I think he's the athletic trainer or something. Honestly, I was too distracted by the players all decked out in their gear in the locker room to fully pay attention when Macklin introduced us. Still, the guy was nice enough to let me shadow Mack for the evening, so I'm not complaining.

With his hand pressed to my lower back, Macklin follows behind the players and guides me down the tunnel to the ice. His partner, Felix, is here as well. He's giving us a wide berth, though. I'm not sure if it's because he isn't close with Mack or because I'm here, and Mack asked for a little more space than usual. Regardless, he's texting someone, completely oblivious to the chaos around us.

And Professor Buchanan is here. I'm not sure why. We haven't really spoken, but I assume it has something to do with his latest endeavor. The guy comes from money and power and has shifted his occupation on more than one occasion. He's LAU alumni and worked as the CEO of B-

Tech Enterprises. It's a major software company his father started when he was a kid. When Henry Buchanan grew bored with his role as CEO, he passed it to his brother-in-law, Jake Jensen, and pursued his doctorate, choosing to become a professor instead. And now? Apparently, he's decided owning a hockey team in the NHL is the next item on his bucket list. The Lions will start playing next season, and the community is stoked to have a local NHL team they can cheer for. Now that I think about it, Buchanan's probably here to observe two of the key players on LAU's team who will be playing professionally for him next year. Theo and Colt signed their contracts a while back. It's crazy. Yet kind of awesome too.

I tear my gaze from the suave billionaire hidden in the shadows and turn to the arena.

It's packed with fans. LAU's red, black, and white school colors brand the crowds' faces, their clothes, and the poster boards peppered throughout the seating. Most of which have Theo's and Colt's numbers scrawled across them in thick, bold fonts.

It's insane. And loud. And chaotic.

Awe floods my system as I take it all in.

"Do you come to many games?" Mack asks while the referee blows his whistle and drops the puck in the center of the rink, starting the first period.

I shake my head, too mesmerized by the players on the ice to give Mack my full attention. "A few but never this close." Tugging my jacket tighter around me, I add, "It's cooler down here than in the stands."

"Yeah." He glances at the ice thoughtfully. "I guess it is. Did you ever play sports when you were little?"

I shake my head. "Not really. I was always more of a book nerd kind of girl."

"Yet I see you at the gym multiple times a week."

"You can blame Blake for that one." I hesitate. "Actually, scratch that. Pretty sure Ash is the culprit."

He chuckles, his eyes on the game, but only out of obligation in case he sees a hit or something, making it clear I'm the main subject of his entertainment. "How so?"

"She's the one who read up on anything and everything to do with…" I pause, nibbling on my lower lip, unsure what to say. It's weird. Talking about this. Epilepsy. I've never been open about it, but with Mack? He kind of makes me want to be.

"She's the one who read up on everything to do with my condition," I finish, my tone stronger than before.

Mack cocks his head, well aware we're talking about my least favorite subject on the planet. "And?"

"After the incident at the restaurant, Ash did a deep dive into everything and decided my morning walks should be a little more vigorous. So, Blake volunteered to help me step it up a bit."

"And you agreed?"

With a smirk, I admit, "The girls can be pretty persuasive when they want to be."

"Definitely," he replies. "They can be *very* persuasive when they want to be. Any seizures since?"

My anxiety spikes as the word slips past his lips, but I keep my eyes glued to the game in front of me, the players blurring into jumbled streaks of red, black, and white.

"Nope," I answer.

I can feel him staring at me, but I don't look at him. I'm too anxious. I shouldn't be. I know I shouldn't. But it's weird. Talking about epilepsy out in the open like this when I've spent who knows how many years avoiding it like the Plague, especially with a guy I'm kind of, sort of dating.

"Look at you, my prickly little porcupine," Mack murmurs dryly.

I can hear the smile in his voice. The teasing lilt I've come to recognize. I look at him from the corner of my eye and take in the shit-eating grin I knew would be there.

"Look at what?" I mutter.

"You not biting off my head when I ask you questions about your epilepsy."

"I'm thinking about it," I grumble under my breath.

His chuckle turns my insides to goo as he wraps his arms around my waist, pressing my back to his front. "Do you wanna know what *I'm* thinking about?"

"What?"

"How attractive you are when you're fired up about something."

"I think you take too much pride in ruffling my feathers," I announce, turning back to the game in time to see Colt pass the puck to Theo, who slaps it toward the net, but he misses.

"I think the more we talk about epilepsy, the easier it becomes," he tells me.

"And I think you're delusional."

"And I think I like you, my strong, stubborn, impenetrable Kate Winchester."

My lips purse. "And I think you should be paying attention to the game."

"Probably," he says with a laugh. "But you have a way of stealing my focus, Kate. And do you want to know a secret?" He bends closer, his lips brushing against the shell of my ear. "I like it. Because when I focus on you, the world around me doesn't seem so shitty."

The referee blows his whistle in time for us to catch a tussle on the ice. Depp, one of the players I've met at Theo's house, is on the ice clutching his wrist as Theo shoves an opposing player, and Colt skates up to them, his arm cocked back, ready to deck the guy. It happens so fast I'm not even sure I register everything. Theo, Colt, and the player on the opposing team are taken to the penalty boxes on the other side of the rink while Depp skates back to the bench.

"Fuck," he yells as Russ orders him to take off his glove.

"I'm fine," Depp seethes.

"Get your ass up, Depp," Russ demands. "Let's take a look—"

"I said I'm fine!"

"Mack!" Russ calls over his shoulder, his weathered face wrinkled and angry.

Mack drops a kiss to my head. "Be right back. Stay here."

I nod while he heads toward the bench as the opposite team scores a goal, and Depp curses all over again.

After analyzing Depp's wrist, Mack demands, "All right, let's go. We need a closer look."

"It's nothing," Depp grits out, ignoring Mack as he collapses on the bench and watches the opposing team make another dash toward our goalie, Tukani.

"Listen up, man." Mack steps in front of Depp, blocking his view of the ice. "You can play the rest of the game, gritting through the pain, potentially fucking up your wrist even more, *and* wind up needing surgery. Or, you can get off your ass, walk with me to the back room so Russ and I can take a better look, and be back on the ice before you know it."

"Back the hell up, Mack," Depp argues, pushing to his feet. "I can still play. It doesn't even hurt much."

His face is red, and sweat is clinging to his forehead. I can't decide if it's because he's in pain or if he's mad he's standing by the bench when he clearly wants to be on the ice right now.

"Then, you might even be able to finish the game," Mack offers. "But we need to take a closer look to be sure you aren't playing with a broken wrist."

Depp shakes his head, refusing to give in to Mack and Russ's request. "If it's broken, you can fix it after."

"Or you can fuck it up so much during the next two periods you spend the rest of the season in a cast warming the bench."

Depp's upper lip curls as he tears his attention from the ice and gives Mack an angry stare. But even with his skates, Depp doesn't tower over him. Nope. They're the same height, and clearly, Mack isn't afraid of the player. In fact, it looks like he's ready to go head-to-head if he needs to. And it's hot as hell.

"I'm not a pussy," Depp growls.

"Never said you were. But if you cause permanent damage to your hand because you want to look like a man to the other guys on the ice, you're letting your team down. They deserve better. Come on."

This time, Depp shakes his head but storms down the tunnel, passing me in the shadows while Mack, Felix, and Russ follow behind him.

Blake was right. Mack's level-headed. Compassionate. He didn't even bat an eye at Depp being a dick. He saw what needed to be done and handled it.

I can't help but envy the bastard, though I refuse to acknowledge why.

There have been so many times I've seen what needed to be done but was too much of a coward to acknowledge it, let alone handle it the way it needed to be.

Arms folded, I try to make myself small as the team finishes the rest of the game. Depp doesn't return with Mack or Felix.

LAU loses one to three. The rest of the team files to the locker room, and the stands slowly clear out, leaving Theo and Colt on the bench staring at the scuffed-up rink, the loss heavy on their shoulders.

I should leave. Give them a minute to lick their wounds. But Theo's supposed to be my ride since Macklin's gone, and

I don't know where to go or what to do. Instead, I stay quiet, hidden in the shadows of the tunnel, giving them space until they're ready to leave.

"You gonna tell Ash?" Theo asks Colt.

I frown, surprised.

Tell Ash about what?

"Nah." Taking a swig of water from his red and black bottle, Colt shakes his head. "The asshole didn't know what he was talking about."

"You sure?" Theo takes off his helmet, his wavy blonde hair clinging to his forehead as he scrubs his hand over his face. "If what he said is true––"

"It's not," Colt snaps. "Can't be."

"But if it is––"

"Let it go, man. I'm not gonna stir shit up with Ash because some asshole was trying to get in my head during a game, and you shouldn't, either," he warns. With his elbows on his knees, he hangs his head and adds, "It was all bullshit."

Theo doesn't answer him. He just stares at Colt, eventually muttering, "Yeah, man. You're probably right. A bunch of bullshit."

I have no idea what they're talking about. Clearly, it's none of my business, and they obviously have no idea I've overheard their conversation.

Before they have a chance to spot me, I tiptoe back into the tunnel, unsure where to go or what to do. I don't want to run into anyone because I most definitely shouldn't be down here. Especially without Macklin. But if I head into the stands, I'll have to pass Theo and Colt.

Thanks, but no thanks.

A broom closet is off to one side. I jiggle the door handle, finding it unlocked. Releasing a sigh of relief, I slip inside and close the door behind me with a quiet click. Twenty to thirty minutes should be enough time for everyone to shower. I'll wait here for a while, head back into the tunnel, and text someone to pick me up. Mia's definitely working, but maybe Ash or Blake are free? One thing's for sure. I won't be asking Theo or Colt for a ride. Not after overhearing that little tidbit. I'd rather walk home.

With my back pressed against the closed door, I slide down onto my ass and pull my knees to my chest.

Yup. This is definitely not how I anticipated my evening ending.

Then again, I could've always wound up having a seizure or something, so...

Hello, bright side.

29

MACKLIN

The air is cold as I walk back to my car in the hospital's parking lot. I hit the remote start on my key fob so the engine can begin heating up. Depp's wrist definitely needed an x-ray, so Felix and I drove him here in the ambulance, despite his protests. Now, the sun has set, and the winter chill hangs in the air, my breath swirling in the night sky as I climb into my car, anxious to call Kate. When my phone rings, I dig it out of my pocket and press it to my ear.

"Hello?" I answer.

"Hey, it's Russ."

"Hey, what's up?" I ask.

"How's Depp?"

"He'll be fine. Told the doctor to forward you the x-rays."

"Thanks."

A weighted silence follows, and I frown. "Everything okay?"

"Yeah," he rushes out. "Had an interesting conversation after you left."

I stay quiet as I start the vehicle and the call switches to

Bluetooth. The air is still frigid as it comes out of the vents, and I anxiously wait for it to warm up. When Russ doesn't continue, I prod, "With who?"

"Henry Buchanan. You know him?"

"I know *of* him," I clarify dryly. The guy's a billionaire and has been featured in *Forbes* magazine on more than one occasion. It'd be more strange if I *didn't* know of him.

"Yeah, well, he wants to meet with you," Russ tells me.

"About what?"

"About a potential job opportunity."

"What kind of job opportunity?" I probe.

"I'll let him explain the details. Does next Friday work?"

I mentally check my schedule while putting my phone in the cupholder and shifting in my seat to get comfortable. "Uh, yeah. Yeah, that should work."

"Good." He rattles off the details, and I hang up.

Why would Henry Buchanan want to meet with me?

Realizing I won't have any answers tonight, I pull up my text thread with Kate, anxious to see where she is and how she's doing. I hated leaving her at the rink on her own, but I texted Theo, asking if he'd drive her home, so I assume she's taken care of. I still miss her, though.

Unable to help myself, I send her a text.

ME

> Hey. Sorry I had to bail. You make it home all right?

Her response is almost instant.

KATE

> Actually…I may or may not be holed up at the arena. Any chance you could swing by and give me a ride home?

I pull up her contact info and press the call icon without

another thought. It rings once before her familiar voice rings through the speaker.

"Hey."

"You're still at the arena?" I demand.

"Well, yeah, but--"

"Why didn't Theo give you a ride home?"

"Um, so…it's kind of complicated?"

I shove my car into drive and pull out of the parking spot. "Explain it to me. Because if Theo ditched you 'cause he was too pissed about the loss--"

"That wasn't it," she interrupts. "He was having a conversation with Colt, and I realized if I spoke up, it would look like I was eavesdropping, and it was kind of a serious, cryptic conversation, so I decided to hide in a broom closet instead, after I sent him a text and lied, saying I caught a ride with someone else so he wouldn't have to worry about me, and now, it looks like all the lights are off in the arena, and I have no idea if this place is locked or anything, and…yeah. I'm kind of freaking out."

I pull onto the main road leading back to the arena, more amused than I probably should be. I can't help it. The girl's adorable as shit, and she has no idea. Honestly, I should probably be annoyed, but I'm not. Not at all.

"I'll be there in ten," I tell her.

"Thanks."

"Russ and Sanderson are probably still in their offices. I'm sure if you can find one of them, they'll escort you to the front--"

"And get in trouble for hiding in the broom closet like a lunatic?" she hisses, trying to keep her voice quiet. "No, thank you."

"I'd hardly call you a troublemaker." I bite back my amusement and shake my head.

"What? The sweet nerd can't cause trouble?" she argues.

"Now, I kind of want to break something so I can prove you wrong."

"Wouldn't put it past you, Kate." I press the gas pedal a little harder. "Stay put. I think I know which broom closet you're talking about. I'll be there in five and will sneak you out, okay?"

"Okay," she breathes, her relief filtering through the speaker. "And, Mack?"

"Yeah?"

"Thanks."

~

AFTER A BULLSHIT EXCUSE TO RUSS, HE LETS ME IN, AND I walk down the tunnel, glancing over my shoulder to make sure I'm alone when I stop at the broom closet. I open the door to find Kate's soft gray eyes glowing in the tunnel's fluorescent lights as she peeks up at me like a little mouse.

"Hi," she whispers, a shy smile toying at the edge of her lips.

"Hey." Offering my hand, I pull her up and out into the hallway. I close the door behind her in hopes of covering our tracks, though I doubt Russ would care too much.

"You all right?" I ask.

"Better now that I've seen a familiar face." She pinches my chin playfully, tickling the scruff along my jaw, and drops her hand to her side. "Shall we?"

"Yeah."

Snow crunches beneath my boots as little white flakes drift down from the dark sky, landing in Kate's hair as we reach my car.

"Thanks again for picking me up," she comments as she climbs into the passenger seat.

"No problem. Do you want me to take you home or…?" I

grip the edge of the door but don't close it. Her cheeks are a little red from the icy wind, and her straight, dark hair hangs in messy strands around her shoulders.

Peeking up at me, she prods, "Or?"

"Or...you could come back to my place. We could watch a movie. Talk. Bake cookies. Whatever you want."

"You want to watch a movie?" she questions me.

"I want to do whatever you want to do."

"Ya know, if I didn't know any better, I'd say it sounds an awful lot like an invitation to hook up."

"Already told you I need to earn you first," I remind her.

"Yeah, well, in my book, you're well on your way." She scoots further into the leather seat and rests her elbow on the center console, waiting for me to close the door. When I don't, she bats her lashes up at me. "In case it isn't clear, yes. I'd love to come over."

"Good." I close her door, jog around the front of the car, then hop inside, turning the heat to full blast as I head east. Billy Joel plays in the background as we make our way toward the canyon road leading to my place.

And I can't get over how nice it is. Being with her. Talking to her.

"Tell me something," I start. "Are you always afraid to rock the boat?"

She turns to me, her little brows furrowed. "Huh?"

"Earlier tonight," I clarify. "You didn't want to ask Theo for a ride, so you hid in the closet. You didn't come out because you didn't want to get in trouble with Russ or Coach Sanderson. You *also* didn't call me to tell me you'd locked yourself in a closet. Instead, you waited until I reached out to you. Call it a hunch, but I think you didn't want to rock the boat or be an inconvenience to anyone. Am I right?"

She grimaces. "Is it really so obvious?"

"A little," I answer with a laugh. "But I get it. My youngest daughter's the same way. A people-pleaser through and through."

"Yeah. Don't get me wrong. I'm working on it. But it's like you said, I don't like to rock the boat, and I *really* don't like standing out when it's an inconvenience."

"Such as when you have a seizure," I point out.

Her lips pull into a thin line. "Maybe."

"Or when you left your pills at home."

The steely façade breaks almost instantly, and she covers her face, groaning loudly. "I still can't believe you were nice enough to take me home in the middle of the night."

"I was happy to help, Kate."

"Because you're a sweet golden retriever who's always looking out for others," she tells me, setting her hands back in her lap. "Speaking of looking out for others, do you miss your daughters?" She shakes her head. "Actually, forget I asked such a stupid question. Of course, you miss them."

"More than anything," I admit. "I was so involved in their lives for such a long time it's hard for me to respect their requests to keep my distance when all I want to do is hold them and tell them I love them."

I turn off the main road, but Kate stays quiet, letting my words settle around us. I can feel her stare on the side of my face, the wheels turning like always. I wish I knew what she was thinking. If she thinks I'm a terrible dad for staying away.

"I think the fact you respect them and their decisions is huge," she decides, reaching her conclusion. "I love my parents, Mack. But ever since I was diagnosed with epilepsy, they've been a bit on the overbearing side. And I know it's because they love me and want me to be safe, but I also want them to see me as a normal daughter instead of a broken one."

"You aren't broken, Kate," I remind her.

"Debatable." Her smile is forced at best. "I've proven them right, though."

"How?"

"When I switched to my new AEDs, uh, anti-epileptic drugs," she clarifies, "my memory broke, too, and they were given front-row seats to help me pick up the pieces."

Surprised by her honesty, I turn down the music a little, desperate for her to tell me more. To stop hiding the details of her diagnosis. Because this conversation? This honesty? It's refreshing. Addictive. I was given a glimpse at the arena earlier tonight when she didn't shy away from the topic. But I could see how much she wanted to.

I want her to trust me. I want her to let me in.

"What do you mean your memory broke?" I coax, checking my blind spot despite knowing exactly how empty this road is this time of night.

"My seizure medicine can have some not-so-great side effects," Kate explains. "And memory problems are one of them. I used to be super on top of things. And it was pretty easy, ya know? I had straight A's. My room was always spotless. I never lost anything or forgot anything. And even though the doctors warned me about the potential side effects, I was determined not to let the medicine affect me. Honestly, I had pretty good results––memory-wise––with the medication I was on during high school and my first couple of college years. Then, I started having absence seizures, so they decided to switch up my medicine during my junior year, and everything went downhill."

"What's an absence seizure?" I ask.

"It's basically a mini-seizure. Only with these, I don't physically shake or fall to the ground. They're…smaller, I guess?" She hesitates. "I start blinking super fast and kind of zone out without even realizing it."

"Got it. So you switched up your medicine?" I prod.

"Yeah, during my junior year and after I was accepted into the master's program," she repeats. "And even though this new medicine stopped the absence seizures––actually, seizures in general unless I miss a pill––it messed with my memory more than my previous one, which has made my classes feel…impossible."

"Is that why you've been struggling with studying?"

"Yeah," she admits. "I can't tell you how many times I've questioned my major since the switch."

"To be fair, biochemistry isn't for the faint of heart, generally speaking. But trying to learn everything while struggling to actually absorb it? It's gotta be hard."

"You have no idea," she murmurs.

"Have you ever considered switching medication again?"

"Not really. It's a huge pain requiring a ton of doctor's visits, blood tests, and monitoring, and"––she shivers–– "yeah, no thank you. Anyway, after the initial switch, I refused to use the planner my mom bought me. I refused to set alarms or reminders. I refused to do anything I felt was a crutch because I was determined to handle it all on my own." She laughs and shakes her head. "Unfortunately, it doesn't matter how much you want something or how stubborn you are when you have epilepsy, Mack. It *still* has a way of screwing you over."

"How so?"

"Like when I forgot to pick up my prescription a few weeks ago, or when I didn't refill my emergency pills in my backpack, and you had to take me home. And that's only the tip of the iceberg. But what really sucks is every time I screw up, it only solidifies my parents' decision to basically babysit me. Needless to say, it doesn't exactly cultivate independence, ya know?"

"And that's what you want," I conclude. "To feel independence."

"Isn't it what everyone wants? Don't get me wrong. I know they're doing it out of love, and I know I need their help because I *can't* do it on my own. But it still sucks dealing with their constant reminders while attempting to study and focus on school, even if I'm still seeing my grades slowly slip, thanks to how hard it is to retain the information I'm spending so much time learning. It's…a lot sometimes."

"I'm sorry, Kate."

"Don't be. I know this is the hand I was dealt, and honestly? Being around you and seeing your confidence in me has been pretty eye-opening. So, thank you." Her shy smile greets me as she reaches over and squeezes my hand, lacing our fingers together.

She has no idea what it means to me. To have her trust.

As I glance back to the road, she clears her throat. But when she tries to pull her hand away from mine, I hold on tight, refusing to let her go. She gives up on our little tugging match and rests our entwined hands on the center console.

"Long story short," she continues, "I think it's cool you're listening to your daughters' wants and needs and putting them ahead of your own."

"I try. I'm gonna be honest with you, Kate. If it came to their health, you better damn well believe I'd be on them like white on rice to make sure they were taking care of themselves."

A breath of laughter slips out of her as she glances at me and rolls her eyes. "Yeah, I know. And clearly, my parents are doing the same, so here I am."

"Here you are," I quip.

"Can I ask you something?"

"Sure."

"Is it weird? Dating someone close to your daughters' ages?"

I hesitate, tapping my free hand's thumb against the steering wheel as I consider her question. "Honestly?"

She nods.

"Being married to the wrong person puts into perspective what the right person looks like. And I don't think age has shit to do with it. Are you kind? Are you considerate? Are you generous? Do you make me happy? Do we have fun together? Do we see eye to eye on most things? If the answer's yes, what else matters? I know what I want, Kate. And I know what I don't want. But overcomplicating the list with something as superficial as age?" I snort and pull into the garage. "As long as both parties are consenting adults, I don't give a shit. The question is... Do you?"

Her lips lift softly. "Do I give a shit?"

"Yeah."

"I guess not."

She lets go of my hand, pushes the passenger door open, and heads inside my home like she's always belonged there.

30

KATE

With my feet in Mack's lap, the fire roaring across the room, and my stomach full of home-made chicken noodle soup Mack threw together as soon as we walked in the door, I'm a happy camper through and through.

He squeezes my feet, massaging them as I moan softly and snuggle into the cushions, my eyelids growing heavy.

"You like that?" he teases.

Fighting the urge to close my eyes and succumb to his perfection, I reply, "I'm having a foot massage by a hot guy after he fed me something he cooked himself while lounging on the most comfortable couch I've ever been on as a fire crackles in the corner. Yeah, I'd say I like this."

"What else do you like?" he prods.

"I like your mom's cookies," I offer.

"And pumpkins spice lattes on campus."

"And movies."

"What kind of movies?" he questions.

"I dunno? I'm not too picky. Documentaries are always fun."

"Documentaries?" He quirks his brow as if he can't quite figure me out.

"I also like reading," I add.

"Reading, huh?" He perks up, digging his thumbs into the arch of my foot and making me moan even louder.

Seriously. It's official. This guy has magic fingers.

"What kind of books?" he asks.

"A little bit of everything, I guess."

"Textbooks don't count."

I clutch at my chest. "I don't *only* read textbooks."

"Self-help books don't count, either."

"Who says textbooks and self-help books are all I read?"

"Call it a hunch."

The guy looks more confident than the king of England as he smirks back at me, daring me to defend myself. But the truth is, Mack knows me too well, and he's proven it. But allowing him room to gloat? I don't think so.

Tugging my foot from his grasp, I sit up fully, tuck my feet under my butt, and tilt my head to one side. "Okay, Mr. Smarty Pants, what kinds of books do you read?"

"A little bit of everything," he quips, throwing my own response back at me.

"Such as?"

"Mystery, sci-fi, romance, historical fiction. No horror, though." His nose scrunches. "I don't do scary."

With a light laugh, I raise my hand in a stop gesture. "I'm sorry, did you say romance?"

His mouth lifts. "You caught that, huh?"

Realizing he's serious, my jaw drops. "You actually read romance?"

"Hey, don't knock it 'til you try it."

Scooting closer, I lean my head against my hand propped up on the back of the couch as I stare at the man in front of me.

Who the hell is this guy?

He's joking. He has to be.

"You're not joking with me, are you?" I push.

"Is there a problem with romance novels, my prickly porcupine?"

"Not at all," I rush out. "I'm surprised, is all. I've never met a guy who reads romance, let alone one who admits it out loud."

With a shrug, he scratches his jaw. "To be fair, I started reading romance books when Miley posted the cover of a book on her Instagram. I bought it hoping we could discuss it."

He read a romance book in hopes of connecting with his daughter?

Swoon.

"That's really sweet," I murmur, my heart close to bursting at how freaking thoughtful Mack is, even when he hides behind nonchalance. Like it isn't a big deal. Following his daughter's Instagram. Showing interest in her hobbies. Trying to connect with her on a level deeper than most people will ever recognize.

"So, what'd you think?" I press.

"Honestly? I thought it was pretty good. All guys should read romance."

I pull back, surprised. "Oh?"

"Yeah. It's literally a roadmap written by women, explaining exactly what a girl wants in her perfect guy."

"Ah, so that's where you learned all your magic tricks," I quip.

He winks at me. "There's nothing wrong with a guy trying to understand a woman's psyche."

"And apparently, it's also why you're so swoon-worthy."

His chuckle is deep and throaty, causing butterflies to take flight in my stomach. "You think I'm swoon-worthy?"

"You're charming. Charismatic. Thoughtful. Caring. Kind." I count a few of his characteristics off on one hand before running out of fingers and fluttering my lashes at him. "Need I go on, Mr. Golden Retriever?"

"I mean if you insist."

With a light laugh, I shake my head. "Tell me this. Did you learn anything else from those books?"

His attention drops to my mouth. "Maybe a thing or two."

"Such as?"

"Foreplay is key."

I laugh a little harder. "Okay. What kind of foreplay?"

"You want me to show you?"

"For research purposes, I feel obligated to say yes."

"For research, huh?" He inches closer, his gaze darkening a shade.

My heart rate thrums a little faster, and I look down at his mouth, the memory of our kiss tempting me even further. "Yeah."

"Okay." He scoots a bit closer to me. "For starters, girls like it when you touch their cheek." Running his hand along my arm, he cups my cheek, his calloused fingers brushing against my sensitive skin. "Like this. Am I right?"

I gulp and nod.

His mouth twitches. "They also like it when you lean in close but don't kiss them right away."

"Uh-huh," I confirm, my gaze dropping to his lips.

So. Freaking. Close.

"Good breath is key," he adds.

Practically panting, I nod again and breathe out, "Always a solid perk."

Ever so slowly, he leans in, leaving the tiniest of gaps between us. Waiting. Driving me insane. The warmth from his breath making me want to taste him even more.

Kiss me, Mack. Freaking kiss me, dammit!

We've kissed before. And it was good. Really freaking good. Pretty sure the memory alone is enough to drive me insane. Still, the fact he's so freaking close to letting me relive the moment yet refuses to put me out of my misery?

If I wasn't so turned on, I'd probably stand up and leave, just to get some fresh air and think clearly for two seconds.

It's not like I've ever been able to think clearly when Mack's around, though.

His eyes crinkle slightly in the corners as if he can read my thoughts. "You still in your head, Kate?"

"Mm-hmm." My tongue darts out and moistens my bottom lip. "Maybe I need something else to focus––"

He kisses me, cutting off my snarky response. It's soft. Sweet. Perfect. Straight out of a freaking romance novel. Gently, he rubs his thumb against my cheek, then drags his tongue along the seam of my mouth, and I part my lips, lost in his touch. How? How is it so different with him? It isn't fair. Deepening the kiss, Mack slips his tongue into my mouth, and I gasp softly.

Yes.

This. This is what I want––times ten––but I'm not picky. As long as he doesn't stop kissing me, I'll be a happy little porcupine. I smile against his mouth, relishing the feel of his lips on mine. Because it *is* different with Mack. More intimate. Less about a physical connection and more about an emotional one.

And this is only a kiss.

Making love to Mack? My breath hitches, and my pulse goes wild against his pinky resting on my neck. He can probably feel it drumming away, rivaling a hummingbird's. But he keeps kissing me, driving me wild while slowly lying me down on my back. And I'm ready. So freaking ready. Because I feel like we've been stuck in foreplay since the moment we met, and there are only so many steamy scenarios I can play out in the darkness of my own room before growing impatient and desperate for the real thing.

And right now, the real thing is on top of me, his weight pressing into my thighs and stomach. A hard ridge rubs against my pubic bone, and dammit if it isn't the best thing I've ever felt. But I need more. I need Mack.

His arms cage me in on both sides as he pulls away slightly and looks down at me, his light eyes bluer than ever. "They also recommend worshipping the girl with your mouth. Mind if I give it a try, Kate?"

"I mean, if it's what the romance novel says," I whisper. It takes everything inside of me not to squirm beneath him at the idea alone, no matter how terrifying it is. It shouldn't be. I'm a grown-ass adult. And I want this. I want this with Mack. I want *everything* with Mack.

As if I've thrown down the gauntlet, Mack grins and kisses me again. He's peppering kisses along my throat when he slips his hand beneath my T-shirt. It's warm as he slides it along my soft abdomen. He stops on my biggest insecurity. I hold my breath and squeeze my eyes shut.

Keep on moving, buddy, I want to tell him. Instead, I freeze.

"You have no idea how sexy you are," Mack rasps, leaving open-mouthed kisses along my stomach. I don't look at him. I don't want to. Not when he's zeroed in on the least favorite part of my body.

"Was that in the novel too?" I whisper, looking up at the ceiling. "Complimenting a girl's biggest insecurities?"

Lifting his head, he stares at me, his brows stitched in confusion. When he realizes how uncomfortable I am, he murmurs, "You don't have any idea, do you?"

My lips part, but I can't say anything.

"Look at me, Kate."

I grit my teeth and tilt my head toward him.

Determination flashes in those blue eyes. "Don't worry,

my prickly little porcupine. I'll help you see what I do anytime I look at you."

With a light laugh, I mutter, "That nickname."

"Is it growing on you yet?"

I shake my head, not giving him a reply. I'm too lost in the feel of his hand as it trails north, leaving my stomach alone. Finding my breast, he squeezes it through my cotton bra.

"Those, you can touch," I announce. My back bows off the couch as I get lost in the feel of his hand on me. Because it feels so freaking good. *He* feels so freaking good. Touching me. Kissing me.

With a groan, he palms me harder, and a gasp slips out of me. "Yes."

"Fuck, Kate. You have no idea how long I've wanted to touch these."

I laugh and look up at the ceiling as he pushes the cups of my bra down and touches my bare skin.

"Fucking perfect," he growls.

His mouth replaces his hand, and my back arches even more. He nibbles my flesh, sucking on my nipples and driving me absolutely crazy. The heat of his tongue against me is out of this world, and my clit pulses as I tangle my fingers in his hair, savoring the feel of his mouth and the way his hand slides up and down my side like he's committing my shape to memory. Every curve. Every divot.

With another groan, he lets go of my breast and moves to unbutton my jeans, tugging them off. Once I'm bare from the waist down, my shirt still shoved up to my armpits and my breasts on full display, he drags his hands along my bare thighs. I keep them closed, my insecurities getting the best of me.

Brows pulled low, Mack lifts his head, pins me with his stare, and waits.

When I don't say anything, he asks, "There a problem, Porcupine?"

"You don't have to--"

"Sorry, but the romance novels insist."

"We aren't in a romance novel."

"It seems you're missing the entire point, Kate." He cocks his head to the side. Waiting. For me to take the bait. For me to give in.

"And what point is that?" I finally whisper.

"You deserve the romance novel kind of love. The one where you can't get enough, and you're convinced a guy like that doesn't exist in the real world when the truth is..." He pauses and lifts my hips, shoving a pillow beneath my ass until I'm propped up for him like a buffet. "My mouth is literally watering at the idea of tasting you."

Fuck. Me.

I bite my lip, my entrance practically weeping from his words alone.

"Let me be selfish, Kate," Mack begs. "Let me taste you."

I look up at the ceiling again and part my thighs, my fingers gripping the edge of the leather cushion as the heat of his mouth brands my entrance. A jolt of pleasure shoots through me, shocking me to my literal core.

Ooookay.

His tongue laps at me, licking me over and over again as my eyes roll back in my head.

"Holy freaking..." My voice trails off, and my back bows, pushing my hips closer to this man's magic mouth. It's so good. The tempo. The pressure. The way he knows exactly where to go and what to do.

Wes went down on me once. It lasted about thirty seconds before he slipped on a condom and pushed into me. Don't get me wrong. I understood. Going down on someone isn't everyone's cup of tea, but Mack? Well, apparently, it's his.

I'm not complaining. Nope. Not at all. In fact, I think it's the new standard.

I clutch my thighs around his head, rolling my hips against him as one of his hands digs into my ass while the other finds my entrance. He pushes a finger into me, his mouth finding my clit, and I gasp. Because it feels good. Oh, so good. I don't want it to stop. Not now. Not ever. Using the tip of his tongue, he flicks my sensitive nub over and over while dragging his finger against the bundle of nerves inside me, playing with me like I was made for him.

And in this moment, I think I might've been.

"Oh. Oh. Oh," I chant, blown away by the fact I might actually have an orgasm while in the presence of someone else when before this? It was only in the privacy of my own bedroom with zero––and I mean zero––people around to witness it.

His groan vibrates against my clit as he licks my juices, adding another finger to my core, pumping them in and out of me in rhythm with his tongue.

"Mack," I moan. "Oh, my gosh, Mack. Yes. Yes. Yes."

Squeezing his head harder with my thighs, I tug at his hair, holding him against me, and I come around his fingers and against his tongue.

So good.

So. Freaking. Good.

I swear I see stars, which is ridiculous but true. Either that or I officially blacked out from coming so hard. To be fair, it's definitely possible, considering how amazing it felt to have his mouth on me. Regardless, my chest heaves as I stare at the ceiling, blown away at actually having an orgasm while a guy went down on me.

A few seconds later, Mack lifts himself up and climbs on

top of me, kissing my neck softly. As I catch my breath, he relaxes against me, getting comfortable.

"What are you doing?" I murmur.

The weight from his body presses me into the couch cushions as he finds the crook in my neck and rubs his nose against it. "Snuggling."

"I'm sorry, is this it?"

He pushes himself up and stares down at me. "Is *what* it?"

"No sex?" I challenge. "Is this what the romance novels are telling you? That I don't want to have sex after you gave me the best orgasm of my freaking life? If so, we need to find you a few different authors."

His chuckle is warm but dry as he argues, "To be fair, the novels say you shouldn't push the girl unless she wants--"

"Oh, I want," I interrupt, sliding my arms around his neck and tugging him closer to me. "I want right now."

The cotton from his shirt rubs against my bare nipples, and I dig my teeth into my bottom lip, daring him to turn me down. To not give in.

His gaze heats, and he slips his hands between us to unbutton his jeans, pushing them down and over his ass. I lift my foot and snag the hem of his pants, shoving them down to his ankles. Then, I spread my thighs around him. Feeling his skin against mine is like a blanket in the dead of winter. Comforting. Warm. I want to curl up in him. And it should be scary. Wanting to feel close to him. Wanting to let down a few of the walls I've surrounded myself with. But I can't help it. Mack is different. He's always been different. I want all of him.

"Condom," he warns.

"On the pill," I volley, daring him to hold back when all I want to do is give in and feel him inside me without any barriers. Without any reservations. Only me and him.

"I'm clean, Kate."

"Me too. Although, I gotta ask. Is there this much chitchat in romance novels? Or––"

He thrusts into me, and my mouth falls slack with a gasp as my head falls back to the cushion.

Ooookay.

My mouth forms an 'o' as I remind myself to breathe while attempting to adjust to the guy's massive dick.

Welp. It's official. He's big. Like, really freaking big. I feel so full stretching around him. Every nerve is on fire, battling between pain and pleasure.

Mack presses a kiss to my neck and lifts his head, his gaze boring into me, "You okay?"

"You just *had* to shut me up, didn't you?"

He grins and kisses my nose. "Guess so."

I shift slightly beneath him, pulling another groan from his throat as I slowly adjust to his size.

"You have no idea how good you feel, Kate," he grinds out. "No idea."

"You can move now." My fingers flutter beneath his shirt, and I move them upward along his spine, dragging them back to his ass. His muscles flex beneath my fingertips as Mack thrusts his hips into me. And I love it. How gentle he is. Like he doesn't want to hurt me. I squeeze my core, spurring him on. His chest rumbles with a grunt, and he slowly picks up his pace.

It feels different. Like he isn't inside me because he wants an orgasm or a warm body to thrust into. He's inside me because he wants to be close to me. The same way I'm desperate to be close to him.

"Mack," I breathe out, my skin slick with sweat. I writhe beneath him, craving the closeness. The intimacy. The wet sounds of him pumping in and out of me and the crackling fire are enough to make me feel like I'm literally in a romance novel. The combination leaves me dizzy as he burrows his head against my neck and sucks softly.

"Yes," I moan. "Yes, just like that."

I can feel it. Another orgasm. It's right there. Toying with me. His thrusts grow faster and faster as he chases our bliss. And I love it. The desperation. The need. Hooking my ankles around his waist, I hold on tight, panting, moaning, and rambling about how good it feels.

"Come for me, Kate," Mack rasps. "Let me feel you squeeze my cock."

His dirty words push me over the edge. My core tightens around him as I come. Hard.

With another low groan, he grabs my hips, his muscles turning rigid. Then, he's pulsing inside me.

I've never let a guy come inside me without a condom. I've never wanted to. But this? It's more. As he said at the coffee shop, it's like we're connected. Like we're one.

We stay this way for a few minutes, catching our breath, our heart rates slowing, my mind reeling.

This wasn't sex. Not to me.

I should be scared, but I'm not.

Which is even scarier when I think about it.

I'm too tired to analyze what it all means.

Later.

Mindlessly, I drag my fingers along his spine, savoring his weight pressing me into the leather cushions. I feel like I'm in a cocoon. Protected. Safe. Safer than I've ever been in my entire life.

As I slowly come back down to Earth, I cover my face with my arm and mutter, "You win."

Mack lifts himself into a half push-up and looks down at me, a question in his baby blues, though he doesn't say a word.

"Apparently, I need to start reading romance," I clarify.

With a dry laugh, he lifts himself up the rest of the way, and his softening erection slips out of me.

"Stay here," he orders. "I'll grab a towel so I can clean you up."

"Clean me up?" My brow cocks. "Is this also in the How to be an Awesome Guy 101 course?"

"Maybe." He drops another kiss on my forehead. "I'll be back."

His tight ass makes me smile shamelessly as I check him out while he heads to the bathroom and returns with a towel. Once I'm cleaned up and have taken care of business, Mack tugs me against him, grabs the remote, and turns on a documentary all because I said I like them.

Snuggling against his bare chest, a single word crosses my mind.

Swoon.

❧

AN HOUR LATER, MY EYELIDS ARE HEAVY, AND I CATCH MYSELF falling asleep. The documentary's over. At least, I think it is. I peel my eyes open, seeing Netflix's home screen. The glow from the television and fireplace light up the dark family room. But the kitchen and the hallway are blanketed in shadows.

What time is it?

My muscles are deliciously sore as I shift slightly against Mack's bare chest, attempting to wake up. But I don't want to move. I want to stay in his arms and sleep the night away.

And I might…*after* I take my medicine.

"What time do you need to take your med?" he grumbles, his voice thick with sleep.

I smile against his chest. "Usually around ten. What time is it?"

The light from his Apple watch glows in the dark room as he lifts his wrist and looks at the time. "9:55."

"Guess I should get it then." With a quiet groan, I push myself up, but Mack tightens his arms around me.

"Where is it? I'll get it for you."

"You don't have to--"

"Stay," he orders, slipping from beneath me. Once he's on his feet, he repeats, "Where is it?"

"Backpack. Side pouch."

Stretching my arms over my head, I yawn on the couch while listening to Mack's bare feet padding across the hardwood floor. With a little orange bottle in one hand and a glass of water in the other, he rounds the edge of the couch a minute later and sits on the coffee table across from me.

"Here." The cap comes off with a soft pop, and he hands me a single pill.

"Thanks." It glides down my throat with ease as I take a sip of water, watching him rummage through my pants on the ground.

"What are you doing?" I ask.

Finding my phone in one of the pockets, he hands it to me. "Text your mom and let her know you took your medicine."

My brow arches. "You trying to get on her good side?"

"Gotta show her I'm a catch."

I roll my eyes. Taking the phone, I send her a quick text anyway.

ME

Just took my medicine.

MOM

Thanks for the update. Love you, baby!

ME

Love you too.

I turn off my phone and toss it back onto the heap of clothes on the floor.

"Now what, Mr. Golden Retriever?"

"Now, it's bedtime." Tangling his fingers with mine, he pulls me to my feet. "Come on. Let's get some sleep."

31

KATE

A dull ache settles above my pubic bone, and I wake up groggily. It's still late. Or early, depending on how you look at things. There isn't any light coming in through the windows, but I'm not quite as exhausted as I should be. It must be early morning. Shifting onto my side, I pull my knees to my chest before I realize my thighs are slick. I freeze.

Maybe it's the remnants from my tryst with Macklin.

Or maybe it's my worst nightmare.

I do the math in my head, dread filling my system as the numbers check out.

Quietly, I slip out from under the covers, my footsteps muffled by the thick carpet in Mack's bedroom as I tiptoe toward the bathroom. Once the door is closed behind me, I flick on the lights and head to the toilet.

I gasp.

No!

No, no, no, no.

I started my period.

And it's everywhere.

Shit!

Apparently, sleeping naked was a bad idea.

I shove my hair away from my face and peek at my legs again.

A terrible idea.

Crimson coats my inner thighs, and I close my eyes, fighting back tears as wave after wave of embarrassment floods through me. If it's all over me, it's probably all over his sheets. It has to be. The question is, how do I clean them when Mack's currently sleeping in them?

My stomach rolls, and I cover my mouth.

Why? Why does this have to happen to me?

Cradling my head in my hands, I'm trying to devise a plan that leaves Mack in the dark when a soft knock echoes from the door.

"Kate?" Macklin calls. His voice is still rusty from sleep.

My head falls. "Yeah?"

"You okay?"

"Yeah," I repeat. "I, uh…" My voice trails off. I don't know what to say.

"Kate, what's wrong?"

"Nothing, I…"

Kill me now.

I seriously want to cry.

"Kate?" he prods.

I shove my hair away from my face again, desperate for a freaking elastic or something, and reach for the toilet paper, wiping myself up. I stare at the stained material, feeling more helpless than ever. I can't walk around naked. Not like this. But I can't stay in here the rest of the night, either. My clothes are in the family room. Not that it would fix the situation in the long run. I don't have any supplies with me. No pads. No tampons. I don't even have any in my backpack. I have some in my glove compartment, but since I don't have my car...

Tears spring to my eyes, but I swallow them back.

Why me?

Why now?

After the amazing night we had, why did this have to happen?

"Kate, talk to me. What's going on?" His words are laced with worry, threatening to choke me with more guilt. More embarrassment.

"I'm fine," I call out, my voice cracking. "I, uh, I had a little issue."

"What kind of issue?" His voice rises with panic. "Did you have a seizure?"

"No, nothing like that." I look down at the inside of my thighs, paralyzed.

"What is it?"

A laundry basket sits next to the bathroom counter, and I eye it warily. I could always steal some of his clothes. Slip them on and make sure I'm locked and loaded with plenty of toilet paper while I try to find my own in the family room. What about after, though? What do I do? I can't go anywhere without Mack driving me there.

"Kate, open the door," he demands, his patience dissipating.

Shoving a ball of toilet paper between my thighs, I flush the toilet and grab one of his shirts from the laundry, not caring how dirty it is. I slip it over my head and keep my legs pressed together.

As I open the door, Mack squints from the light. Once his eyes adjust to the brightness, he scans every inch of me, searching for any bumps or bruises or hints as to why I'm hiding in his bathroom. When he comes up empty, he asks, "What's going on?"

"Nothing. I um…" I cross my arms and lean against the doorjamb. "Is there any chance I can borrow your car?"

"Why would you need to borrow my car?"

"I need to grab something from the store."

"It's four in the morning––"

"I know. I…need something."

"What do you need? I might have it––"

"Trust me. You don't," I interrupt, keeping my head down as I try to slip past him.

He steps in front of me. "Stop. You're freaking me out."

"I'm fine."

"Kate." His calloused finger brushes beneath my chin as he lifts my head up. "What's going on? Have you been crying? Did I do something wrong?"

The concern in his gaze hits like a sucker punch to the gut. Oh, how easily I've fallen for this man. Despite our age difference. Despite working with his daughter. Despite *everything*.

"Tell me," he begs.

"You didn't do anything wrong."

"Then, what is it? What do you need from the store?"

Just say it, Kate.

"I started my period, and I don't have any pads or tampons, and I made a mess of your bed and probably this shirt, and I'm pretty sure I'm two seconds away from dying of embarrassment, and I can't even do that right now, because I can already feel myself bleeding through this toilet paper, so…"

He reaches for the hem of the shirt I'd thrown on, but I stop him. "Mack, don't. I'm gross."

"I'm a paramedic, Kate. I think I can handle a little blood." He pulls the shirt up more forcefully, and this time, I let him slip it off of me. My hair spills around my shoulders as I stand naked as the day I was born and more vulnerable than

251

I've ever felt in my entire life. At least when I have a seizure, I wake up without any memory of the event. But this? Yeah. Pretty sure it's tattooed on my brain forever.

And the kindness in his eyes? The gentleness in his touch? Those will be tattooed there, too. And I'm okay with that.

"How are you feeling?" he murmurs, his warm hand caressing beneath my belly button where I'm most achy.

"Crampy."

"A hot shower should help." His hand drops to his side, leaving me cold. "I'll be back in an hour." He turns on his heel.

I reach out to stop him. "Wait. Where are you going?"

"To pick up the stuff you need."

"You don't have to––"

"It's not a big deal, Kate."

"Uh, trust me. It kind of is. Periods are gross."

"I was married for sixteen years, witnessed my two children being born, and both daughters started their periods when they were twelve. I think I can handle this. Periods aren't gross. They're natural." He tucks my hair behind my ear, kisses my forehead, and gently urges me toward his shower. "Take your time. I'll lay some of my clothes on the bed for you to change into until I get back."

"I can use my own."

"You can change into yours once you have the stuff you need. No use getting them dirty."

"Um…speaking of your bed…" I grimace. "I may have gotten some blood on the sheets."

"You already mentioned it," he reminds me with a smirk. "Not a big deal. Promise. I'll put them in the wash before I leave. Do you prefer pads, tampons, or the D-cup thing?"

"Uh, I––"

"I'll get them all."

"Mack."

"Kate," he mimics as he opens the glass door and turns on the water until steam billows from the shower head.

"Now, go clean up. I'll take care of the rest." He kisses my cheek like he can't stand not to and walks out of the bathroom, leaving me more confused––yet grateful––than ever.

32

MACKLIN

After getting dressed, treating the stains on the sheets, and starting the load of laundry, I head to the nearest gas station and grab everything they have to offer. I'm driving back up the mountain toward home a few minutes later.

With a grocery sack hanging on my arm, I walk inside the house to find the scent of bacon and eggs wafting through the air. Kate's behind the stove in a pair of my boxers and the T-shirt I'd laid out for her hanging off one of her shoulders. Her hair hangs in a damp braid down her back, and her feet are bare.

The view makes me pause. She looks so natural. In her element. Relaxed. Like she belongs here. With me. In our house.

It should be terrifying.

The idea of building a future with her. Of creating a life together. One where I don't fuck it up. Where we have each other.

But it doesn't frighten me. At all.

As if she can feel me staring, she peeks over her bare shoulder and smiles. "Hey."

"Hey," I greet her, setting the bag on the counter and rummaging through it. Finding the box of tampons and package of pads, I pull them out and hand them to her. "These were the only things I could find. Hope they're all right. I know some brands are better than others."

"They're great. Thank you." She replaces the boxes of products with an overflowing plate of bacon and eggs and rounds the kitchen island, ready to escape to the bathroom. Even though I know I should let her, I grab her waist and pull her against me, kissing her cheek.

With a shy smile, she closes her eyes, sighs, and gives in, leaning into me and wrapping her arms around my neck. "Thank you."

"You're welcome." I peck her lips. "Thanks for making breakfast."

"You're welcome," she returns and wiggles out of my grasp. "Now, if you'll excuse me, I should probably take care of this."

Reluctantly, I let her go. Her hips sway back and forth as she heads to the guest bathroom, closing the door behind her.

Grabbing a fork from the utensil drawer, I cut off a small bite of the eggs and almost groan as soon as it hits my tongue. Damn. The girl can cook.

Kate returns a few minutes later dressed in her clothes from last night, with mine wadded into a ball in her hands. Hooking her thumb over her shoulder, she mutters, "I'm gonna…" She clears her throat and heads toward the laundry room without another word.

She's cute when she's embarrassed, but I don't call her out for it. She's probably used to guys being squeamish over this shit. Like how she's used to dating guys who break it off as soon as they find out about her epilepsy.

Bunch of pussies.

Determination floods my veins, and my hand tightens around my fork as I stare at the crispy bacon on my plate. I'm not like other guys. I refuse to be. I can only imagine how much shame she must've felt this morning. I'd heard her slip out of bed and tiptoe into the bathroom. Noticed the minutes tick by as she stayed locked away, refusing to come back to bed.

I didn't want to pry, but I also couldn't help myself. Not when it comes to her.

Kate's different.

I care about her.

And even if it takes every single day for the rest of my life, I'm stubborn enough to prove it to her. That she doesn't need to feel shame around me. That she doesn't need to be embarrassed.

And I know I'm walking a fine line. I know she's young and probably wants to have fun before settling down. But I also know myself. I'm not the hit-it-and-quit-it type. Not the no-strings-attached kind of guy. I'm the love-you-forever and take-you-home-to-meet-the-parents type. I don't quit. Not when things get complicated. And I'm a stubborn sono-fabitch.

It's one of the reasons why I married Summer despite knowing we weren't a good fit. It's one of the reasons why online dating has been a bitch. Hell, it's why I never wanted to move into an apartment after the divorce. Why I haven't left my job since I was hired all those years ago. I'm loyal. And when I get attached to things, well, it's been known to bite me in the ass a time or two.

But with every moment I spend with Kate, I can't help

growing more and more attached. I'm not gonna quit on her. I'm too stubborn for that shit.

I glance at the hallway, waiting for Kate to appear again, but she doesn't. Finally, I give in and walk down the hall. I find her in my bedroom, attempting to stretch the fitted sheet onto the mattress.

I rest my shoulder against the doorjamb. "What are you doing?"

She jumps at the sound of my voice and turns to me. "Making your bed."

"Why?"

"Uh, because I made a mess of your other sheets?" she answers with a look telling me I'm an idiot for even asking.

I chuckle, pushing myself upright and stalking toward her. "All right, my prickly little porcupine." I wrap my arms around her waist and press my front to hers, her curves molding against me in all the right places. "Don't get me wrong. You look sexy as hell in my bedroom, but unless we're married and partners, you don't lift a finger in this house. We clear?"

"That's very un-golden retriever-y of you."

I grin and drag my nose along hers. "And your actions are very prickly of you, my little porcupine."

"Only with you," she murmurs, her muscles melting against me as the sheet slips from her fingers, and she wraps her arms around my shoulders.

"Is this you surrendering?"

"About what?"

"About not making the bed."

"Maybe."

We sway back and forth as I press my forehead to hers, breathing in the hint of my body wash clinging to her skin. And fuck, if it doesn't make me hard.

"What is it?" she asks.

"You smell like me."

"Is smelling like you a good thing or a bad thing?"

"A very good thing." I kiss her softly, reminding myself to be gentle, and she smiles against my lips.

"You know, if I wasn't on my period, I'd say you were trying to get in my pants again."

"You honestly think your period would stop me?" I challenge.

She laughs and shakes her head. "You're ridiculous."

"And you're too tempting for your own good."

"Mm-hmm." Rising onto her tiptoes, she kisses me again and pats my chest softly. "If only I didn't have to go to work today, I'd make you prove it. Any chance you can take me home?"

"Yeah." I let her go but grab her hand and guide her toward the kitchen, leaving my room a mess. It would normally drive me nuts. I like order. Always have. But for some reason, seeing the sheets in a pile on the mattress makes me smile, knowing it's because she gave in. She let herself be an inconvenience today, which means she trusts me. And it means more to me than she'll ever understand.

"How are you feeling?" I question her. "Can I get you any Tylenol or Ibuprofen or anything? I looked for Midol, but they didn't have any at the gas station."

"You know what Midol is?"

"Two daughters, remember?"

"Ah, so there are benefits to dating an old guy," she teases.

A low growl rumbles up my throat. "Careful. You might give me a complex."

"I think you'll survive. And as for my cramps, I may have already stolen some Tylenol from your bathroom." She grimaces, meeting my eyes.

"Not a problem, Kate. I'm glad you found some."

"Me too. Cramps are the worst."

"I can imagine." As we round the kitchen island, making our way toward the garage, I grab the sack of goodies on the counter and hand them to her. "This is for you."

Confused, she looks down at the bag, shaking her head. "What's this?"

"Didn't know if you were a chocolate girl or not, so I grabbed a few things."

Her gaze softens as she searches the contents, then looks at me. "Why are you so sweet to me, Mack?"

"'Cause I'm a golden retriever, remember?" She laughs, and I grab her hand again, tugging her toward the garage. "Come on. Let's get you home."

Once we're in the SUV, I start the engine, turn on her seat heater, and we drive down the road, the bag of goodies sitting in her lap as she hums along to the song on the stereo.

It's nice.

Peaceful.

Like freshly fallen snow.

A little while later, she clears her throat. "So...question."

"Yeah?"

"Are you busy next weekend?"

"I have a meeting with Henry Buchanan, but otherwise, I'm free. Why?"

"Hold up. You're meeting with Professor Buchanan?"

I nod.

"Why?" she asks.

"No idea. He reached out to Russ after the last hockey game and asked if I was interested in meeting him. I said yes, so Russ sent me the date and where I was supposed to meet Buchanan, and that was it."

"It's kind of cool," she decides. "Don't you think?"

I shrug as I pull onto her street. "I guess so. But to answer your question, yeah, I'm free after the meeting. Why do you ask?"

Looking down at her lap, she twists the sack in her fingers, suddenly shy. "My parents have been begging me to come home, and since I don't have a car and I like being with you, I was wondering if…" Her voice trails off as she bites her bottom lip and looks up at me, her eyes almost hopeful if it wasn't for the fear diluting it.

The girl looks like she's about to have a colonoscopy or some shit, and I can't help but laugh as I reach over and grab her hand, stopping her fidgeting. "Are you asking for a ride, or are you asking if I want to meet your parents, Kate?"

Nibbling her bottom lip, she stares at our entwined fingers, a soft smile slipping past her nerves. "Both, I think." Her eyes meet mine. "I mean, yes. Technically, I need a ride since I still can't drive, but also…if you think you're ready and willing to meet them, I know they'd love to meet you too."

Bringing our locked hands to my lips, I kiss her knuckles softly. "Yeah, Kate. I'd love to meet them."

"Really?"

I laugh. "Yeah. Really."

Her expression lights up. "Okay."

33

KATE

The door opens with a soft creak as I walk inside my house and stop dead in my tracks.

Blake's munching on cinnamon toast, Mia's making a pot of coffee, and Ash is pouring herself a bowl of cereal.

With a grin, Blake greets me. "Look who finally came home."

"Hi, guys." I close the front door, keeping the cold out.

"We were worried about you," Ash tells me.

"I know I should've texted to tell you I wouldn't be home. I'm sorry."

"No worries," Ash replies.

"So, where were you?" Blakely quizzes me.

My gaze narrows. I'm well aware of the game she's playing. But the girl doesn't cower. She stares back at me, daring me to admit the truth.

And, like a stack of cards, I fold almost instantly. "I was with Mack."

"Oh?" Ash exchanges a knowing look with the rest of the girls.

"Yup." I hook my thumb over my shoulder. "I should probably get ready for work. So…"

"Uh-uh. No deal. You think we're gonna let you off the hook so easily?" Mia laughs and adds some half-and-half to her Snoopy mug. "Come on. You should know us better than that by now."

With a groan, I slip my backpack off my shoulder and set it by my feet, keeping the sack of goodies in my hand. If I don't, they'll sniff them out like a bunch of bloodhounds and steal the chocolate for themselves.

"Fine," I grumble, dragging my feet. "Let's get it over with."

Three pairs of eyes light up as Blake grabs the kitchen chair beside hers and shoves it away from the table. "Take a seat."

I collapse onto the wooden chair and fold my arms, bracing myself for the inevitable with the bag of snacks pressed to my chest.

"So, what'd you guys do?" Mia starts the inquisition.

"We hung out. He made me soup. Then we…" --I clear my throat--"watched a documentary."

"I'm sorry, you"--Blake fake coughs, mimicking me-- "what's that code for?"

"It means they totally had sex," Mia announces shamelessly.

"Shut up." Ash's spoon clatters in her bowl. "You did?"

My nose scrunches, and I squeeze my eyes shut. "Maybe?"

Blake laughs even harder. "Yeah, they totally did it." Raising her hand, she offers Ash a high-five, and I roll my eyes.

"Are you serious right now?" I yell.

"Come on! Don't leave me hanging!" Blake pleads to Ash.

Ash's lips purse, but she gives into Blake's antics, slapping her palm against Blake's raised hand in a half-assed high-five so Blake will leave me alone. Then, she turns back to me. "And? What happened? Obviously, you slept over…"

"Yeah." I deflate more into the seat, my stomach knotting at the memory, no matter how sweet Mack was this morning. "And then, I almost died of embarrassment."

"What happened?" Ash prods, her cereal forgotten.

"Let's just say I'm on shark week, and Flo was *not* subtle when showing up this month."

Blake and Mia exchange curious glances.

Ash blurts out, "Okay, we're gonna all need some more details, Kate."

A groan escapes me as I shove aside my embarrassment and rip it off like a Band-Aid. "After we hooked up, we watched a movie and fell asleep. I woke up to find I'd started my period. In his *bed*."

"No!" Mia gasps.

"Yup. I bled all over his sheets and didn't have any tampons in my backpack, so he had to drive to the gas station at the base of the mountain to pick some up for me. I offered to take his car and do it myself, but he insisted I take a shower and promised he'd be back in a few. While he was gone, I cleaned myself up and made him breakfast, and he drove me home when we finished eating. Now, here I am."

Silence ensues, and I peek over at them.

Blake's grinning like the Cheshire cat, Mia's eyes are wide with surprise, and Ash looks like she might literally swoon at any second.

"Say something," I snap.

Blowing softly on her hot mug of coffee, Mia murmurs, "If you don't marry him, I will."

Blake snorts. "Yeah, I'm totally calling Theo to remind him how he's starting to look like the lesser Taylor and needs to up his game. Because that?" Blake's mouth makes a tiny circle as she whistles. "Is the sweetest thing I've ever heard."

Biting the inside of my cheek to keep from grinning, I mutter, "I didn't get to the best part."

"There's a better part?" Ash asks.

I toss the grocery sack of goodies toward them. "He also bought me chocolate and apologized when there wasn't any Midol at the gas station."

"Mack knows what Midol is?" Ash asks.

"He has two daughters, remember?" Blake chimes in.

"Oh, yeah." Ash grabs the sack and searches its contents, clearly impressed with the selection. "I forgot."

"Speaking of which." The time glares at me as I check my phone. "I have to get ready for work. Can anyone drive me?"

Steam billows from Mia's Snoopy cup, and she blows on it as she collapses into the chair next to mine. "I can take you."

"Thanks."

34
MACKLIN

MY PRICKLY PORCUPINE

Got my grade for Litwak's test. Not great.

ME

Damn. I'm sorry, Kate.

MY PRICKLY PORCUPINE

It's fine.

ME

Liar. Anything I can do to help?

MY PRICKLY PORCUPINE

Not unless you can make it easier for me to memorize stuff.

ME

I'd be happy to help you study.

MY PRICKLY PORCUPINE

Pretty sure you'd distract me with all your manly muscles.

I chuckle and type my response.

> You gotta learn about human anatomy, right? Happy to take one for the team.

> Of course, you would be. Unfortunately, I already passed anatomy before my medication swap, so...I guess I won't need your services this time around. Maybe next time. ;) Good luck with your meeting. I'll see you soon.

There's a buzz beneath my skin as I open the door to B-Tech Enterprises. It's been a week since Kate and I had sex for the first time, and even though she's been busy with school, we've spent almost every night together. Whether it's at her place or mine, it hasn't mattered. And it's been nice. Being with someone. Being with her.

After this meeting, we'll have the whole weekend together. We're driving up to her parents' house. I'm trying to tell myself it isn't a big deal, but I'm excited. Excited to meet her parents. Excited to learn more about her and how she was raised. Excited to prove I'm in this for the long haul, even if she isn't ready to put a label on our relationship.

But first, I have to get through this meeting, and I have no idea why I'm here.

The building is flashy and luxurious. Steel beams. Dark leather. Glass windows. And black marble. Hell, I can almost smell the money wafting through the heated air as I walk toward the receptionist's desk in the center of the open main floor.

With a pair of glasses propped on her nose, the young

woman stops clicking her manicured fingernails against the keyboard and looks up at me.

"Hello, sir. How can I help you?"

"I'm here to see Mr.––Dr.––Buchanan?" I offer.

Fuck, I sound like an idiot.

She smiles and points to an elevator on her left. "Take the elevator to the twenty-fifth floor. His personal assistant will help you from there."

"Thanks."

I follow the receptionist's directions until the elevator opens, revealing the twenty-fifth floor. Huge windows line the walls from the floor to the ceiling, showcasing an excellent view of the city below. It's different than my view at home. More buildings. Fewer trees. But just as memorable.

If Buchanan wanted to make a statement by asking to meet here instead of on campus, it's working.

A pretty brunette sits behind a black desk and smiles when she sees me. "You must be Mr. Taylor, correct?"

"Yeah." I wipe my sweaty palms onto my jeans, trying not to look like a fish out of water. I doubt I'm successful. It doesn't matter if I was raised in an upper-middle-class family. It doesn't matter if I have more money in the bank than I could ever need. This atmosphere? It reeks of wealth, security, and power in a way I'll never be able to replicate.

I don't want to.

I don't need to.

But it does fan my curiosity.

Why did Buchanan reach out to Russ and schedule this meeting?

The assistant pushes a button on her phone system and speaks quietly into her headset. Standing, she motions to a large set of black doors. They must be ten feet tall.

"Dr. Buchanan will see you now," she announces.

"Thanks." I clear my throat and open the heavy doors, my

anxiety getting the best of me. Buchanan's office is a lot like the rest of the building. Black. Chrome. Leather. Money. It touches everything. Even the man behind the desk as he stands and rounds the edge of it, striding toward me with his hand outstretched.

"Macklin Taylor," he greets me. "Nice to meet you."

I shake his hand and nod. "You, too, Dr. Buchanan."

"Call me Henry." He motions to a pair of couches separated by a glass coffee table in front of his desk. "Please, take a seat. Can I get you anything? Whiskey? Water? Soda? Coffee?"

"Water's fine," I answer.

A minibar lines one side of the room, and he walks toward it, retrieving my beverage and pouring himself a tumbler of bourbon. Pappy Van Winkle. That shit is *not* cheap.

"Thanks for coming down," he continues. "I considered asking if you wanted to meet on campus but decided against it. I'm trying to keep my business endeavors separate from my teaching. I'm sure you understand."

"Of course."

"You're probably wondering why I asked Russ to set up a meeting," he adds, handing me the cool glass and sitting down on the couch opposite mine.

Staring at him over the rim of my glass, I take a swallow of water and clear my throat. "You could say that."

"Then, I guess I'll cut to the chase. As I'm sure you're aware, I'm the owner of a new NHL team and am building it from the ground up. Would you be interested in joining the Lions this upcoming season?"

My eyes narrow. "As what?"

"I want you on our physician's team."

"I don't have a sports medicine degree. Honestly, I have *no* degree. I'm a certified paramedic, but––"

"Not a problem."

"Yeah, but--" I pause and shake my head. "Why?"

"I saw how you handled the situation with Depp the other night."

I cock my brow, still confused.

"Hockey players are stubborn, Mr. Taylor. And, while I might not have as much experience as some of the other owners in the NHL, I know the importance of keeping my roster healthy. Players have a habit of pushing themselves too far, especially when they're young and stupid. The Lions' roster is full of young bucks who have something to prove. Most of them are exactly like Depp. They'd rather play on a broken arm than sit out and look like a pussy who can't take the pain. It's why I want you. You know how to talk to players and help them see the big picture. I think you know how to spot serious injuries and understand when the risk isn't worth the final score of one game with the rest of the season on the line. To put it bluntly, I think you'd be a great addition to the Lions this upcoming season, and I want you with us."

He's serious. I can see it in his eyes. The no-bullshit attitude wafting off him and mixing with his expensive cologne. Clearly, the man's used to getting what he wants, and for some reason, he wants me.

The ice clinks against my glass as I take another swig of water, my mind racing as I consider his offer.

"And what happens when I tell the coach or the manager they need to pull someone from the ice because of an injury, and the team loses the game because of my decision?" I lean forward, resting my elbows on my knees. "We both know players aren't the only ones putting themselves at risk during the season. The organization wants to make money. And in order to make money, they need to win games. Sometimes--

and let's be honest, it's far too often––winning is at the expense of their players. What then?"

"That's where I'm different. I won't stand in your way when you make a call. And if anyone else in the organization does, you reach out to me, and I'll take care of it. You have my full support."

"No matter what?"

"I trust Russ, and he tells me you know your shit. Call yourself a consultant or a specialist. Honestly, I don't care, but I want you behind the bench, and I want you in the locker room. Do you think this is something you'd be interested in?"

I sit back on the couch, my legs spread wide as I take him in. He's serious. The motherfucker's serious. I can see it in his eyes. Feel it in the room, emanating off his tailored suit and the bourbon in his glass.

"I, uh, I don't know," I answer candidly.

"You don't know?"

"It's a lot to think about."

"What do you need to think about?"

"Uh, travel," I start. "Being away from home."

"You're divorced? Two kids? Sixteen and eighteen?"

My eyes widen. I guess I shouldn't be surprised. A man like Buchanan does his research. He's sharp. Direct. Thorough. Of course, he would know my history before offering me a job, especially when I don't have the degree to back it up.

"This is an opportunity to travel," he continues. "To see new places. To help keep young men like your brother and his friend healthy. And you'd still have your home base here in case you decide to put down any more roots." With a knowing look, he searches for something in his suit pocket and hands it to me. "Oh, and our benefits were curated with health in mind. You know, for chronic illnesses and such.

Think about it."

I take his card, lost in thought. Chronic illnesses?

Kate.

Buchanan must've seen us at the hockey game. Talking. He's probably assuming too much, but... Is he? I want a future with her. I don't know what it is yet, but I do want it, whatever it is. And I care about her. I care about her well-being. I care about her health and whether or not she's taken care of. But insurance? Benefits? It would mean marriage again. We're not there yet. But the prospect of knowing she'll be taken care of if we get to that point is comforting.

A little weird. But comforting.

"I'll think about it," I answer, shoving his card into my pocket. "Thank you."

"Sure thing."

THE DRIVE BACK TO KATE'S HOUSE IS QUIET AS I CONSIDER Buchanan's offer. The pros and cons list is endless. But is it? I love my job. I love helping people. I love saving people. And the idea of keeping dumbasses like my brother and his friends from pushing themselves too hard and potentially causing life-altering mistakes? It sounds good. Fulfilling.

Lost in thought, I almost miss my phone buzzing. Checking the navigation screen, I see it's Kate's calling.

"Hello?" I answer through the Bluetooth speaker.

"Hey! How'd it go?"

"Good." I pause, replaying the conversation for the hundredth time. "I think?"

Her laugh eases the tightness in my chest. "You think?"

"Honestly, I'm not sure. It was...unexpected."

"Well, what did he say? What did he want?"

"He offered me a job."

"A job?" she clarifies, sounding as dumbfounded as I am. "Doing what?"

"Working with the Lions next season. He wants me to be a consultant to the sports physician. Someone who can rein in the players when they're being dumbasses or need medical attention."

"Mack, that's amazing," Kate gushes. "Seriously, it sounds like the perfect job for you."

"You think?"

"Of course. I saw how you treated Depp during the game the other day. The way you were firm but understanding. Are you going to take it?"

"I don't know." I scratch my jaw. "Do you think I should?"

"I mean..." She hesitates. "You do you, boo. But if it's something you're interested in taking, then heck yes, you most definitely should accept his offer."

"I'd be away more. Traveling with the team." I let the words hang in the air, unsure what else to say. We haven't been together long, but the time we've spent getting to know each other has meant more to me than anything I've done in the past two years. But pushing her on this? On us? I scrub my hand over my face, her silence killing me. I dunno what the fuck I'm doing.

"I'm sure those closest to you will be understanding throughout all of it," she murmurs.

I can hear the smile in her voice. It makes me breathe a little easier.

"Heck, maybe they'll even tag along," she adds dryly.

Relief floods my veins as I sag further into the leather seat. "You think?"

"Uh-huh. I kind of do. You got this, Mack. Do it for yourself. Do it because you can. And have a little faith in the people around you. They've got your back."

No one's ever had my back the way she does. Summer sure as hell didn't. Not in the end.

But Kate?

I have a hunch she'd do almost anything to see me happy. And it means more than she'll ever know.

"Thanks, Kate," I murmur. "And I'm sorry about your test score."

"It's fine. Actually, it isn't, but there's nothing I can do about it, so…" Her voice trails off, leaving only the sound of the freeway as I head toward her house. I hate how I can hear what she isn't saying. How she feels helpless. How she feels like she's always swimming upstream. How she feels like no matter how much time and effort she puts into school, she still won't be enough. And it's the furthest thing from the truth.

I check my blind spot, merging between cars. "Can I ask you something?"

"Sure."

"Why'd you choose biochemistry in the beginning?"

"Oof. Um…probably because it came easy, made my parents proud, and I thought I could make a lot of money," she answers with a laugh.

"If you could go back, would you choose it again?"

"I can't go back."

"Yeah, but if you could," I push. "Do you even like it anymore?"

Her silence rings louder than any response she could give.

"Kate?"

"I don't have any other options, Mack."

"Why'd you decide to get your master's?" I ask. "You must have realized you didn't like it by then."

"Who says I don't like it?" She's defensive. I can hear it in her voice. The slight hitch. The short, sharp response.

Recognizing how fine of a line I'm walking, I hedge, "Just a hunch. I see how much school stresses you out."

"It's familiar. I like familiar."

"And the idea of graduating?" I probe.

"Terrifies me," she admits with another laugh, but it's forced. Laced with defeat. With brutal honesty.

"Do your doctors know how much the medication messes with your memory?" I ask.

She hesitates. "No."

"I think you should tell them."

"It's not a big deal, Mack."

"I think it's been affecting you for so long you've grown accustomed to it."

"Maybe I have. So, what?"

"All I'm saying is I think you might be surprised by what would happen if you decided to switch things up."

"If I switch things up, I'll potentially have more seizures for everyone to deal with, and I'll have more doctor appointments, and I'll have to have my blood drawn constantly to make sure my organs aren't shutting down. So, no. No, thank you. Switching things up and rocking the boat sounds pretty freaking miserable."

"So, you'd rather have a shit memory affecting your day-to-day life?" I challenge.

"Better it messes with me than with everyone else around me too."

"Everyone else around you wants you to be happy."

"I am happy," she argues. "Just a little forgetful sometimes."

"And the idea of trying new medication...?"

"Sounds like more effort than it's worth," she finishes.

"You do you, boo," I murmur, repeating her words from a few minutes ago. "No matter what it is. No matter how long it takes to find what makes you happy. You do you. Even if it's outside of biochemistry. Even if it's something simple and doesn't make much money or is outside the box. Even if it involves switching up your medication so you can focus better. You do *you*. Okay?"

Her sigh echoes through the speaker. "I'll try."

"Good. I'll pick you up in a few."

"Yup." Relief fills her words like she's grateful for the subject change. And to be honest, so am I.

"I'm all packed and ready," she adds.

"Good. Me too. See you soon."

"Bye."

I hang up and push the gas pedal a little harder--anything to see Kate as soon as possible.

Because fuck me, I miss her.

I miss her a lot.

35

MACKLIN

She's been chewing on her nails the entire drive. I shouldn't find it adorable, but I do. The way she fidgets in the passenger seat. Glancing at me. Staring out the window. Shifting. Crossing her legs. Folding her arms. Picking at her split ends.

Adorable.

Not great for my own nerves, but hey. I guess I'll take it.

I haven't met someone's parents in almost two decades. Doing it when you're fifteen versus thirty-four are two different experiences. I didn't care when I was a teenager. Didn't think they'd be my in-laws one day. Didn't think in general unless it was with my dick.

Man, I was a freaking kid before.

Now, though?

When I'm capable of understanding my own feelings and where I want my future to go, along with my desire to have Kate in it?

I tap my fingers against the steering wheel and bring my attention back to the road.

It's a different beast. One I'm not familiar with.

What if Hazel brought someone my age home? Even if he made her happy? Even if I could see how happy she made him? Would I be okay with it?

Shit, I don't know.

So much for not stressing.

"It's the house on the left," Kate speaks up, pointing to a tan stucco house with a large Maple tree out front. The driveway looks freshly shoveled, and there's a pine wreath on the door. It looks nice. Homey.

Pulling up next to the curb, I put the car in park and round the hood to open Kate's door. I offer her my hand. With a smile, she takes it and guides me toward the front porch while the snow drifts down from the sky, and the sun sets in the distance.

"You ready?" she asks.

"Did you bring Wes home?" I'm not sure where the question comes from, but now it's out there, and I want to know. I want to know if he met her parents. If they liked him. If they thought he was good for their daughter.

Kate stops walking and looks up at me. "No, why?"

"Curious whether they'd compare." I smooth down my black coat and let out a deep breath.

"Why are you suddenly stressed? I was the mess in the car. Not you."

"I was fine until I started thinking about Hazel and how I'd react if she brought a guy my age home." I glance at the window. The blinds are closed, proving we're still alone. "Wes has to sound pretty good to them compared to me."

Tugging my hand away from my coat, she tangles our fingers together and forces me to look at her. "Even if they had met Wes, which they haven't, they'd still be able to see there's no comparison between you and him."

"You sure?" I press.

"All they care about is how you treat me, Mack. And trust

me." She rises onto her tiptoes and kisses my cheek. "Once they realize you're basically perfect, you'll be golden."

"Far from perfect, Kate," I remind her.

"Maybe in general. But for me? Pretty sure you cross everything that matters off the list. Now, come on." She shivers and tugs me toward the door again. "It's cold out here."

When we reach the front door, she pushes it open and calls out, "We're here!"

I stomp my snow-covered boots on the welcome mat outside. Kate does the same as a petite Asian woman rounds the corner, followed by an older man with ashy gray hair and the build of a football player. He stretches out his hand for me to shake while Kate's mom drags her into a hug.

"My baby!" she gushes, kissing Kate's cheek with a loud smack.

I laugh, surprised at her show of affection, and take Kate's father's hand, shaking it. "Hi. Nice to meet you."

"You too. I'm Dan, Kate's dad."

"And I'm Lily," Kate's mom interjects, finally releasing Kate so she can look at me.

"Nice to meet you," I repeat.

"Mom. Dad," Kate interjects. "This is Macklin, Mack. My…"

"Friend?" Lily offers.

"Boyfriend," I correct, shaking her hand as well. "Thanks for inviting me."

"Of course. Do you…go to school with Kate?" she asks.

The woman's kind enough to pretend I'm not a decade older than her daughter, and I'm grateful for it. Maybe they'll give me an honest chance instead of making assumptions.

Maybe.

"Actually, I'm a paramedic," I tell her.

"Oh." Lily's eyes widen in surprise, and she shoots Dan a

look. "A paramedic, huh? Well, if that isn't a nice fit for our daughter, I don't know what is."

"Mom," Kate snaps.

She lifts her hands in defense. "I'm just saying…"

"He knows what you're saying," Kate grits out, turning to me. "I'm so sorry."

"Don't be." Snaking my hand around Kate's lower back, I pull her into my side, hoping to calm her down. Her fingers fist the back of my shirt, and she shakes her head but stays quiet.

The girl's definitely prickly. I think it's cute how she wants to stand up for me. How she wants to defend me even though she doesn't need to.

Satisfied she isn't going to bite her parents' heads off, I turn back to Kate's parents and explain, "I have two daughters myself. If one of them had a medical condition, I'd be pretty happy if they wound up with someone familiar enough with it to take care of them. It's not why I'm dating your daughter, but I get it."

"Exactly," Lily announces, dipping her chin as if that's that. "Now. Let's eat. I hope you like Chinese food."

"Yeah, it's delicious. Thank you." With our fingers tangled together, Kate leads me into the dining room, and her parents follow.

"So, where are you from?" Dan quizzes.

"I grew up in Lockwood Height, not far from LAU's campus. How about you both?" I pull the chair out for Kate, and she sits.

"I'm actually from Los Angeles," Lily tells me. "I met Kate's father there. He was the whitest of all the boys my parents would've chosen for me," she adds cheekily. She sits on the opposite side of the table next to her husband. "And Dan is from Texas."

"Born and raised before going to college," her dad mentions.

The table is already set, littered with plates, cutlery, and a few takeout containers filled with Chinese food. Kate motions to everything. "Dig in."

I start scooping ham fried rice, orange chicken, and chicken lo mein onto Kate's plate. I'm dishing some up for myself when Dan speaks again. "So, Macklin. You mentioned you have kids?"

"Yeah. Two daughters," I repeat. "One is sixteen. The other turned eighteen recently."

"And how old are you?" he asks.

"Dad!" Kate practically squeals.

"I'm thirty-four," I answer, not giving Kate a chance to jump across the table and throttle him. I understand where they're coming from. Why they want to know my background and if I'm a good fit for their daughter, despite the initial brownie points I earned by being a paramedic.

Reaching beneath the table, I squeeze Kate's thigh. "My ex-wife and I had been dating for a year in high school when we found out she was pregnant. We got married, started our family pretty young, raised two beautiful daughters, and decided to divorce a couple of years ago."

"And why'd you divorce?" he prods.

"Dad," Kate snaps, giving him a death stare. "Are you serious right now?"

"It's only a question," Lily defends her husband.

"It's fine, Porcupine," I reassure her. "And honestly, I'm not exactly sure what the final blow to our marriage was. I think a big part of the problem was how young we were when we first married. We made a lot of mistakes. Our marriage was based solely on an obligation to each other. When I came into some money, she realized she didn't need me to provide for her any longer in order to stay at home. She took half of my winnings and sent me divorce papers."

Resting his fork on the edge of his plate, Dan stares at me from across the table, his gaze impenetrable. "And you didn't fight for her?"

"I stopped fighting for her a long time ago. Long before our marriage ended," I admit. "But I learned what was worth fighting for because of it. And your daughter?" I turn to Kate. "She's pretty incredible."

"How'd you meet our Kate?" Lily asks, picking up a piece of orange chicken with her chopsticks.

Kate grabs my hand and digs her fingernails into my skin as if she might actually kill me if I dare to bring up her seizure. Hoping it'll be enough to ease her anxiety, I hold her gaze and smile.

"My younger brother goes to school with Kate and is dating one of her roommates. Since I was the lonely, recently divorced older brother with no friends, my brother invited me to tag along to one of their get-togethers, which is where I met Kate. Neither one of us is a big party animal, so we decided to start hanging out as friends. Things progressed from there."

"Really?" Lily asks, turning to Kate.

Kate forces a smile and takes a massive bite of her rice, mumbling, "Yup."

"Well, I think it's lovely," Lily decides.

"Thank you," I reply.

"I *am* going to make you sleep in separate rooms, though," Dan adds.

I chuckle and dip my chin. "I think that's a fair arrangement."

Satisfied, Dan grabs the white container of lo mein in the center of the table and adds another scoop to his plate.

Guess that's it, then.

3 6

KATE

Since you introduced yourself to my parents as my boyfriend, is sexting now allowed?

MACKLIN

You caught that, huh?

ME

Sure did. Although I notice you didn't answer my question about sexting...

MACKLIN

Not sure it's a good idea.

I frown, reading his words as another text pops up.

MACKLIN

Not when I know you're only a few rooms away.

Another message follows right after.

MACKLIN

Not when I want to sneak in and slide my
hands up your bare thighs.

ME

And if I wasn't a few rooms away from you?

MACKLIN

I'd ask what you're wearing.

ME

I mean, you did mention bare thighs…

MACKLIN

What are you wearing, Kate?

ME

One of your shirts.

MACKLIN

Fuck.

I smile and move onto my side, staring at my bedroom door as I prop my head on the pillow. The hallway's quiet. And he wouldn't sneak in here, anyway. Not when he's too damn respectful for his own good.

ME

Do you want to see it? Me in your shirt?

MACKLIN

I don't think it's a good idea.

ME

Personally, I think it's a great one.

Before I can talk myself out of it, I toss the comforter off my body and tiptoe toward my bedroom door. It creaks quietly as I pull it open, and I hold my breath, waiting for my parents' door to open and my dad's angry face to come into view. Instead? Silence.

Yeah. I most definitely should not be doing this. But I can't help it. I sneak down the hall toward Mack's room.

He was so sweet with my parents tonight. Withstanding their interrogation. Answering their questions. Saying all the right things.

I didn't know how much I needed their approval until my dad gave it during dinner. He might not have said it in so many words, but the look in his eyes? The way he accepted Mack's past? I couldn't have been more grateful for my mom and dad than at that moment.

I peek over my shoulder and down the dark hallway where my parents are sleeping one more time. Grabbing the guest bedroom door handle and taking a deep breath, I open it.

It's dark inside the room. Only a faint glow streams in from the streetlight outside the window. Mack's in the bed. His shirt is off, his hands are behind his head, and his attention is solely focused on me. As if he knew I'd come despite his feeble protest. As if he was waiting for me. The realization makes me smile.

"Hey," I whisper, sneaking the rest of the way into the guest room. I close the door quietly behind me and press my back to it. "Sorry they cornered you earlier."

"Don't apologize. I would've done the same thing if my girls brought a guy home." He smiles and crooks his finger, urging me closer. As my bare feet scuff against the carpet, it muffles my footsteps, and he adds, "I like your parents."

"Thanks. I like them too."

"Do you know what else I like?" he asks.

"Hmm?"

"You."

With a laugh, I say, "I like you too. Although you should know, you're a terrible sexter."

"Only because I'm in your parents' house, Kate," he

reminds me dryly. "Do you know what I'd do to one of Hazel's or Miley's boyfriends if I caught them sneaking into my daughter's room?"

"I guess it's a good thing you're not the one doing the sneaking," I quip.

"Yeah, because that makes it better." He shakes his head, but his gaze heats as he watches me step closer.

"They said we couldn't sleep in the same bed." When I'm within his reach, I stop and pull my hair over one shoulder, playing with the hem of the T-shirt I'd stolen to use as my pajamas, smiling as he stares at my fingers. "They never said we couldn't dirty the sheets a bit."

He chuckles and glances at the closed door again as he drags his hands along the back of my thighs. "Pretty sure it's exactly what they were talking about."

"Then, they probably should've been more specific." Pushing him back onto the bed, I straddle his hips and grin down at him.

"You trying to get me in trouble, Kate?"

"Maybe I want what I can't have."

His hands slide up my thighs and toy with the string on my shorts. "Hate to disappoint you, my little porcupine, but I think that ship has sailed. You have me wrapped around your little finger."

"I do, huh?"

"Mm-hmm," he hums. The sound is so low, so throaty, it practically vibrates through the air, turning me on and brushing against *all* the right places.

I run my hands along his tight abs, grateful for his lack of a shirt and the sheets bunched around his waist. My lips lift with appreciation as I shamelessly check him out. Seriously, though. This guy? He's something else. And I have him wrapped around my little finger.

"Then, you probably won't mind if we break another rule or two, will you?" I murmur.

He hesitates, his attention darting to the closed bedroom door once more. "Kate..."

"Macklin..."

"I respect your father too much to--"

"I'm sure you do." I roll my hips against him, feeling him harden under me despite his best efforts to keep things PG. "But this is about you and me and how freaking charming you were."

"I was trying to impress your parents and convince them to let me date their daughter."

"And you did an excellent job." I rub myself against him another time and bite my lip as he tries to hold back a groan.

Damn, his groan.

Damn, those blue eyes.

Damn, the way he's looking at me. Like I'm good enough to eat when he's the one who's about to be swallowed whole.

"Kate," he warns. Again. Only this time, it's less sure. More desperate.

"Let me thank you for being so sweet today," I whisper.

His gaze darkens as he watches me scoot lower, dragging my hands from his belly button to the hem of his boxers. Maybe he honestly didn't expect me to sneak in here. The realization only turns me on more.

"If he finds out, he'll kill me," Mack grunts.

I bend closer, rub my nose against the ridge of him, and peek up at Macklin propped against the headboard. "In that case, I suggest you be quiet."

Slowly, I pull him out of his black boxers, my trepidation begging me to stop and run back to my room. But I don't. Because it's what the old Kate would've done. The Kate who doesn't know what it's like to be looked at the way Mack's looking at me at this moment. The Kate who thinks she's a burden. Someone unlovable. Unlikable. Someone who isn't worth the effort when Macklin's done nothing but prove the opposite.

Yeah. The girl I was before Macklin came into my life would've bolted to her room and locked her door. But now? I know what it's like to be accepted, flaws and all, and the confidence that comes with it is indescribable, but I'll do my best to thank Mack anyway.

I lick my lips and touch the head of his cock with my hand, watching as the precum glistens in the light filtering in from the window. He's turned on. He wants this. Despite his own apprehension, he likes this. Likes me. Likes me sneaking into his room. Likes what I'm about to do. It's a turn-on for him as much as it is for me.

And damn, if this isn't a turn-on.

I smile softly, dragging my tongue along the base of him. He tastes good. Smells good. Warm and thick and hot. When I reach the head, I kiss it softly and open my mouth, swirling my tongue around the tip.

Mack curses under his breath and fists the sheets pooled around us, but he doesn't tell me to stop. And he sure as shit doesn't mention my dad or how easily we could be caught. And I like this. How I can make him weak with a simple drag of my tongue. I peer up at him again, taking him deeper, adrenaline shooting through me. His jaw is tight, and a tiny vein is throbbing in his forehead as he watches.

Me.

He's watching me.

He's watching what I do to him.

How I make him feel.

"You're playing a dangerous game, baby," he warns.

With a smile, I cup his balls, massaging them gently and bobbing my head up and down his erection. Salt teases my taste buds as I continue my assault. Licking. Sucking. Moaning.

I've given a few blow jobs. They're not my cup of tea. At least, they weren't. With Macklin, though? It's different. More intimate somehow. It's playful yet meaningful. Like he's committing the moment to memory. Not because it's hot--which it is--but because it's me. It isn't some random girl between his legs. It's Kate. His Kate. His prickly little porcupine.

My jaw aches as I continue sucking him, so I lift myself off him, dragging my tongue along the tiny slit and licking him like an ice cream cone. With a soft groan, he tosses his head back but lifts it again as if he can't help himself. As if he doesn't want to miss a moment. So, I take him deeper, sucking harder as he slowly lifts his hips and matches my rhythm.

"Gonna come," he growls, his breath hitching.

I continue my pace, over and over, before he warns, "Seriously, Kate, I'm gonna--"

Hot cum hits the back of my throat, and I swallow it greedily. Savoring it. Savoring *him.* The way his breathing is ragged. The feel of his hands in my hair. I'm not sure when they moved there or how long he's been tugging on the roots, but my hair's a mess, and there's water leaking from the corner of my eyes. It doesn't matter. None of it does. Because I made this man break for me. And I plan to put him back together.

Yanking me off him, he drags me up his body and kisses me, tasting himself on my lips as he shoves his tongue into my mouth.

I moan, pressing my thighs together. He pulls away and grunts, "I think it's your turn."

My hair drags across his bare chest as I shake my head. "Nope. We wouldn't want to disrespect Dan and Lily

Winchester's daughter, would we?" I grin and peck his lips one more time. "I'll see you in the morning."

As I slip out of bed, he holds onto my fingers, keeping me in place.

I glance over my shoulder and smile. "Yes?"

"Will you go to Rowdy's again with me next weekend?"

"Do you even have to ask?"

"Okay." He squeezes my fingers again as if he can't help himself, then lets me go. "Miss you already, Kate."

The stupid organ in my chest skips a beat, and I bite my lower lip to keep from grinning like a lunatic, though he sees right through it.

"Miss you too," I murmur and sneak back to my room.

MACKLIN

Fucking gorgeous.

My eyes drag down Kate's body as she leans against the doorjamb. It's been another perfect yet uneventful week. And last night, we went to the LAU game. Sat with her friends. Hung out. Afterward, she came home with me, and we made love by the fire. The next morning, I dropped her off at work, promising to pick her up later for our date night at Rowdy's.

And now, here I am. Nearly swallowing my tongue.

Long, curvy legs. Tight, dark jeans. White, flowy top. Gold necklace. Thick, black jacket. Dark, jet-black hair hanging down her back. Fucking gorgeous.

When I finally meet her eye, Kate grins. "Like what you see?"

"Mm-hmm," I hum. "Only...you're missing something."

She quirks her brow and steps aside, letting me into her place. I offer her the box tucked beneath my arm.

As she takes it carefully from me, she questions, "What's this?"

"What you're missing."

Curious, she lifts the lid off the large box and gasps. "Shut up. You didn't."

"Told you we were going to Rowdy's."

"Yeah, but you didn't need to buy me cowgirl boots." She sets the box on the kitchen table and runs her hands along the stitched brown leather. A sweet smile teases her lips. "Aww...seriously, Mack?"

"Do you like them?"

She takes them from the box and hugs the boots to her chest. "Like them? I *love* them. Seriously."

"Put 'em on," I urge.

She slips them over her white socks, modeling them for me with a cheesy grin. "What do you think?"

"I think you look beautiful, Kate."

Her grin softens as she pauses, staring at me. "And I think you're dangerous, Mack."

"How so?"

Her eyes hold mine for the briefest of seconds, like she doesn't know whether or not she wants to answer me. Like she's scared to tell me the truth.

"Tell me," I push.

Her attention falls to the ground, and she untucks her hair from behind her ear, shielding herself from me as she bends down and picks up the box. "Pretty sure you have the power to break me." The box scuffs softly against the floor as she sets it near the recycling bin. She grabs a small purse from the counter and slips it over her head, her wariness replaced with fake excitement. "Shall we?"

She tries to sneak out the front door, but I grab her arm, keeping her in place. "Not gonna break you, Kate. Not after all the work it took to put you back together again."

Her laugh eases the knot in my chest as she peeks up at me. "Promise?"

"Yeah."

She swallows thickly and smiles. This time, it's genuine.

"Okay," she whispers.

Dipping my head, I kiss her softly, savoring her taste like all the other times I've been lucky enough to kiss her. And it's almost as good as the first time. Almost as unbelievable that I get to kiss her, I get to hold her, and I get to see her smile and make her laugh.

"Now, the real question is," I add, "are you ready to give those boots some time to shine on the dance floor tonight?"

Her eyes thin. "Are you saying what I think you're saying?"

"Maybe."

"Did you brush up on your dancing skills?"

"I've been practicing," I announce.

"Yes!" she gushes. "I'm so ready. Okay, what do I do? What are the moves? How do I not look like an idiot?" She shakes her arms out and rolls her head back and forth as if she's preparing for a fight, and I can't help but laugh as I usher her toward the door.

"Just trust me and follow my lead. I only know like six moves, and they're pretty easy to catch onto. I'll show you after dinner."

As I open the passenger door, she grabs the edge of my coat and tugs me closer to her, kissing me like she can't help herself. And I like it. The fact she feels secure around me. Secure enough to take what she wants instead of asking. Secure enough to laugh and tease. I smile against her lips and wrap my arm around her waist, kissing her harder. It isn't sensual. It's playful. And real. And effortless.

When she pulls away, she smooths the front of my jacket down. "You, my dear Macklin, are the best surprise I've ever had. Thank you."

"You're welcome."

~

TWIST, GRAB, FLICK THE WRIST, TUG HER BACK, AND DIP, I silently chant, pressing my hand against Kate's back. I wasn't kidding when I said it'd been a while since I'd practiced any country dancing, but I wanted to make Kate happy, and with the massive grin on her face, I'd say it's working.

The lights are dim, and the scent of smoked meats hangs in the air, but the dance floor lacks any peanut shells--for now--and we figured dancing before dinner might be a smart idea. After a single drink at the bar, which she assured me was fine, she insisted I teach her some moves, and here we are.

"Okay, what now?" she asks, turning to me.

I grab her hands but keep my elbows tucked at my sides. "All right. Step one. The basic step. You keep your hands on top, and I keep mine on the bottom. Got it?"

"Yup."

"Good. Take your left foot and step in front of me while angling it to your right." She does as she's told, and I follow suit, causing our legs to mirror each other as I help her pull away slightly, then tug her back to me. Slowly, we move in a circle as she gets used to it. Once she's comfortable, I announce, "Now, let's do the back slide."

"Okay?"

I demonstrate it, and she slides her hand against my lower back, stepping behind me as I catch her palm, spin her around, and bring her back to our original position. The girl's a natural and pieces the moves together almost instantly. We practice it a few more times when she says, "Okay. Next move."

She's a quick learner. And soon, we're both spinning around the dance floor. She looks so carefree like this.

Happy. Relaxed. Another song comes on, and I can't help but pull her close, leaning forward and murmuring, "Trust me?"

She nods. "Yeah, why?"

"I have another move in mind."

"Okay?"

"We're gonna do another dip, but this time, I'm going to grab your throat."

"Oh, really?" She quirks her brow, intrigued.

"Hold onto my wrist with both hands when I bring you to the floor and keep your legs straight instead of bending your grounded leg. Got it?"

"Grab your wrist and keep my legs straight. Got it."

Around and around, we go, twisting and turning and backsliding as the beat turns a little darker. Sexier. I spin her around, grab her throat, and dip her. Down she goes, the lights casting shadows along her gorgeous parted lips. I pull her back up and kiss the shit out of her, my hand still wrapped around her throat. I can't help it. This girl. She's unlike anyone I've ever met. And seeing her come out of her shell? Seeing her break down those walls?

Fuck.

I might love her.

She slips her hands around my shoulders, tangling her fingers in the short strands of hair at the nape of my neck, and scrapes them gently against my scalp. I nearly groan. The feeling shoots straight to my groin as we sway back and forth. When a throat clears, it breaks through the haze we'd been lost in.

As if she's been caught sneaking out after curfew, Kate jerks away from me, folds her arms, and leaves a solid foot of distance between us while I wipe my mouth with the back of my hand, finding a worried Rowdy behind me.

Confused by the interruption, I clear my throat. "Uh, hey, Rowdy. Sorry, if we--"

"A girl who looked a shit-ton like Hazel just ran out of here, man," Rowdy warns. His cowboy hat is pulled low, but it doesn't stop me from noticing his eyes darting toward the exit. "Figured you'd wanna know."

My brows furrow. "Hazel? M-my Hazel?"

Rowdy nods.

"Crap," Kate mutters, looking shy and nervous as shit, twisting her hands in front of her as she stares at the exit.

Scrubbing my hand over my face, I shake my head and stride back to our table, finding my keys and ushering Kate to the car. If Hazel saw me with Kate, she'll be pissed. She might even think I orchestrated it or some shit, and our relationship is already shaky enough as it is.

There aren't any texts from Hazel, Summer, or Miley when I check my phone, but it doesn't make me feel any better. I need to talk to Hazel. I need to explain. I need to make sure she's okay.

Hazel's contact info lights up the screen, and I push the call button after I turn on the car. I need to clear this up. I need to fix this.

"Pick up, Haze," I mutter. "Please pick up."

The call goes straight to voicemail.

I slam my hand against the steering wheel, and Kate flinches beside me.

"Fuck!" I yell, dropping my phone onto my lap.

"What can I do?" Kate whispers. "How can I help?"

"I dunno. I dunno what to do. If Rowdy saw her leave, she's probably pissed, but..." I scrub my hand over my face again, defeat settling into my bones. "I dunno. What if it wasn't her? Maybe Rowdy got it wrong. He hasn't seen her in a couple of years now. But if it was her?" I scrub my hand over my face. "Shit."

"I can try calling her if you want. To make sure she's okay. Or would it be weird? If Hazel did recognize me, it's not like she'll answer, but it's not like I've called her on the phone to chat before tonight, either, so…"

"We should leave it," I decide. "I'll call her again in a few. Send her a text. Try to explain everything. But…"

"But, what?" Her touch is gentle as she reaches over and squeezes my thigh. Like she doesn't want to push. Yet, she also doesn't want me to feel alone. And I'm surprised by how much I need it. Her touch. Her presence. I've been dealing with this shit alone for so long I almost forgot what it was like to have a partner. Even before Summer and I divorced, we weren't partners. We were…roommates. Cohabitating. Sharing the responsibilities of the household. But I stopped feeling anything for her, and she stopped feeling anything for me long before the lottery. I think it's why I didn't care when she left.

But Kate? If she got out of my car right now and left me, I'm not sure I could handle it. The idea sobers me.

"I'm sorry she saw us, Mack."

"Guess I'm just surprised," I mutter, admitting the truth.

"Surprised by what?"

"By her response. She left. She cared enough to leave in the first place. The girl hasn't had a conversation with me lasting more than a couple texts in two years, but she was so hurt by seeing me she left." I rub at my temple, lost in thought. "I dunno what to think about it."

"You're her dad, Mack. I'm not sure the *seeing you* part spooked her. I think the whole seeing you with someone other than her mother did the trick."

I frown, mulling it over and shaking my head. "Why would she care? Summer left me, Kate. Not the other way around."

"Still," Kate argues. "It had to have brought up some mixed emotions. Especially after the gossip train from your ex and how she made you sound to Hazel and Miley from the last time we were seen together. It's probably confusing."

"Yeah." I close my eyes and hang my head. I'm so fucking exhausted. Exhausted by my past. Exhausted by the desire to have a relationship with my daughters while maintaining one with the woman beside me.

"What are you thinking?" Kate whispers.

"I feel guilty, but I don't know why."

"Maybe you should reach out again. Tell her you love her, you miss her, and you'd love to meet up so you can explain things?"

"Yeah." I nod, pull up the limited conversations I've had with Hazel via text, then type a message.

ME

> Hey, Haze. Heard you were at Rowdy's tonight. Wish you would've said hello. I miss you and want to introduce you to someone. Or not, if you're not ready. I hate to see you hurting. I wasn't trying to keep my relationship from you or anything. I didn't know…

I sigh, delete the last sentence, and press send.

"Do you want me to call Ash or Mia or someone else and get a ride?" Kate offers. "So you can maybe stop by Summer's house and see if Hazel went home?"

"I don't want to corner her," I mutter, staring at the screen, hoping to find a response. Hell, I'd even take the little blue dots hinting Hazel's typing something. But nothing happens.

Nothing.

With a sigh, I set my phone in the cupholder.

"What can I do?" Kate questions, her breath swirling in the cold air. "How can I help?"

Her hand is still on my thigh, and I grab it, bringing her

cool fingertips to my lips, and blow my warm breath against them.

Her smile is sad yet comforting. As if she can feel my pain and anxiety. As if it's her own. As if she'd do anything to take it away. To make me feel better.

And fuck. It's nice. Being able to lean on her when I need it most. Her stormy eyes are reassuring in a way I never could've anticipated. And right now, they're solely focused on me. It means more than she'll ever understand.

"I don't wanna be alone tonight," I tell her.

"Okay."

"Do you have your medicine?"

She lifts her purse and jiggles it back and forth. "Way ahead of you."

"All right." I turn on the car, blast the heat, and pull onto the main road, heading back to my place.

3 8

KATE

"What do you want to do?" I ask, flicking on the kitchen light.

Mack's home seems a little less inviting tonight. A little more stark. Part of me wonders if it's because the man who makes the space a home is too preoccupied. Too distracted by Hazel and her lack of response to his text. Or texts, considering he pulled over twice on our way up to his house so he could send her a couple more. I don't know what they said, and honestly, it doesn't even matter. He's hurting. And I hate how he's hurting.

Squeezing the back of his neck, Mack tosses his keys onto the counter and shrugs. "No idea."

"Are you saying you need something else to *focus* on?" I prop my hip against the kitchen island and quirk my brow.

His chuckle is pathetic at best, but he nods. "Yeah, my prickly little porcupine. Looks like it's your turn to distract me."

My tongue clicks against the roof of my mouth as I wrack my brain for options. My mouth tilts up in a sly smile as I announce, "I have an idea."

"Yeah?"

"Mm-hmm," I hum, tucking my thumbs into the back pockets of my jeans. "Do you have blankets?"

His eyebrow arches. "Yes?"

"Like, a lot of them?"

"Yes?" he repeats, still unsure where I'm going with this line of questioning.

I clap my hands together. "Then, chop-chop, my sad little golden retriever. We have a fort to build."

His laughter is less forced than earlier and eases the tightness in my chest that had settled there on the silent drive to his house. Without a word, he heads to a closet down the hall and returns with his arms full of blankets. Together, we drag his couch closer to the fire and bring in his kitchen chairs, throwing blankets on all the furniture and stretching the fabric from one side of the room to the other. In a stroke of genius, Mack grabs some clips from the pantry. Usually, they're used for keeping potato chip bags closed, but tonight, we use them to keep the blankets in place on top of the chairs. They secure the fabric perfectly. It's messy and childish and kind of ridiculous, but by the end, Mack is smiling. His eyes are crinkled at the corners, and his shoulders aren't quite as tight as they were. Which means Operation Distraction is a success.

When he catches me staring, my grin widens. "Hi."

"Hey," he returns. "What are you lookin' at?"

"My handiwork." Without giving him a chance to respond, I dart down the hallway, steal the pillows off his bed, and create a comfy oasis beneath the canopy while Mack boots up his laptop and turns on a show.

It's perfect.

The familiar opening song from *The Office* echoes throughout the room as I pour some freshly microwaved popcorn into a bowl and head back to the fort, finding Macklin snuggled inside.

"You comin'?" he asks, lifting the edge of one of the blankets while giving me a sneak peek of his bare torso.

"You seem to be missing your shirt," I point out.

"Don't get me wrong, Kate, the idea of snuggling with you in a fort of blankets sounds amazing. But it's gonna get hot as hell in here with the fire. Figured stripping the clothes would help cut down on the heat for a bit."

"Oh, so it had nothing to do with you wanting to get laid?" I quip.

His eyes soften, and he laughs, shaking his head. "Never gonna turn down being naked with you, Kate. But tonight, I'm happy to just lie here with you."

My heart clenches.

He's telling the truth. I can see it in his eyes. The hint of vulnerability. The slight hesitation.

It kind of makes me want to jump his bones right here, right now. But surprisingly, I don't think an orgasm is what he needs. He needs a deeper connection. A simple one. A *real* one. A reminder that his value isn't in things or sex or money or…anything. Simply being with him is enough.

And it is.

I strip naked, climb beneath the sheets, and snuggle against his bare chest. He's so warm. So comfortable. So…*safe*. Like home.

Slowly, the tension eases from his muscles as one episode turns into four. Neither of us says a word. We munch on popcorn until the bowl is empty. Later, we kick off the blanket, the heat rising with every second, and I snuggle into his chest again. My eyelids feel heavy, the rhythm of his heart against my ear lulling me to sleep when I force my eyes open to find him looking at his phone. Again.

"Did she text you back?" I ask.

He shakes his head and sets his cell back onto the floor beneath his thigh. "It was Theo. The girls wanted to make sure you were okay."

"That was sweet of them."

"Yeah." He threads his hand through a few strands of my hair and tugs softly. "Told them you were good."

"Thank you." I drag my fingers against his bare chest, the firelight dancing off his tan skin, casting shadows along the walls of our fort. "Can I...say something?"

"Yeah?" he rumbles.

"I don't like to see you hurting." He squeezes his arm tighter around my shoulders, so I burrow into him even more. "I'm sorry they've pulled away since the divorce." And I am. I hate it so much. Can't they see how much he wants to be part of their lives? Don't they know he'd do anything to be with them? To talk to them? And if it kills me, a bystander, I can't even imagine how much it guts Mack. I close my eyes and breathe him in deeply, his familiar scent of pine and spice grounding me.

He lifts his head and kisses the crown of mine.

"I'm sorry she saw us together," I add. The apology hurts as it slips past my lips, leaving me raw and vulnerable. Because I was never one to like standing out. Blending in always seemed easier. But once Mack and I started dating, those insecurities slowly fell away. I like being playful and silly sometimes. I like riding the mechanical bull and learning how to dance, even when there are witnesses. I like how Mack makes me feel special and worth seeing. Worthy of attention. Worthy of making a splash. Yet here I am, apologizing for it, the stark reminder of why I prefer to keep my head down rearing its ugly head.

Is it my fault Hazel ran away? Would she have done it if Mack was dating anyone else? Does it even matter? I can't change the past, and honestly, I don't want to. How selfish does it make me?

The sheets rustle slightly as Mack pulls away from me, sits up, rests his weight on his forearm, and stares down at me. "Don't ever be sorry for that, Kate."

"But−−"

"My shit with my daughters and my ex is *my* shit. Don't let the drama surrounding them ruin what we have. I'm begging you." His fingers glide across my cheek. Softly. Carefully. "Because if they screw this up for me…" The pain in his eyes almost breaks me, the cerulean color practically glowing in the dim light, so I nod anyway.

"I'm not going anywhere, Mack. I promise."

With another kiss to my forehead, he settles back onto the floor and tugs the covers over us, his exhaustion finally getting the best of him. "Let's get some rest. It's late, and you have work in the morning."

Work. With his daughter. Yeah…should be a real treat. But he's right. I'm tired. And I'm sure he is too.

Tomorrow's worries can wait.

"Goodnight," I whisper.

"Goodnight, Kate."

39

MACKLIN

I can't sleep. Not anymore. I got some solid shut-eye for a few hours, but now, the fire's out, and the morning light is spilling in from the windows, the sun reflecting off the fresh snow and filtering through the blankets.

To be fair, I should be happy I slept at all. After the issue with Hazel and her lack of response, I was convinced I'd be a mess for the rest of the night. Instead, Kate distracted me. And not with sex, which I wouldn't have complained about. With a different kind of comfort. One I didn't even know I needed until my not-so-prickly porcupine slipped beneath the sheets and burrowed closer to me. As if I was her lifeline. Her rock. When in reality, she's slowly becoming mine.

Her dark hair is splayed across my chest, and her lips are parted as she breathes slowly, still lost in sleep.

Fucking beautiful.

Pushing her hair away from her face, I brush my thumb along her cheek, and she moans softly, leaning into my touch. The sheets hug every curve of her body, showcasing her pebbled nipples and the apex of her thighs.

Craving her, I slip the covers over my head and drag my hands along her bare skin, watching as it leaves a trail of goosebumps along every inch. Leaning closer, I kiss her clavicle, then move lower, brushing my lips against her nipples before sucking on the little patch of skin beneath her belly button.

Her thighs tighten, and she squirms slightly, her breathing remaining deep and even.

She's still asleep.

Softly, I bite at her hip bone, and she moans again. "Macklin."

I smile against her skin, letting my fingers dip into the heat between her thighs. Her legs part, giving me better access, so I slide lower, finding her core. My fingertips brush along the slit, playing with the heat and finding her wet.

Fuck.

I dip into her again, circling my fingers and bringing her juices to her clit.

"Mack," she gasps. It's breathy and sweet but almost crackly too. Probably from sleep. She's awake now.

Good.

Instead of answering her, I scoot lower and kiss her pubic bone, positioning myself between her parted thighs. The sheets rustle around us more as she arches her back. Desperate. Needy.

"Lift your hips, Kate," I order. "Wanna have my breakfast served properly."

She snorts but raises her hips, and I stuff a pillow beneath them, parting her lips and kissing her softly.

It's funny. How intimate oral sex can be. It's not about getting off. It's about pleasuring the person you're with. The person you care about. It's about tasting them. Peeling away every single layer. Making them helpless. Making them crave you. What you can do. How you can make them feel. Without any expectations of whether or not they'll return the favor. It's about making the other person feel good.

And I want to make Kate feel good.

I want it more than anything.

Dipping my tongue into her slit again, I lick her slowly, add a finger, and curl it, finding the little bundle of nerves inside her.

She moans again.

This time, it's louder. More breathy. I close my eyes and breathe in deeply, savoring her taste. Her scent. Her hips lift, meeting my mouth as I continue sucking and licking, adding a second finger and scissoring them back and forth. Slowly. Rhythmically.

With another gasp, she tangles her fingers into my hair, pushing me against her pussy as her thighs clench around my ears. And fuck, does it feel good. To be needed. Wanted. I continue my assault, playing with her, toying with her, bringing her closer to the edge as her mewls and pants grow louder and louder, mingling with my name on her parted lips.

Her juices cling to my chin, and I savor the taste, refusing to let up or give her an ounce of breathing room as her heels dig into my shoulder blades and her back arches off the ground.

"Mack, I'm coming. Ah, I'm coming." She bucks against my face, riding out her orgasm as I continue licking, biting, and suckling her clit, committing the taste, the smell, and the feel to memory.

I don't want to forget it. The way it feels when I'm with her. How different it is compared to my past relationship. How much more she means to me despite the shitstorm we created by falling for each other. And we did create a shitstorm. But I don't want to think about it. I only want to think about her. Kate. And what she means to me.

As the grip on my hair lessens, Kate's thighs fall limp. I kiss her swollen clit one more time and crawl up her body.

With both arms on either side of her head, I cage her in. "Kissing after oral, yay or nay?"

Her eyes widen in surprise as she considers my question. After a moment, she shrugs. "Never tried it."

"Seriously?"

"Don't make me feel self-conscious," she scolds.

Laughing, I bend closer, giving her plenty of time to turn her head before I kiss her. Our tongues dance together as I allow her to taste herself, and she hums softly, running her fingers along the back of my head and down my neck.

I almost groan at how good it feels. Like heaven. It's strange. Being with someone who's as considerate as Kate. As caring. She makes it seem effortless. Like it's who she is. Like she's unable to turn it off, even if she wanted to.

"I love how innocent you are, Kate Winchester."

"And I love how you accept me through and through, Macklin Taylor."

"Wanna know what else I love?" I ask.

"What?"

"How you knew exactly what I needed last night."

Her legs part, and she cradles me between them, rubbing herself against my erection.

"Mmm," she hums. "Want to know what I think you need?"

"What?" I return.

"A solid orgasm."

I laugh a little harder, though it takes everything inside of me to keep from thrusting into her. She's so damn warm. So damn inviting.

"Oh, you think?" I quip.

"Yup. You should definitely get inside me now."

"I should, huh?"

"Mm-hmm. I'm ready for my second orgasm."

I chuckle dryly and line myself up with her entrance. "As you wish."

40

KATE

With a frown, Macklin types another message into his phone as I brush my fingers through my damp hair hanging in ropes down my back. "Everything okay?" I question him.

"Still no word from Hazel," he mutters, setting his phone back on the bathroom counter. After our little tryst in the makeshift fort, we cleaned everything up and took a shower. Unfortunately, reality can only be pushed off for so long, and it seems it's caught up with us.

Stupid reality.

Everything had felt so perfect and natural I'd almost forgotten the drama from last night.

Almost.

As I take in the slight frown marring his lips, I murmur, "I'm sorry."

"Don't be." He grabs a white towel from the hook and wipes the steam from the mirror, his eyes meeting mine in our reflection. "Can I give you a ride to work today?"

"Yes, please." The answer startles me as it slips past my lips. Because the old Kate would've lied and told him I already had a ride. The old Kate would've deflected. The old Kate would've ridden the bus instead of asking for help––from anyone, let alone the guy she's most definitely falling for. But thanks to Mack, I've...*changed*. And it's nice. Refreshing even. To allow myself to ask for help.

"I do need to stop by my place and grab a change of clothes, if you don't mind," I add. "Look at me, remembering my pills but forgetting an outfit."

"Because you know I like it when you wear my clothes."

"Oh, I do?" I challenge.

"Well, if you didn't, you do now. You should steal one of my hoodies."

"Are you sure it's okay?" I ask, holding his gaze in the mirror as he steps around me and hangs the towel back in its place. There's something intimate about wearing a man's clothes. And even though this wouldn't be my first time stealing Mack's, it still makes me feel all warm and fuzzy inside.

"Positive." He snakes his hands around my waist and pulls my back to his front.

"But I feel bad," I argue.

As I angle my head to the side, giving him access to my neck, he kisses beneath my ear. And despite it being the sweetest gesture and making my ovaries want to burst, it also tickles, so I squirm against him.

"Stop, stop, stop," I beg through bouts of laughter. He keeps his grip firm around my waist and blows raspberries on my neck.

"You gonna steal my hoodie?" he demands.

"Yes! Yes, I'll steal your hoodie!"

"Good girl." He lifts his head, but he keeps me glued against him and kisses my cheek with a cocky smirk.

"Speaking of stealing things..." I continue. "I'm thinking of making some breakfast before we leave. Is that okay?"

"Let me do it. I have to chop some wood first, though."

Chop wood? Seriously. Who the hell chops wood these days? Sexy mountain men, that's who.

My gaze slides down his toned body as I shamelessly check him out. "So that's where all the manly muscles come from."

He flexes, wiggling his eyebrows. I playfully shove him away from me.

"Why don't you chop the wood while I cook breakfast?" I suggest. "You know, two birds with one stone and all that jazz."

"You sure?"

"Of course. What sounds good to you? Pancakes? Omelets? Bacon?"

"Is all of the above an option?"

I roll my eyes, turning and facing him fully. "So needy."

"Only when it comes to you." With another kiss on my cheek, he pulls away. Suddenly, the world spins, and I grab onto his shoulders, squeezing my eyes shut.

"Whoa," I breathe out.

His hands grab my elbows, steadying me. "You okay?"

I nod but keep my eyes closed. "Yeah. Give me a second."

"What's wrong?"

"Dizzy."

"Kate, you okay?" His tone is sharper. More concerned. More anxious.

I nod again and open my eyes. "Yeah, I'm okay."

"You sure?" he confirms as if he doesn't believe me.

"Yeah. I'm sure."

"Would you tell me if you weren't?" His brows are knitted together as he grips the side of my face, and I lean into him.

My smile stretches as I nod against his hand. "Actually, I think I would tell you if I wasn't okay. And that's saying something."

311

The worry in his eyes softens, and he runs his thumb back and forth against my cheek. "Sounds like a miracle."

"Go," I tell him. "Seriously, I'm okay. Sometimes I get a little dizzy, but it doesn't mean I'm going to have a seizure. And even if I did, as long as I don't hit my head or anything, it would *still* be okay."

"You took your medicine last night?" he prods.

"Yes, Macklin, I took my medicine at 10:00 pm like I'm supposed to. I'm fine. Promise. Go." I shove him gently, and he slips on a dark T-shirt, casting me one last look as he leaves. Once he's gone, I steal one of his hoodies from his closet and a pair of his sweats from the dresser, loving how small and weirdly feminine they make me feel. Like I'm being swallowed by all things Mack.

Yes, please.

The scent. The soft fabric against my bare skin. They make me want to cuddle up next to the fire and never leave.

We'll have to stop at my place before he can take me to work, but it isn't a big deal. And even if it was, Mack would be okay with it. The realization is staggering, yet so damn comforting. In fact, it makes me want to hug him all over again.

My bare feet scuff against the hardwood as I make my way to the kitchen and look out the giant windows. It's so beautiful here. So peaceful. Like a world of its own. One where all expectations are moot, and I can just be me.

Me and Macklin.

Sitting in a tree.

K-I-S-S-I-N——

Dammit, Blakely. You're rubbing off on me.

My eyes thin as I catch Mack in the scenery outside. Somehow, he's managed to blend into the white, brown, and pine green seamlessly. Like he always belonged here. Out in the wild. Away from the world. Away from obligations and chaos and traffic and bills. Away from all of it.

The man looks like a lumberjack, swinging an ax into an already cut stump, making the pieces smaller and more manageable for the house. The sun glistens off the sharp blade as it slices through the air, mesmerizing me. He isn't wearing a coat, despite the freshly fallen snow. Probably because he's already worked up a sweat thanks to his little workout, but what do I know? His arms are on full display, showcasing his biceps, triceps, and every other muscle made to make a woman's mouth water. Well, that and actually accomplishing hard work such as cutting wood. But still.

My mouth *is* watering.

And it doesn't matter that I already had him this morning. It doesn't matter that I'll probably have him again tonight and the day after. Because it's surreal. He's mine. All mine.

And I never want to let him go.

Forcing myself to stay in reality, I look away from the sexy mountain man outside and make breakfast. A little while later, the bacon is sizzling, and the pancakes are on the griddle when Macklin returns with some logs for the fireplace.

"Breakfast is almost ready," I announce.

"Smells great. Let me grab another quick shower and––"

"Again?"

"I mean, I did chop a shit-ton of wood," he reminds me, striding closer and inspecting the variety of food I've thrown together.

"Why didn't you do it before the first shower?"

"And miss an opportunity to see you naked?" He chuckles and dips his head in for a kiss. "I think not. I'll be back in five."

"Okay."

A few minutes later, we're both dished up and are sitting

at the kitchen island, our plates in front of us. A freshly-showered Mack tells me, "I have to be on-site for the LAU game tonight. Want to catch a ride with Ash or Blake, and I'll drive you home after?"

"You sure you won't ditch me again and leave me in a broom closet?"

He snorts. "The likelihood of another injury happening is relatively small, but if it happens, I'll make sure Theo knows he's not allowed to leave you there even if you lie and say you found a ride like last time. Deal?"

"Yup. Deal."

41

KATE

Hazel's car is in the parking lot as Macklin pulls in.

I didn't know whether or not she was scheduled to work today. Part of me had hoped she wasn't. The other part feels guilty for even wishing for such a thing. Besides, I like Hazel. I really do. The question is, does she still like me after possibly seeing me with her dad last night?

I glance at Mack, curious if he also saw her car, but he's oblivious. Then again, he might not know what car she drives in the first place. The realization makes me frown. Why did she run away last night, avoiding him like the Plague, when she's been doing it since the divorce? Maybe she wasn't disappointed in seeing Mack with someone. Maybe she didn't want to see him, period? The thought doesn't make me feel any better. Because their tumultuous relationship is killing Mack. I've noticed it since the first time I saw him in the grocery store. And after last night? My assumption only solidified.

Come on, Hazel. Give the guy a chance.

I peek at Mack again, my heart swelling. She's so freaking

lucky, and she has no idea. No idea how awesome her dad is. No idea he'd do anything for her and for Miley.

"What?" he questions, feeling my stare.

"Nothing, it's..." I tilt my head toward the brand new, pearly white Jetta parked near Butter and Grace's entrance. "Hazel's here."

His eyes widen, and he forces out a slow breath, examining the car with a new level of interest. "Oh."

"Do you want to come in? Talk to her or something?" I ask.

"I shouldn't." He shakes his head. "I don't want her to feel cornered."

"Me either." I unbuckle my seatbelt and stare at the building like it's a dungeon instead of a busy food establishment. I don't want to go inside. I don't want to face Hazel.

Not that it matters. I can't ditch work for no reason. I mean, I could. But I won't. Not when Anna is counting on me for my shift. Besides, I'm still not sure whether Hazel saw me with Mack or if she only saw a faceless woman with her father last night.

"Do you want me to come in?" Mack reaches out and touches my thigh. The warmth from his hand seeps through my jeans, grounding me instantly.

"No, you're okay."

"Are you sure? Because I will. I might not want Hazel to feel cornered by me, but I don't want you to feel cornered by Hazel, either."

"I'm a big girl, Mack," I remind him. "And you're right. Letting Hazel see us together for the first time at my workplace probably isn't the brightest thing we could do right now, especially when we don't know if she recognized me in the first place."

"Yeah, but sending you in alone..."

"We don't want to make her feel like she's being ganged

up on or anything. Best case scenario, she doesn't know I was the girl with you last night, and we'll figure out a way to tell her on our terms when we aren't working. Worst case scenario, she knows I'm dating you and will spill nachos on me or something to get back at me. It's not the end of the world."

His expression falls. "Dammit, Kate."

"It's fine," I rush out, smoothing out my jacket while avoiding Mack's gaze. "Don't get me wrong. I'm not going to lie to her or anything if it comes up, but I think, for now, we should wait until she reaches out to you. Until she's ready to talk."

His eyes fall to his lap. "What if she isn't? What if she's never ready?"

"Then, it's on her," I remind him. "You're literally doing everything you can, Mack. As long as you keep trying to communicate, the ball's in her court."

He sighs, squeezing my thigh again. "You're right. Come here."

I lean over the center console to kiss him softly, push the passenger door open, and brace myself for the inevitable.

"I'll see you at the game," he calls out.

"See you at the game." I close the passenger door, hoist my purse over my shoulder, and walk inside.

Behind the hostess table, Hazel's playing with her phone as she looks up and sees me.

My spine feels like a steel rod as I try to keep my expression blank, but my feet dig into the ground nonetheless. I'm on edge. I'm jumpy. I'm nervous. I feel like I'm in trouble, even though I shouldn't be. I can't help it. Because I don't know what to say. Or do. Or...anything. Not until I can tell whether or not Hazel knows I'm dating her dad.

My knuckles turn white as I squeeze the strap of my purse.

How screwed up is this?

I'm dating Hazel's dad.

She would have every right to throw nachos in my face. Or to yell at me and cause a scene. I should've told her. Mack should've told her. She probably feels betrayed. Like I stabbed her in the back.

If she knows.

"Hey, Kate," she greets me, setting her phone down and giving me her full attention.

Forcing my legs to move, I stride toward her and paste on a smile. "Hey."

"How was your weekend?"

My breathing feels staggered, but I try to keep it in check. "Fine. How was yours?"

"Well, you know." She shrugs and rounds the edge of the hostess stand, leaning her hip against it. "Anything new?"

Dammit!

Does she know? Does she not? I can't tell. She seems like she's in a decent mood, but still. Something's off. Or maybe it's my imagination. It's not like I'm good at keeping secrets or anything. And even if she doesn't know, it's not like I can keep this from her. But telling her doesn't exactly sound like a walk in the park. Not at the beginning of our shift. And not when Mack and I agreed to wait until we were together to rip off the Band-Aid.

I suck my bottom lip into my mouth and scan her expression carefully.

Why do I feel like I'm seconds from being interrogated? Like I'm an enemy spy and am about to have a hood thrown over my head as I'm carted off to the nearest basement where they can torture me for answers?

Picking at her cuticles, she prods, "You feeling okay? You look a little…"––her gaze flicks up to mine––"pale."

"Honestly, I'm not feeling great," I admit. And boy, if it isn't the truth. I seriously might puke. Or faint.

"Why not?" she asks.

"Because." I let the word hang in the air, unable to follow up with anything at all. None of it feels right. Nothing. Nada. I'm fresh out of ideas and have no clue where to go from here without either dying of guilt, crumbling from the pressure, or causing a scene that could get us both fired if I'm not careful.

Dammit!

I should've most definitely called in sick.

"So, do you remember how I was telling you about my dad?" she continues, clicking her fingers against the top of the hostess stand.

"Yes?"

Click. Click. Click.

"Yeah. Well." *Click.* "I ran into him last night." *Click. Click.* "How weird, right?"

I gulp.

She knows.

She has to know.

I step closer to her and look over my shoulder, scanning Butter and Grace for our manager. Dropping my voice low, I start, "Listen––"

"Yeah. Saw him up close and personal with his new fuck bunny." Her nose scrunches as if she's smelled something foul. "Fun times."

"Hazel," I try again.

"My mom was right. He's definitely dating someone who's half his age––"

"Haz––"

"Which I should've expected, honestly. He's never exactly been father of the year, so––"

"Hazel," I snap, but she continues barrelling over me.

"Who would've thought it'd be with a girl from my work? A girl who, from what I assumed, was my actual friend, ya know? Like what the fuck?" She laughs, shaking her head back and forth as if caught between denial, frustration, and absolute disgust.

The strap slips from my shoulder, and my purse clatters to the ground, but I don't reach for it. I don't move. I just stare at her. Hazel. Because the girl doesn't look pissed. I mean, she does, but underneath all the hatred and contempt is hurt.

She's hurting.

And it's all because of me.

"I didn't know he was your dad," I whisper. "Not in the beginning."

She laughs again, shaking her head. "Because that makes it better."

"I'm serious, Hazel. I didn't know, and neither did Mack––"

"Don't say his name." Her bright blue gaze shines with fury. It's the first time she's ever looked like him. I've never seen Mack truly mad in the first place, but the color? The way it gleams? The passion? The hint of stubbornness? The hurt? Yeah. Those are all too familiar, especially after last night and how much he was hurting when she ghosted him.

"What do you have against him?" I demand, her resemblance causing a spark of protectiveness inside of me. "He's sweet and thoughtful. He's always looking out for others and goes out of his way to help people. Why do you hate him so much?"

"I don't hate him."

"Then, why don't you talk to him? Why do you ignore his texts? And I'm not only talking about last night. I'm talking about in general."

Her upper lip curls in disgust. "Don't act like you know anything about me or my relationship with my dad."

"What relationship?" I push. "Because all I've seen is him reaching out to you. Wanting to connect with you. To get to know you again. And yet he's never gotten anything in return."

"Shut up," she warns.

But I don't. Because I want to know. I want to know why she's so hard on him yet so accepting of her mom and all the lies she's been told.

"Tell me, Haz––"

"I said *stop*," she spits, her pitch rising until I can feel the people around us staring. Eavesdropping.

"Okay." I lift my hands in the air and take a step back. "I'll stop. But you need to give him a chance to explain himself."

"Why? So he can tell me how great it is to date someone his daughter's age?" Her upper lip curls again as her gaze rolls over me. "Do you have any idea how disgusting it is?"

I bite my tongue and keep myself from pointing out we aren't exactly the same age. She's barely eighteen. I'm twenty-five. Her dad is thirty-four. Admittedly, it's a decent age gap between us, but it's not like I went to high school with Hazel or anything. I didn't know they were related until after we'd started hanging out. It's only a coincidence. A shitty one, but still. We're both consenting adults, and I love him.

My breath hitches.

I love him.

I love Macklin Taylor.

"What? Nothing to say?" she grits out.

"Oh, I have plenty to say." I look around us as the customers go back to their meals. Satisfied with our limited privacy, I step closer, keeping my voice low. "But you're not in the right headspace to listen, and honestly? What I have to say doesn't matter, anyway. You don't owe me an opportunity to explain myself, but you do owe it to your dad."

"Don't talk about him," she warns.

"If you took two seconds to hear him out and give him another chance, you'd recognize he isn't trying to hurt you, and he never would've lied to you or gone out of his way to piss you off the way he clearly has. He loves you, Hazel. Hell, he's your dad."

"So?" She scoffs and folds her arms. "He ruined any chance of us having a relationship as soon as he started dating someone my age."

"I'm not your age," I point out. "I'm twenty-five, Hazel. And yeah, a nine-year age gap isn't exactly tiny, but I care about him––"

"Stop." She raises her hand, her chest heaving. Like she can't catch her breath. Like she can't hold back her tears much longer. Like she's hanging on by a thread, and I'm waving a pair of scissors around.

I don't listen. I can't. Because Macklin deserves an opportunity to explain himself. He deserves a chance. And Hazel's refusing to give him one.

"Why?" I demand. "Why should I stop? It's not like you want a relationship with him anyway. If you did, you'd answer his texts. You'd take his calls. Instead, all you've done is ignore him. Do you have any idea how much it kills him every time he sends you a text, and you don't even respond?"

"Yeah, like he's one to talk. He's dating *you*, remember?" She waves her hand at me like I'm nothing but scum.

Not sure what it has to do with our conversation, but…

Pinching the bridge of my nose, I dig deep for another ounce of patience. "He's your father, Hazel. And he loves the crap out of you."

Another scoff slips out of her as she shakes her head back and forth. "Oh, really?"

"Yes, Hazel. He really does."

"Fine. Tell him it's over. Leave my dad alone, and I'll give him a chance to be my father again. I'll talk to him. Call him. Even take him out to Sunday brunch if it will get you away from him."

I jerk away as if I've been slapped, my mind reeling. "Are you serious?"

"Yes."

"You want me to break up with your dad?"

"Yeah." She squares her shoulders like the idea sounds better and better to her as it marinates in the air around us. "I do."

"I'm not going to do that."

"Then, I guess he can kiss his daughter goodbye. And I guarantee Miley will say the same thing when she finds out about our father's new whore."

Her eyes spark with determination and leave a heavy stone in my gut. Still, I ignore the jab, too distracted by the twisted predicament she's gifted me with.

"This isn't fair, Hazel," I grit out.

"Yeah, I don't give a shit."

"Kate! Hazel!" Our manager storms toward us. "What the hell is going on?"

"Nothing," we utter in unison, despite the fissure in my chest and how much it feels like I'm being ripped in two.

"Damn right, it's nothing." Anna turns to me. "Now get your shit in the breakroom. Your shift started ten minutes ago."

"Yes, ma'am."

I turn on my heel and walk away.

4 2
KATE

"Hey-o!" Blakely greets me. Her face is painted LAU's red and black colors, and her curly red hair is pulled on top of her head in a messy bun as she pushes the back door of Ash's car open. I climb inside.

Anna was on my ass all day, so I didn't dare pull out my phone during my shift, and I knew if I hid in the bathroom for a minute to myself, I'd probably burst into tears, so I stayed distracted instead. It didn't help. I feel awful, and I miss Mack more than anything else in the world.

Exhaustion curdles in my stomach as I pull out my phone and scan the messages from Mack, desperate to talk to him. To tell him what happened.

> **MACKLIN**
>
> I should've come inside. I feel guilty as shit for leaving you. I'm sorry.
>
> Hey. Everything okay?
>
> I'm stressing over here.
>
> Did you talk to her? What'd she say? Does she know?

Sorry. I know you're at work. I'll stop bugging you. Just stressed. I'm definitely thinking about you. Hope you're okay. Text me when you're off work.

Missing you like crazy, Kate.

My lips pull into a sad smile as I reread his last message. I don't text him back. Not yet. Because I don't know what to say anymore.

Part of me wants to go home, curl into a ball, and pretend today never happened, but I miss Mack too much to go through with it.

I miss him so much.

Ash glances at me in her rearview mirror, frowning. "You okay?"

"Fine. Exhausted," I clarify, tucking my phone back into my lap, "but fine."

"You sure?" she prods.

"Positive."

"Then, what's wrong?" Blake interjects beside me.

"Nothing," I lie.

"Kate," Ash warns.

Mia twists in the passenger seat, her eyes thinning. "Seriously. Tell us."

The window feels cold as I rest my forehead against it and let out a sigh, desperate to relieve a bit of the pressure in my chest that took up residence as soon as Hazel opened her mouth this morning. The old Kate would've stayed quiet. And I'm tired of staying quiet.

"Mack's daughter works at Butter and Grace with me and found out I'm dating him." The words feel good to say. Cathartic somehow. No matter how unbelievable it feels.

Mia gasps as Ash turns on her blinker. "Yikes."

"It's not even the worst part," I tell them. "I don't know

how much you've heard about Mack and his relationship with his daughters, but *rocky* would be an understatement. During today's shift, Hazel informed me if I want her to have a relationship with her dad, *I* need to have zero relationship with her dad."

Blake's jaw drops. "Are you shitting me?"

Pinching the bridge of my nose, I close my eyes and search for a modicum of serenity when all I want to do is cry and maybe hit something. The combination isn't exactly making me feel very Zen.

"What did you tell her?" Ash questions when I've been silent too long.

"I told her I'm not going to break up with her dad just because she wants me to."

"Good," Blakely announces. "We don't negotiate with terrorists."

I laugh, but it doesn't make me feel much better. Actually, I kind of still want to cry. A lot. Especially when I can feel my stupid head getting dizzy and heavy and...I feel like I'm over-stimulated. Stress is a trigger, and I'm fucking stressed out of my mind.

Breathe, I remind myself as Mia inquires, "What did Mack say?"

"I haven't talked to him about it yet," I answer.

"Are you going to tell him?"

"Of course," I mutter. "But I don't know if he'll be proud or pissed at me for standing up for myself."

"Why would he be pissed?" Mia quizzes me.

"I mean, Hazel's his daughter. And he was so great with my family, and now I'm causing a rift between him and his child, and––"

"You didn't cause the rift, Kate," Blake argues. "It was already there."

With a one-shouldered shrug, I rest my head against the window and close my eyes. "Yeah, but I made it worse."

"We're here for you," Ash reminds me, turning into the arena.

And they are. I know they are. Even when I'm a recluse. Even when I push them away. They've been the best friends a girl could ask for, and I refuse to ever take them for granted again.

"Thanks, guys. For putting up with me like you do."

"Trust us,"--Blake nudges her shoulder against mine--"it isn't exactly a chore. And trust Mack too. He loves you. I can see it."

"So can I," Ash adds.

"Me too," Mia chimes in. "Not gonna lie. It makes me jealous as hell."

"Ah, don't worry, Mia." Ash grins at her best friend. "We'll find you someone."

"Someone who isn't an ass and doesn't air my dirty laundry to everyone on the internet?" She rolls her eyes. "Yeah. Good luck."

ONCE ASH FINDS A PARKING SPOT, WE HEAD INTO THE ARENA. The place is busy, like always, as we make our way to our seats. Students are packed into the student section, while the other fans are scattered around the rest of the oval, munching on hotdogs and popcorn while juggling posters with different teammates' names scrawled across them.

My attention catches on a poster with Colt's jersey number and the words, *Can I have your babies?* written in bold, black sharpie. I glance at Ash, my stomach knotting for her. She's staring at the poster, too, her expression unreadable.

327

"You okay?" I ask.

"At least that one's pretty tame." She tears her attention from the poster and sits down on one of the plastic seats. "Blah. Dating a famous hockey player is kind of the worst. Not gonna lie."

"It's a good thing Colt loves you," I remind her.

"Yup. And don't get me wrong. I trust him," she clarifies, "but it doesn't always make those"––she waves her hand toward the gaggle of half-dressed girls, Colt's number painted on their cheeks as they raise their posters high in the air––"situations any easier to swallow."

"I'm sorry."

"You're lucky Macklin isn't famous, Kate." Ash tucks her long blonde hair behind her ear, sitting beside Mia and Blake.

She's right. At least when it comes to that particular aspect. The idea of women ogling the love of my life behind my back sounds pretty terrible. Doing it in front of me? Yeah,…even worse, especially with Ashlyn's history. Before Colt, she dated Logan, another hockey player. Except he was an ass. Because he cheated on her all the time with puck bunnies, and she had no idea. Honestly, none of us did. And the fact Ash was willing to open up her heart again––to a hockey player who literally has a section of women in the stands who would love to hook up with him no less––proves how much she loves the guy.

I settle into my seat and watch as the announcer's voice crackles through the speakers. One by one, the players head onto the ice. Theo and Colt search the stands as they line up next to their teammates. Colt spots us and leans closer to Theo, saying something to him. Their expressions light up almost instantly, and they wave. Cupping her hands over her mouth, Blake shouts Theo's name while Ash waves her hand back and forth shyly, not wanting to cause a scene.

The girl's always been a wallflower. I can only imagine what it's like to date someone like Colt, who was born to be in the limelight. It must be hard. Damn near impossible some days.

I look at Ash again.

I guess everyone has their shit, don't they?

43

KATE

Mia left during the second period, borrowing Ash's car to drive to work since Ash said she'd catch a ride with Colt after the game. LAU wins four to one. Colt and Theo both killed it, and even I can feel the victory buzzing through the air as the crowd heads to the parking lot.

Blake and Ash are heading down to the back area where their boys promised to meet them after they shower, and I follow behind. Unsure where to go or what to do. Thankfully, no one was injured during the game, so I assume I'll catch a ride with Mack as we'd discussed, but I haven't messaged him yet. I still don't know what to say. Because he's going to ask questions. He's going to want to know about my conversation with Hazel. And when I inevitably spill the beans...what then?

I dig my teeth into my cheek as another wave of anxiety barrels through me.

What am I going to do?

What is he going to say?

My phone rings, and I dig it out of my back pocket, Mack's name flashing on the screeen.

"Hey," I answer.

"Hey, where are you?"

"Walking with Ash and Blake––"

"I see you," he interrupts.

The crowd trickles out of the exits, revealing a very sexy Mack heading toward us.

His hair is pushed away from his face, and his icy blue eyes feel like a homing beacon as he strides toward me.

"Hey, Mack!" Blake greets him.

"Hey, Blake. Hey, Ash." His gaze finds mine again. "Hey, Kate."

I force a smile and pull my long sleeves into my sweaty palms. "Hi."

Blake laughs, unperturbed by Mack's lack of manners, and hooks her arm through Ash's. "Aaaand, we're gonna go find our boys. See you guys later!"

"Bye," Mack calls. He doesn't bother watching them leave. He's too busy looking at me.

Li'l ol' me.

I fold my arms, still unsure what to say or how to bring up Hazel's ultimatum or if I even should.

"How was work?" he asks.

"Good," I lie. "You?"

"Good. No injuries. Felix offered to drive the ambulance back to the hospital since I met him here so I could have my car after the game. Thankfully, Remi wanted to hang out with him even though she wasn't on call, so it worked out."

"Convenient," I note.

"Yeah." He hooks his arm around my neck and starts walking me toward the exit. "Now, I can spend the rest of my night with you. How was Hazel?" A hint of reservation seeps into his innocent question, and my steps falter. It's like he already knows something happened. Like he knows why I didn't answer his texts despite the fact I've been off work for hours now. Like he knows his daughter is the cause of my silence.

And she is.

"Should we wait 'til we get home?" I hedge, staring down at my sneakers against the concrete arena floor.

"Pretty sure I'm gonna go crazy if I have to wait another minute." He guides me toward the nearest wall and pins me with his stare. It's quieter now. Most of the fans have already left. Only a few stragglers are scattered throughout the area, leaving the space almost cold and empty.

"So, she knew it was you?" he concludes, reading my silence loud and clear.

I nod.

"And?"

"And she gave me an ultimatum." I peek up at him. "Gave *us* an ultimatum."

His frown deepens. "What kind of ultimatum, Kate?"

I don't want to do this. I don't want to say this. Even voicing the words aloud feels like it'll give them power. And I don't want to give them power.

I shake my head, my vision blurring.

"Tell me," he demands.

"She says if I break up with you, she'll try to have a relationship with you again."

He pauses, battling confusion, indecision, and frustration the same way I have for hours.

"And if you don't?" he asks.

"Then, that's it." I look up at him again. "She won't have a relationship with you."

A whoosh of air leaves his lungs, the severity of the situation hitting full force. He doesn't say anything. Just lets the ultimatum hang in the air. Tainting it. Tainting *us*. And I hate it. I hate it more than anything. The space between us grows as he takes a step back, runs his hands over his face, and rests them on the crown of his head, his fingers woven together, his expression looking nothing less than helpless.

"What did you tell her?" His voice is hollow. Empty.

"I told her I couldn't do it."

His eyes widen as he drops his hands to his sides. "*What?*"

"I mean, I can't do that, right?" I confirm, finally gathering enough courage to look him in the eye.

"She's my daughter, Kate."

"I know," I whisper. "I know she is. And I know you love her more than anything. More than me. More than Theo. But if she wanted a relationship with you, she would've been cultivating it before she found out about us, right?"

A curse slips past his lips as Mack's chin drops to his chest. Because he knows I make a good point. He knows Hazel is far from innocent in this entire situation. But he also knows it doesn't matter whether or not she's innocent because he's her father. And dads? They're supposed to be there for their kids and do anything for them––no matter what.

But at what cost?

Shoving aside the tiny voice in my head telling me to walk away, to make this easier for him, I step closer to Mack and repeat, "Mack, if she wanted a relationship with you, she would've been cultivating it before she found out about us. *Right?*"

"Yeah, but…" His voice trails off, leaving a crack in my chest the size of the Grand Canyon.

But.

He said but.

"She's my daughter," he argues, looking more broken than I've ever witnessed. "I'm her father. I'd do anything for her. I have to be willing to do anything for her."

"And I get it," I breathe out. The bite from my nails making tiny crescent shapes in my palms grounds me as I fist my hands at my sides. "I do. I get that I should walk away and leave you alone. I should make this decision easier for you. I should bow out and say it's okay. She deserves your love more than I ever could. But here's the thing, Mack." I wipe at my cheeks, finding them damp. "I don't want to."

His eyes are bloodshot as he looks up at me again. Tortured. Broken. Defeated.

"I don't want you to either, Kate. Trust me. I don't want it at all. The past couple of months? They've been...fuck, Kate. They've meant everything to me. But what choice do I have? She's my daughter."

"Your daughter who has had every opportunity to reach out to you, yet she hasn't."

The words slice through the last of his defenses, and he hangs his head. "Let me think for a minute. Let me find a solution."

A solution. I'd laugh if I wasn't so close to having a full-blown breakdown right here. Right now. Doesn't he get it? She's pushing him into a corner, leveraging their relationship to get what she wants. She won't back down from it. Not if she realizes how much power she has over him. And if he breaks up with me? It won't fix anything. It won't mend their relationship. He has to see it.

Doesn't he?

"There isn't a solution," I choke out. "Not one that lets you have your cake and eat it too."

He shakes his head, determined to keep the truth from sinking into his stubborn bones. "Let me think." He paces slowly. Back and forth. Back and forth. "Maybe we can keep this under the radar for a bit. Only for a little while. Until I can talk to her. Until she can see I'm not the guy her mother painted me to be. We'll keep our relationship under wraps for a little while. It'll be fine."

"You know what's crazy, Mack?" My tears clog my throat, and he stops pacing, standing in front of me. "I was broken before we met. So fucking broken. If Hazel would've approached me then, I would've walked away. I wouldn't have even tried fighting for you because I didn't think I was worth it."

I reach up and touch the side of his face, refusing to acknowledge it might be the last time I'm allowed to do so. His five o'clock shadow tickles my fingertips, and I almost smile. "But we met, and you showed me I'm worth it. I'm worth the effort. I'm worth the inconveniences. You put me back together, Mack." My voice cracks on a sob, and I wipe at my tears. "You put me back together, and yet, here I am, asking you––*begging you*––to pick me. Even when it's inconvenient. Even when it isn't fair. Because I'm worth it. Because you love me. Because I'm not broken. And I *know* it isn't fair," I repeat. "But this isn't on me. It's on Hazel. She shouldn't have the power to decide who you do or don't date. She's a fucking adult, Macklin. An adult who's still listening to her stupid mom, letting her warp Hazel's perspective of you and now me. I'm begging you, Mack. Please don't let her do this to you. Don't let her come between us. Don't let her ruin what we have. Don't give me up. Don't break me. Please. Please don't break me." I'm rambling. I know I am, but I can't stop. I can't stop pleading my case. I can't stop begging him to see things from my point of view. Because if I do, I'm terrified I'll lose him. I'm terrified I'll lose the potential future we could've had together. The future I know we would've had together if given a chance.

"I'm not asking you to choose," I continue. "I'm asking you to stand up to her. To stand up to your ex, who we both know is pulling the strings. I'm asking you to set boundaries and stand up for what you want. Because I know you want me. I know you could maybe even love me one day. And do you want to know how I know it, Mack?"

He squeezes his eyes shut but rasps, "How?"

"Because you've shown me I'm lovable. And I know you love your daughters, and I know you deserve to have a relationship with them. I *want* you to have a relationship with them, Mack. More than anything, I do, but this isn't fair. You can't let them control you. You *can't*."

My chest heaves with a sob, but I choke it back and stare at the ceiling as a stream of tears cascades down my cheeks and drips off my chin. There's no point wiping them away. They'll only be replaced with more. And there's no point hiding how broken I feel, either. Not now. Not anymore. Because if I've learned anything from my relationship with Mack, it's that I'm allowed to feel. I'm allowed to be vulnerable. I'm allowed to fight for what I want instead of taking it on the chin and slinking back to my own cave of loneliness I've been shrouded in since my initial diagnosis.

"You're killing me, Kate." He watches the tears fall down my face, but he doesn't reach out and wipe them away. He doesn't tell me everything's going to be okay. He simply watches me. My pain. My fears. As if his hands are tied when they aren't. Why can't he see it?

I laugh dryly and shake my head, wiping beneath my nose with the back of my hand. "Ditto."

Tortured, he paces back and forth again like he's too amped up to stand still. His hand runs over his face, then pinches the bridge of his nose.

Clearly, I'm not the only one close to breaking, but the situation isn't exactly in my favor, either.

"I don't want to choose," he grits out. "You can't ask me to choose."

"They're the ones asking you to choose!" I yell. The last of my restraint finally snaps as I wave my hand through the air. "I don't want you to pick. You shouldn't have to pick."

"But I do!" he returns. "They've left me no choice!"

"There's always a choice, Mack. Stand up for yourself. Stand up for me. Don't let them push you around. Set boundaries. Tell them you love me. You're an adult, Mack. You're allowed to be happy. You're allowed to have a relationship with your daughters *and* your girlfriend. What they're doing? It isn't fair."

"You think I don't know how unfair this is?" he snaps. "You think I'm not dying inside at the idea of losing you?"

"You don't have to, though."

"At what expense, Kate?" he rasps. His head hangs low, and his shoulders hunch. "At what expense?"

"I don't know, Mack." I inch closer to him, my fingers brushing against the zipper on his coat. I want to touch him. I want to hold him. I want to cry on his shoulder and feel his arms around me. Sliding my hands higher, I place my hand on his heart, the unsteady *thump-thump* matching my own.

"But it shouldn't be at your expense, and it sure as hell shouldn't be at mine." I drop my hand and release a slow, shuddered breath. "Let me know what you decide. I'll respect your decision, whatever it is. I promise."

"Wait." He grabs my wrist, holding me in place.

"I'm not going to hide our relationship." I gently tug myself from his grasp. "I deserve more than that. And so do you."

I walk away and pull out my phone, praying Ash or Blake is still here so I can catch a ride with one of them. If not, I'll walk if I have to, but there's no way I'm turning around and walking back to Mack.

If I do, I'll cave.

And I'm stronger than that.

Aren't I?

44

KATE

I left my medicine at his house. The realization feels like the cherry on top of a thoroughly craptastic day, but I don't have the energy to call him. Not after walking away at the rink.

Besides, what good will it do? It's not like I can ask someone to swing by his place and grab it for me, especially when no one's available anyway. And the idea of Macklin making a special trip down the mountain to drop it off feels like salt in my wounds with everything happening between us.

After our fight at the rink, I'm not ready to see him again. Not yet. Not until he's had time to make a decision.

I hate how a small part of me already knows what he's going to say. Who he's going to choose. I hate how I can't blame him for picking his daughters over me. I hate how I'd almost be disappointed if he surprised me by choosing me instead of them. Because I know him. I know how much he loves his daughters. And I know it would bite us both in the butt down the road. Maybe not tomorrow or even a month or a year from now. But in the long run? He'd resent me. Hell, *I'd* resent myself.

What I hate the most is how much I miss him. It's only been a few hours, but I can't help it. I do. I miss the way he knew how to get me out of my own head. I miss the way he'd hold me and kiss my forehead. I miss how he made me feel sexy and desirable yet never made me feel like I was an object or a thing to be used.

I miss the way he knew how to push me without pissing me off. Okay, scratch that. He pissed me off on multiple occasions, but he did it in a way that almost made me like him more for it. Which is insane. I also miss the way he made me feel important. Special. The way he managed to put all of the broken pieces back together that had fallen apart after my diagnosis. The way he slipped past my defenses and made me feel accepted.

I puff out my cheeks and shove aside the thought, bottling up my emotions like *before*. Before we met. Before I fell for him. Before I thought I was worthy of feeling *anything*, afraid it would inconvenience someone.

Then again, I guess it has, so...

Mack was supposed to pick me up from work tomorrow. Since that most likely isn't happening after today's events, I need a ride. Sometimes, I hate being responsible. Sometimes, I hate caring. If I was smart, I'd call in sick, having already learned my lesson from earlier today. But nope. Instead, I have to care about Anna and the other waitresses who would have to step up if I was a no-show. I can't do it. It isn't fair to them.

However, finding a ride for tomorrow's shift when it's two in the morning isn't exactly an easy feat. Ash is sleeping at Colt's place, and Blake and Theo are tucked inside her bedroom. Mia's door is half open, the glow from her bedroom light seeping into the hallway.

I tiptoe closer and tap my knuckles against the hard wooden surface. "Hey."

Mia's head snaps up, and she tucks her phone under her thigh as if she's been caught doing something she shouldn't. "Oh." Her expression fills with relief. "Hey."

"Hey," I repeat.

With an awkward smile, she asks, "What's up?"

"I was wondering if you're busy tomorrow afternoon?"

"Um…" Her phone dings with a message, and she flinches but doesn't answer it. "What time?"

"Four or so?"

"My shift doesn't start until seven, so nope. Not busy." She shifts slightly on the mattress, almost uncomfortable, though I can't figure out why. Seriously, the girl's acting weird. Shifty. On edge.

Suspicion flares in my gut. "Everything okay?"

"Yup. Why are you asking about my schedule?"

"Blake's taking me, but I kind of need a ride home from work."

"Oh. Sure thing." She waves me off. "I can pick you up before my shift."

I breathe out a sigh of relief. "Perfect. Thanks. Also…"

"Yes?"

"Any chance you'd be willing to swing by Mack's place afterward with me? It's about a thirty-minute drive."

"Yeah, no problem," she replies, glancing down at her lap, distracted.

"Perfect. Thanks. And Mia?"

She looks up at me again. "Yeah?"

"You sure you're okay?"

With a shrug, she gives in and explains, "Somehow, an OnlyFans supporter found my phone number and is sending me dick pics, so I was blocking him when you walked in. It's why my phone won't stop ringing."

"Yikes. Can I help?"

"Nah. I'll figure it out." She grabs her phone and silences another call. "It's late, and I had a long shift tonight, so I should probably get some rest."

"Me too," I mutter, running my hands up and down my bare arms.

"I'll see you tomorrow at four."

"Okay. Thanks again."

"No problem."

                          ∽

HAZEL'S JETTA IS IN THE PARKING LOT. I DON'T KNOW WHY I'M surprised, but I am. When Blake catches me staring, she asks, "You okay?"

"Yup. Thanks again for the ride."

"No problem."

I tug my jacket close around me and step out of Blake's car, walking into the restaurant. It smells like bacon and cinnamon, and I'm oddly comforted until Hazel comes into view.

She's staring at me.

Glaring at me.

Like she has a bone to pick with me.

Not today.

Keeping my head down, I walk around her and head to the breakroom, shoving my purse into my locker and tying a black apron around my waist. Once my nametag is pinned to my shirt, I head to my station but stop short.

You've got to be kidding me.

Rage, fear, and anxiety battle inside me, turning my stomach into a jumbled knot of regret as I turn on my heel and run smack-dab into Anna.

"Sorry," I mutter, staring at my white Nikes.

"Where are you going?"

"I was--"

She grabs my shoulders and twists me around. "Tables are over there. Hazel has already started placing customers in your section. Danny grabbed them some drinks for you, but her hands are already full with her tables, so chop-chop, Kate. It's gonna be a busy day."

I take a few steps toward my tables, then glance over my shoulder, confirming Anna has already found a new employee to terrorize. Satisfied, I beeline it toward Hazel and spit, "Tell me you're joking."

She quirks her brow. "Why would I be joking?"

"Why are your mom and little sister sitting in my section?"

"They wanted brunch. So sue me."

"And you decided me waiting on them was a good idea?"

"It's not my fault you thought it would be a good idea to date my dad."

"For the last time, I didn't know he was your dad when we started seeing each other," I seethe, my head pounding. "But even if I did, your father's a grown-ass adult, and so am I."

"Yeah, well, I guess you won't mind being a grown-ass adult who does her job." She flicks her fingers toward her mom and sister, who are waiting in a booth a few yards away. "You should probably get to it."

My teeth grind together, but I don't move a muscle as I try to find the words to fix this. Words to make Summer and her youngest daughter go away. Words to remove the chip clearly on Hazel's shoulder. Words to ease the haze in my vision and the tingling in my limbs.

Oh, shit. Not now.

I clench my hands and blink slowly, letting out a soft, slow breath in hopes of grounding myself.

"He chose you, ya know," I whisper, ignoring the way my legs feel weak and how fast my heart is racing. "So, if you could…let me work in peace…that'd be…"

It's coming. I can feel it.

Sometimes they hit out of nowhere. Other times, it builds. Mocking me. Torturing me. Prickling beneath my skin. Like a weird, agonizing sixth sense.

I need to sit down.

My palm slaps against the hostess table as I try to steady myself, preparing for the inevitable when everything goes black.

45

MACKLIN

After Kate walked away from me at the arena last night, I'd confirmed with Theo that she'd caught a ride home with him and Blake, and I drove to my house--alone.

After sending my nightly text to Miley and Hazel, I turned off my cell and climbed into bed. I slept like shit. I'm not surprised. My sheets smell like her, and it's messing with my head.

I take another whiff of the pillow, Kate's scent clinging to it. Turning onto my back, I stare up at the wood beams strewn across my ceiling.

I should've slept on the couch. Maybe I would've been able to get my head out of my ass for two minutes, though I doubt it.

After a hot shower, I tug on some clothes, shove my phone into my back pocket, and head to the kitchen in search of coffee. I pause when a little orange bottle sitting on the counter grabs my attention.

Kate's medicine.

She must've left it yesterday morning since we'd been

planning on her staying the night after the game. This means she didn't take it before bed or this morning. Unless she has some more stashed at her house. It's possible. My molars grind together, the little orange bottle taunting me for another thirty seconds. I pull out my phone and turn it back on. Like always, Miley's response is scrawled across the screen, wishing me goodnight. Only this time, there's a second message.

From Hazel.

HAZEL

Goodnight, Dad.

I close my eyes, unable to appreciate the momentous text. Because it's corrupted. Ruined by her selfishness.

I screwed up last night. Kate was right. I shouldn't have had to choose. It was an impossible situation Hazel assumed she could put me in without repercussions. I shouldn't have given her so much power. Not because I don't love her, but rather because I do.

The plastic is slightly cool against my palm as I grab the bottle from the counter and dial Kate's number. The call goes straight to voicemail. Checking the time, I try again. When it immediately goes to voicemail again, I pull up Blake's contact info.

She answers on the first ring. "Hey, Jerkface."

"Hey."

"I shouldn't be talking to you."

"Why not?"

"Because you're a jerkface," she tells me. "Don't get me wrong. I still love you and all since you're going to be my brother-in-law at some point, but––"

Someone cuts her off on the other end, and her voice muffles. "Oh, shush. You know you love me and are going to put a ring on it one day, so don't even bother arguing,

Teddy." Then she talks into the speaker again, addressing me. "But I'm still mad at you, Macklin."

"Yeah, I'm pissed at me too," I mutter. "Any chance you're going to the gym with Kate this morning?"

"Nope. Already dropped her off at Butter and Grace. She has the early shift. You know how brunch is. Hell, maybe she'll run into Summer, who will ruin her life even more," she quips. "Seems Hazel's already doing a bang-up job--"

A low voice rumbles in the background, and I swear I can hear Blake making a face. "Okay, okay. I'm being unfair. I'll stop. But to answer your question. No. I'm not going to the gym with Kate this morning. I dropped her off at the restaurant a half hour ago, and Mia's supposed to pick her up at four. Any more questions, Jerkface?"

"Maybe stop calling me jerkface?"

She snorts. "Yeah. Not until you make it up to Kate. And P.S., Theo says hi."

"No, I didn't!" he yells. "You made Kate cry--"

"Bye," Blake interrupts.

The call ends, and I drop my hand to my side.

I made her cry.

The words roll around in my head, over and over, gaining momentum as an image of Kate and her tear-stained cheeks from last night rises to the surface.

I fucked up.

And she's right.

Fuck, she's right.

I can't let Hazel manipulate me like this. I can't let her hold our relationship hostage. I can't let her mom twist her perception of me or how I feel about Kate. I've done nothing wrong. *We've* done nothing wrong.

And I'm not choosing Kate over Hazel. I love my daughters. I love them more than anything. But it's *my* life. And despite wanting them to be a part of it, I refuse to let them hold this over my head. I can't.

If I do, I'll lose Kate.

I can't lose Kate.

With my keys in one hand and her meds in the other, I push the garage door open and head to my car.

IT'S SNOWING NOW. THE TINY FLAKES FLOAT DOWN FROM THE cloudy sky, dusting the winding road in white. As I reach the base of the mountain, my phone lights up with Hazel's name. She's calling.

Curious, I slide my thumb across the screen. "Hello?"

"Dad! Dad, it's Kate!"

"What's going on?"

"I was wrong, okay? I screwed up, and I was wrong, and Kate, she's…" A sob slips through the speaker, and I press my foot harder on the gas pedal.

Something's wrong.

"What's going on with Kate?" I demand.

"She's…she's shaking, Dad. We're at work, and I was a bitch, and I invited Mom, and––"

"Don't touch her," I order.

"But Dad, the blood…" Her voice is nothing but a squeak, and I know she's looking at it. Staring. Unable to turn away from it or focus on our conversation. Too lost in the sight in front of her and what it means.

My heart nearly stops. "What blood?"

"It's everywhere. We were talking, and she just…fell," Hazel chokes out. "She hit her head on the hostess stand, and s-she…she's bleeding and jerking around, and her eyes are rolled back, and, and…" Hazel sobs a little harder. The girl's going into shock. I've seen it a hundred times while on the job. The way their skin turns pale and clammy. The way their pulse increases and their breathing turns rapid and uneven. Fuck, I can almost see it now, the vision blurring the road and making it hard to focus. But there isn't anything I can do to help her. To calm her down so she can help Kate.

Fuck.

Kate.

"How much blood, Hazel?" I demand.

"A-a lot. There's a lot."

"Did someone call an ambulance?"

"Y-yes." She hiccups. "Our manager called."

"What'd they say?"

"I don't...I don't know."

"Breathe," I order, though I'm not sure who I'm telling at this point. The veins bulge in the back of my hands as I throttle the steering wheel, check my blind spot, and change lanes. I drive around the person in front of me and swerve into oncoming traffic so I can get to the restaurant faster. So I can get to Kate faster.

"Dad, I'm freaking out!"

"It's gonna be okay, Haze," I promise her, knowing it's a bald-faced lie. Because I don't know if it's going to be okay. I don't know if Kate's going to be okay. I've seen enough shit on the job to know nothing is guaranteed, and life is far from fair.

"I'll be there in two." I end the call and take a sharp right turn, cutting off a minivan without giving a shit. My tires squeal in protest, but I push the gas pedal harder.

In ninety seconds flat, I pull into the parking lot and shove my car into park next to the curb. An ambulance is already there. Felix and Remi are rushing out of the rig, armed and ready for whatever they find inside. Regret pools in my gut as I follow them through the main entrance.

The metallic scent of blood causes my stomach to churn

when Kate comes into view. She's on the ground, convulsing. Her limbs are flailing, her muscles are tightened like rubber bands stretched too tight, and the whites of her eyes are on full display. A pool of blood surrounds her, and I stop short. Remi is on her knees beside her in an instant, pressing her gloved hand to Kate's head as Felix appears with a thick bandage.

And for the first time ever, I freeze. I can't move. I can't help. I've never battled being unable to act under pressure. Yet seeing someone you love––someone you can't lose–– struggling, it hits differently. Like my world is being ripped away, and there isn't a single fucking thing I can do about it. Her shirt is drenched in blood, her black apron is damp with urine, and her legs are splayed out in front of her.

In an instant, Kate stops shaking, and her head falls to one side. The seizure's over. But the repercussions? The embarrassment? The shame? It's there. It's all fucking there in front of me. And I'd do anything to fix it.

Ripping off my jacket, I throw it over her lower half to cover her soiled jeans, then collapse onto my knees, cupping the back of my head with my hands. Felix takes Kate's vitals, and Remi tends to the wound on the side of her head.

Head wounds are bleeders. I know this. But it doesn't make me feel any better. Doesn't make me feel any less help-less. What if this one's worse? What if she isn't okay? What if it's too much?

Kate's bottom lip quivers as she opens her stormy gray eyes, wincing at the bright fluorescent lights. Relief, fear, anxiety, and every other fucking emotion in the book assaults me, one after the other, as I stare at her. Desperate to feel her, to make sure she's okay, I crawl toward her on my hands and knees. I touch her cheek and rub my thumb against it as Remi finishes wrapping the bandage around

349

Kate's head. She looks so lost. So broken. So damn vulnerable and small. It kills me.

"Talk to her," Remi murmurs. Her voice is quiet, but it's enough. Enough to snap me out of my daze. Enough to bring me back from the edge.

"Hey," I rasp.

Kate forces her eyelids open again, attempting to focus on her surroundings despite looking lost. "M-Mack?"

"Hey," I repeat, swallowing the lump in my throat.

Her wince wrecks me as her eyelids close again. "My head."

"I know, Kate. I know."

A single tear falls down her cheek and runs onto my thumb when she leans into my touch like she can't help herself.

"Everything hurts," she mumbles.

"Let's get her out of here," Felix orders.

He leaves, returning with the stretcher a few moments later, but it feels like a lifetime. I move aside, lost, as Remi and Felix load Kate onto it.

Once she's settled, Felix asks, "You comin'?"

I reach for her limp hand on the cotton sheets and squeeze softly. "Yeah. Let's go."

"Dad," a familiar voice calls.

I look up to find Hazel, Miley, and Summer staring back at me. I don't know how long they've been standing there. Watching me. Judging me for crying over Kate. For fucking breaking. But I don't care. Let them watch me break. Let them see how much I care about the girl they're determined to rip away from me.

They don't look pleased with themselves, though. The girls look...scared. And young. Younger than their years. Like the little girls I remember. The little girls who used to call me Daddy and would wrap their arms around my neck, begging for a piggyback ride or an extra story at bedtime. They look like the little girls who trusted their parents to protect them. To keep them safe. And here they are, huddled against their mother's side. Watching me.

"If I call you later, will you answer?" I ask Miley.

Without hesitation, she tells me, "Yeah. Go. Be with her."

"And you?" I demand, holding Hazel's gaze.

She bites her bottom lip, her blue eyes glassy with unshed tears as she nods. "Yeah, Dad. I'll answer."

"Good."

Without another word, I walk beside the stretcher, holding Kate's limp hand as I follow Felix and Remi back to the rig and climb inside.

Kate's asleep. Or at least drowsy. She keeps fighting it. The need to give in and rest. Her eyelids flutter, and she shifts slightly on the stretcher, wincing when her head lolls too much to one side and puts pressure on her wound.

"Will she need stitches?" I ask Remi.

Remi nods. "Yeah, definitely."

"She was more awake last time."

"Every seizure's different."

Remi's right. I know this. Every seizure is different. Most wouldn't even warrant a ride in an ambulance. Not unless it lasted more than five minutes. But today, Kate hit her head. She injured herself. It's always possible with seizures, which is why she was willing to sacrifice her memory for the medication that prevents episodes like this. But it's my fault she missed two doses. My fault her shirt is covered in blood.

My fucking fault.

I squeeze Kate's hand again, taking in her trimmed fingernails and how dainty they look in my grasp.

"You okay?" Remi checks on me.

I sniff and lean back in my seat while refusing to let go of Kate's hand. "Yeah."

"You sure?"

"It's different," I mutter. "When it's someone you love."

With a sigh, she glances at Kate's prone position and nods. "It is."

The rest of the ride is silent as we make our way to the hospital and settle Kate into a room.

Remi was right. Kate needs twelve stitches. They also give her some pain meds for the splitting headache and sore muscles, along with a dressing gown since she'd soiled her clothes. I text Blake, asking her to bring Kate a clean pair of pants, and she promises to drop something off.

But the silence kills me.

Because I almost lost her today.

And I've never been more terrified in my entire life.

KATE

My body aches from head to toe, but my skull? Yeah. It takes the cake. The nurse told me I hit it on the hostess stand when I started convulsing. It makes sense, even if I have no memory of it.

Mack's here. In the hospital. He won't stop looking at me. I feel like I'm under a microscope, and I don't like it.

"Stop staring at me, please," I whisper, resting my throbbing head against the ice pack a nurse delivered earlier. The sheets feel itchy against my skin, but I'm too exhausted to care. I just want to go home.

"Kate," Mack starts.

"Did you call my parents?"

He shakes his head. "No."

"Why?"

"Didn't think you'd want them to worry."

"They're my parents," I remind him dryly. "A wise man once told me it's what they're supposed to do."

His mouth lifts in a ghost of a smile, but it looks forced as he pushes himself to his feet. "I'll be right back."

The familiar beeping from the machines keeps me

company. Mack returns a few minutes later. At least, I think it's a few minutes. For all I know, it could've been an hour or a year. Honestly, I have no idea. I pry my eyelids open and look at him.

"They're on their way," he tells me.

"Thanks." I close my eyes again. It's weird. Having Mack here after how we left things. The nurse told me he hasn't left my side since Butter and Grace. But even that's fuzzy. I have no idea why he was at the restaurant or why he decided to ride with me in the ambulance. I have no idea why he reached out to Blake and asked her to drop off a change of clothes at the hospital or why he's waiting for my parents to drive here so I won't be alone.

I also have no idea what he expects me to say or if he spoke with Hazel while I was busy seizing on the floor.

I've gathered he's spooked. Unlike the last time he saw me have a seizure.

It should piss me off, should make me feel guilty, but it doesn't. Right now, I'm too exhausted to care.

"I love you, Kate," he rasps from the edge of the hospital bed.

My lips part as I register his words, convinced I'm still lost in la-la land. "W-what did you say?"

"I said I love--"

"Stop." I fight the heaviness of my eyelids as I hold his gaze.

He pauses. "What?"

"Don't tell me. Not now. Not after today."

"But--"

"I scared you," I mumble. "That's all."

He reaches for my hand, tangles our fingers together, and brings them to his lips. The heat from his mouth warms me as he presses a kiss to each of them. "I loved you before the seizure, Kate."

He should know this isn't fair. The way he's kissing me and how much I need it. Especially after today. The way he's looking at me. Like he really does love me. It isn't fair.

"Mack," I breathe out his name. Exhausted. Emotional. Burnt out.

"Yeah, you scared me," he adds. "Because loving you is scary. You have the power to break me, Kate."

"Can we talk about this later? Please? When my brain doesn't feel like it was put through a blender? When I don't have to worry if you're only telling me these things because of…" I gulp and close my eyes, attempting to focus. "Because of what you saw."

"I'm not––"

"Please," I beg. "Please stop. Please…wait. *Please.*"

He stays quiet. Doesn't argue. Doesn't drive his point home. He just watches me. Rubbing his thumb back and forth against the back of my hand, the rhythmic touch soothing.

"Okay, my prickly porcupine," he decides. "I'll wait."

MY PARENTS' VOICES ECHO FROM THE HALL A LITTLE WHILE later. I have no idea how long it's been. Time still feels sporadic. I must've fallen asleep again.

I'm still too tired to care. Too tired to focus on anything except rest. After the day I've had, I need it.

"Tell Kate I'll call her tomorrow." Macklin's voice cuts through the thick haze in my brain, though I don't open my eyes.

"Sure thing," a deep voice returns.

Dad?

I fall back to sleep.

47
MACKLIN

After Kate was released from the hospital, she left with her parents, and I drove home alone. Again.

My phone vibrates as I sip a beer in front of the fireplace.

It feels strange being here without her. Like she was the heart of this place. But she was right for making me wait instead of spilling out all my feelings in the middle of her hospital room. It wasn't fair to her. And it sure as shit wasn't about her episode or how much it scared me.

I told her parents I'd pick her up at their place tomorrow, but I plan to text Kate to confirm she's okay with it too. The idea of seeing her again is the only thing giving me an ounce of peace when all I want to do is crawl out of my own skin.

I scrub my hand over my face, balancing the beer bottle on my lap as I pull out my phone.

There's a message from Hazel.

HAZEL
Hey. How's she doing?

I pull back, surprised by her question. It's been over

twelve hours since the incident. Part of me was sure she'd block my number. But this? Her concern? It's the last thing I expected.

Which means I'm an asshole.

I shove the thought aside and type my response.

> **ME**
> She's good. At her parents' tonight.

> **HAZEL**
> Good.

> **ME**
> You ready for that phone call yet?

> **HAZEL**
> Yes.

I press call.

The phone rings at least six times. Convinced Hazel has cold feet, I put my thumb over the end button when the ringing stops and is replaced with silence.

I pull my cell away from my ear and check to see whether or not the call disconnected. Sure enough, she's there.

"Haze?" I murmur.

Silence.

"Haze, you there?"

"Hi," she whispers.

"Hey. You okay?"

Silence.

"Haze?" I repeat.

"I'm so sorry, Dad."

Like a knife to the chest, I ignore the stab of pain, the sentiment hanging in the air. And I know she can feel it too. The regret. The distance. The time and how quickly it passed.

"Why are you sorry?" I rasp.

"I invited Mom. I was being a bitch and wanted to make Kate uncomfortable." She sniffles. "It's my fault––"

"What happened to Kate isn't your fault."

"Don't try to make me feel better. I was such a––"

"Kate has epilepsy. She'd left her meds at my place the day before, and I didn't notice until this morning. Even if you hadn't invited Mom to the restaurant, it's possible Kate would've *still* had a seizure."

"You don't know––" Hazel tries to argue.

"You're right. I don't know for sure, but my assumption has a hell of a lot more merit than yours. The medication keeps her from having episodes. Even though she only missed two doses, it makes sense that she was more likely to have an issue, especially when she's always been sensitive with her dosing. The doctors said the same thing at the ER."

Hazel's shallow, unsteady breaths filter out, but she doesn't argue with me. Not this time. Instead, she lets my words sink in, recognizing how little she knows about the woman I've been seeing, the woman she's hated since the moment she found out I was dating someone other than her mother.

I stay quiet, unsure of what to say, while fighting my disbelief over actually having a conversation with my oldest daughter. It's been two years. Two years of the cold shoulder. Two years of unanswered messages and brutal stonewalling.

I was blindsided when Hazel told Kate she'd be willing to give our relationship another try if I ended things with her. But I'm not going to end things with Kate. Even before the shitshow from this morning, I'd already made up my mind. So where does it leave me with Hazel? Does she know where I stand?

It's hard. Balancing respect and distance while still proving you care. After the divorce, I spent most of my nights tossing and turning, debating whether or not I should push Hazel. Whether or not I should push Miley. Whether or not they knew I loved them and would do anything for them. But was it enough? Was I enough? There was so much left unsaid, and I'm not sure if I'll ever have another opportunity to apologize for how things ended, no matter how much it hurts.

"I'm sorry, Hazel," I rasp. "I'm sorry it didn't work out between your mom and me. I'm sorry I moved out. I'm sorry for the yelling and the fights. I'm sorry you had to witness it. I'm sorry if you ever felt like your home wasn't a safe space. And I'm sorry I wasn't there afterward. I was trying to respect your wishes, but…" I lean my head against the back of the sofa, my body feeling drained and heavy. So damn heavy. "I'm sorry."

"I don't have work tomorrow," she whispers.

I lift my head and clear my throat. "Oh?"

"Yeah. You know, if you want to have breakfast or dinner or…"

An olive branch has never felt so sweet, and I let out another slow, controlled breath, terrified of spooking her like a baby deer.

"Yeah, Haze," I murmur. "I'd like that."

"Miley's gonna be there too," she says. "So, it's not like a big deal or anything."

I smile at the defensiveness in her voice. "Okay, Haze. Not a big deal. But I feel like I should clarify something…" My voice trails off, another wave of fear humming beneath my skin as the words catch in my throat.

"You're not going to break up with her, are you?"

"No. I'm not," I answer honestly. "Do you still want to meet somewhere?"

"Yeah," she returns. "Wherever's fine. Well, maybe not Rowdy's."

I chuckle. "Still have PTSD?"

Her light laugh washes over me. "Ew, don't make it weird, Dad."

Dad.

Pretty sure I'll never get over how sweet the word sounds.

"How 'bout Dotties?" I offer, mentioning the small diner we used to go to when she was little.

I swear I can hear the smile in her voice as she murmurs, "Okay. I'll tell Miley."

"Okay. I'll see you tomorrow. Meet at 9?"

"In the *morning*?" she nearly screeches.

"Uh, yeah?" I laugh. "Isn't that when most people eat breakfast?"

"Let's do eleven."

With a grin, I shake my head but let it go. "Okay. Eleven it is. Love you, Haze."

"You too."

The call ends.

48

MACKLIN

Breakfast is good. A little awkward here and there, but good. I find out Miley has a boyfriend named Court, and Hazel is busy with work and writing college applications. She wants to go to LAU and plans to pursue a degree in marketing or graphic design.

I toss my used napkin on the plate and settle back into the booth as I take in Hazel and Miley on the opposite side.

"He's doing it again," Miley chirps, glancing at Hazel.

"Yeah. Seriously, old man, you gotta stop looking at us like we're ghosts or something."

Not bothering to hide my amusement, I shake my head as I sit forward and rest my elbows on the table. "You'll have to cut me a little slack. It's been a while since I've seen you guys. Thanks again for inviting me today."

"Sure thing. I've been"––Miley gives Hazel another pointed look––"wanting to do this for a while now."

"All of us are different," I interject, defending my oldest. "And that's okay. I'm glad you guys waited until you were ready. I know this doesn't mean everything is good on all

361

fronts, but it feels like a step in the right direction to me. What do you guys think?"

With a grin, Miley lifts her glass of orange juice as if toasting me. "Definitely." She takes a sip of the tart liquid.

"Yeah," Hazel adds. But her tone is softer than her sister's. She reaches for her glass and mumbles, "Definitely," as she brings it to her lips.

Hazel's always been this way. More stubborn. More like her mother. I don't know if I'm expected to ask how Summer's doing or if it's a no-fly zone. I'm not sure it even matters at this point. I care about Summer. I'll always care about her. For giving me two beautiful daughters. For helping me become the man I am today. But the idea of keeping her in my past and cultivating relationships with my daughters outside of their mother is appealing as shit.

Miley adds, "You'll have to bring Kate next time. I'd love to officially meet her."

My eyes widen in surprise. "You sure?"

"Yeah, of course. Right, Haze?" Miley bumps her shoulder against Hazel's.

"Definitely," Hazel repeats, though it's as unsure as earlier.

"Letting me in doesn't mean you have to let Kate in. Not in the beginning. You know that, right?" I confirm.

Hazel closes her eyes, looking like she's seconds from crying.

"It's not that," Miley interjects. "Seriously."

"Miley's right," Hazel explains. "It's not that I don't like her or whatever. I'm...embarrassed."

"Don't be embarrassed," I start, but Hazel cuts me off.

"Stop."

My mouth snaps closed.

"It's, well,...you know Mom," Miley adds. "She isn't afraid to tell everyone her opinion about anything, and when she

362

heard you were dating again, let alone someone a little... younger than her, she kind of freaked out, and..."

With her gaze glued to her lap, Hazel mutters, "And I guess it rubbed off on me." She gulps and looks up at me again. "Does she hate me?"

"Kate?" I question.

Hazel nods.

"I'm sure she doesn't."

"Did I ruin everything between you two?" she questions me.

"Not at all, Haze."

"Are you lying to make me feel better?"

I chuckle, but it doesn't stop the sharp twinge of pain between my ribs. Because the truth is, I have no idea where I stand with Kate. I have no idea if she's pissed at me or if she'll forgive me. I have no idea if she even wants to give me another chance or if I've lost her forever. I don't know a lot of things right now, but I do know Hazel doesn't deserve to carry this kind of regret on her shoulders. It isn't fair.

Reaching across the table, I touch Hazel's hand and squeeze it softly. "My relationship with Kate is independent of yours, Haze." I glance at Miley. "Yours too. Even if it doesn't work out between us, it won't be your fault. Understood?"

Miley nods, and Hazel joins in.

"Good," I tell them.

"Does this mean you two aren't okay?" Miley asks.

"You think I'm gonna let her go so easily?" I pull a few twenties from my wallet and toss them onto the table. "I'm gonna see her later today."

"Good," Miley decides. "Because you deserve to be happy, Dad."

"You really do," Hazel adds. The sincerity in her eyes makes me pause. Because they have no idea how much I needed to hear them say it. To see them sitting across the table from me. To have their support, even when I probably don't deserve it.

"Thanks, girls."

"The question is," Miley muses, "what are you going to do to win her back?"

KATE

MACKLIN

I want to see you today. Can I stop by?

I just finished breakfast. What time works for you?

Come on, my prickly porcupine. Please don't shut me out.

The messages blur together as I stare at them, allowing the screen to go black under my thumbs. I miss him.

A lot, actually.

And I know we need to talk.

But I'm scared. Scared my episode spooked him. Scared I imagined his declaration of love or his reason behind it. Scared he changed his mind and is going to tell me I'm not worth it. Not worth the effort or the anxiety or the fear that comes with loving someone like me. Scared I reminded him how hard it can be to love someone with a chronic disease. And combining it with his own shitty baggage? It doesn't matter how manly his muscles are. I'm not sure he's interested in carrying all of the weight. Not anymore.

My phone buzzes again.

MACKLIN

Kate.

Missing you like crazy.

I know you're awake.

Kate.

Kate.

Kate.

Kate.

I'm gonna keep texting you until you respond, so I hope you're ready for a thousand messages.

Even if it gives me carpal tunnel.

Kate.

Katey Kat.

Katey Cutie Kitty Kat.

What did the Macklin say to the Kate?

I wanna kiss the shit out of you.

Okay, it's not my best joke, but I've been a bit preoccupied worrying about you.

If I bring a present, will you answer my texts?

And trust me. It's a good one. Might even be worth a kidney on the black market.

Am I bugging you yet?

Tell me to stop texting.

> Because if you don't, I'm not gonna stop.

> Please let me come see you.

> Let me hold you.

> I can bring you back to my place, and we can make another fort.

> Please?

> Don't you dare make me say the "L" word via text, my prickly porcupine.

> Because I'll do it.

> You know I will.

With a light laugh, I sit on the edge of my childhood bed and push the call button, finally giving in to the insanity. It barely rings once before Macklin answers.

"You sick of my texts yet, Porcupine?" his low, silky voice asks in lieu of a greeting.

"Thought I'd give your thumbs a break. Wouldn't want you to get arthritis for another year or so. Ya know, since you're so old and all."

"I said carpal tunnel, not arthritis," he grumbles.

"Toe-may-toe, toe-mah-toe."

"Ah, so the porcupine's feeling prickly today. Noted."

I smile and fall back onto the bed, staring at the ceiling. "And someone's feeling particularly needy."

"So damn needy," he agrees.

"I'm surprised you didn't just show up on my parents' doorstep."

"I was gonna give you until five to respond to my texts. Then I was driving over no matter what."

I laugh a little harder, turning onto my stomach and kicking my feet into the air, careful of my stitches. "I'm seriously fine, Mack."

"You think this is about you, Kate? You're fucking perfect, and you would be with or without me. *I'm* the mess when we aren't together," he argues. "Not you."

"Mack," I whisper.

"Is your head clear enough for us to talk today? 'Cause I told you I don't play games, and I'm not about to start now."

The determination in his voice makes my mouth twitch as I close my eyes, savoring it. What it's like to have Mack want me. Fight for me. Even though he's owned me for months.

"Okay, Mack," I murmur. "You win. You can come over."

"Can I pick up food for you and your parents? If I leave now, I'll get there around dinnertime."

"You don't need to feed my parents––"

"Do they like Indian food? Or should I bring a pizza? What toppings do they like?"

"Seriously, Mack."

"I'll pick a few options," he decides.

"You don't have to––"

"See you in a bit."

Then, he hangs up the phone.

ONE HOUR AND FIFTEEN MINUTES LATER, A LOUD KNOCK echoes from the main floor. Heavy footsteps make their way from the family room to the front door as I slowly walk down the stairs. Dad's already there, opening the door and revealing a slightly disheveled Macklin. His hair is a mess as he runs his fingers through it while balancing three pizzas in his opposite hand. Still handsome. Still swoony.

"Mr. Winchester," Macklin greets my dad, dipping his chin.

"Hey, Macklin. Good to see you again. Come on in." Dad opens the door the rest of the way, and Mack steps inside, offering him the pizzas.

"I wasn't sure what you liked on your pizza, so I bought one meat lover's, one vegetarian, and one pepperoni. Debated on Hawaiian, too, but––"

"Pineapple doesn't belong on pizza," my dad agrees as he takes the boxes. "Let me grab Kate."

"I'm here," I announce.

My father's head snaps behind him, finding me on the staircase. He lifts the boxes to showcase Mack's offerings. "He brought pizza."

"I heard," I reply with a smile.

"Guess I'll…" Dad hooks his thumb over his shoulder toward the family room. "Lily!"

Before my mom has a chance to bombard Mack, I speak up again. "Come on, Mack. Let's chat in my room."

The stairs creak underneath Mack's feet as he walks up the stairs, a sense of foreboding swirling in the air with every step. Because this is the moment. The moment when he decides if my illness is too much. If I'm too much.

Once we're in my room, I sit on the edge of the bed, unsure what to say now that he's here.

Choose me. Pick me.

The words flash through my mind, matching the unsteady rhythm of my heart as he makes his way around my room.

In silence, he examines the photographs on my magnet board along with the medal for winning the fourth-grade spelling bee and the bookshelf littered with textbooks from high school, mystery novels, and a lava lamp. He runs his fingers along the edge of the glass, watching the purple and pink blobs of lava bubble up inside and rise to the top of the cylinder.

"I asked my doctor if I could switch up my medication," I announce, unable to take the silence for a second longer.

He drops his hand and looks at me. "You did?"

"Yeah. I told them how much the side effects were messing with me, and they agreed that finding a different avenue was worth the effort."

His smile loosens the pressure in my chest. "That's great, Kate."

"Yeah." I pick at the edge of my baby pink comforter. "Have you talked to Hazel?"

"I had breakfast with her and Miley this morning."

"She sent me a text," I murmur.

His brows shoot up. "She did?"

"Yeah. Apologized for the ultimatum and for telling her mom about me, er, that she knew who you were dating. Said she gave her blessing, even though it sounded weird to both of us, but..."

"What did you say?" he asks.

"I told her I understood and apologized for not telling her in the first place."

"It was my responsibility to tell her. Not yours." The bed dips slightly as Mack sits beside me, keeping enough space between us to make me wonder where he stands or if he meant the words he said to me in the hospital.

"Yeah, well, apparently, we both kind of failed," I tell him.

"Yeah, I guess we did."

"Thanks for bringing me my medicine. The nurse told me it's why you were at Butter and Grace. The fact you noticed it in the first place was sweet, so…"

"I'd do anything for you, Kate."

Dammit, Mack!

The words act like a noose around my throat, making it hard to breathe as I dig my nails into my palms.

"I'm sorry if I scared you," I whisper.

"Don't ever apologize for something like that. Ever." He grabs my chin, forcing me to look at him. "You hear me?"

"I feel bad. For scaring you." And I hate how hard the words hit. How often I've felt the need to say them. But especially after yesterday. After seeing the fear in his eyes. The blood on his jeans at the hospital. My blood. Another wave of guilt cripples me, leaving me speechless as I hold his gaze.

"Don't you get it, Kate?" Mack whispers. "You're worth the risk. Worth the fear. Because every single day I get to spend in your presence is a day worth having. Before you, I was lost. Lost in monotony. Lost in my job. And the gym. And the cabin."

"You like all those things," I point out.

"Yeah. But I like them better when I'm with you. I like *me* better when I'm with you."

"Don't say those things just because you saw me have a seizure yesterday."

"I'm not."

"You sure?" I demand.

"Yeah, Kate." He smiles, running his thumb against my cheek and dragging his fingers further up to where my stitches are. His concern makes my breath hitch as he examines the damage and meets my eyes again. "I love you. All of you."

"Even the broken parts?"

He leans closer, carefully touching the back of my neck and pulling me toward him. And I love it. His hands on me. His touch, no matter how innocent it is. It's addictive. But calming too.

Magic.

With his forehead pressed against mine, he tells me, "It's like I said, Kate, we all have our shit. I have a meddling ex and two daughters who don't know what to do with you, and you have a perfect little brain that likes to wig out on occasion."

He kisses my forehead as if to prove his point, and I laugh, closing my eyes and savoring the feel of his lips on me.

"A perfect little brain that likes to wig out on occasion?" I repeat his words back to him.

"Yeah."

"That's what we're calling it?"

"Uh-huh."

I roll my eyes, but he kisses me again, cupping the side of my face and brushing his nose against mine in an Eskimo kiss. My lips pull up into a smile as my stomach flip-flops at the innocent contact.

"Love you, Kate Winchester."

"Love you, too, Macklin Taylor."

His smile widens. "Ah, so now she admits it."

And for the first time ever, I don't feel broken anymore.

In fact, Macklin Taylor might actually make me feel whole again. And while it should be scary as hell, it's comforting. Because I have a feeling I make him whole too.

"So, are we good?" he asks.

I nod.

"Good. 'Cause I have something for you."

"What do you have?"

"I told you I brought you a present." He shifts on the mattress and pulls something from his back pocket, handing it to me.

"What's this?" My eyes bounce around the little index card. One cup of salted butter, softened. One cup of white sugar. One cup of light brown sugar, packed. Two teaspoons of vanilla extract. The list goes on and on.

I look up at Mack and shake my head, confused.

"Is this..." My lips part, but my voice is lost as I scan the list of ingredients again.

It can't be.

There's no way.

"It's Mama Taylor's recipe," Macklin tells me. His chest swells with pride.

"But you said--"

"It was impossible to get?"

My gaze narrows. "You said she wouldn't even give it to your wife when you were married."

"Yeah, well, I told her I found the love of my life but had kind of screwed it up, so I needed help with a Hail Mary."

"And your sob story was enough to pry the recipe from her?"

"Well, that and I told her you wouldn't come to Sunday dinner unless she coughed it up."

I snort and cover my face. "Please tell me you're joking."

"Had to pull out the big guns, Kate."

"You made an awfully huge assumption there, Macklin."

"And what assumption did I make?"

"You assumed she'd want to meet me in the first place."

"Ah, my sweet, innocent porcupine." He hooks his arm around my neck, kissing the crown of my head. "Of course, she'd want to meet you."

"Why?"

"Because I never called Summer the love of my life. I said I cared about her. And I loved her. But the love of my *life?*" He shakes his head. "Not once. The real reason my mom never handed the recipe over to Summer was because she knew as well as I did I might work my ass off to make her happy, but it wasn't because we were soulmates. It's because I was a stubborn asshole who hated disappointing people. But guess what you taught me, Kate?"

"What?"

"My happiness is worth fighting for. And no one should

have the power to control or manipulate it but me. I love you, Kate. You make me happy."

"You make me happy too," I admit.

"Wanna know what else would make me happy?"

"What?"

"If we took our pizza to go and spent the night in my bed."

My cheeks pinch from smiling so hard. "I think that sounds pretty perfect."

He leans in for another kiss. "Me too."

EPILOGUE

MACKLIN

She looks beautiful standing on the stage in her black cap and gown, the dark red tassel hanging by her cheek.

Kate didn't want to walk today. Didn't think it was worth the fanfare or the time I asked off work so I could be here. But my girl's graduating with a Master's degree in biochemistry. If that isn't worth celebrating, I don't know what is.

It's been a few months since her medication was changed, and her grades skyrocketed soon after. She wants to become a pharmacologist. Wants to help people. People like herself. People with chronic diseases who deserve medicine to help them live their best lives without side effects screwing them over. And she's going to crush her internship at ModernLabs this summer.

I took the job Buchanan offered me. And as Kate promised, she's been nothing but supportive. Not sure how we're going to handle me traveling so much. I already miss her, and she's thirty feet in front of me. She's adamant we'll figure it out once the hockey season starts in the fall, and I know we will.

Placing my thumb and forefinger between my lips, I whistle loudly as Kate takes her diploma from the dean. Her parents cheer beside me, clapping their hands while their only child gives them a half-wave from the center of the stage before finding her seat again.

The rest of the graduation ceremony crawls by at a snail's pace until hats are tossed into the air and a blanket of unbridled enthusiasm falls over the crowd.

Afterward, we go to dinner with Kate's parents, and I drop them off at their house. Then, we head to my place. Kate's been staying with me more days than she stays at home. But we haven't made anything official. Yet. I haven't wanted to rush her.

She's still young.

She still has hopes and dreams. Things she wants to do. Places she wants to go. And I want to support her through all of it. But I'm not one who likes to play games, and the idea of not being with her, of not claiming her, is more than I can stomach now that she's graduated and we're starting the next chapter of our lives.

Kate's head bobs slightly to the music as my car climbs up the mountain. It's warmer now, and her creamy thighs tease me, her baby blue knee-length dress riding up in the passenger seat. I reach over and squeeze her leg, her skin warm beneath my touch.

These fucking thighs. Pretty sure they'll be the death of me.

She smiles, looking at the trees lining the road. "It's pretty out here. The full trees. The sunset. The ambiance. I can't decide if I like the view more in winter or spring."

I take in the skyline peeking through the trees on the side of the mountain. "Yeah. It's something else."

"Have you decided what you want to do with the place?" she asks.

When I accepted Buchanan's offer, I debated whether to put the house up for sale and find a more central location. But Kate hated the idea of all my hard work being sold to the highest bidder. Part of me thinks she knows how much I love this place. Part of me thinks she loves it as much as I do and would be sad to see it go. Part of me wonders if all those assumptions are nothing more than wishful thinking on my part. Guess I'll find out soon enough.

"I haven't decided what I'm gonna do yet," I tell her. "Still looking at all my options." I drive around the final bend, and the house comes into view. The wood beams and large windows combined with the gray stone siding make the green trees surrounding the driveway even brighter somehow. Even more beautiful. More serene. More saturated. I can't believe how much the foliage has grown over the past year. Hell, the giant pines and sequoias have practically swallowed the yard whole, making the home look like it's always belonged here. Like it was made to be here.

"I'm still saying you should keep it," she murmurs. "You love this house."

"I do." I pull into the driveway but don't open the garage door as I shove the car into park. "The question is...do you love it?"

She turns to me, her brows pinched. "You know I love your house."

"And if I wanted it to be *our* house?" I probe.

Disbelief paints her features as she stares at me, those stormy gray eyes more turbulent than ever. "What are you saying?"

"I'm saying I'm looking into my options."

"And those options are...?"

"Do you want a commute? Do you feel comfortable being up here alone when I'm gone? Would you prefer to move closer to the city or live near your parents?"

"Those are an awful lot of options, Mack." She places her hand on top of mine. "But I haven't heard you mention yourself in any of them."

My dark chuckle fills the cab as I shake my head back and forth. She doesn't get it. She's never understood. And it doesn't matter how many times I've tried to explain my feelings. I'm not sure she'll ever fully grasp how much she means to me. "I don't matter, Kate. Not with this. I wanna be where you are. Whether it's in this house or across the street from ModernLabs. I wanna be with you."

"I want to be with you, too, but where you live doesn't affect that. Not unless..." She chews on her bottom lip, her eyes brimming with hope.

"I want us under the same roof when I'm not traveling for work. And I want to keep doing that for as long as you'll have me."

"Are you asking if I want to move in with you?" she whispers.

"Yeah. I am."

"And the house?" she prods.

"I want to be where you are. Wherever it is, Kate. And if you say yes, and agree to live with me, I think what happens to this house is both of our decision." I flip my palm up and tangle our fingers together, resting the back of my hand against her thigh. "So what do you say? Where do you wanna live?"

Her teeth dig into her bottom lip as she looks at the front of the house again. The stained wood door. The pot of marigolds she'd planted on the front porch. A small stack of wood lining the side of the house.

She turns to me again and nods. "I fell in love in this house, Macklin. I want to stay here. With you."

"And the commute?"

"I mean, I might have to get a more reliable car for the winter, but––"

The garage door whirs into motion with the click of a button, and I pull inside, turning off the SUV's engine. A shiny, white Jeep Grand Cherokee is parked on the right-hand side, and Kate stares at it carefully.

"Mack?"

"One of the best four-wheel drive vehicles on the market. It's yours."

"Mack," she repeats, her voice nothing but a breath.

It doesn't matter how long we've been dating. She's never once asked about my money from the lottery. She hasn't cared. Being with me was enough. And even though accepting the gifts I've purchased over the last few months has made her prickly, it's only made me want to buy her more.

"A graduation gift," I clarify.

"Mm-hmm." Her lips purse as she stares at the SUV for another minute.

"Do you like it?"

She nods, meeting my eyes. "I love it, Mack. Just like how I love this house and how I love you."

I hook her neck and tug her into me, kissing the shit out of her. Because I love this girl. And she loves me. Loves me enough to move to the middle of fucking nowhere. Loves me enough to commute to her new job on the opposite side of town. Loves me enough to put up with my bullshit and embrace me and all my flaws.

And fuck me.

It might not be today, but I swear I'm gonna marry her because of it.

And if she keeps kissing me like this?

It might be one day soon.

The End

Don't Let Me Down
Chapter One
Mia

THE BAND IS KILLING IT ON THE STAGE. THEY'RE NOT BROKEN Vows, but they're pretty good. Alternative rock with a dash of blues. My head bobs up and down with the beat as I wipe out a freshly washed glass with a clean towel when someone approaches me at the bar.

If it isn't the devil himself.

"Hello again, Professor," I greet him. "Two trips to SeaBird in one week?"

"It's been a tough week," he grumbles.

"You know, if you lost the suit, you might not stick out like a sore thumb around here."

"Yeah." He looks down at his dark, fitted suit that makes him look like a GQ model. As he smooths down the rich fabric, light reflects off the Rolex wrapped around his sexy wrist and catches my attention. I didn't know wrists could be sexy, but with the dapple of dark hair and veins popping along the top of his hand, I stand corrected. Not that I'm surprised. The man's even been voted as sexiest bachelor alive before his girlfriend took him off the market. If that isn't an accomplishment, I don't know what is.

"Guess I forget I don't look like a student anymore," he adds, dryly, assessing his odd choice of clothes compared to everyone else around him.

Yeah, no. Not even close. I started paying attention to the Buchanan name when I found out Evelyn Buchanan, Henry's little sister, was dating my father's killer. Well, technically two men were arrested for my dad's murder, but still.

Thankfully, the Buchanan's weren't involved in my

father's disappearance, but their names were still dragged through the dirt thanks to Henry's dad running for Senator at the time.

After the police made the connection, the Buchanan name hit the newspapers for weeks. Henry was friends with the guy, too. Troy McAdams. The frat boy asshole who became friends with the lowlife loan shark who killed my dad and asked Troy to help him cover his tracks.

And what would you know? I ended up having Professor Buchanan, Troy McAdams' friend, as a teacher a few years later.

It's eerie how small the world feels sometimes.

Then again, I could've always moved across the country to get away from it all. I could still move across the country to get away from it all.

But I won't.

Because what little family I have is here. In this small town, including my friends, and I doubt they're going anywhere.

"Missing the good ol' days, Professor?" I quip. "When you'd blend in with the rest of the students at SeaBird instead of sticking out like a sore thumb?"

Apparently, Henry Buchanan went to LAU, too. Rumor has it, this is the same bar his little sister met her husband, Jake Jensen. And it's a good thing she found such a perfect fit for her snooty tooty family, because the guy's a software nerd who took over B-Tech Enterprises after Henry passed along the responsibilities and decided to become a professor instead.

Henry's full lips press together as he scans the bar, barely casting me a glance as he reminds me, "You've graduated. You don't need to call me professor anymore."

"And what would you prefer I call you? Professor? Daddy? Doctor Buchanan?" My sultry voice hangs in the air as my mouth pulls into a shameless grin. But I can't help it. The guy's grumpier and more guarded than a rhinoceros. He's always had his guard up high around me. Which is fine. My guard's high around everyone. But it does make me want to poke at him for it.

"Henry's fine," he grunts, refusing to give into my teasing.

"Okay, Henry," I purr. "What can I get ya?"

The guy scans the bar again, not bothering to look at me. "Whiskey. Top shelf."

I turn around and stand on my tiptoes, reaching for the nicest bottle SeaBird owns before pouring two fingers of the caramel colored liquid into the freshly cleaned glass tumbler.

"So what brings you in? Looking for another chat with Theo and Colt?" I ask.

He doesn't answer me as he shoots back the liquid before setting it in front of him again. With a dark look, he waits for me to refill it, so I do.

"Or maybe you're looking for your girlfriend," I add.

His gaze narrows. "Has she been in here?"

"Yup."

"Was she with a guy?" he grits out.

And damn. I can see why he's such a shark in the business world. The hair along the back of my neck raises, as if he's daring me to lie. To withhold what he wants. To push him when he's clearly not in the mood to be pushed.

I know that look, though. The look that already knows the truth without needing to witness it firsthand. The look that shows he's already seen the red flags, but wants proof. More proof. But he won't get it here. Not when I have less faith in the opposite sex than I do in aliens or God.

"She was out with her friends," I lie. I shouldn't. He deserves to know the truth. But it isn't my place, and I don't know the full story. Hell, maybe Henry's had someone on the side for months now, and his girlfriend just found out and is looking for revenge. Maybe he's stalking her and they already broke up. Not that I think he'd do that, but... I cock my head, examining his tight jaw and the vein throbbing in his neck. Actually, scratch that. Professor Buchanan definitely looks like someone who isn't afraid to get his hands dirty to get what he wants.

"So she left?" he demands.

"Yup."

His ever perfect posture slumps slightly, and he turns to me fully, giving up on his search as he takes another sip of whiskey from his glass. "How's your mother?"

My expression sours. Not because I hate my mother, but because Henry's the one asking about her.

"She's fine."

"And your uncle?"

"Fine," I repeat.

Henry Buchanan knows me too. Mia Rutherford. The girl with the murdered daddy. To be fair, most of Lockwood Heights knows me. My face was splashed all over the news for weeks after my dad's body was found, just like the Buchanan name. If I was smart I would've moved away. But I didn't want to give the assholes who took my father from me the pleasure.

"You find a job yet?" he questions.

Sometimes I hate the way he keeps tabs on me. Hell, he's worse than Uncle Fen. Part of me wonders if it's because he feels guilty. For knowing Troy McAdams. For being friends with him. For not spotting the red flags or just how dangerous his friend really was. Not that I blame Henry. I've fallen for a wolf in sheep's clothes on more than one occasion.

"No," I answer.

"Why not?"

Resting my elbows on the counter separating us, I steeple my fingers in front of me and hold his dark gaze. "Because I started selling pictures of my body on the internet to make ends meet, and now every doctor's office and hospital within a hundred mile radius knows about it and wants nothing to do with me."

I don't know why I say it. I shouldn't. It's none of his business anyway, and shining a light on the mess of my life probably isn't the brightest thing I've ever done, but I can't help it. Wanting to shock the impenetrable bastard in front of me. To see him flinch. To see him feel. Something. Anything. Even if it's only disgust.

His dark, flinty eyes dip to my low cut, black tank top before traveling south, along my waist and hips, leaving me squirming.

I'm used to being checked out.

Call it a blessing or a curse, but it is what it is. I'm pretty in an emo, untouchable, this girl's got daddy issues, kind of way. Add to the fact that I'm a bartender who looks like she enjoys getting freaky in the sheets, and I've been hit on more times than I can count.

But being checked out by Henry Buchanan? That's new. And I'm not sure how I feel about it.

"Eyes up here, Professor," I warn.

His nostrils flare as his eyes meet mine again, and he tips the rest of his drink back. The glass clinks against the bartop once he's finished. "Selling pictures of your body on the internet was a poor decision."

"One of many," I point out.

Without a word, he pulls out a small stack of bills and sets them on the counter. "Keep the change."

Then he walks out of the bar without a backward glance. When the door closes behind him, I pick up the bills, my jaw dropping.

Five hundred bucks.

His tab was maybe a hundred.

Sometimes, I hate his pity.

Always, I hate his charity.

And lately? I've hated the way he gets under my skin whenever he's around.

Buy Now

ALSO BY KELSIE RAE

Kelsie Rae tries to keep her books formatted with an updated list of her releases, but every once in a while she falls behind.

If you'd like to check out a complete list of her up-to-date published books, visit her website at www.authorkelsierae.com/books

Or you can join her newsletter to hear about her latest releases, get exclusive content, and participate in fun giveaways.

Interested in reading more by Kelsie Rae?

Don't Let Me Series

(Steamy Contemporary Romance Standalone Series)

Don't Let Me Fall - Ashlyn and Colt's Story

Don't Let Me Go - Blakely and Theo's Story

Don't Let Me Break - Kate and Macklin's Story

Let Me Love You - A Don't Let Me Sequel

Don't Let Me Down - Mia and Henry's Story

Wrecked Roommates Series

(Steamy Contemporary Romance Standalone Series)

Model Behavior

Forbidden Lyrics

Messy Strokes

Risky Business

Broken Instrument

Signature Sweethearts Series

(Sweet Contemporary Romance Standalone Series)

Taking the Chance

Taking the Backseat - Download now for FREE

Taking the Job

Taking the Leap

Get Baked Sweethearts Series

(Sweet Contemporary Romance Standalone Series)

Off Limits

Stand Off

Hands Off

Hired Hottie (A *Steamy* Get Baked Sweethearts Spin-Off)

Swenson Sweethearts Series

(Sweet Contemporary Romance Standalone Series)

Finding You

Fooling You

Hating You

Cruising with You (A *Steamy* Swenson Sweethearts Novella)

Crush (A *Steamy* Swenson Sweethearts Spin-Off)

Advantage Play Series

(Steamy Romantic Suspense/Mafia Series)

Wild Card

Little Bird

Bitter Queen

Black Jack

Royal Flush - Download now for FREE

Stand Alones

Fifty-Fifty

Sign up for Kelsie's newsletter to receive exclusive content, including the first two chapters of every new book two weeks before its release date!

Dear Reader,

I want to thank you guys from the bottom of my heart for taking a chance on Don't Let Me Break, and for giving me the opportunity to share this story with you. I couldn't do this without you!

I would also be very grateful if you could take the time to leave a review. It's amazing how such a little thing like a review can be such a huge help to an author!

Thank you so much!!!

-Kelsie

ABOUT THE AUTHOR

Kelsie is a sucker for a love story with all the feels. When she's not chasing words for her next book, you will probably find her reading or, more likely, hanging out with her husband and playing with her three kiddos who love to drive her crazy.

She adores photography, baking, her two pups, and her cat who thinks she's a dog. Now that she's actively pursuing her writing dreams, she's set her sights on someday finding the self-discipline to not binge-watch an entire series on Netflix in one sitting.

If you'd like to connect with Kelsie, follow her on Facebook, sign up for her newsletter, or join Kelsie Rae's Reader Group to stay up to date on new releases, exclusive content, give-aways, and her crazy publishing journey.